M000310078

THE KLONDIKE
BAKE-OVEN DEATHS

Allen M. Hornblum

MILFORD
HOUSE

an imprint of Sunbury Press, Inc.
Mechanicsburg, PA USA

MILFORD HOUSE

an imprint of Sunbury Press, Inc.
Mechanicsburg, PA USA

For information about special discounts for bulk purchases, please contact Sunbury Press Orders Dept. at (855) 338-8359 or orders@sunburypress.com.

To request one of our authors for speaking engagements or book signings, please contact Sunbury Press Publicity Dept. at publicity@sunburypress.com.

FIRST MILFORD HOUSE PRESS EDITION: February 2021

Set in Adobe Garamond | Interior design by Crystal Devine | Cover by Terry Kennedy | Edited by Jennifer Cappello.

Publisher's Cataloging-in-Publication Data
Names: Hornblum, Allen M., author.
Title: The Klondike bake-oven deaths / Allen M. Hornblum.
Description: First trade paperback edition. | Mechanicsburg, PA : Milford House Press, 2021.
Summary: The discovery of eight bizarrely discolored inmate corpses jolts an unschooled county coroner who owes his job to an unscrupulous mayor and a political machine that ensured his election.
Identifiers: ISBN 978-1-620064-28-3 (softcover).
Subjects: FICTION / Thrillers / Crime | FICTION / Mystery & Detective / Historical | FICTION / Thrillers / Historical.

Product of the United States of America
0 1 1 2 3 5 8 13 21 34 55

Continue the Enlightenment!

PART I

Chapter 1

Cauldron of Anger

Philadelphia: Monday morning, August 22, 1938

Death was more than his business; it was his legal responsibility. During his nearly four years on the job, he had observed just about every imaginable manner of accident and depravity that can befall or be inflicted upon a human being. From the bullet-riddled bodies of mafiosi caught up in gangland warfare, to smashed remains of businessmen who lost everything in the economic collapse and threw themselves out the windows of thirty-story buildings, to the mangled corpses of children run over by electric streetcars, to defenseless housewives who had been garroted by their intoxicated husbands, Heshel Glass had seen it all.

But what he now viewed on the sweltering concrete floor of the city's largest prison literally took his breath away. Almost otherworldly in appearance, the vision of shriveled bodies with a conspicuous indigo cast was nothing short of hair-raising. Even for someone whose position routinely brought him in close proximity with cadavers of all sizes and descriptions, Glass was stunned. More alien than human at first glance, the discolored corpses were an unnerving spectacle. After a quick inspection of the deceased, he still wasn't sure what he was dealing with. Discovered earlier that morning, the presumably once-human remains would ultimately present Glass, and one of the nation's largest cities, with a moral and political challenge of unprecedented complexity and importance.

⤮

The day had begun like most others during what was turning out to be an unusually long and uncomfortable summer heatwave. Blue-collar workers

1

cursed a blazing sun they'd be forced to labor under, office workers dreaded a code of professional decorum requiring ties and jackets, and ladies applied an extra layer of perfumed talc and lilac water for added protection. With temperatures once again expected to climb into the mid-nineties, many took the day off and traveled to the Jersey Shore for a relaxing day on the beach and a refreshing dip in the ocean. Others were forced to make do with a favorite lawn chair under a shady tree and a glass of iced tea by their side.

For those returning to work after a listless weekend, it is unlikely that any of them would have predicted that before the day was over Philadelphia—"the City of Brotherly Love"—would become synonymous with villainy and emblematic of man's capacity for cruel and callous behavior.

Heshel Glass, the county coroner, began his day before eight A.M. at the home of a South Philadelphia ward leader seeking a job for a new constituent just arrived from Galway. A second appointment took him across town to Philadelphia General Hospital, where a dyspeptic hospital administrator expressed his annoyance with new city regulations on the storage of cadavers. Such early morning meetings weren't unusual, and neither were the subjects under discussion. As the elected coroner of the nation's third-largest city, his days tended to be dominated by mundane ward politics and issues involving the dead.

Between a fitful night's sleep, a demanding Monday schedule, and temperatures that blanketed the region in oppressive humidity, Glass was in an irritable mood. His disposition wasn't helped when he entered the sixth-floor City Hall office suite and was handed a stack of messages by his secretary. Glass showed little interest and continued to his private office.

"You better look at that first one," advised his secretary.

Glass did as Miss Renwick, a gruff but competent woman, suggested. He immediately stopped in his tracks. "Any more than this?" he inquired as he shifted his focus from the small slip of paper to his secretary.

"No, but it didn't sound good."

"Never is," replied the coroner, his hawklike face disclosing sudden foreboding.

Glass examined the note again. The two-sentence memo read, "Get the coroner up here immediately. It's an emergency." The call had come from the city's superintendent of prisons.

"Carl went up there a little while ago," said Miss Renwick, referring to Carl Ferencz, Glass's chief deputy. "He took the intern with him. You want to wait until they call in or are you going to go up there?"

Glass didn't reply but just continued to gaze at the ominous nine-word message. Trips up to Holmesburg in the far northeast section of the city were always unsettling affairs. It wasn't just the corpses or the threatening prison atmosphere. He had grown used to seeing lifeless bodies. Holmesburg corpses, however, were usually mangled in some distinct and cruel way. The institution had a knack for leaving its mark on both the living and the dead. After instructing his secretary to cancel any appointments he had scheduled that morning, Glass departed the building, went to his car, and began the long drive up to Holmesburg, Philadelphia's largest prison.

A formidable relic of the Victorian era, the walled facility was the city's toughest penal establishment and customarily held the area's most dangerous criminals. Al Capone, Bugsy Siegel, Legs Diamond, Willie Sutton, Waxy Gordon, and thousands of lesser-known but equally dangerous felons had all been guests of the institution. Glass's last visit was just two weeks earlier when guards discovered an inmate hanging from a wire noose fastened to a ceiling air vent. The issue of whether the inmate's death had been a suicide or possible homicide had yet to be resolved. Penal authorities subscribed to the former, but the coroner's investigators had their doubts.

As he drove up Broad Street to Roosevelt Boulevard and the outer reaches of the city that had yet to be developed, the coroner loosened his tie and repeatedly mopped perspiration from his brow and neck while pondering what he was about to encounter. Normally, he was given a clue as to why he was being summoned. There was not even a hint this time, a worrisome departure from standard practice, especially since it was Holmesburg. But one thing was certain; there'd be a dead body to examine.

Holmesburg had been in the news for the last few days. No surprise this time of year. A seething cauldron of anger and discontent on the best of days, late-summer hot spells combined with acute overcrowding could always be counted on to spark dissatisfaction, foster grievances, and incite some form of violence. Escape attempts, cellblock fights, and hostage dramas were practically routine incidents in recent years. Oddly, however, newspaper accounts over the weekend—even those in the *New York Times*—centered around inmate disgruntlement with their meals; prisoners were tired of a steady menu of hamburger steak, spaghetti and cheese, soup, bologna, and fried eggplant.

When Glass first read of the prisoners' grievances on Saturday morning while drinking coffee at the kitchen table, he shook his head in disbelief. The part about the strikers demanding ice cream and cake every Sunday really galled him. *What chutzpah*, he thought to himself. The coroner was no rigid disciplinarian; he didn't embrace punitive lock 'em up and throw away the key practices, but neither was he a mollycoddler interested in showering public miscreants with cookies and kindness. And the inmates' additional demand for a say in how the prison was run was clearly ludicrous.

It was all too absurd. Just a few years earlier during the height of the Depression, many a destitute family in Philadelphia would have considered hamburgers, spaghetti, and eggplant a real treat. Maybe it was just another sign of the times; the economy had improved so much prison inmates felt they deserved more varied and lavish offerings. *The next thing they'll be asking for*, he thought to himself, *is a chef skilled in French cuisine and chocolate éclairs served for dessert at supper.*

Though hundreds of Holmesburg inmates had reportedly gone on a hunger strike to show their displeasure with the lack of variety in their weekly menu, the coroner had a hard time linking their peaceful protest with the reason he was being summoned to the facility. Besides, according to news accounts he had read on Sunday and just that very morning, the food strike was over. Only a handful of inmates continued to protest their rations.

It was while he traveled on Rhawn Street that he first heard the police sirens. Barely audible at first, as he approached Torresdale Avenue the sirens grew louder and more numerous. Periodically, a police wagon and hospital ambulance would zoom past him. He remained skeptical they were all headed to the same destination until they turned north on Torresdale Avenue, the location of the medieval fortress known as Holmesburg Prison.

Police and fire department vehicles lined the street near the base of Holmesburg's daunting thirty-five-foot fieldstone walls and imposing turrets. Such an outpouring of city police, hospital vehicles, and support personnel indicated a major conflagration of some type, possibly a riot, a mass escape, or a significant fire. But there was no smoke or gunshots or signs of turmoil to justify such a formidable collection of municipal vehicles and personnel.

As he approached the three-story administration building that sat just in front of the entrance to the prison, Glass was moved by the traffic flowing into and out of the facility. Prison guards, police, and medical personnel, all sweat-stained and grim-faced, came and went, including stretcher-bearers who hurriedly entered through the institution's front portal. Holmesburg's front gates had always impressed Glass. Their immense size—almost two stories in height and nearly a foot thick—combined with an impressive latticework of steel and heavy oak made for an imposing sight. He was always reminded of the thousand-pound doors of a seventeenth-century Welsh or Bavarian castle, but now the doors were flung open to reveal mass mayhem.

As he entered the sally port, he immediately came upon two stretchers on the ground, white bedsheets covering their lifeless contents. Glass's concern heightened. Prison guards and police skirted around the bodies as if they were articles of trash and litter rather than people. Glass spotted David Sandler, a recent college graduate who was interning in the coroner's office during the summer before going off to medical school. The slim, well-mannered lad was flush against a far wall; he was pale, soaked in perspiration, and staring into space as if in a trance, apparently in shell shock. Before going over to him and asking where his deputy, Carl Ferencz, was, the coroner bent down over one of the stretchers and pulled the sheet back to inspect the corpse. He was desperate to know if the deceased were inmates or guards.

Stunned, Glass drew back. It was a prisoner, and though the individual's face was unscathed, at least with regard to any obvious signs of a slashing or blunt-force trauma—the usual remnants of a fatal Holmesburg beat down—there was still something that shocked him, something the coroner had never seen before. In addition to the blistered lips and swollen tongue, the deceased inmate's face was blue. Glass pulled back the rest of the sheet to reveal a naked corpse. Much of the inmate's skin from head to waist appeared shriveled, but the most striking feature was the body's light-blue tint.

"What the hell . . . ?" Glass murmured to himself.

The coroner quickly moved to the adjoining stretcher and ripped off the sheet. Once again, a practically nude, shriveled corpse, with a purplish-blue hue. The decedent's face was battered, and the feet of the victim exhibited definite burn marks. Both bodies appeared partially mummified and bathed in what could only be described as a ghostly blue veneer. Glass was dumbstruck. Trips to Holmesburg to examine deceased prisoners were always enlightening, but this macabre oddity won the prize.

He now looked up at his young intern along the far wall. Sandler hadn't moved; he seemed frozen. Glass approached him, put his hand on the boy's shoulder, and asked, "Where's Carl? Where's Ferencz?"

Obviously frightened, the youth remained mute, almost catatonic.

"Are you all right?" the coroner inquired. No reply. Louder this time, "Where's Ferencz?"

Sandler, never making eye contact, slowly raised his left arm and pointed toward the prison yard. "There's more of them," he responded in a halting whisper. "There are more bodies inside."

Chapter 2

The Klondike Killing Field

Built in the last decade of the nineteenth century, Holmesburg Prison was modeled along the lines of its famous architectural ancestor, Eastern State Penitentiary in the Fairmount section of the city. Built at a cost of $1.5 million on a seventeen-acre plot of ground between the Delaware River and Pennypack Creek in the Holmesburg section of Northeast Philadelphia, the facility was designed to be "the embodiment of enlightened penal philosophy." That optimistic vision, however, was quickly proven unrealistic, if not fanciful. Newspaper reporters covering periodic instances of bloodshed and mayhem had their own impressions of the place. One scribe familiar with the brutality and violence told his readers a plaque should be installed over Holmesburg's entryway that read, "Abandon hope all ye who enter here." As another newspaperman mused on the occasion of the facility's opening: "Not a window can be seen, and a spectator gathers the impression that light, too, is denied the unfortunate who are condemned to spend years of seclusion within these abhorrent limits."

Borrowing the classic spoke-and-wheel architectural design popularized by Eastern State decades earlier, Holmesburg contained ten cellblocks that radiated out from a central hub or rotunda. The cellblocks were constructed in varying lengths, some consisting of sixty-eight cells, some seventy-four, and others seventy-eight. Each cell was six feet by eight feet, and though designed to hold one inmate, the cells usually housed two or three men and on occasion as many as five. Built to contain 738 troublemakers, reprobates, and outright felons, the institution normally held over 1,200 and as many as 1,500 at times. Most of the prison's inhabitants were sentenced, but rough customers awaiting trial could also find themselves interned at "the Burg."

Well into its fourth decade of operation, Holmesburg could claim more than its fair share of bloody riots, clever escapes, and violent encounters between inmates and guards. Rules and regulations were vigorously enforced by the institution's complement of seasoned guards. The hundred-man force consisted of mostly Irish ruffians and other ethnic roughnecks who could handle themselves with both fist and club. On some violence-prone cellblocks, guards carried truncheons and blackjacks to better maintain order. When that didn't work, some superintendents were known to resort to more innovative methods. One superintendent during the 1920s, for example, established his own crew of law and order enforcers. Nicknamed the "Black Musketeers," they were a collection of vicious colored head-bangers and ass-kickers who received small favors including additional rations of tobacco for welcoming new misfits, malcontents, and prospective troublemakers to the institution.

Two other penal institutions—Moyamensing Prison at 10th and Reed Streets in South Philadelphia, and the House of Correction also along Pennypack Creek—presently served Philadelphia's criminal justice system, but it was Holmesburg that earned a reputation for toughness and brutality. In the aftermath of bloody riots in the nineteen-twenties and early thirties, many aggressive and disruptive prisoners were sent off to distant county prisons throughout the commonwealth to cool off while order was reestablished and destruction repaired at Holmesburg. Invariably, wardens across the state threw up their hands and admitted their new Holmesburg inmates were "too tough," "too much trouble," and all too quick to establish "a reputation for hardness." Wardens from Elk, Potter, Clarion, Luzerne, and other upstate counties sent the motley collection of criminals back to Philadelphia with the simple proviso, "Never again. We won't take any more of your intractable thugs."

Heshel Glass was no novice when it came to Holmesburg's history, practices, or reputation. A lifelong Philadelphian and resident of a tough, working-class section of the city for more years than he cared to recall, the coroner was quite familiar with both the institution's criminal clientele and its brutal overseers. No angel growing up, Glass had luckily escaped the many opportunities the city's criminal justice system afforded him to call Holmesburg home. But he knew many who hadn't been as fortunate, heard the grim stories, and now as coroner, saw the chilling results.

As soon as he stepped out of the shady confines of the sally port, he felt the heat. The intense sunlight momentarily blinded him. Prison guards, city police, and what appeared to be medical personnel from nearby hospitals scurried across the lawn, some to the hub or center control area of the prison, while others circled A Block. Recognized by a sergeant of the guard, he was advised to follow those who were running near the wall and around the various cellblocks. The prison had been locked down, and moving through interior checkpoints would prove frustrating and time-consuming.

"What the hell happened?" Glass inquired.

"A real mess," said the sergeant. "They really fucked up this time."

As he trotted along the interior of the north wall, Glass was reminded he was not the athlete he had once been. He was quickly out of breath, and a blistering sun wasn't helping. More importantly, he tried to imagine what had caused such a large disturbance and loss of life. Again, he couldn't conceive of what was obviously a crisis in the making without some indication of a fire, gunshots, or armed insurrection. Angry curses and shouts from inmates, many expressing indignation over their treatment, periodically echoed across the triangular plots of grass that separated one cellblock from another. As he passed the exterior of B and C Blocks, Glass observed emergency personnel carrying two survivors on stretchers to what he assumed were waiting hospital ambulances on Torresdale Avenue. His sense of dread increased with each step.

When he finally turned at the corner of D Block, he was met with a scene only imaginable on a battlefield: nearly two-dozen dead and injured men lay on a parched piece of earth between D and E Blocks. Alongside them was an even larger number of frantic city support personnel, some administering water, others fanning survivors, and some placing bodies on stretchers or slabs of wood to be carried off to a hospital or morgue. A connoisseur of military history, Glass couldn't help but associate the disturbing sight before him with the scenes captured in nineteenth-century lithographs of bloated corpses that littered the ground in the aftermath of bloody battles at Antietam and Gettysburg.

The dead were covered in white bedsheets from head to foot and remained unattended, while those with any sign of life lay naked, barely moving, or writhing in pain and gasping for air. Glass bent over one heavily panting survivor who grabbed the lapel of his jacket, pulled him close, and whispered in a raspy voice, "They almost killed me. It was so hot, so hot . . . but I . . . I made it out. Thank God, I made it out."

The coroner worked to loosen the man's surprisingly strong grip on his jacket. He then asked one of those attending the injured man, a Holmesburg guard, what had happened. He was met with a shoulder shrug and silence.

Glass knelt alongside another man whose face appeared to be creased and weathered well beyond his years. He was being given repeated cups of water and whimpered incoherently. When Glass asked what happened, he heard the man plead, "Please, no more. Please don't put me back in there again."

Glass looked throughout the small exercise yard for his deputy or one of the higher-ranking prison officials he was familiar with, but without success. As he walked past the many prone bodies—some dead, others soon to be—he realized something extraordinary had taken place, but he was still at a loss as to what. Recognizing a white-shirted officer of the guard, the coroner went over to him and pointedly asked, "What the hell happened?"

"Talk to Stryker and Davis," barked the officer. "Leave me the hell out of this. I wasn't any part of it."

Furious, Glass demanded to know where the warden and superintendent were. Just then, the officer pointed to a group of men coming from a small building situated between the two cellblocks. Glass recognized most of them; Superintendent Davis and Warden Stryker were out front, followed by investigators for the district attorney's office, and Philadelphia Police Department detectives. Carl Ferencz, his deputy, was in the rear.

"Hi, Hesh," said one of the city's top detectives as he fanned himself and walked past the coroner. "Hot goddamn day, isn't it?"

The coroner was taken aback; the detective's greeting was as casual as if they had crossed paths on busy Chestnut Street in Center City Philadelphia at lunchtime.

Glass was amazed by the detective's cavalier manner, like the man hadn't a care in the world and there weren't a number of dead and near-dead littering the ground. Superintendent Davis, cigarette in hand and looking shaken, briefly greeted the coroner and thanked him for coming up but was cut short when a panicked guard informed him newspapermen and photographers were gathering outside the walls on Torresdale Avenue. "They're demanding answers and asking questions about men being cooked alive," he told his superior. "They want to be let in."

"No one, absolutely no one is to be let into the institution," Davis told the officer. He then excused himself to deal with the press.

Glass wanted answers as well, and he hoped to get some from his deputy. Ferencz approached him looking exhausted and dripping in perspiration.

"My God, Carl, what happened here?" said Glass emotionally. "It looks like a battlefield."

"Six dead, four unconscious, and five others in pretty bad shape," replied Ferencz. "Many need to be hospitalized, but the superintendent refuses to let any out. I wouldn't be surprised if a few more expire before—"

"Jesus Christ almighty," said the coroner. "Can't I get a straight answer from anyone? Don't give me an accountant's balance sheet. What the hell happened?"

Ferencz appeared to be momentarily offended—Glass was usually quite civil with his subordinate—but then he exhaled his emotion and replied with one word: "There." Ferencz nodded toward the small brick-and-mortar building he had just departed. "Davis and Stryker call it an isolation unit," said Ferencz. "The inmates have a few names for it, but most of them call it Klondike. Whatever it's called, I think it's actually a torture chamber. I think they tried to roast these men in there."

A guard at the entrance to the low, coffin-shaped building tried to block the tall, well-dressed intruder from entering, but all of Glass's six-foot-three, 212-pound frame boldly pushed the guard's arm aside while informing him he was the city coroner and he had every right to examine the premises. The prison guard, a middle-aged, red-faced man, appeared unsure but didn't try to stop him. Ferencz followed behind and told his boss what he knew of the facility.

On entering, Glass was met with overbearing heat and an inescapable stench. He took out his handkerchief to wipe the sweat from his face and used his straw hat as a fan. The air was thick, foul, and overpowering. Glass thought if he spent any length of time on the block he'd become ill and vomit. From periodic trips through Philadelphia's prisons and mental asylums, Glass was not unfamiliar with stomach-turning odors—the ones that come from hundreds of unsanitary men in close quarters mixing with gallons of cleansers and disinfectant all competing for dominance—but the air in this small structure was beyond putrid.

A narrow, dark corridor no more than three-and-a-half-feet wide ran the length of the fifty-foot structure. On the left were a dozen cells. The doors to the small cells were open and hot. Glass quickly removed his hand from the first door as he pushed it back in order to see inside. There were no windows, just a slight air vent in the ceiling of each cell. And the cell was cluttered with chairs, tables, pieces of wood, and lengths of pipe, as was the next cell. The third cell— no more than eight-by-five feet in size—was empty but littered with articles of clothing, puddles of dirty water, and what he suspected was a repulsive mixture of urine, vomit, and feces. He was forced to strike a match to negotiate his object-strewn path. Several large bolts were attached to the wall that was once used to fasten inmate beds in place. A toilet—filled with urine and feces—and a small sink appeared battered and inoperable. When the coroner put his hand to the spigot's rim, all he felt was hot metal; the spigot was bone dry. Both the spigot and the toilet, according to Ferencz, were operated automatically from the outside. Prisoners were unable to control either of them.

The coroner was forced to hold a handkerchief to his nose as he examined the other cells; four more like the last, and then another five at the far end filled with paint cans, building supplies, and maintenance material. Based on the mayhem he had observed since walking through Holmesburg's front gate, Glass calculated that the operable cells in the small brick-and-concrete hotbox he was now walking through must have contained sixteen men. *Was such a thing possible*, he thought to himself. That prospect as well as the noxious results horrified him.

As he walked back along the corridor to exit the building, he couldn't help but notice that opposite the cells and suspended against the wall were numerous large banks of steam radiators that ran the length of the building. They protruded from the wall, reminding him of organ pipes, but auditory pleasure was not their purpose. Above the radiators were three small windows, all out of the prisoners' reach. Additional pipes ran above them and along what could have been no more than an eight-foot ceiling. The heat they threw off was intense, and the Glass didn't dare get too close. "Incredible," was the coroner's only comment as he walked down the corridor.

When his deputy informed him the radiators had been turned off as soon as the prisoners had been discovered dead and unconscious, he paused, dubious. He then spit on one bank of radiators. Ferencz and the prison guard watched the coroner's saliva sizzle and evaporate in a matter of seconds. "Must have been hot in here last night," said Glass, stone-faced, turning to the guard. "Why the hell would the heat be turned on in the midst of an August heatwave?"

The prison guard walked off without comment.

Upon exiting the structure, the coroner took off the jacket to his now-sweat-soaked seersucker suit and felt immediate relief. Though the sun was directly overhead and the temperature still climbing, it was a vast improvement over the unbearable heat inside the miniature cellblock. Glass was also pleased by the reappearance of David Sandler. The coroner's young summer intern had recovered from the shock of coming upon a penal killing field. Though still perspiring profusely, color had returned to his cheeks and his eyes were once again alert if not bright.

"I want to apologize for . . . for my behavior," said Sandler. "I don't know what came over me. It must have been . . ."

"The heat," interjected the coroner. "It's brutally hot out here, and this mess," he scanned the Antietam-like plot of ground next to them. After apologizing once more for his loss of control and promising it wouldn't happen again, Sandler reported that police detectives had informed members of the various news agencies gathered outside Holmesburg that prison malcontents sequestered in an isolation unit had turned on each other, fought violently, and ended up killing each other.

"My God," Glass murmured.

"Suicide was also mentioned," said Sandler.

"Christ almighty," uttered Glass. "What did Davis and Stryker say?"

"Not much," replied Sandler. "The superintendent and warden sort of backed up the detectives. They seemed to agree that the inmates who organized the food strike argued amongst themselves. Some wanted to continue the protest and others expressed their desire for food and a return to their normal cells. The superintendent claimed many prisoners wanted to end the protest and some of the more violent men wouldn't let them. According to the police, it boiled down to the inmates dying from exhaustion after fighting among themselves."

The coroner grimaced and emitted a few whispered obscenities. "Unbelievable," was the only comment clearly discerned as he pondered the possibility that prison overseers first tried to roast the men and then blamed their devastating handiwork on the victims.

"I should tell you something," Ferencz told his boss somewhat sheepishly. "When I got here, many of the men kept in the punishment unit were strung out on the ground like you see now. The dead were still in their cells. The survivors were all in pretty bad shape. When we were given the tour of the cells, there were dead men all around. It was pretty ugly. While we're in there, Detective Sergeant Hennessey pulls me aside, looks me in the eye, and says, 'I guess we'll have to see that our stories coincide when we turn in our reports.' I knew what he meant. He gave me a knowing nod, but I didn't say anything."

The scowl on Glass's face grew in intensity, and he took a few steps to think things through but remained silent.

Everyone was quiet for a few moments before Ferencz asked, "How do you want to proceed?"

The coroner narrowed his gaze on a nearby cellblock where the muffled shouts of angry inmates could be heard. They were cursing and hurling epithets at authorities. Judging by the stifled protests, the inmates knew there were people in the prison yard. Something had happened, something big; rumors were running rampant through the cellblocks of many dead and injured. The lockdown confirmed it.

Turning back, Ferencz and Sandler could see rivulets of sweat on their boss's face. His expression underscored the seriousness of the moment.

"How do you want to handle this?" Ferencz asked once more.

Glass gazed at the physically depleted men being attended to by guards and medical personnel, and then back at the small cellblock where the dead had been discovered.

Recognizing his boss's indecision, Ferencz slowly approached the coroner and said, "You know how something like this is normally handled. Do you want to leave?"

The coroner gave his deputy an angry look and then stared back at the grim spectacle of corpses covered with white sheets in the midst of feverish activity.

"What do you want to do?" asked Ferencz almost pleadingly. "We don't have a lot of time."

"Okay," said Glass, turning back to his two aides, "this is what I want you to do."

Chapter 3

The Investigation

Holmesburg Prison: Monday afternoon, August 22

"Are you sure about this, Hesh?" said Ferencz.

Glass didn't reply.

"You can see what the mayor and police are up to. If we start digging in this . . ."

"What do you want me to do?" asked the coroner. "Should we just walk out of here and leave it to the police and the mayor? You know what will happen."

"There's going to be hell to pay if we expose what I think . . . what we both think happened here."

"I know," said Glass as he turned away and took a few unsure steps in the exercise yard.

"If we dig into this," said Ferencz, "we're liable to face greater repercussions than Davis and his men. It could get ugly, and it'll be the coroner's office that pays."

"What do you want me to do, Carl?"

Both men were silent for a time. Finally, Ferencz spoke up and said, "Okay, I'll start doing the interviews."

Glass nodded and gave Ferencz and Sandler their marching orders: "Interview anyone who had some knowledge of events over the past weekend. Inmate survivors, if they're strong enough, and prison guards if they're willing to talk.

"We won't have much time, so we'll have to work quickly before the injured are removed to a hospital or back to another secure cellblock in the jail. Take detailed notes so we can build a chronology of events as best we can. Was it the food strike or something else that sparked prison administrators to punish the men so harshly? If there was a confrontation between two groups of inmates over ending or continuing the protest, that, too, has to be documented.

"And find out what you can about this . . . this damn sweatbox," ordered the coroner while eyeing the small, single-story isolation building. "When was it built, what was its purpose, and how often was it used? And why the hell does it have more radiators than the Bellevue-Stratford Hotel?"

After watching Ferencz and Sandler walk off, Glass took one last glance at the building where the sick and dead prisoners were discovered and then went directly to the administration building outside the wall on Torresdale Avenue. Due to the commotion, prison staff had congregated in different parts of the building, allowing Glass to find an empty office and begin a series of phone calls. His first call was to his secretary in City Hall. "This is important," said Glass impatiently. "Take this down."

He asked Miss Renwick to get word to the office's two pathologists that they were to drop everything and get up to Holmesburg immediately. To bring whatever vehicle or truck was available to transport anywhere from six to a dozen bodies of inmates who had died over the weekend.

"My God," blurted Miss Renwick, stunned by the news.

The coroner then told her the dead needed to be moved to the morgue at 13th and Wood Streets. Autopsies were to commence immediately.

"Tell Mattingly," said Glass, "I've got some bizarre-looking bodies up here, and I want to know what killed these men." He then told her to prepare staff to notify relatives of the deceased that a loved one had passed and to assign someone else to collect any newspaper articles printed over the last week that mentioned the inmate food strike at Holmesburg. In addition, he wanted her to make known to the mayor, the district attorney, and the chief of police that he'd be calling about the deadly prison fiasco. "Tell them I suggested they need to get up here themselves, and that I have questions about the initial reports of their investigators," said Glass. "And also make it known I have some concerns about the safety of the survivors. I don't want them to spend another night in this place."

Miss Renwick reported that there were already rumors spreading through the City Hall corridors of a riot and numerous dead up at the prison. "How bad is it?" she inquired.

"Bad enough," said the coroner, "that some may think twice about committing a crime in Philadelphia."

Glass had just started dialing another phone number when Superintendent Davis, followed by a large entourage, walked into the office. The coroner would have preferred a more private conversation, but it appeared unlikely with so many guards, police, and reporters tuned to the superintendent's every word and action.

"Hesh, this is a real mess," said Davis, obviously weary and perspiring freely from the heat and turbulence swirling around him. "Thanks for getting up here so quick. I appreciate your support."

"It looks like Verdun out there, Warren," Glass said through his teeth in an effort not to be overheard by the gathering throng of reporters. "What the hell happened up here? There are bodies all over the place. And that punishment building you've got out there. What the hell is that?"

The sixty-one-year-old prison superintendent was taken aback. They were clearly questions the superintendent didn't want to hear, especially with all the reporters in the room. "Not now, Hesh," said Davis. "And it's an isolation unit, not a punishment block. We'll talk later and I'll explain everything."

Glass was dissatisfied with the superintendent's response but understood this was neither the place nor time for a frank discussion. He was insistent, however, that the deceased be removed to the city morgue. Autopsies needed to be done. Davis took a long drag on his cigarette. He looked worried, undecided.

"Fine," the coroner conceded—for now. "In the meantime, all inmates who were held in the isolation unit should be taken to PGH or a hospital nearby if their injuries require further assessment."

"Afraid we can't do that, Mr. Glass," interjected Victor Stryker, the warden of Holmesburg, who had a well-established reputation as a tough, no-nonsense administrator. "These are dangerous men. Any injured prisoners will be placed on the medical block here at Holmesburg. Our doctors will see to them."

Glass looked at Davis, but the superintendent remained silent. Troubled, Glass tried to maintain his composure. "Where the hell were the prison physicians when these men were on the punishment block?"

Neither the superintendent nor the warden replied, but their expressions disclosed their annoyance with the question.

"Some of these men are in grave condition," said Glass, pushing the inmate transfer issue once again. "They require treatment that can only be found in a hospital—a real hospital. They can't get that at a makeshift first-aid station on a prison cellblock."

"You know the prison medical unit is more than that," Davis replied.

"But these men need—"

"No one is leaving," Stryker interjected.

"I'm going to—"

"No one is leaving," Stryker repeated with a menacing glare.

"Well, the deceased certainly are," Glass shot back, looking first at Stryker and then Superintendent Davis.

Warden Stryker, a short, dark-haired, forty-three-year-old bundle of German-Irish certitude opposed this as well. He began to state why this was impossible when the coroner interrupted him.

"I'm the duly elected coroner of this city," announced Glass. "These men are dead. No one can tell me they have not come to a shocking and untimely end. I don't know just how many there are or what killed them, but if there are any people on city property without a pulse, they're now the province of my office. If you care to challenge my authority you can take it up with the city solicitor and Common Pleas Court."

Stryker, his ruddy face turning redder, was obviously surprised by the coroner's uncharacteristic vehemence. He looked to the superintendent for support. Davis appeared anxious and unsure but finally said the coroner was in his right to take the deceased to the city morgue.

Reporters overhearing the conversation were stunned by the exchange. No less surprising was the coroner's insistence that all injured survivors be removed from the jail. His assertiveness triggered a series of questions.

"Coroner Glass, what do you believe happened here?"

"Mr. Glass, do you agree with police detectives that the inmates killed each other?"

Newsmen sensing friction between city officials sought answers. It was clear to all that something grave—possibly unprecedented—had occurred at Holmesburg over the weekend. City leaders had made themselves scarce and unresponsive. The comments of police investigators were unconvincing. Reporters were further incensed that they weren't allowed to enter the institution and see for themselves what was occurring; prison guards had orders that reporters and photographers were to be kept outside the walls.

Glass was repeatedly asked what he believed to have taken place. When one news scribe asked, "Coroner Glass, is there any merit to the claim prison officials and investigators are making that the loss of life is due to communistic influences in the inmate population?" the coroner grew agitated. He excused himself and quickly left the room. Before leaving the building, however, he located another empty office and dialed his secretary. Miss Renwick was given one more task to fulfill. "Get any lawyer you can find in the city solicitor's office and have him research municipal and state law as to the coroner's constitutional authority to assume additional functions and responsibilities in times of crisis. Specifically, I want to know if there's precedent for the coroner taking over the operations of another county agency or department."

Chapter 4

Initial Survivor Interviews

"Yeah, I was one of the strikers, but Jesus Christ, they didn't have to murder us like this. Hell, we didn't kill nobody . . . we didn't harm nobody. Ain't no one thought they would do us like this."

Practically naked, and much of his skin discolored and wrinkled, Wesley Hickok was gasping for air. As the inmate lay on a patch of grass and dirt, he was fanned and given water by first-aid attendants. Hickok was one of the lucky ones. He made it out alive, but just barely. Though wheezing badly and appearing as if he'd just trekked across the Gobi Desert, he tried to answer the questions of his earnest young interrogator. Afraid of possible consequences, Hickok initially refused to make any official statement.

"Listen, I work for the Philadelphia Coroner's Office," said the inquisitor. "My name is David Sandler. We're here to investigate what happened. How did you end up like this?"

Unshaven, with matted hair, bloodshot eyes, and too weak to even prop himself up on his elbows, Hickok lay on the ground, his head in the lap of an attendant who periodically wiped his face with a handkerchief. The inmate admitted it was all about the hunger strike, his dry, raspy voice barely audible. "You'da thought if they wanted to punish us, they'd just lock us on the block without food, but they . . . they wanted to get us. You know . . . teach us a lesson. They thought I was one of the ringleaders, so they threw me in that hellhole Saturday evening. Weren't necessary—the protest was collapsing all by itself. Guys were hungry, thirsty. Some were already breaking, you know, going down to the mess hall for chow. There was only a handful of us left. It probably would've been over in a day or two. But they wanted to get us, you know, show us who's boss, who runs the jail."

Kneeling on one knee and taking notes as best he could with sweat falling from his face onto his notepad, Sandler was intent on redeeming himself. Embarrassed by his emotional response to seeing so many dead and disfigured when he walked into Holmesburg, he feared the coroner would now think less of him. He imagined Coroner Glass suggesting he rethink his goal of a career in medicine.

As a youngster, Sandler had played with a chemistry set his parents had given him as a birthday present. Later, he enjoyed classical music and poetry and developed an appreciation for Italian opera, but it would be science and stories of scientific triumph that captured his imagination. The heroic men of microbiology challenging themselves and nature in the quest to solve age-old medical riddles increasingly dominated his reading agenda. Unlike the footballs and baseball gloves other boys kept by their bedsides, Paul de Kruif's *Microbe Hunters* and Sinclair Lewis's *Arrowsmith* adorned Sandler's night table growing up. He often fell asleep in the evening with visions of a properly schooled and credentialed David Sandler joining the likes of Walter Reed, Theobald Smith, and Paul Ehrlich in conquering the deadly diseases threatening mankind.

He had done well in college, his parents were proud of him, and his goal of becoming a physician made them proud. His father, a successful businessman, had become a supporter of the coroner after following Glass's earlier athletic exploits. He thought working in a city coroner's office would be good experience for his son before going off to medical school.

Since coming on board earlier that summer, Sandler had observed many autopsies with no ill effects, but seeing so many dead and others on the verge of death had unnerved him. He couldn't explain it; maybe it was the abnormally hot weather or the unearthly sight of so many strange blue corpses. Whatever it was, he was now intent on proving his mettle to the coroner.

Sandler asked the exhausted inmate a series of questions regarding the small punishment unit.

"How many men were locked in each cell?"

"How were you treated by guards?"

"Were you given adequate food and water?"

Hickok struggled to get the words out. In several halting, cough-filled attempts, he tried to form sentences, but his lungs were damaged. On a few occasions, Sandler thought he heard gurgling emanating from the inmate's chest cavity. Though willing in spirit, Hickok was physically unable to communicate. Sandler grew frustrated. He knew the importance of acquiring inmate accounts of their treatment and didn't want to disappoint his boss. His first time in a prison and his first time conducting an interview in what was actually a murder investigation, the young college grad gently coaxed the inmate to say what he could about his time in the punishment unit.

Carl Ferencz was having similar difficulty. Though he had worked in the coroner's office for nearly a dozen years and had been at the forefront of many investigations, the Holmesburg debacle broke new ground for depravity and outright cruelty. The first couple of survivors he attempted to question were barely conscious. The third, just ten yards away from Sandler and Hickok, gulped air as if his lungs had shriveled to the size of peas. The inmate's face was so pale he appeared white as paste, and attendants repeatedly poured water over the man's head in a desperate attempt to keep him conscious and to lower his body temperature. The inmate, James Walters, was from Harrowgate, a working-class section of the city near Kensington.

"I knew most of the guys in there," said Walters, swallowing big gulps of air between sentences. "They were in bad shape. It was terrible. God, was it hot. The guards shut all the windows, closed the air vents. Then they turned on the heat. By sundown, I thought I was a goner. I started screaming. We were dying. You couldn't breathe. We were suffocating. The radiators . . . they were so hot you could hear and see the steam coming out of 'em. If you touched a piece of metal you got burnt."

"Did you or the other men in the Klondike receive any food or water?" Ferencz asked.

"We got nothin'," said Walters. "Hell, we couldn't even flush the fuckin' hopper. And the spigot, forget it, everything was turned off except the heat."

Ferencz scribbled Walters's testimony onto his notepad as he eyed two guards approaching them. "Were any of the prisoners who were put into the Klondike uninvolved in the food strike?" he asked quickly. "Why were you placed there if reports in the newspapers say the protest had been broken?" But before Walters could answer the deputy coroner's questions, the guards escorted the injured prisoner to the infirmary on C Block.

While Ferencz and Sandler informed the coroner of their findings and busily sought out those inmates who were conscious and willing to talk before they were taken away, Glass concerned himself with collecting the dead and getting them down to the city morgue as quickly as possible. He was anxious to learn the exact cause of death. Philip Mattingly and William Harvey, the coroner's office's two physicians, arrived at Holmesburg's front gate with a borrowed sheriff's truck just before noon. Even though both men had years of experience observing a wide variety of human remains, they reacted like most others who saw the disfigured bodies that morning.

After first inspecting the bluish, desiccated skin of several dead men, they examined their nasal cavities, bulging eyes, and parched throats, the cracked lips and swollen tongues, and finally the hands and feet of the victims. Occasionally they would murmur a comment to each other, but few outside their number understood the medical jargon in which they communicated. Dr. Mattingly, the chief coroner's physician and a professor at the University of Pennsylvania School of Medicine, took note of several unusual burn marks on the legs and torsos of the deceased. At one point, he took off his gold wire eyeglasses to more closely examine severe burn marks on the toes, soles, and heels of the men's feet.

Pressed by their boss for an opinion, the doctors' initial examination of the deceased resulted in a preliminary determination of death by some form of scalding.

"These deaths were violent," Mattingly concluded. "They appear to have been scalded. There's nasal congestion, typical of death by gas, steam, or hot water."

"What about the unusual azure color of the corpses?" Coroner Glass asked.

At this, the pathologists were less certain.

"The cause of death," Dr. Harvey offered, "can only be established by a thorough autopsy, but our best guess is a lethal combination of intense steam and extremely hot liquid as the killing agent."

"A number of the deceased had serious bruising and scrape marks," Dr. Mattingly said, "but they were probably secondary to the actual cause of death. Rigor mortis was well established—several of the men had been dead for some time—but that, too, would best be determined in a lab."

"I want you to take the deceased to 13th and Wood Streets," Glass ordered, "and begin your examinations once next of kin have been given an opportunity to view their loved ones. Also, be warned that there might be additional bodies to examine before the day is over." Before departing with the remains of six inmates, the pathologists received one more assignment: "I want you to pay a visit to a small building in the prison yard located between D and E Blocks."

Chapter 5

The List of Dead

Newspaper reporters were growing increasingly exasperated. They had been seeking specifics about the Holmesburg affair, including the names of the deceased and injured, without success. In addition, they had to contend with a fierce Great Dane that a prison guard periodically employed to disburse reporters and residents blocking the street. Prison administrators and city officials were reluctant to release any information.

Glass, too, had sought the names and been rebuffed. Like members of various news-gathering organizations, he had grown frustrated by the inexplicable delay and outright obfuscation, but he was adamant on notifying relatives of the deceased that autopsies were in order and they'd only have a short window of opportunity before the postmortem process began. His persistence and status as a city official were finally rewarded. He was given a list of the sixteen inmates who had been assigned to the punishment unit. With the help of some officers and inmates, he was able to determine the identities of the six deceased. Glass read each entry carefully.

James McBride, 28, serving 18 months to 3 years for public intoxication and assault on a policeman. McBride lived on Somerset Street in North Philadelphia and worked at the Cramp Shipyard in Kensington.

Bruno Palumbo, 24, of Morris Street near Broad, was serving an 18-to-40-month sentence for two grocery store burglaries on Snyder Avenue. His older brother Patrick was also one of the inmates involved in the Holmesburg food strike and locked in the punishment unit.

John Webster, 46, formerly of Pittsburgh, with an extensive criminal history, was serving a 25-to-50-year sentence for a pharmacy hold-up in South Philadelphia that left the proprietor with two gunshot wounds.

Paul Oteri, 25, a resident of Disston Street in Tacony, was serving a 3-to-10-year sentence for a series of Frankford burglaries.

Jake Smyzak, 32, of the 2300 block of Washington Avenue in South Philadelphia, was serving a 5-to-16-year sentence for disorderly conduct, public intoxication, and severely injuring a police officer during a car chase.

Timothy O'Shea, 27, of Lippincott Street in Port Richmond, a welder at the Baldwin Locomotive plant, was serving a 3-to-10-year sentence for a series of nighttime burglaries of commercial establishments on Kensington Avenue.

None of the deceased were well known, nor were their crimes—with the exception of Webster—particularly noteworthy. When it was announced in the early afternoon that the coroner was about to release the names of the dead, even Glass was surprised by the number of information-starved newsmen— both radio and print—who quickly assembled to record names and addresses.

The swarm of reporters gathering on the street and in a basement shot-and-beer joint across from the prison was not only large but diverse. There were some familiar faces in the crowd, reporters representing the city's major papers including the *Public Ledger, Philadelphia Inquirer, Evening Bulletin, Daily News,* and *Philadelphia Record.* To the coroner's surprise, however, there were also reporters from out-of-state newspapers and radio stations. It was only when Glass started to field reporters' excited questions and they identified themselves that it suddenly dawned on him that representatives of the *New York Times, Wilmington Journal, Trenton Times, Baltimore Herald, Pittsburgh Post-Gazette,* and *Washington Post* had hurriedly journeyed to Philadelphia to cover the unfolding drama. But Mayor Clarke, District Attorney Campbell, and Chief of Police Gleason were nowhere to be found. Though a fairly minor row office functionary, Glass realized he was the highest-ranking elected official on-site. The realization wasn't comforting. The city's most important representatives were shunning what had become a major news story with national implications.

Reporters were growing disgruntled; some were openly skeptical of official pronouncements. Forced to stand around for several hours under an unforgiving sun waiting on information from city officials, they couldn't help but notice the sharply divergent accounts they were hearing from guards and medical personnel attending to the dead and injured. With each hour's passage, more and more reporters let it be known that the official version was having difficulty passing the smell test. Talk of bizarre-looking corpses, inmates being "cooked to death," and prison protesters "roasted" in some kind of "house of horrors" increased.

Though many local journalists viewed the coroner as a rather insignificant party loyalist, he was also seen by some as a straight shooter, a generally honest broker who was less inclined to wave the flag and blindly follow party dictates. When he appeared before them, reporters didn't hide their reservations about the official line being trumpeted by police detectives and Superintendent Davis.

"Coroner Glass," inquired one, "do you believe it was really fights between inmates that resulted in so many dead?"

"What proof is there that overexertion and malnutrition contributed to the deaths of the inmates?" asked another.

"And, Coroner Glass, is there any credence to the claim that communist organizers among the inmate population provoked the violence?" queried a third.

Each time a question laden with distrust was uttered, the growing mob of neighborhood residents that had gathered on the street and around the bar across the street from the prison voiced their approval. It was clear their allegiance to one of the largest employers in the area was minimal. Shouts of a cover-up and mass murder were frequent, along with demands for the where-abouts of the city's key officials.

"Where's the mayor?"

"Where's Mayor Clarke, where's Councilman Green?"

"When are we gonna get the real story of what happened here?"

Glass had his own reservations. A terrible calamity had occurred, and he suspected criminal behavior was a key element, but he had other concerns as well. His political survival was central among them. He held no aspirations for higher office and generally avoided controversy. Comfortable being a team player, he wanted to be viewed that way by his City Hall colleagues. The reputa-tions of the prison superintendent and the city administration were on the line. Caught in a tense battle between his official ethical obligation and party loyalty, Glass knew he had a difficult course to navigate. But the magnitude and nature of the human devastation he had observed—and was now obligated to investigate—was becoming increasingly uncomfortable.

"Yes, a deadly tragedy has occurred, and I'm not satisfied with any of the stories I have heard," said the coroner in response to reporters' and citizens' questions. "Six men are dead in rather horrible circumstances. Many others were discovered unconscious and near death. What happened here will be thoroughly investigated, I think I can assure you of that."

Skeptical newsmen continued to demand access to the institution, but Glass said he did not have the legal authority to grant such a request.

"Holmesburg is a crime scene, and the proper authorities need to conduct their investigation. Again, I assure you, my office is part of the investigatory process, and I hope we can shed light on the tragedy very soon."

When the coroner finished divulging the names of the deceased and taking questions from newsmen, several reporters tried to engage him in private conversation, but Glass managed to pull himself away. He was uncomfortable with the entire situation. Unsure himself with what had transpired over the weekend, he didn't want to harm the reputations of his municipal colleagues. He wasn't prepared to make any definitive pronouncements. In addition, he was preoccupied with his other conundrum, one that the crowd had already identified: Why was he the only elected official at the site? Where were the city's leaders at such a critical time? Even the local councilman whose district Holmesburg resided in was a no-show.

Intent on finding out, Glass called his secretary. Her reply proved unsettling.

"I made calls to the mayor, DA, and police chief some hours ago, with little to report. Their offices are monitoring the situation, and they say they'll be in touch at the appropriate time," Miss Renwick informed him.

Glass sensed what was occurring. He feared the knot in the pit of his stomach that had been building throughout the day would eventually consume him.

His secretary continued: "Pennsylvania Secretary of Welfare Enteen has called a couple of times to express his concern, however." She then proceeded to inform him of some relevant constitutional precedents he had inquired about earlier. He wrote down the pertinent citations as she informed him of several calls from Enteen and other members of the governor's office in Harrisburg. "They're aghast at the loss of life and want answers. There are also a growing number of interview requests, several from out-of-state news agencies . . ."

Miss Renwick's voice trailed on, but the coroner was distracted. He recognized the cowardly and often-used stratagem that was being played out by the city's political leaders. He wondered if there was anything he could do about it . . .

After thanking his secretary, Glass quickly dialed the mayor's office. The mayor's private secretary said he was in a meeting, but she would take a message. Wondering what could be more important than what was occurring in Northeast Philadelphia, Glass insisted on speaking to the mayor. His argumentative tone resulted in one of the mayor's top deputies, Harold Jennings, getting on the line.

"Hesh, I understand you have quite a situation on your hands up there?"

"That's an understatement if I ever heard one," said Glass crossly. "There are bodies all over the place. I can't be sure, but it appears the actions of Davis and his guards may have contributed to the death of some half-dozen men up here this weekend. Reporters from as far away as New York and Washington are now camped out on Torresdale Avenue. They want to know what the mayor has to say about this . . . this damn mess. When the hell is the mayor going to make an appearance or a statement?"

"Calm down, Hesh," said Jennings. "It's a delicate situation. We don't want to act rashly."

"Rashly?" Glass bellowed. "The bodies were discovered at sun-up. It's mid-afternoon. A comment from the mayor now would hardly be considered rash!"

"Listen," said the mayor's advisor, "we'd recommend you not get ahead of yourself. You can't assume causation to Superintendent Davis. There could be a reasonable explanation and . . . and think of the consequences . . ."

"What are you talking about?" asked Glass. "What consequences?"

"You don't want to hurt your friends, Hesh."

Momentarily speechless, Glass suspected what Jennings was referring to.

"We need to be cautious," said Jennings calmly. "This situation needs to be properly managed."

"Well, what do you suggest, Harold? How 'bout I tell everyone it was all a big mistake and they should just go home? Besides, Holmesburg's been overcrowded for years. What's the big deal about the loss of a half-dozen neighborhood hoodlums?"

"No need for sarcasm, Hesh. That won't help resolve anything."

"And neither will the city's top elected officials hiding in their offices," said Glass angrily. "I'm up here by myself."

"I know, I know. Take it easy."

"Autopsies will begin shortly, and the pathology report will be released to the press. I'm not gonna hide it," said Glass. "I have no intention of shading the truth in order to protect the image of the county prison system. I'm not gonna be part of any cover-up."

When Jennings objected to the coroner's characterization of what he was suggesting, Glass quickly interrupted and denounced the falsehoods police investigators were disseminating regarding the cause of the deaths.

"Harold, those men didn't die from exhaustion, undernourishment, or any disagreement over ending a food strike!" Glass screamed into the phone. "And they certainly didn't take their own lives because Joe Stalin told them to. I think they were roasted on a spit like slabs of beef at a country fair. I know because I was in that oven, that little torture chamber the inmates call Klondike. Christ, it's a brick furnace. I'm afraid Davis must periodically use the damn thing to punish troublemakers."

"Is that what you're going to tell newspaper reporters?" Jennings replied warily.

"Listen, Harold," said Glass, "I don't know the building's original purpose or how it's been used, but over this past weekend it would seem to have been used for one thing—to roast people."

"Rubbish."

"Rubbish?" Glass repeated angrily. "I've got a half-dozen black corpses up here. Now, that may not be such a big deal, but guess what? They're not colored inmates—they're actually white men. That's right, they're Caucasians like you and me. But over the weekend they've become as dark as Jesse Owens. Don't you think that's a bit peculiar?"

Glass gathered himself when there was no reply. He continued: "My office will do a thorough investigation, and I won't say anything I can't support with substantial evidence." He sighed. "Listen, Harold, I'm paid $8,000 a year as the city's coroner, and I have sworn an oath . . . If city detectives continue to propagate such ridiculous explanations as mass suicide, fighting among themselves, and inmate exhaustion, I'll . . . let's just say don't count on me to back them up. I have no intention of being the fall guy in a purposely bungled homicide investigation."

There were several seconds of uncomfortable silence before Jennings inquired, "What do you want?"

"Get the mayor up here," said Glass. "If you can't do that, get him to at least make a statement. And I want the mayor's cooperation in ensuring those in bad shape are immediately transferred out of Holmesburg and sent to Philadelphia General Hospital. Some of these men are in dire condition and require proper medical care."

"I don't know, Hesh—"

"And one more thing: I'm concerned for the safety of the survivors if they remain at Holmesburg under the custody of men who obviously tried to kill them. They're scared to death," said Glass, "and I can't blame them. I can't get them to talk if—"

"That will be Superintendent Davis's call," said Jennings matter-of-factly.

"But I'm trying to conduct an investigation, and men won't tell me what happened if they're stuck on a Holmesburg cellblock. I'm telling you their lives are at risk."

"It's a police matter, Hesh. You're not a cop; you don't have to investigate anything."

"You don't get it, do you?" Glass shot back. "If you were up here, you'd know this isn't your standard municipal screw-up. It's not something you can cover up. A bunch of disfigured bodies are laying out under the sun, and what seems like half the news reporters in America are gathered on Torresdale Avenue seeking answers."

After a few moments of silence, Jennings again asked, "What do you want, Hesh?"

"I want the survivors to be moved to Moyamensing or another secure location."

"It's the superintendent's decision," Jennings once again repeated. "It's up to Davis."

"You should inform the mayor that Davis's career as a prison superintendent is probably over," barked the coroner. "In fact, he'll be lucky if he escapes a prison sentence. This is not your typical gambling beef or kickback scandal, Harold. If you were up here, you'd know that. As I've already said, we've got some peculiar-looking bodies up here and a growing number of reporters who want answers. I don't think the mayor's silence is going to be viewed well when the truth comes out."

Though both men attempted to end the conversation in a civil fashion, their mutual distrust could not be masked. The coroner's disappointment with the mayor's office was immediately aggravated by further bad news when Ferencz and Sandler informed him two more inmates had died. Taken out of the punishment unit with the other survivors, the men never regained consciousness.

Their bodies were now being prepared for transport to the morgue. The Klondike had claimed the lives of eight men, and there were still several hours of daylight left.

Chapter 6

A City Consumed by Ethical Challenges

Though the majority of the city's citizens may not have known it was Lincoln Steffens who authored the infamous assessment that Philadelphia was "corrupt and contented," they well knew the ethical swamp that was being referenced. The city had a long and unhealthy tolerance for machine politics and public corruption. "Bossism" had surely found a home.

The Depression years only further cemented that noxious tradition. During the 1930s, a series of either incompetent or outright corrupt mayoral administrations experienced an embarrassing number of political scandals, grand jury investigations, and high-profile convictions. Much consternation, hand wringing, and calls for reform followed suit. Despite the endless governmental miasma, law enforcement ineptitude, and cries for change by good government groups, business continued as usual. Steffens had written at the turn of the century that Philadelphia was "politically benighted," a city whose citizens were "proud . . . to defend corruption and boast of their machine." The passage of several decades hadn't changed the toxic civic dynamic.

Mayor G. Thomas Clarke was a product of that system. Flexible philosophically, prone to controversy, and seemingly fond of a wide array of liquid spirits, Clarke's short time in office since his election in 1935 was anything but boring. He was currently the centerpiece of a political firestorm concerning new kickback allegations; newspaper headlines screamed of widespread police department corruption that stretched from gambling dens to police precincts to City Hall. "Gambling Kingpins Accuse City Officials," "Police Linked to Gamblers," and "Payoffs to Police Allowed 136 Gambling Houses to Flourish," were front-page headlines that greeted readers of the city's many daily newspapers in recent days.

Though over a hundred gangsters, bootleggers, and gambling kingpins were named in a Special Grand Jury presentment, there were also the names of "Philadelphia's Finest," prominent members of the police department. In fact, the grand jury recommended the dismissal of an inspector, a captain, two lieutenants, and eleven policemen attached to the 12th and Pine police station in Center City. It was further suggested that numerous others, including three sergeants and nearly a dozen policemen, be demoted and a few others suspended. Apparently, everyone at the precinct was on the take. Worse still, the grand jury flatly stated that if top members of the city administration were not on the pad themselves, they at least knew of the payoffs by various gambling houses and kept their mouths shut.

Silence, in fact, seemed a press strategy much embraced by Mayor Clarke. Usually ensconced in his second-floor office and unavailable for comment, on those rare occasions when reporters caught up to him in the corridors of City Hall, Clarke replied, "I have no comment to make. I am very busy running the city government. And I won't have any comment to make later." By late summer, the heat and his declining health were getting to him, however. As proof, Clarke threatened to take an extended vacation. Newspaper headlines captured the absurdity of the situation: "Mayor to Leave Job for Two Months," and "Clarke Off to the Mountains to Escape Heat."

Department heads and other underlings got the message and followed suit. The director of public safety, for example, informed the press, simply, "I have nothing to say." Superintendent of Police Walter Gleason responded much the same and threatened to arrest any reporter who came to his office. 'The less said the better' became an office holder's first, second, and third line of defense.

Commonly known a century earlier as the "Athens of America," Philadelphia by the late 1930s was more a commercial and shipping hub like Rotterdam and Hamburg than an enlightened Hellenic hilltop. A shining example of public rectitude it was not. A city of over two million people with a robust industrial economy that was home to such diverse manufacturing giants as Stetson Hats, Baldwin Locomotive, and Cramp Shipyard, Philadelphia was also characterized by major contrasts, constantly shifting alliances, and Byzantine complexity. With large, varied constituencies reflecting affluence and poverty, criminality and tranquility, Philadelphia was an East Coast metropolis whose many assets were only exceeded by its even greater challenges. Often trading on its historic social, economic, and political contributions, the city—to the consternation of many forward thinkers—kept a respectful distance from anything that smacked of modernity and innovation. An economic powerhouse whose wide-ranging and mighty industries produced everything from electronics and battleships to textiles and chemicals, Philadelphia weathered the Depression better than many large American cities, such as Pittsburgh and Detroit, that were primarily one-industry towns.

Philadelphia was far from unscathed, however. Unemployment skyrocketed, banks closed their doors, mortgage foreclosures exploded, and shantytowns filled with the homeless emerged overnight. Many sophisticated financial observers saw the city on the verge of collapse. In addition to the economic impact, the Depression had another significant effect: it propelled the city's inexorable journey from a one-party town dominated by Republicans to a competitive two-party city where Democrats actually competed and occasionally won elective office. Franklin Roosevelt's optimistic spirit and programmatic vision offered a New Deal to thousands who were brought down by the economic crash. The city's changing political landscape was fostered by a Republican machine that put men in the mayor's office who either threw their hands up in exasperation at the financial turmoil surrounding them or scolded the city's unemployed citizens for their lethargy and willingness to go on the public dole. Mayor Clarke's predecessor, for example, had the temerity to denounce those in financial difficulty as "living well despite their claims of distress. They drive automobiles, go to restaurants, and have nice homes. I don't see any poverty or blight. Talk of a national depression," he bellowed, "is much overblown." Hard to explain then why that same mayor fired nearly 4,000 city workers to save salaries and put police and firemen on mandatory vacation for two weeks at a time to save additional millions in tax revenue.

Such insensitive talk and hard-hearted action resulted in hundreds of thousands of new registrants annually joining the Democratic Party. The once-solid foundation of Philadelphia's Republican Party was definitely showing fissures, the structural fault lines thereby allowing several minor row office positions like city coroner to go Democratic. Republicans still controlled major offices like mayor and district attorney, but one could see in the not-too-distant future where Democratic candidates would have a real shot at winning those higher offices.

In the meantime, the political structure was as corrupt as it was when Steffens called Philadelphia "hopelessly ring-ruled," and "the worst-governed city in America." Election fraud complaints were routine, as were phantom voters, payoffs on election day, and outright intimidation and manhandling of voters. The city's magistrates' courts further weakened an already ethically challenged legal system. More conniving politicians than prudent jurists, the magistrates usually had no legal education, were small-minded in outlook, and were forever beholden to the key political players and organizations that put them in office. Opportunities for payoffs and bribes were abundant, and many magistrates made out like bandits, but despite the periodic charges of corruption and tabloid revelations of self-enrichment, the institution remained a key part of the city's legal apparatus.

Criminal activity flourished; why wouldn't it? It was protected. Just a decade earlier, a much-frustrated, high-ranking city jurist called for a "sweeping investigation into the deplorable criminal conditions in Philadelphia." It was to no one's surprise that members of the police force of all ranks had obtained graft which totaled millions of dollars. It was estimated that protection payments of $2,000,000, not counting sums received by high-ranking police officials, were paid to ensure the continued operation of illegal gambling establishments. Police officials were growing rich; one captain deposited $8,500 in his bank account within ten weeks; another received $200,000 in less than two years.

Calls for reform were pervasive, and grand jury investigations seemed an annual exercise. Police corruption was often the target of the investigations. One grand jury presentment ordered three police inspectors, eighteen captains, and fifteen lieutenants to stand trial. An additional twenty-two officers were suspended for failure to explain their accumulations of wealth. As one document argued, "the operation of 1,170 saloons, thousands of speakeasies, many houses of prostitution, and large gambling establishments—all of which have been in existence for years—indicated that police acquiescence was essential for these thriving operations."

One Philadelphia mayor was so distressed by the intractable corruption and criminal activity that he asked the president to send World War I hero General Smedley Butler to clean up the city. Butler vigorously attacked criminal activity with military-like precision in an effort to transform Philadelphia into a law-abiding community. However, with all his arrests of bootleggers, speakeasy operators, corrupt magistrates, and so forth, he was accused of only skimming the surface. Crime and public corruption continued unfazed. General Butler finally threw up his hands, called it quits, and went back to the Marine Corps. "Trying to enforce the law in Philadelphia," said Butler, "was worse than any battle I was ever in."

For law-abiding Philadelphians, the problem seemed hopeless. Just a week before the Holmesburg incident, inmates initiated their widely publicized food strike, and local newspaper headlines announced the results of the Ruth Commission, a fifteen-month state legislative investigation that documented everything from jury fixing and parole payoff schemes to widespread racketeer influence and judges on the pad. Justice in Philadelphia was declared, "riddled with dangers," including jury fixing and notorious criminals continually receiving paroles. Crime, argued the commission report, "was destroying the whole fabric of society," thereby ensuring Philadelphia remained "submerged in an ethical swamp" and irretrievably lost as a decent place to live, work, and raise a family.

Commission members not only referred "to the outright sale of public justice for a cash consideration, but also to the subtle system of barter, which conceals the real elements of these corrupt transactions while trading upon a multitude of social, economic, and political ties." The report went on to underscore the depth of the problem by acknowledging the integrity of the judicial system as a key safeguard against brazen illegality, but in Philadelphia, many of the judges paid as little attention to the law as did the criminals. Hanging over all like a Damocles Sword was a special commonwealth grand jury investigating public corruption and its ties to organized crime. Investigators had been pursuing leads and witnesses for months. Both county elected officials and police administrators were bracing themselves; the grand jury's report was expected before the end of September.

Glass had witnessed much of the moral morass but was never particularly moved by it. He, too, was a product of the system. Fearful the administration would attempt to handle the Holmesburg deaths as it had other scandals garnering front-page attention, Glass realized he'd have to move quickly if he wanted to collect evidence and take witness statements. The threat of being barred from the penal facility loomed over him like an ominous cloud. In an effort to control the news, he didn't put it past Clarke and Davis to sever his access to the institution even though he had every legal right to carry out his investigation. Uncomfortable with his own decision, he informed Ferencz and Sandler they'd have to immediately interview as many survivors as possible.

Guards would be interviewed as well, although the prospect of them informing on superiors or fellow guards was unlikely. The trio would work through the night if necessary; it was imperative that they piece together as much as they could from inmate accounts.

While Ferencz and Sandler went directly to the prison hospital on C Block and began interviewing all who were willing and able to recount the events of the last thirty-six hours, the coroner went out onto Torresdale Avenue to inform the press that the death toll had risen to eight. In addition, he wanted to ensure that radio broadcasts as well as those newspapers with evening editions contained the names of the deceased. He was anxious for the results of the autopsies, but families of the deceased men deserved time with their loved ones.

Under a fusillade of reporters' questions, the coroner made no attempt to defend the initial police assessment of the inmate deaths. Initially mute, he was eventually forced to give a statement. "It's all very suspicious, and to be honest, I'm not satisfied with any of the stories I have heard by investigators today," said Glass rather bluntly. "There is no question that these men met their deaths by some type of scalding or proximity to extreme heat. Various body parts of the deceased were shriveled, indicating immersion in hot water or exposure to intense steam. I am sure it was not fire in their cells. That would have burned the victims over larger areas of their bodies and left definite burn marks on cell bars and walls. There was no fire. I believe it was some form of steam, tear gas, vapor, or something else of destructive intensity. My physicians should be able to nail it down."

"What about police reports and those statements of prison authorities regarding inmate fights over continuing or ending the food strike?" asked one reporter.

Glass managed to maintain his composure, but others followed. He deflected the questions as best he could. However, when he was asked if he supported Superintendent Davis's decision to keep all of the survivors at Holmesburg and not send any to nearby hospitals, and whether the investigation would be affected by politics, Glass had difficulty holding to script.

"My deputies are interviewing prisoners as we speak," said Glass. "I shall be joining them once I leave you. If necessary, we will interview the occupants of the entire jail throughout the night in order to get the true story of what happened here. There will be no whitewash or cover-up. The truth will come out. No one, including the mayor, can abrogate or curtail this investigation."

Reporters immediately responded with questions and comments regarding the city's long history of obstructing investigative commissions, abiding corruption, and generally showing little interest in rooting out illegal activity.

Frustrated and intent on demonstrating his independence as well as not being tainted by the pervasive odor of corruption that saturated Philadelphia politics, the coroner announced a legal bombshell that was sure to resonate with the powers that be. "According to an Act of the General Assembly of March 29, 1819," stated Glass, "the coroner has authority to make investigations of all murders, suicides, manslaughters, or deaths in prisons. In addition, there is also a State Supreme Court decision of 1809, which holds that the coroner has the common law duty to investigate prison deaths and prison breaches. There are some other interesting aspects of that decision, but I will save those for another time. The bottom line is this: Whatever nefarious activity occurred over the weekend and in whatever way it may have contributed to the deaths of these eight men will be revealed for all to see."

The huge crowd, in which there were almost two dozen reporters frantically scribbling on notepads, voiced their approval, but there were still doubters among them. Like most party operatives, Glass had never been viewed as a beacon of independence. And for the many skeptics all too familiar with high-level municipal investigations that tended to produce little, or even worse—exonerate the guilty—there was ample reason for doubt. But the coroner reiterated, "I am going to interview prisoners, and I expect to do it without the interference of the superintendent, the warden, and any guards. If necessary, we will interview the occupants of entire cellblocks and the entire prison population in order to get the true story of who and what killed these men."

There were a few supportive cheers from the crowd, but the coroner didn't bother to take a bow, expand on his comments, or entertain any sidebar conversations. He immediately re-entered the institution and went directly to C Block to assist with the interview process.

After hearing the coroner's bold remarks from his corner office in the administration building, Superintendent Davis felt compelled to defend his honor and respond to what he had just heard. In shirtsleeves, the knot of his necktie coming undone, and his white hair blowing in the stifling afternoon breeze, Superintendent Davis took to the street, stamped out his cigarette, and claimed to be incredulous at the coroner's statements.

"I can't see how the coroner's theory of the deaths could have taken place," said the superintendent with a perplexed expression as newsmen gathered around him. "We certainly used no steam or hot water on the men and there are no steam or hot water pipes in the building in which they were confined. In my mind, there were no marks on the bodies of these men sufficient to have caused death. They were placed in what the prisoners call Klondike. It's really an isolation block for significant troublemakers and violent felons who present a danger to other inmates and guards."

"Are we permitted to see the structure where the men died?" a reporter called out.

"No, no, that would be impossible as it is still a crime scene. Not until the police investigation is complete would I consider giving newsmen access to it." Davis went on to explain the Klondike's location between D and E Blocks and described its size, contents, and purpose. "It is imperative that you note the structure's radiators and the supply lines were all out of reach of the prisoners and none of the pipes had been touched or broken. In other words, the coroner's theories of the deaths are inaccurate."

"Superintendent Davis, can you explain the shriveled bodies of the deceased men, their creepy blue tint, and the unusually high number of victims?"

Davis had no answer. He hesitated, then reiterated, "The prisoners in isolation cells were placed there Sunday morning after they insisted on agitating the other prisoners to keep up their hunger strike, which began Friday. Some of these men were strike leaders and others were your regular troublemakers. No one saw them until they were given breakfast yesterday morning, since there are no guards in or about the building. It's an isolation block. Warden Stryker heard the prisoners talking at about ten-thirty on Sunday evening, and everything seemed normal at that time. No one else could have gotten into the building, as I have the only key. After the bodies were found and police were notified, the entire prison was turned over to the city detectives, and every aid was given them."

Though some reporters were accepting of the superintendent's argument, many evidently harbored reservations and continued to pepper the city's top prison official with questions he couldn't or wouldn't answer. Local newsmen knew Davis as a competent and experienced municipal official with an impressive resume. Born in Upland, near Chester, Pennsylvania, in 1878, Davis quit school at an early age and began working in his father's cotton mill. He was quick to master every machine and device in the plant and only left due to the outbreak of war. He distinguished himself in the Philippines during the Spanish-American conflict and was nicknamed "Rough-and-Ready" Davis by the cavalry troops he commanded in the 6th Pennsylvania Infantry. He'd return home in 1901 to knock about for a couple of years before enrolling at Temple University. Tall and rugged, he was talked into becoming a fullback on the college's first football team, but the classroom never held much interest for him, and he'd leave school without earning a degree. Friends in South Philadelphia political circles, however, recognized his talents—especially as a cavalry officer—and assisted him in becoming a Philadelphia mounted police officer in 1904. He'd remain on the force for the next three decades. No shrinking violet, he'd oversee significant investigations and departmental advancements, all the while contending with dangerous criminals and demanding politicians.

On several occasions, he was nearly killed in deadly bombings. In the hunt for communists and anarchists after World War I, radicals retaliated and twice blew up his home. One nighttime blast tossed him out of bed and into a hospital gurney. Years later, just after christening a new police boat on the Delaware, the vessel exploded, forcing Davis to swim to shore despite suffering a broken ankle. When asked about his attraction to such a dangerous line of work, he replied, "Guess I'm just a sucker for a uniform and adventure." Repeatedly promoted in rank, Davis proved himself a sound manager and was credited with doing pioneer work on developing the department's first traffic squad, instituting electric traffic signals, training mounted police, and introducing police radios and teletype machines to the local force.

In 1929, he was promoted to superintendent of police and enjoyed the command of a 4,000-member force, but four years later and as a favor to the mayor, he agreed to take the prison superintendent's position after a series of scandals and disturbances rocked the city penal system. Davis was not thrilled with the switch—keeping prisoners under lock and key was never as interesting as police work—but he owed his political sponsors. Politics was the lifeblood of most big cities, and everyone with a job, whether elected or appointed, had to follow their patrons' wishes.

A war hero, an innovative city administrator, and someone who up to now had been relatively scandal-free—at least by Philadelphia standards—Davis had earned the goodwill of even the most cynical tabloid scribe. However, eight men were dead in a most brutal fashion, and Davis had no explanation. Adding to the confusion was a police department account that stretched plausibility to the breaking point.

Chapter 7

The Morgue

"My poor boy, my poor boy, what have they done to you?" cried the distraught middle-aged woman being aided by relatives as they exited the city morgue on 13th Street. In a drab housedress, her salt-and-pepper hair uncombed, tears falling freely down her cheeks, Mrs. Maria Oteri had just paid her last respects to her youngest son, Paul. "He was a good boy," sobbed Mrs. Oteri. "He never hurt no one. But look what they did to him. Look what they did."

"He's a mess, all battered up. I can barely recognize him and I'm his brother," added Dante Oteri. "His skin is like an alligator's, all wrinkly and scaly, and his left eye is totally misshapen. It's at least three or four times its regular size. He looks like somebody worked him over with a crowbar. They're all monsters up there at that prison. They destroy people at will."

Dante Oteri and Paul's wife—now a widow at twenty-three, with a three-year-old child to care for—placed the matriarch of the family against a parked automobile to gather herself before the journey home to the Tacony section of the city. Though emotionally battered, Mrs. Oteri continued to plead her case to the small crowd of reporters who had gathered for the emotionally wrenching identification process.

Paul Oteri, according to what his mother had been told by doctors, was one of the last to die that day. She informed reporters he had been arrested in February for burglarizing homes in the Frankford and Torresdale sections of the city. He had managed to escape the Ruan Street police station and had gotten as far as Harrisburg when his conscience got the better of him and told him to turn back. "He knew what it would mean to be a fugitive and never see his wife and baby or his brothers and sisters," said Mrs. Oteri, her bloodshot eyes filled with tears. "He came back on his own, went to see a priest at St. Leo's, and made his confession. He said he would surrender voluntarily if he could first see me. He came home February 21 and said he had done wrong. I always told him the importance of faith and belief in the Lord.

"He asked me if I'd go with him and stick close by until this was over. He said that if I did, he'd swear he'd never give me another heartache. He was in that terrible Holmesburg Prison nearly six months. And now this, and I was the one who talked him into coming back. Oh my God, look what I did."

Mrs. Oteri admitted to newsmen that her son had presented her with a "long series of heartaches" over the years. His trouble with the law, according to his police record, had started in 1931 when he was picked up for "loitering and mischievous behavior," and soon after for "suspicion of burglary." In 1933, he was sentenced from eighteen months to three years on a burglary conviction. After completing his minimum he was set free, but other people's possessions became his passion, and he was arrested again for a series of burglaries in Northeast Philadelphia. He escaped from the police lockup and fled, but pangs of conscience and regret brought him back two days later. "I always told him," said Mrs. Oteri, "that if he got right with God, God would get right with him. And now he's gone."

Imprisonment was designed to both punish and end criminal behavior; it certainly had in Paul Oteri's case.

Just as the Oteri family departed, three members of the McBride family exited the one-story, nearly block-long building less than a mile from City Hall. More angry than sorrowful, Herbert McBride, the brother of the late James, spewed a series of venomous comments toward the news reporters. "They're just a bunch of murderers," yelled Herbert McBride of the prison administrators. "What they did to my brother is a crime. The look of agony on Jim's face—his corpse—was horrible. I fought in the last war. I was overseas and saw combat firsthand. I saw some pretty hideous things. But nothing was half as bad as what I have just seen in this morgue. My brother looked as if he'd been tortured. His face was all battered and many of his teeth were out. And his color . . . I can't even describe it. It didn't even look like him. I couldn't recognize my own brother. Who does a thing like that? What kind of people are they? Are we still in America?"

The older McBride, father of the deceased, was pale, unsteady, and the picture of confusion. A former high-ranking official in the fire department, the old man looked as if he were about to faint. Assisted to a nearby step to gather himself, he slowly shook his head and repeatedly mumbled, "They killed him . . . they killed my boy."

Next to leave the building and join others on the cluttered sidewalk was Henry Hazlit, who was a familiar face to many of the newsmen covering the Holmesburg story. Hazlit was an *Evening Bulletin* reporter who had covered the criminal trial of John Webster, aka Ernie Lombardo, from Pittsburgh. A career criminal whose normal field of operations stretched from Youngstown, Ohio, to Johnstown, Pennsylvania, Webster had a long criminal history with pinches in Illinois and New York and everywhere in between. He had done time in tough state institutions such as Stateville and Sing Sing. Assuming more than a dozen aliases over the years, Webster was also tagged with the moniker "One Inch Johnny" in the Pittsburgh area for his deft work with a penknife. It was said he could break into a residence or business with a dull, snub-nose knife quicker than a homeowner could unlock his front door with a key. Sought by Allegheny County police for a series of burglaries, Lombardo fled to Philadelphia where he soon ran afoul of the law. Hazlit had covered his conviction in a City Hall courtroom and was there the day Webster received a 25-to-50-year sentence for shooting a North Philadelphia pharmacist during the commission of a robbery. Hazlit volunteered to identify Lombardo's body, as the decedent had no known relatives. The reporter also predicted to his fellow scribes that since the newly deceased was apparently without family, it was quite likely he would become a permanent resident of Philadelphia, residing in the potter's field in the far northeast section of the city.

Shortly after Hazlit departed, Shirley O'Shea exited the building with an unidentified male. O'Shea was the mother of Timothy O'Shea, a Fishtown welder employed at the Baldwin Locomotive Works before being found guilty of a series of commercial burglaries along Kensington Avenue. "Somebody's gonna pay for this," snapped Mrs. O'Shea as she walked past reporters toward Broad Street. "They murdered my boy. One look and you can see they baked him alive up there at Holmesburg. That's right; baked him alive. Somebody is gonna pay dearly for this."

Unable to hide her anger, Mrs. O'Shea attacked the entire prison system. "The courtesies visitors receive at Holmesburg are terrible. They have a couple guards up there who treat you as if you were a dog. You'da thought I was a criminal, that I did something wrong every time I went up there to visit my son. Yeah, my boy broke the law and he was serving his punishment, but this . . . No one had the right to do this to him. They killed him for a couple of burglaries."

For the next couple of hours, friends and relatives of the deceased, having been notified by the coroner's office that they needed to immediately go to the city morgue, endured the painful gauntlet of gawkers and reporters before seeing the corpse of a loved one laid out on a marble slab. They then had to field questions hurled at them by aggressive newsmen.

It was only when a deceased individual's family had left that Drs. Mattingly and Harvey commenced what would prove a very long night performing autopsies. Though little known or appreciated by city residents, the 13th and Wood Streets facility was one of the most up-to-date municipal morgues in the nation. With modern laboratory equipment capable of testing everything from poisons to knife and bullet wounds, the morgue possessed state-of-the-art X-ray and photographic technology, a comprehensive medical library, and the latest ballistics equipment. Dr. Mattingly had been personally trained by the office's former chief physician and was routinely sought out by other jurisdictions for his opinion on difficult cases requiring expertise on cause of death.

A graduate of Villanova College and the University of Pennsylvania Medical School, Philip Donald Mattingly had been the chief coroner's physician for nearly five years. Though also a connoisseur of nineteenth-century British fiction—he had pursued a graduate degree in English literature at St. Joseph's University prior to entering medical school—Mattingly had chosen medicine as his life's work after spending a series of summers working as an intern for the longtime chief pathologist of the city. An accomplished student with an inquisitive mind, he'd studied abroad after graduating from medical school. Taking advanced courses in dermatopathology at the University of Edinburgh and Leipzig University, blood preservation techniques at Leningrad University in the Soviet Union, and tropical diseases in the West Indies, Mattingly's academic credentials were some of the most impressive of any physician to have worked in the coroner's office.

The Leipzig experience would prove distressing, however. "The country is now in the hands of thugs and maniacs," he cautioned his colleagues regarding the growth of Hitler and the Nazi Party in Germany. "The best academic minds are being kicked out and replaced by undistinguished bottom-feeders and party hacks. Medicine in Germany is becoming a racket run by imposters. A hundred years of academic rigor and scientific excellence is going to hell."

Such bombast, however, was unusual for the office's chief physician; he normally stayed clear of politics. In addition to the $3,500 he earned from his city job, Mattingly was also the chief of medical service at Misericordia Hospital in West Philadelphia, plus his duties at Penn. Unmarried, in his late thirties, and without any time-consuming hobbies besides his appreciation of nineteenth-century British writers, Dr. Mattingly was known for putting in prodigious work hours—a trait that would be of immense value considering the office's current challenge.

While staff discreetly shuttled family members of the deceased to private rooms where they could identify the corpses and pay their last respects, Mattingly and Harvey took to adjoining operating rooms in the rear of the building and began conducting the laborious postmortem investigations. Adorned in surgeon's gowns, large rubber gloves, and rubber aprons, with scalpels in hand and microscopes by their sides, the doctors literally cut into the deadly Holmesburg mystery.

Slowly and meticulously, the two men made large incisions in the chest cavities of the first two prisoners to undergo a "Viennese post," as Dr. Mattingly referred to the procedure. Because of their collective suspicions, the doctors focused their attentions on the lungs of the deceased. A "gross examination," or one without a lot of sophisticated instrumentation, was designed to see if water was present in the lungs. They then placed the lungs in water to see if they would float, further allowing them to determine the amount of water or other fluids that might have been ingested prior to death. If the prisoners had inhaled steam before they died, the lungs would be red and irritated. Pus and mucous—similar to what is found in blisters caused by burned skin—might also be present. If the men had inhaled tear gas or some other type of toxic material, the lungs would also become red and show signs of irritation.

Mattingly and Harvey then moved on to the next step, the microscopic examination of lung tissue. By first freezing sections of the lungs in dry ice and then slicing several thin sections with a microtone (or surgical meat cleaver), and placing them under a microscope, the doctors would be able to determine if the cell structure had been altered before death. The same procedure would be followed with other vital organs of the body such as the liver, heart, and kidneys.

The doctors were sure that any foreign matter such as arsenic, strychnine, or other poison that entered the bodies of the deceased would be discovered.

A stickler for the highest standards of propriety when performing any surgical procedure, Dr. Mattingly didn't countenance shortcuts or slipshod methodology in his laboratory, even when the patient was deceased. As he frequently told his Penn pathology students, "You mustn't hazard a guess or let the evidence get away from you in difficult, controversial cases. Someone might say your work was below par, shoddy, or tampered with while you weren't looking. You must have the samples in your control at all times and be precise in your examination."

Though neither a politician nor law enforcement official, Mattingly well knew the importance of his judgment regarding the cause of death of the Klondike inmates.

Chapter 8

Interviews with Survivors in the Prison Hospital

August 22, 1939, Monday Evening

"Hey, cutie, I've never seen you before," whispered an inmate with a pronounced effeminate swagger. "What's going on out there, honey? Y'all seem very busy. Maybe you be interested in some company tonight? Whaddaya say, sugar?"

"Now, what do we got here? Aren't you a special treat on a warm summer evening," chimed in a more masculine inmate.

"Yo, slim, you lookin' for some action?" said a third sweaty prisoner pushing a broom across the expansive rotunda floor.

Wolf whistles soon followed. Though the catcalls unnerved him, the young college grad didn't dare look to see their origin. His first time crossing Holmesburg's large center control area, David Sandler put on his most professional expression, the one that resonated purpose and self-assurance. But the young man felt anything but confident. His heart was racing; he was determined not to lose control as he had hours earlier. Refusing to look at the ruffians whistling and hurling sexual comments at him, he focused on the officer escorting the deputy coroner and himself to the prison medical unit.

Tall, trim, and not yet twenty-two years of age, Sandler's youth and good looks made him a natural object of desire for imprisoned men with lusty but truncated sexual appetites. Although his anxiety-provoking walk across the rotunda to C Block may have felt inordinately long and embarrassing, his exposure to wolf whistles and sexual ridicule was actually rather tame compared to what he would have encountered on a normal day when scores of inmates would have been crossing the same piece of Holmesburg real estate. At the moment, however, there were no prisoners going to the chow hall, the auditorium, or the gym; the prison was locked down and only a handful of prison workers—kitchen staff, hospital orderlies, and cellblock workers—were allowed out of their cells.

There were catcalls, however, to upset him. He wondered what Ferencz was thinking. Should he make a remark to the deputy coroner or just try and mask his insecurity in an air of resolve and determination? Fortunately, their entrance on to C Block quickly reintroduced them to their mission as well as the intimidating gaze of Warden Victor Stryker. Sandler was overseeing the placement of the eight Klondike survivors, and it was more than obvious to inmates and guards alike that Stryker saw the coroners' men as meddlers, if not trespassers.

A career prison official, Stryker had worked his way up the chain of command with little help from the political establishment. Dependable, forthright, and not easily intimidated, he had proven a reliable, conscientious administrator in every job he held from tower guard and K-9 officer to sergeant and eventually warden. He knew every inch of the city's three penal institutions and could still name just about every criminal and guard he came upon during his twenty-three years in the system. Even more impressive to those under lock and key was Stryker's Gibraltar-like fixation on rules, regulations, and especially his own importance in the city penal system. If steadfastness was his strength, adaptability and receptivity to change were concerted enemies.

"I was put in the hole Saturday around sundown," said the inmate lying in the bed, his chest heaving as he strained to talk. Next to him was a large fan and a variety of fluids. Young Sandler dutifully jotted down every item of import. Prevented from going to a nearby hospital by the superintendent, Klondike survivors were taken to the prison infirmary on C Block. Basically a series of large cell rooms that had been transformed into a primitive dispensary, the prison hospital performed minor surgical procedures, cared for the sick and disabled, and offered a slightly cleaner, less-hostile environment than the other nine cellblocks in the institution.

There, survivors were hydrated with cold drinks, their bodies sponged with cool water, and they were given intravenous saline solution to restore their normal salt levels. Large fans had been brought in and placed in strategic locations to ameliorate the stifling heat that clung to Holmesburg's cellblock walls like a thick wool sweater on a hot, sweaty marathon runner. Ferencz and Sandler felt pressed to collect as many personal accounts as time and the authorities allowed. Both men initially sought out those they had first started to question in the prison yard. Sandler began with Wesley Hickok.

Still hyperventilating and floating somewhere between exhaustion and comatose, the inmate struggled to recount his ordeal. He said it all began two days earlier when he was taken off his cellblock and placed in the punishment unit. "The guards pulled me off the block and threw me in Klondike just because I was one of the holdouts who refused to go down to the chow hall," Hickok told Sandler. "I was hungry—we all were. But I believed in the strike. They threw me in a cell that already had a couple guys in it. They had been brought in the night before and looked bad, you know . . . really weak and wasted. It was crazy hot. They told me to take my clothes off and wrap them around any parts of my body that might touch the walls and floor. It was just too hot to wear anything, and you couldn't touch a thing or you'd get burnt bad. They said we were getting the heat treatment. I didn't know what that meant. I ain't never been in a place like Klondike before."

A Virginian by birth, Hickok was no stranger to penal colonies. He haltingly related his experience in several Virginia and North Carolina county jails and state penitentiaries. Convicted of a few burglaries, he had spent time on several chain gangs, the cornerstone of most Southern penal systems. Picking cotton, clearing canals of debris, and hauling lumber in all sorts of weather was brutal work even for young men in good physical shape. Rule breakers and runaways were dealt with harshly. Whippings, beatings, and being thrown in small, dark isolation cages just large enough for a dog were common.

Hickok said he had come north looking for work but found the wrong crowd to hang with instead. Second-story work proved more appealing than an honest day's pay in a textile or locomotive factory, and he soon found himself back in jail. But an 18-to-36-month stint in a Northern prison was comparatively "easy living," according to Hickok. The food and the accommodations were better, plus there were no striped canvas uniforms, roadwork assignments, river leeches, or cat-o'-nine-tails to contend with. Moyamensing—or Moko, as the hundred-year-old facility was more commonly called—had been his home for ten months until a fight on a cellblock with another inmate had him classified a troublemaker and reassigned to Holmesburg. Though it was clearly a tougher joint than Moyamensing, it was still a step or two above what he had known below the Mason-Dixon line in terms of penal accommodations. That was until he was thrown in the small brick punishment unit between D and E

Blocks. "Ain't seen or heard nothin' like it before," said Hickok. "That Klondike is a fuckin' oven. I'm thankful to still be alive. Another hour and I'da been dead. Roasted like a rabbit on a spit."

In another section of C Block, Carl Ferencz was interviewing James Walters. Serving a five-year sentence for robbing a John Wanamaker Department Store payroll truck, Walters admitted to being one of the few holdouts still in support of the protest. "They threw me in Klondike on Sunday afternoon, I figure, because I was sticking with the cause. July was a bad month in Holmesburg. Overcrowding. Midsummer heat taking a toll on everyone. I heard we're up to over 1,500 of us prisoners, and most cells're packed with four or five men. By August, space was real tight, and it didn't take much for guys to get on each other's nerves. Arguments and fights all the time. I never thought much about the food because it was the same slop every day. Most of us men had come to hate it. Fried eggplant, stale bologna sandwiches, same crap all the time," said Walters. "Guys started to complain more than usual, and pretty soon some started calling for a strike. They said if we united and protested, we could get rid of the lousy rubber spaghetti for some decent food. Maybe even ice cream and cake on Sundays. At the time it sounded pretty good, so I joined up."

"Who were the inmate leaders?" Ferencz asked.

Walters shook his head, keeping that bit of information off the record. "I will say, though, that there was a group of a dozen or so men that led the protest. They even got a meeting with the superintendent and warden. The inmate representatives presented their demands, including one that would give the prisoners a role in how the prison was run. But the superintendent just laughed at us. He told the men they were crazy and that we'll eat what we're served and like it. That's when the strike started," said Walters. "We stopped going down to the mess hall on Thursday. Christ, seemed like most of the joint stopped goin' to chow. Even some of the cooks and kitchen staff sat down and refused to work. It was really something."

Walters waited while Ferencz jotted down the pertinent notes, then he continued. "The prison administration probably could have lived with that, but what really angered them was the fact that the protest made the front page of the newspapers. Articles came out describing the hundreds of men supporting the strike and the prisoners' list of demands. Hell, we even heard the *New York Times* was running articles about the strike. We were pretty impressed with ourselves, but then Davis and Stryker started in on us. They wanted to make us pay, you know, for giving them a bad name.

"They locked down the entire joint," Walters claimed, "and the spirits and enthusiasm of the striking inmates began to wane. Hour after hour in hot, overcrowded cells with just bread and a cup of warm water took its toll. There was no movement. The men just stewed, perspired, and grumbled in their cells. Gradually, support for the protest began to fade away. More and more men over the weekend asked to go to the mess hall for some real food as well as the yard for fresh air. Hell, some guys would have probably killed for a glass of ice water. By Sunday afternoon the strike was over. We were played out. But, for a few hacks who took the challenge personally, there was still some unresolved business. It was payback time, and there were some scores to settle."

"What were the conditions like inside Klondike?" Ferencz asked, studying the prisoner, whose strength was noticeably ebbing. There was no reply. He pushed onward: "Tell me," asked Ferencz, "which guards and administrators oversaw the operations of the punishment unit? Who gave the orders?"

Walters withdrew even more, but the deputy coroner kept at it. Eventually, Ferencz was able to learn the names of key participants of the carnage—particularly the roles of guards Bridges and Smoot.

When Coroner Glass rejoined his assistants in the prison hospital, they gave him a quick update on what they were learning.

"Most of those housed in Klondike over the weekend were either dead, unconscious, or too afraid to talk, but a few were willing to recount what had transpired over the days leading up to the shocking discovery earlier this morning," Ferencz stated. "Also, we've acquired a shadow in Warden Stryker. He's been a bit of a lurker and even followed us through Center and on to C Block. He's been paying careful attention to everyone we interviewed. He's furious with our presence here," Ferencz concluded. "I'm expecting him to have us thrown out at any moment."

"I agree, we appear to be working on borrowed time," said Glass. "The warden is probably our most ardent foe at the present time. Stryker hasn't earned a hard-edge reputation for nothing," added Glass. "Hopefully he's smart enough to know kicking us out would be the worst thing for his boss and the mayor.

"Perhaps the ever-increasing number of reporters and curiosity seekers gathered outside on Torresdale Avenue are providing some protection. Without them, I don't think we'd be in here now."

"We've got another problem," observed Ferencz. "Getting witnesses to open up with the warden watching."

Glass understood his deputy's concern but was powerless to alter the situation. He had tried, pressed the mayor to hospitalize survivors, but without success. "We'll have to do the best we can, knowing some prisoners will refuse to make any statements, and others will outright lie to prevent any further abuse while incarcerated. Hopefully, we'll get enough truthful statements to figure it all out."

Before interviewing any inmates, the coroner approached Samuel Moretti, the longtime chief physician of Holmesburg Prison. Prematurely bald and overweight, the fifty-two-year-old was from a large and well-known Italian family from South Philadelphia. Originally confectionary workers, the family had thrived both socially and economically and was now producing as many doctors, lawyers, and politicians as bakers. All, it seemed, had developed political connections. In his few meetings with Dr. Moretti in recent years, Glass had found the doctor competent and knowledgeable, but there was also that nagging feeling that Moretti rarely took a position that conflicted with his political patrons. "Not now," replied Dr. Moretti brusquely when the coroner asked for a word with him. "We've got to get these men rehydrated and stabilized."

Glass understood the urgency of the prison medical director's abruptness, but there was something else. He always had the feeling Moretti looked down on him and considered him something of an imposter. Moretti had both a college degree and a medical degree; Glass had neither. He believed Moretti was one of those in the medical community who felt the coroner of Philadelphia should be a medical man and not an uncredentialed political hack with patrons in high places.

Regardless as to whether it was his own insecurities or Moretti's superior attitude, Glass had what he thought were valid questions about the doctors' involvement—or lack thereof—in the inmate deaths. He then sought out another doctor on the hospital block to query.

Oliver Hankins was one of the prison medical personnel tending to the Klondike survivors. Of average height, in his mid-forties, and wearing a white lab coat, Hankins was like most prison physicians Glass had come upon: adequate from a professional standpoint but lacking in ambition, energy, and entrepreneurial talent. A part-time contract with the city to provide bare-bones medical care to hundreds of risk-taking, ill-mannered, high school drop-outs behind bars added economic stability to an income stream already diminished by the devastating Depression years.

After inquiring how the men were doing, the coroner asked Dr. Hankins, "How could such a deadly event have occurred? Aren't there any rules regarding physicians periodically checking on the health of those kept in that punishment unit?"

"Of course there are such rules, and I may have even been in a position to save these men had I been permitted to carry out my job," Hankins sniffed. "I visited Holmesburg over the weekend, and while performing my duties, I learned there were men in the isolation cells. I came upon Warden Stryker yesterday afternoon and told him I heard the isolation cells were in use, and because of the extremely hot weather, I thought I better go out there and see how the prisoners were coming along. The warden told me 'I'll let you know when we're ready for you to go out there.'"

"And then what happened?"

"Nothing," the doctor replied. "That was all the answer I got, and after performing my usual tasks I left. I went home."

"So you never bothered to see the men in Klondike," asked Glass, "even though you were in the institution?"

"Prison physicians can't inspect the place at will," Hankins quickly answered, obviously offended by the question. "Everywhere we go inside the walls we must be accompanied by a guard to lock and unlock gates, doors, and cells. So we can go only where we're told to go and where the guards are allowed to take us." The doctor went on to admit, "I have taken men out of there sick. But there was never anything like this."

Glass followed Dr. Hankins's gaze as he looked around the hectic cell room infirmary. Doctors and nurses were treating Klondike survivors connected to intravenous solutions, and orderlies were busy fanning, sponging down, and giving water to those in need. For the somewhat cowed doctor who was one of the first to attend to the survivors in the prison yard, the frantic scene epitomized something he had never experienced before—a cataclysmic event with a significant loss of life. "I don't know for sure," said Hankins with a fretful expression on his face, "but it could be the most devastating thing that ever happened in a penal institution, at least around here."

"I don't know whether it is or not," replied the coroner, "but until I learn of something more fiendish, this Klondike mess can probably claim the honor."

Just when Glass was about to ask if the doctor had witnessed the so-called heat treatment being used to discipline prisoners on other occasions, he noticed the warden intently watching them. Irritated by Stryker's disapproving glare, Glass decided to confront him with the information he had just received. He walked over and pointedly asked, "Is it true you didn't allow Dr. Hankins to see the men in the punishment unit?"

"When do you think you'll be done here?" the warden forcefully replied. "These men have gone through a lot. They should get some rest."

In what amounted to a daylong series of stunning surprises and chilling discoveries, Glass thought the warden's comment might have been the most flabbergasting for its sheer chutzpah.

"We'll be here as long as it takes us," replied Glass.

"My men need a break," said Stryker, "and your presence here isn't helping them get one."

Glass was tempted to lecture the warden on everything from his skewed priorities to his warped sense of penal punishment, but he realized a small victory now could impede his overall goal. Without saying a word, the coroner turned and walked to one of the large cells holding Klondike survivors. He had no doubt that the answers to this weekend's carnage would come from the men who were forced to endure it.

The first inmate the coroner approached was like the others pulled out of Klondike; flat on his back, hyperventilating, and tucked between two large bags of ice. The inmate looked ghostlike; a vacant gaze, labored breathing, and lack of response to repeated queries gave the strong impression the inmate may yet succumb to his injuries. An attendant's disapproving glance further encouraged the coroner to move on.

Glass approached another survivor who appeared a bit more resilient, but when asked a question the prisoner turned his head away. Whether honoring the criminal's code of silence or frightened of retribution, the prisoner remained unwilling to even acknowledge the coroner's presence.

Glass moved to a third bed. Burn marks on the inmate's shoulders and arms were plainly visible. Even the tip of the inmate's nose appeared singed. Glass cautiously approached the prisoner, who was sipping cold water through cracked, parched lips, with one arm hooked up to an intravenous line. Dark-haired with muscular, tattooed arms, the inmate examined his visitor warily. Glass imagined the inmate was wondering whether the stranger walking in his direction in a sweat-stained suit and tie was a doctor, police detective, or prison official.

"My name's Glass. I'm the county coroner. I'm trying to figure out what happened here. Mind if I ask you a couple questions?" When the prisoner didn't object, Glass continued: "May I have your name and your description of what happened?" Receiving no reply, Glass asked, "How did you come to be incarcerated at Holmesburg?"

The inmate remained silent, but a pronounced sneer spoke volumes. "Police investigators say you fought among yourselves," said Glass. "They say you fought over whether to end the food strike. Is that true?"

The inmate just glared back at him. Growing frustrated, Glass asked, "Are you gonna let those who did this to you get off scot-free?" When the inmate remained mute, Glass angrily added, "Are you that much of a sap that you'll let those who perpetrated this hideous crime get away with it? Are you really that much of a chump?"

"Who the fuck are you?" spit the gravelly voiced prisoner. "You don't know nothin' about what goes on in here. What do you care what happened?"

"I told you, I'm the county coroner. It's my job to investigate suspicious deaths. By my reckoning, what happened here this morning qualifies."

"Yeah, well I wanna talk to the guy who stops this fuckin' shit from happenin'. Where the hell is that guy?"

"Maybe I can help you find him," said Glass in a more measured tone. "You tell me what took place here, and I'll work to find some people who will see this doesn't happen again."

"Bullshit," said the inmate. "It's all bullshit." Breathing heavily and sweating profusely, he eyed his interrogator with contempt. The coroner, however, pressed on. Despite the inmate's condition and distrust, at least he was talking. Now Glass had to figure out how to get the angry prisoner to recount what happened in the punishment unit.

"The police investigators said you guys fought among yourselves over whether to end the strike. Did you tell them that?"

"Hell no," said the inmate, raising his voice so that others in the room took notice. "No one told 'em anything."

"Well, somebody did," said Glass, "'cause that's what the police are telling everyone, the press included."

"That's a goddamn lie, and they know it. Christ, we didn't even have the strength to stand up, much less fight each other. Hell, it took all our strength just to breathe."

"Are you on the level? There was no arguing or fighting about ending the strike?"

"Do I look like I'm making shit up? Did you see the bodies they pulled out of that oven?"

"Then let me help you get the truth out," said Glass, extending his hand. "My name is Heshel Glass. I've been in Klondike. I've seen it for myself, and I don't buy the police account. I'd like to know what really happened."

The inmate made no effort to shake the coroner's hand but said with a contemptuous sneer, "Heshel, Heshel, what kind of name is that? Are you a Jew?"

"Yeah, what of it?"

The inmate chuckled and turned his head away.

"And what are you, a dumb-ass Polack or Dago happy to turn the other cheek to those that threw you and fifteen others in a lethal sweatbox?"

The coroner expected the inmate to throw a punch at him, but he didn't. They both stared at each other angrily.

"Tell me," said the coroner finally, "what's a person gotta do to get you to open up? Do I need to convert to Catholicism and move to the Vatican for you to show some guts and tell me what really happened?"

"That would be a start," said the inmate, again turning his head away from his wise-cracking interrogator.

"Listen, tough guy," said Glass firmly. "I wanna know what really happened. We can start with what led to this shit-storm."

"It was the damn strike, if you need to know," said the inmate, turning his head back to his persistent inquisitor. "We just stopped going down to chow. We weren't going to eat their crap anymore."

"You mean it was all over food?"

"That's what I said. You heard me."

"But—"

"If you were in here day after day, you'd know what it's like. You'd understand."

"And that got you thrown in that punishment unit?" inquired the coroner skeptically.

"That's it," the inmate replied. "They wanted to put an end to the strike."

"Did they threaten you in there? Did they offer to return you to your cell-block if you promised to end the strike?"

"Shit, who the hell are you kidding?" snapped the inmate. "They didn't offer us nothin'. They just shut the windows, closed the vents, shut off the water, and turned on the steam. They weren't lookin' to make any deals—they wanted to kill us."

Glass was momentarily stunned by the response. "And none of you ever attacked a guard or officer?"

"Go chase yourself," said the inmate angrily. "We didn't lay a hand on anybody."

"But—"

"I'm tellin' you they were pissed off about the strike. They wanted to end it and didn't care how it was done."

The coroner was about to follow up with additional questions when a nurse approached and began removing the IV and checking the inmate's vital signs.

Before stepping aside, the coroner again asked the inmate his name.

"Luzinski. Hank Luzinski. And do me a favor: Don't come back."

Chapter 9

The Threat of Retribution

August 22, 1939, Monday Evening

It was just after Glass left Hank Luzinski's bedside that a captain of the guard walked into the dispensary and informed the coroner he had an important phone call. Glass told the officer he was busy and that the call could wait, but the captain was insistent. "I was told by Superintendent Davis to bring you back to the administration building," said the officer. "Mayor Clarke is on the line. He wants to speak to you."

As Glass crossed the center control area and exited the prison, he realized dusk had settled on the city. He hoped sunset would finally bring some relief to Holmesburg's sweltering cellblocks. He had been at Holmesburg for the entire day, and even now, mid-evening and under increasing darkness, he had no idea when he'd be leaving. He also had no idea why the mayor—seemingly disinterested and unresponsive till now—was so anxious to talk to him.

"Listen, Glass," shouted the mayor when the coroner was handed the phone in the superintendent's office, "who the hell do you think you are telling the press 'the deaths appear very suspicious. The official police version seems very unlikely to me. There are many questions that need answering.'

"Christ, we're probably lucky you didn't promise to interview every inmate and guard in Pennsylvania in your effort to make a show out of this. Damn it, the evening editions are full of it. The *Bulletin, Ledger,* and *Inquirer* have that goddamn prison story all over the front page. The headline of the *Record* has '8 Convicts Roasted to Death; 8 Others Nearly Lost Lives.' How do you think that makes us look? You're even quoted in a couple of them as saying 'the dead appear to have been scalded from gas, steam, or hot vapor.' In fact, they quote you as saying these men suffered an 'extremely violent death' and you're 'determined to get at the truth.' Now I've got folks from the governor's office calling me every hour and news agencies around the country wanting a statement. What the hell are you trying to cause here? Don't we already have enough scandalmongering in this town?"

"Mayor Clarke, with all due respect, you have no idea what we're dealing with," replied Glass. "If you would have come up here—"

"Listen, damn it, I don't have to come up there," barked the mayor. "I've been to Holmesburg a thousand times. I don't need to hike up there every time inmates cause some mischief. Do you really expect that every time some reprobate is found dead in his cell I have to run up there? I'm trying to run a goddamn city."

It was at that point that Superintendent Davis, evidently overhearing the conversation, left the office so the coroner would have some privacy. It was clear the mayor was verbally throttling the coroner and the superintendent's interests were being protected.

"But, Mayor," replied Glass, "we're not talking about some run-of-the-mill inmate rumpus. We've got eight dead and a few others who barely made it out of that . . . that torture chamber Davis has up here. And if that's not bad enough, half the reporters in North America are camped out on Torresdale Avenue."

"And according to those shameless hucksters," said Clarke angrily, "you haven't missed an opportunity to get your name in the papers and make some controversial statements. You seem to be on a mission to malign the police, the prison administration, the city . . ."

"But, Mayor—"

"Listen, Glass, experienced homicide detectives looked at the evidence, interviewed witnesses, and have determined the deaths were accidental, and largely due to the inmates themselves."

"I don't believe that," the coroner replied sharply. "And you wouldn't either if you would have come up here—"

"What . . . What did you say?"

"You heard me," said Glass more assertively now. "I'm sorry, but those men appear to have been cooked alive."

"For God's sake—"

"That's right, cooked alive. And I think prison personnel had a direct role in it."

"You must be out of your mind," screamed Mayor Clarke. "You're crazy, Hesh. No one will believe that story."

"Well, I'm inclined to believe it, and I just might be able to prove it. The men who died were being punished for that damn food strike over the weekend. Christ, I don't even think the inmates took a hostage or laid a hand on a guard. It appears just to have been their refusal to eat the food that started this. And for that, people in your administration put them in that brick oven, that punishment unit, and turned on the heat. They turned a cellblock into a smokehouse. The place got hot enough to cure beef."

"That's not what I hear. What about the report by police investigators claiming it was some kind of inmate riot?" inquired the mayor.

"Bunk, pure bunk," replied the coroner. "Just a manufactured story to confuse the public. They wanted to exonerate Davis and his cronies."

"Enough. Now you listen to me, Hesh," an increasingly agitated Mayor Clarke replied. "You get off your high horse about men being cooked to death or you'll find your dumb ass on the sidewalk. You got a pretty soft job, Hesh. And you're not even a physician. Hell, you don't even have a college diploma. Don't throw it all out the window in an attempt to get headlines. That press ink is like arsenic; swim in enough of it and you'll drown. It'll destroy you. Don't be foolish enough to fall for some slobbering newsman promising to get you on the front page."

"I'm not looking for headlines. That's not my—"

"Let me warn you," continued the mayor, "if you persist in making wild allegations, you'll find yourself pushing a wheelbarrow on Market Street and sweeping manure off the road. Your days of elected office will be over."

"I don't like being threatened," Glass replied. "My office has to follow through on this investigation. I plan on giving my department's findings to the police and the DA."

"Now you listen," barked the mayor. "Neither the police, the DA, nor anyone else in this town will support you. You have no case."

"I think I do," replied Glass. "And as the duly elected coroner of this county I have the power to . . . If the police and district attorney decide to follow your wishes and kill a serious investigation of a major calamity, then I'll have to act."

'What's that mean?" inquired Clarke.

"The law clearly allows coroners to hold inquests. And I'll do it—"

"What . . . what did you say?"

"I know the law," replied Glass. "Anyone who has died violently or under suspicious circumstances can be the subject of an inquest. We've got that right here, and in a county prison no less. Despite what the police department or the DA's men are saying, prisoners—men under lock and key—were murdered at Holmesburg this weekend. I've seen the carnage with my own eyes, and you would have, too, if you had bothered to come up here. And I believe I know how it happened. Now I'm going to find out who did it."

"You're making a big mistake, Hesh," trumpeted the mayor. "Let me remind you of something—you're running for reelection next year. You'll never survive the primary, you can't get reelected without me. I'll bury you. You better quickly realize who your friends are. We put you in that office and we can take you out. And don't you forget it."

The mayor then slammed the phone down, ending the conversation. The coroner was left muttering expletives into a disconnected telephone line.

Incensed by the mayor's threats of political reprisal—as well as his own timidity—the coroner could barely control his anger. Appalled at what he was learning about the brutal treatment of those celled in the punishment unit, Heshel Glass felt compelled to act. He had to do something, at least speak up. But what if the mayor was correct? What if the other city investigative agencies agreed it was some form of inmate confrontation or a prison riot that caused the loss of life? What influence did he have compared to the mayor, police commissioner, and the district attorney, all more well-known and influential than his meager twenty-person office?

Marching quickly past the superintendent without comment, Glass exited the administration building and walked directly toward two-dozen sweaty and irritable news-hungry reporters still milling about on Torresdale Avenue. Another dozen or so mingled outside the tavern directly across the street from the prison, which they periodically visited for liquid nourishment.

Though the mayor had referred to evening edition newspaper headlines concerning the deadly prison debacle, Glass—who had been inside the walls of Holmesburg Prison the entire day—would later discover the enormous coverage the deadly event was receiving. In bold print, newspaper headlines screamed, "Eight Die in Mystery Prison Revolt," "Prison Deaths Attributed to Steam in Cells," and "Police Version Challenged by City Coroner." All of the headlines garnered prominent front-page coverage, many with photographic images of the prison's ominous walled exterior. If that wasn't bad enough from the city administration's point of view, both local and national evening radio broadcasts were making note of the "fatal prison tragedy in Philadelphia."

However, Glass was intent on not confirming unsupportable theories or being part of a cover-up; he was just after the truth. As he appeared on the now-darkened street, photographers' camera lights erupted and newsmen jumped to attention hoping to learn new aspects of the mysterious tragedy. Surrounded by a phalanx of reporters firing a rapid series of questions and several-dozen neighborhood curiosity seekers, the coroner was unsure how he would respond. As he approached an improvised lectern covered with radio equipment and other recording devices, excited reporters with notepads in hand proffered questions on everything from the supposed role of communist agitators and underworld figures in the latest instance of Holmesburg's violence to City Hall's inexplicable "no comment" stance on the deadly affair. When one of the more strident newsmen shouted, "Do you agree with police detectives that inmates fighting amongst themselves broke steam pipes in their cells to use as weapons, and that's what caused so many deaths?" Glass said, "No, that's not my feeling. I don't believe that happened."

A tremor of astonishment rippled through the crowd followed by a moment of collective silence.

"There are no pipes of any kind in the inmate cells," said Glass. "Steam pipes and radiators are in the corridor, but no inmates ever made it out of their cells. The pipes and radiators are intact and functioning as they were designed. In fact, I think the evidence will show they functioned all too well. The prisoners were locked in their cells and forced to endure what . . . what any decent human being would probably consider inhuman conditions. It would appear that over a brutally hot weekend, prisoners were confined in an airtight brick structure with all windows and vents shut tight. There were sixteen prisoners shoved into five small cells. If that wasn't diabolical enough, there's reason to believe guards then shut off the inmates' access to water and turned on the heat. I believe an argument can be made that several banks of radiators created a hothouse effect—a large sweatbox, if you will—of unimaginable intensity. I can't be sure at this point, but the temperature in there must have approached two hundred degrees. Based on my experience in the coroner's office, I'd say these men died of asphyxiation caused by extreme heat."

Aghast at what the coroner just described, reporters mumbled to each other and immediately began firing questions. "What proof do you have to support such an allegation?" yelled one excited scribe.

"After interviewing survivors and seeing what the prisoners call 'Klondike' with my own eyes, it seems pretty clear," replied Glass. "But I'll know more after further interviews and the results of the autopsies. We're still at an early stage of the investigation."

"But what of the detectives' accounts and their timeline?" one reporter called out.

"So this was no ordinary prison scuffle as we've been told?" shouted another.

"Nothing about this incident is normal, ordinary, or run-of-the-mill," Glass soberly replied. "Any objective observer would likely compare the horrific scene that met penal staff this morning to the Black Hole of Calcutta. With each inmate interview, with each hour, it's becoming increasingly clear something extraordinary, something truly horrendous happened here. We certainly can't rule out a criminal component regarding the deaths."

Dutifully capturing every word for their forthcoming articles, reporters intuitively understood an already macabre story was becoming even more newsworthy. Not only did the Holmesburg misfortune entail a shocking loss of life, but there was now the smell of a malicious criminal component and the growing prospect of a full-fledged government cover-up. Adding further gravitas to the story, the allegations were coming from an elected official directly tied to the investigation.

Feverish journalists followed up with a host of questions dealing with the curious findings of police investigators, the silence of high-level elected officials, and the questionable roles of Superintendent Davis and Warden Stryker in what was now taking on the characteristics of a murder investigation. Others wanted to know more about the blue-tinted cadavers.

"We're hearing reports of the deceased looking like Negroes," one reporter stated, "What could make white men appear colored?"

Another cynically asked, "Are you expecting us to believe there is going to be a fair and thorough investigation in a city known for its antipathy to transparency and tolerance of public corruption?"

Glass did the best he could in answering questions and reiterated that much depended on the results of inmate autopsies that were currently being performed. But one thing he stressed in his attempt to alleviate the fear of another botched or partisan municipal investigation was a surprising promise. "Much depends on the determination of the district attorney's office in determining responsibility for this revolting episode, and I hope that investigation goes forward. But everyone will have their day in court. The guilty, I'd like to believe, will be punished," said Glass, his face covered in perspiration and showing the strain of the moment. "After I have established the cause of death, all investigative material and findings of my office will be turned over to the district attorney and open for public comment. There will be no proceedings behind closed doors that include my office. I won't be part of any backroom deals. There will be no effort to cover up crimes or protect lawbreakers regardless of their rank, stature, or party affiliation."

Veteran Philadelphian newsmen were struck by the unusual pledge, and those from out of town were equally impressed. Selwyn Rossman, for example, the respected *New York Times* crime reporter who had been standing on Torresdale Avenue since mid-afternoon, was so taken by the coroner's comments that he asked his *Philadelphia Inquirer* colleague for recommendations regarding hotel accommodations. The savvy *Times* reporter had a hunch his editor back in Manhattan would want him to remain in the Quaker City. His Klondike story was scheduled for the next day's front page, and there was every indication it was going to remain a front-page story for days to come.

When Coroner Glass finally excused himself from the impromptu press conference, he re-entered Holmesburg. Surprised by the boldness of his own statements, he realized he had to back them up with solid proof. He returned to C Block to continue his interrogation of Hank Luzinski and any other survivors willing to talk.

Superintendent Davis and Warden Stryker were bitterly upset, but there was little they could do about it with so many newsmen camped out on their front porch. Stunned by the coroner's series of verbal broadsides, Davis met with reporters to debunk the coroner's absurd allegations. "I can't see how the coroner's account could have taken place," said Davis, obviously annoyed, cigarette in hand, his tie askew. "No one was murdered here by my people. We certainly used no steam or hot water on the men who were confined. We didn't physically pummel or abuse them. We don't really know what happened and won't know until the autopsy results are in. In my mind, there were no marks on the bodies of these men sufficient to have caused death. The prisoners, all of them troublemakers, were placed in the isolation unit over the weekend after they insisted on agitating the other prisoners. Their goal was to keep up their hunger strike. We isolated four or five ringleaders, and the others were strike supporters and general troublemakers."

Reporters interrupted the superintendent several times with pointed questions and requests to enter the prison and see the Klondike building for themselves, but Davis kept to his script. "Nothing untoward took place on my watch. I can assure you," he repeated, "the men have not been murdered. Right now, I cannot tell what caused their deaths. I'm sure Coroner Glass will find nothing suspicious about this after his deputies are through with their investigation. And access to the institution is denied while the investigation is underway."

The response seemed painfully inadequate considering the extensive loss of life and bizarre coloration of the deceased, but Davis continued to argue his absurd version of events.

When asked about the coroner's threat of taking over operation of the prison, Davis became further agitated. "I don't know if he has the right to do that," he replied. "I will, however, turn over the prison to any authoritative body which has the legal right to conduct an investigation." Questioned further on the subject of a coroner's office possible takeover, the superintendent firmly stated, "Look, if anything is wrong here, I'm the guy who wants to know. I have already placed the prison at the disposal of Detective Sergeant Hennessey and the homicide squad, and they have been unhindered in their investigation. They can question anyone they want."

The mayor and the DA were supportive of the city's chief of prison operations, but the usually low-key coroner had emerged as something of a loose cannon; a minor city official, but one they now couldn't control. His alarming bombast before dubious reporters and his re-entry into Holmesburg had prison administrators flustered but helpless. Tossing Glass and his subordinates out of the institution was considered, only to be rejected. The press and the administration's opponents would have a field day with such a heavy-handed approach. Satisfaction would have quickly been replaced by even greater negative publicity.

Recognizing they were working on borrowed time, the coroner, his deputy, and the office's young intern eagerly collected as many accounts as they could concerning the tragedy and the events leading up to it. Glass was intent on getting back to Hank Luzinski's bedside to ask questions, take notes, and catalog every significant act orchestrated by guards and officers over the last forty-eight hours. Carl Ferencz and David Sandler were doing much the same, though it quickly became clear that many men were either too incapacitated or too frightened to speak up.

Guards, staff sergeants, and their white-shirted superiors—lieutenants and captains—proved particularly problematic. If a professional code of silence didn't muzzle them, the fear of prosecution did. Guards repeatedly rebuffed Sandler. Their menacing sneers and comments caused him to finally give up and restrict his interviews to less-threatening inmates.

Ferencz was only slightly more successful. He got the distinct impression, however, that not all of the custodial staff was averse to talking. Some seemed genuinely troubled by the deadly affair but were not about to be seen conversing with investigators inside the institution. One officer admitted, "I feared this would happen one day." Another made the telling statement, "I won't talk unless I can have a lawyer present."

That was not all; Ferencz detected something he hadn't expected concerning institutional pushback. Several guards and officers suggested the incident would be shoved under a municipal rug, while others not only declined to assist the investigators but freely expected that the coroner would pay dearly if he aggressively pursued the Klondike incident as a criminal matter. The prospect of a murder investigation outraged them. "Tell your Jew boss he'll be out of a job if he doesn't fall in line," barked one arrogant officer. Another threatened the deputy coroner, "You better back off. We take care of our friends. We take care of our enemies as well."

When Ferencz approached Sergeant Hartzell, an officer survivors identified as a "Stryker favorite" and as having authority over Klondike operations, he was met with contempt. A cold, menacing glare was all Ferencz received when he asked Hartzell, "What do you think happened here?" It was patently clear that the physically unassuming but steely-faced officer wanted no parts of the coroner's office. When Ferencz followed up with additional questions, the stern, bespectacled officer showed only disdain. Finally, after the deputy coroner claimed the right to investigate suspicious deaths on city property, Hartzell coldly replied, "Get one thing clear, Mr. Ferencz—this is our turf, not yours. We decide what goes on inside these walls, not you. And not that Kosher boss of yours. The sooner you learn that, the better."

Though the sergeant's contempt was evident, the most unsettling interview was with a middle-aged cellblock guard named Derbyshire who reeked of alcohol and moral superiority. When the deputy coroner asked a question about the inmate deaths, the guard replied with one of his own:

"Are you a Christian, Mr. Ferencz?"

"I am," said Ferencz.

"And how well do you know your Bible?"

"Well, not as well as I probably should," replied the deputy, somewhat perplexed by the questions.

"Then I suggest you read the Book of Proverbs, chapter eleven, verse twenty-nine," said the ruddy-faced guard whose gray uniform was soaked with perspiration. "You might learn a thing or two."

"And what would that be?"

The guard stepped toward Ferencz, looked him square in the eye, and said, "He that troubleth his own house shall inherit the wind."

There were a few moments of uncomfortable silence, then Derbyshire added for good measure, "Just watch yourself."

Offended by the warning and the guard's alcohol-fueled breath, Ferencz was tempted to pursue the discussion but then thought better of it. Neither well-versed in scripture nor interested in debating an obvious religious zealot who was not only inebriated but had found some way to overlook roasting prisoners, Ferencz decided to end the conversation and find others to interview.

Besides, the deputy coroner was beginning to wilt. After spending an entire day and evening in an unbearably hot, foul-smelling prison following what increasingly looked like mass murder, he was beyond dispirited. It was not just the nature of the crime he was investigating that had him down but the forces aligning themselves outside the prison walls.

Though the coroner had not yet informed him of the mayor's threat of defeat at the polls, as a party regular Ferencz was experienced enough in Philadelphia's unforgiving and unending political wars to recognize the signs of a serious internecine struggle emerging. The silence—not to mention absence—of the city's highest elected officials at a multiple-homicide event garnering national attention, combined with the coroner's determination to seek out the guilty parties—some that may be allies of the mayor—made for a poisonous state of affairs.

With each hour's passage, Ferencz feared his boss had embarked on something resembling political suicide. A career city employee with a wife and young children to support, Ferencz believed there was a good chance he might end up as collateral damage in any kind of retaliation campaign. Party regulars had lost their jobs for a lot less, and though the coroner's office usually stayed clear of such Byzantine warfare, the Klondike episode was shaping up as a cataclysmic event capable of causing significant damage.

David Sandler, for his part, was oblivious to the shifting forces of Philadelphia politics. He had no idea the coroner's office could become the centerpiece of a controversial firestorm placing everyone in jeopardy.

A novice politically and with no interest in elected office or acquiring a city job, the recent college grad from the suburbs of Philadelphia was exhausted from the most chilling and stressful day of his life. For a lad who had grown up with visions of becoming a great microbiologist fighting germs and advancing science, the Klondike deaths were certainly something unexpected. But there was no question of the import of this case. Lives had been taken, and there was the scientific riddle as to what had killed them.

Unlike most Jewish adolescents growing up in the thirties, whose heroes were sports figures like baseball slugger Hank Greenberg and boxer Barney Ross, Sandler's heroes were renowned men of science like Joseph Goldberger, who conquered the deadly mystery of pellagra. Sandler's exposure to the nuances of a big-city coroner's office had been informative, and no doubt helpful for the forthcoming rigors of medical school, but there was nothing particularly dramatic about the experience—until now.

Sixteen hours earlier, he had walked into the coroner's sixth-floor City Hall office, as he had done every day since the first week of June, with no expectation of anything out of the ordinary occurring. But within minutes of his arrival, a call came in and he was off to Holmesburg Prison. A cauldron of explosive anger and institutional repression would greet him, as well as the terrifying remnants of an unspeakable crime. Stunned and momentarily paralyzed by the initial sight of what looked like casualties on a battlefield—not to mention strange, discolored corpses—Sandler was now focused on helping to solve the bizarre calamity. A willing and committed foot soldier, he unhesitatingly took his lead from Heshel Glass. Though he knew the coroner lacked a college degree and was certainly no highly trained scientist like Dr. Goldberger, Glass was the elected coroner of one of the nation's largest cities, and from Sandler's vantage point his boss had displayed the investigative know-how and moral assurance to tackle the deadly prison mystery.

Even when walking out of the institution well after midnight, Sandler was struck by the coroner's relentlessness in exploring every aspect of the horrid crime. The three men were about to finally exit the prison sally port and step out on the street when the coroner said, "Damn it, I forgot to check something."

Glass then re-entered the facility, boldly walked across the rotunda floor, and had the Center guard open the gate to A Block. Ferencz and Sandler followed and then watched the coroner quickly walk down the block corridor. He never stopped to examine a cell, nor did he attempt to make conversation with anyone. After traversing the lengthy cellblock, he returned to the rotunda and had the guard open the gate to D Block, where he repeated his block-long walk. Puzzled, Sandler turned to Ferencz for an explanation, but he, too, as well as the guards, was mystified. After the third such trip, Sandler noticed a fleeting smile cross the deputy coroner's face.

"What's he doing?" asked Sandler.

"I believe he's checking the plumbing," said Ferencz with a knowing grin.

"What for?" said Sandler.

"I think he wants to compare how many banks of radiators are on these long cellblocks with those in Klondike. I never thought to do it, but he's right. It's important."

Observing his boss perform that early morning deed after a long, physically draining day impressed Sandler. Though unschooled in the traditional sense, the coroner was street smart, seemingly indefatigable, and resolute in building a case.

Ferencz, however, was less in awe of the early morning inspection than his young colleague. He was preoccupied with another Glass initiative; his boss seemed intent on bucking a tough, determined force that had the capability of crushing opponents—and often did. The record was replete with examples of Mayor Clarke and his political machine brazenly opposing tradition and civic advancement and getting away with it. His tolerance of corruption was bad enough, but an even better example of the mayor's ability to thwart progress and withstand criticism was his current stance on the state takeover of the city's mental asylum.

Just a few months earlier, Mayor Clarke had unilaterally decided to block what just about everyone considered a brilliant stroke of government reform: the transfer of Philadelphia Hospital for Mental Diseases—better known as Byberry—to the state. The large complex of hospital buildings near the Bucks County border in Northeast Philadelphia was a morass of human travail, financial grief, and endless embarrassment. In addition to the thousands of lost and delusional souls interned there, the operational upkeep of such a large, poorly managed facility drained the municipal budget of well over a million dollars a year. After a series of scathing newspaper stories and state legislative investigation, state lawmakers grudgingly agreed to take Byberry off the city's hands. They'd make it part of the commonwealth's mental health system.

Mayor Clarke, in a fit of obstinacy, however, decided to oppose the takeover. The transfer of a perpetually troubled governmental entity would have delighted any normal, fiscally prudent chief executive, but Clarke was miffed that his good name had been sullied regarding the mental institution's troubled history. Incredibly, the mayor's wrongheadedness was proving resentment-proof; despite universal agreement that it would be best for all concerned if Byberry became a state-operated facility, the transfer was on hold.

A product of neighborhood ward politics like his boss, such arbitrary political power impressed Ferencz. For all his attributes and good intentions, Heshel Glass, in the mind of his deputy, was no match for Mayor Clarke and his formidable political machine. The district attorney and the police chief seemed to have gotten the message; there would be only superficial involvement by their offices in the Holmesburg calamity. The coroner, however, had either not received or rejected the directive. It appeared he had chosen to take a principled stand, a practically unheard-of exercise by an elected official in Philadelphia during the 1930s. Challenging the mayor and going public in such a brazen manner had only aggravated the situation. There was no question in Ferencz's mind there would be hell to pay.

Several years earlier, Ferencz had nearly garnered the title of Coroner of Philadelphia for himself. But his allies lacked the political muscle to consummate the deal. In Philadelphia's inscrutable world of backroom deal-making, Heshel Glass, a rather insignificant but loyal party activist with no substantive credentials for the office, collected the support to win the coroner's job. Incredibly, he now seemed on the brink of throwing it away. Ferencz wondered about himself—how he would act if he were coroner and pressure was placed on him to bury a criminal investigation. A realist, he was under no illusion he'd do what was morally right. Such acts of civic-minded selflessness were rare in Philadelphia and usually went unrewarded.

A low-wattage elected official to some, an innocuous enigma to others, Heshel Glass had emerged as a pivotal player in an ugly murder mystery being played out in the nation's third-largest city. As Ferencz watched his boss investigate this high-profile case, the coroner's chief deputy pondered what motivated a man to so eagerly place his career, reputation, and economic well-being on the chopping block.

PART II

Chapter 10

Heshel Glass

Milda and Heinrich Glasnitsky left Liverpool, England for America in 1886. They boarded the *S. S. Lapland* with forty dollars, five pieces of luggage, and one newborn. Their son, Heshel Glasnitsky, was born just two months earlier in the Brixton section of London. They had been traveling for some time in hopes of a better life in America. The long trek from a small town near Kiev, Russia, by way of Zurich and Antwerp, to England was a difficult one, but they were not alone. Many from Eastern and Southern Europe were now undertaking similar journeys.

Almost immediately after arriving on Ellis Island in New York Harbor, they were asked by a well-intentioned US immigration official if they'd be willing to take a few letters off the family's awkward last name. "You think you might consider something less challenging like Glasnitz, or better yet, Glass?" inquired the customs official. Ever willing to be hospitable—and unsure what was being asked of them—the couple consented. By the time they left the tiny island for New Jersey and ultimately Philadelphia, Milda and Heinrich Glasnitsky had become Molly and Harry Glass.

One of the oldest and largest cities in America, Philadelphia was a bustling brew of large factories, smoke-belching chimneys, horse-drawn streetcars, and ethnically diverse neighborhoods. Like many young Jewish families new to the city, Molly and Harry Glass were drawn to the lively, ethnically centered neighborhoods of South Philadelphia. Bounded by two rivers, the Delaware and Schuylkill to the south and east, and the city's commercial hub to the north, the section consisting of block after block of tightly packed row houses had become home to a rich mixture of Irish, Italian, Polish, and Jewish immigrants.

Throughout the late 1800s and well into the early decades of the twentieth century, big ocean liners would sail up the Delaware and drop off their wretched human cargo at the South Philadelphia docks, where thousands of exhausted travelers fanned out through the streets and neighborhoods looking for family, shelter, and employment.

Initially, the Glass family would stay with Molly's relatives in the heart of the Jewish quarter, which was situated between large Irish and Italian communities. Running from 3rd to 10th Streets below Snyder Avenue, the section would become the largest Jewish community in America outside of the Lower East Side in New York. Like many struggling immigrant families, the Glasses moved to a series of small cold-water flats. Harry tried his hand at several menial jobs that provided a modest wage and even less security. When he finally found employment at the Navy Yard in South Philadelphia, he earned barely enough money for the family to rent a small row apartment of their own. But there was a definite downside to their new residence; it was located outside the Jewish quarter in a staunch Irish-Catholic section close by the waterfront.

Boyle's Market, Flannigan's Leather and Saddle Supplies, and Brendan's Hardware Store now replaced the more familiar Jewish bakeshops, butchers, and clothing stores they had frequented. Though instances of outright anti-Semitism were infrequent for Mr. and Mrs. Glass—Molly was usually given a cold shoulder by the other women on the street, and Harry was subjected to crude jokes and other indignities at the Navy Yard—it would be young Heshel who would suffer the most.

Not long after moving into their new home the youngest member of the family was given a memorable introduction to the neighborhood. Barely five at the time, Heshel was walking down the street just yards from his family's residence. It was the first occasion Heshel was unaccompanied by a parent, and he was quietly observing the businesses, homes, and people on the street when a door to one house opened and a little boy his age came out. Spying Heshel, the alarmed child suddenly gave out a loud shout, "It's him, it's the Jew," and several older boys ran out. All began screaming, "Get the kike!" and "Beat his Jew ass!"

Astonished by their collective vehemence and too perplexed to know what to do, Heshel stood frozen on the sidewalk and was quickly set upon by five boys and driven to the ground. Pummeled and kicked repeatedly, he tried to block the blows as best he could, but many found their target. If it had not been for the intervention of a passer-by who pulled the attackers off one by one, Hershel would have been beaten to a pulp. Bloody, bruised, and frightened beyond words, Heshel painfully struggled to get himself off the pavement as his youthful attackers continued their verbal barrage. He limped home; a disheveled, tearful mess. His face, head, and ribs were much abused, but what shook him even more than his physical wounds were the anger and vitriol of his assailants. As he would discover many times in coming years, the cuts and welts would gradually heal, but the verbal insults proved resistant to the passage of time. His psyche would be forever scarred, firmly cementing his view of the world as an unpredictable and dangerous place.

At the time of the attack, Heshel had no idea who Jesus Christ was; he had never heard the name before, nor did he understand how he had anything to do with this person's death. But being repeatedly called a "Christ killer," "dirty kike," and "Jew bastard"—and in such angry, violent terms—cut him to the core. Though just a child, he was learning about religious bigotry and ethnic hostility.

Those of Jewish faith were in particular jeopardy, despite Harry and Molly Glass living as non-observant Jews. They didn't wear their religion on their sleeves, nor did they stress its import in their daily lives. For Heshel, however, much of his religious education would come on the streets of an Irish-Catholic neighborhood, and it could come without warning—all too often in the form of a vile epithet or at the end of a clenched fist.

Targeted for both verbal and physical abuse by neighborhood ruffians, Heshel was often alone, homebound by choice, as the streets of his South Philly neighborhood repeatedly proved unsafe. Any gathering of children would provoke concern. "Momma, will I have to go there?" little Heshie often asked his mother as they walked past the local elementary school. The children playing in the schoolyard were loud, large in number, and always frenetically running about, leading Heshel to believe this was the last place he'd want to be. Though his mother tried to reassure him all little children go to school and everything would turn out all right, Heshel knew better. His complaints, fears, and tantrums proved fruitless—he was going, despite his best efforts to postpone the inevitable, and on that first day when his mother escorted him to school he still firmly believed that nothing good would come of it.

This was borne out by the chorus of laughter, guffaws, and crude comments that rang down on him when he was introduced to his new classmates for the first time. The smirking, tow-headed little boys and freckled-faced girls in pigtails all seemed to agree that Hershel Glass was odd and didn't belong.

But if Shawcross Elementary School at Second and Wolf Streets generated unease, Mount Carmel Parochial School just a block away at Third and Wolf proved even more hellish. For the Italian and Irish Catholic students, the shy and retiring little Jew was made to order. Yelling derogatory insults and chasing Heshel down the street became a favorite pastime, and Heshel quickly learned the importance of vigilance, avoiding certain streets, and developing foot speed.

Equally formidable as the Catholic hoards were the Neckers, a semi-civilized assemblage of hog tenders and subsistence farmers who inhabited a fairly desolate stretch of South Philadelphia below Oregon Avenue. An ugly, undeveloped piece of city real estate consisting of ramshackle wood houses, tin sheds, unpaved roads, trash-strewn back alleys, and water-filled ditches—all littered with chickens, pigs, goats, and other farm animals—that gave the area more the flavor of Georgia's Okefenokee Swamp than the third-largest city in the nation.

Children from "the Neck"—as the neglected region was known—didn't go to school and stood out for their backwoods habits, country attire, and general hayseed comportment. But they could fight and cause occasional mayhem. The area's youth, especially teenagers, seemed to take pleasure in periodically amassing along Stonehouse Lane and surreptitiously crossing Oregon Avenue to inflict havoc and destruction to the residences and businesses of the Jewish, Irish, and Italian inhabitants.

It didn't take Heshel long to realize how backward and unusual the Neck was. Whether a misplaced piece of geography or relic of a bygone era, it was strange. But his curiosity was heightened by the chilling stories of bizarre goings-on and children being snatched and held captive there. He would never go there alone, and when he did it was only with children he had a modicum of confidence in. Those infrequent exploratory journeys were always exciting, spiced with an air of danger. But for Heshel, he needn't travel far for heart-pounding excitement.

Just walking to and from school often proved a nerve-racking challenge, and performing the simplest neighborhood chores for his parents as he grew older presented substantial concern. His arrival home bloodied and shaken was far from an unusual occurrence. On one occasion when playing on a back lot with neighborhood children, he was suddenly set upon and thrown off a seven-foot wall. He landed squarely on a cement alleyway, his head and face taking the brunt of the impact.

Dazed, bleeding profusely, and frightened out of his wits, he staggered home and was immediately rushed to the hospital. He was released the following day, told the effects of the concussion would gradually recede, and his stitches would be removed a few days later—but the underlying reasons for his being tossed off the wall would go unaddressed.

Even rather mundane experiences could prove an adventure. Walking to the neighborhood library, for example, proved so dangerous that his father had to escort him in order to prevent a sudden attack by gentile marauders. The need for paternal protection only added to the many embarrassing catcalls that were regularly hurled his way. Eventually, he just gave up on the perilous trek. Books and the pursuit of knowledge meant nothing to the children around him. In fact, spending time on such things became the object of constant derision, not to mention the occasional beating.

Acceptance would come the only way it could have in a stoic, turn-of-the-century working class, community: through the adoption of the Catholic neighborhood's traditional rite of passage—demonstrations of strength and toughness. For juveniles that meant hard-nosed physical play. Lugging a football across a goal line, hitting a home run, winning a foot race, and most importantly, being able to defend oneself with one's fists. Such physical feats were the gold standards of earning a reputation and garnering community respect.

As an outsider—one often accused of being a "Christ killer" and "killing our Lord"—Heshel Glass was regularly reminded of his inferior, if not despised, status in the community. Invariably chosen last when picked at all by the older boys forming teams in backlot baseball games and football scrums, young Glass was routinely snubbed. Many a day he'd walk home in tears. Rejected by his peers, he desperately sought answers to his dilemma. Ever so slowly, however, he began to earn his bona fides as a neighborhood competitor.

One such defining moment occurred when Heshel was just ten years old. The only Jew on the trash-strewn lot that passed for an all-purpose athletic field that day, the often-ridiculed Heshel at a crucial point late in the game was the last defensive player separating Paul Lupinochi—an older and taller boy—from the goal line. Shedding tacklers as he turned the corner and headed for a touchdown, Lupinochi bared down on the little Jew in as menacing and purposeful a stride as he could muster. Lupinochi could have easily avoided Glass, but he wanted to embarrass him. He wanted to scare Hesh off or, better yet, drive him into the ground. With gleeful observers screaming, "Heshie, lookout," and "You're about to get squashed," Heshel Glass, to the amazement of all, didn't flee but steadied himself for a terrible collision. Bracing himself, he drove his head and shoulders into the runner's legs just like the most respected and seasoned players.

Lupinochi slammed into Glass like a freight train hitting an ox cart at a railroad crossing. The impact was severe, sending both players airborne. When the dust cleared, Hesh was flat on his back and dazed. The runner was equally shaken after performing an unexpected cartwheel-like maneuver that underscored the force of the impact. There was a moment of stunned silence; players from both teams were awed by the collision. Suddenly, there were whoops and hollers, and they began singing Hesh's praises. "Hurray for Heshie," "Great tackle, Hesh," and "Can you believe it? Heshie nearly killed Lupo!" were just some of the comments from disbelieving witnesses.

Now seated on his rear end in a state of embarrassment and confusion, Lupinochi was speechless. Heshie—physically shaken, numb from head to toe, and exposing several bloody teeth—attempted to stand but collapsed into the arms of both fellow teammates and opposing players. All were patting him on the back and cheering his unanticipated heroics. Appreciation of his physical feat was near universal. Even Lupinochi—sweat-stained and embarrassed— complimented his often-dismissed Jewish adversary on his tackle.

But that was not the end of it. Astonishingly, the startling feat occurred a second time when later in the game Lupinochi turned the corner and charged upfield with the ball, determined to correct his earlier failing. Once again, a ferocious clash of bodies; but as before he was taken down by Glass. Showered with praise and congratulatory slaps on the back, Hesh was as surprised as anyone. The least-likely figure on the field that day to exhibit spunk and perform a game-saving play was accorded star status. The event's significance did not go unrecognized.

Despite limping off the field with an assortment of painful cuts, ugly bruises, and a splitting headache, Glass had achieved something he had long sought—a modicum of recognition and respect. His display of "guts" and physical prowess had opened a door into a new world, one in which, at least for a moment, he was no longer a shunned outsider. For the first time, he felt like one of the guys. Hearing "See you tomorrow, Hesh," and "Great game, Hesh," as the players left the field was the equivalent of medals and military honors for a battle-weary soldier. As the approval of the other boys washed over him then and in coming days he'd repeatedly reflect on his glorious tackles and the acclaim they brought. There was no hiding the uplift in spirit it fostered. The memory was like no other he had ever experienced. And for an often-shunned youngster, the exhilaration was life-changing. It was a feeling he was determined to retain and nurture.

The formula for neighborhood survival had been discovered. Granted, he would always be different—a "damn Jew" and "dirty kike" in the minds of many—but on the backlots and ballfields of South Philly, the brief interludes of athletic success and camaraderie were as rewarding as a lush oasis for a parched desert traveler. Heshel responded by throwing himself into sports. And if his religion was wanting or skill level questioned, he'd make up for it in grit, displaying the same competitive spirit and physical self-sacrifice as the best gentile players. Though nasty injuries including numerous dislocations and fractured bones would result, Hesh Glass gradually earned a reputation for toughness and athletic ability. The coin of the realm in working-class neighborhoods like South Philadelphia, his hard-nosed physical play was rewarded with grudging respect. Anyone who would run into a wall to make a catch or selflessly dive to make a tackle—and thereby repeatedly sacrifice his body to make a play—deserved respect, even if he was a Jew.

Acceptance would gradually come, and his closest friends would be from families with last names such as O'Brian, Hanlon, Ferguson, Loftus, Martin, and Antonetti. Many a door would still remain closed to him, as would be an array of social events, but that was his life. The indignities were hard to digest, but incremental immersion in the majority culture was undeniable. The assimilation process, however, presented its own conundrums.

One of the more unsettling occurred in a desolate section of South Philly on a warm summer morning when he and several other boys from the neighborhood were exploring a junk-filled part of the Neck. While inspecting a collection of discarded items at a community dump site, they came upon a couple of boys from the Jewish Quarter. No more than ten or twelve in age, they were easy pickings for the street-tough Irish hooligans.

"Get 'em! Get those Jew bastards," yelled Bobby McDevitt as he chased after and quickly tackled one of the boys. "Drag 'em over here," he then called out to his fellow marauders who had taken down the other boy. As the captives screamed for help and pleaded to be let go, McDevitt gathered pieces of rope and scattered strips of discarded saddle leather, and with the aid of his confederates, began tying their two captives to an old poplar tree. McDevitt, obviously enjoying the moment, then grabbed one of the longer leather strips and began swinging it menacingly near the prisoners.

Though appalled by what he was observing, Heshel Glass stood paralyzed. Unable to either take part in or terminate the quickly escalating episode of juvenile shenanigans, he watched in horror as a mischievous prank escalated into something far more ominous. "Lousy Jews," McDevitt screamed as he began whipping the boys. The crack of the leather as it made violent contact with skin and clothing was palpable, causing the captives to cry out in pain and plead for their freedom. Though he had started whipping their pant legs, McDevitt quickly targeted his two captives' torsos. When that did not draw the desired results, he then shifted to their arms and heads. "How's that feel, you lousy bastards?" he shouted at them as red welts began to appear on his victims' arms and faces.

Flushed with anger, his eyes ablaze, McDevitt tormented his captives despite their tears and pleas to stop. He then encouraged his confederates to join in the show of dominance. Jimmy Ivers and Jackie Dougherty each took a few swings of the leather whip as McDevitt urged them on. He then offered the strap to Glass. Chilled by the entire episode, Heshel refused the whip and backed off. "What's wrong?" asked McDevitt, angrily. Perplexed at one of his gang's reluctance to take part in their manly conquest, he asked, "What are you afraid of?"

Glass remained mute and slowly shook his head. Alarmed by both the brazenness and viciousness of his confederates' actions, he wanted no part of it. But he was equally afraid that McDevitt and the others would turn on him. His fear of being called a "gutless kike" and "frightened Jew" was as great as his horror at participating in the torture of two boys guilty of nothing more than being Jews in the wrong place at the wrong time. He had struggled, and occasionally succeeded, in overcoming his cowardice on neighborhood ballfields, but affairs like this remained an immutable challenge.

With the captives pleading for release and the threat of someone hearing their screams increasing, the four troublemakers finally departed the Neck. The two Jewish boys were left tied to the tree.

Heshel was shaken by the incident. He knew he was Jewish, but there was certainly no advantage to being one where he lived. His involvement with an unprovoked attack was serious, maybe even criminal, but the prospect of being called a coward and identified as a Jew himself by those he was always trying to fit in with was equally disturbing. Even if he would have known the right thing to do, he was unsure if he would have had the guts to do it.

The event's significance would only escalate, for later that afternoon he spotted three men and one of the boys who had been tied to a tree walking along 3rd Street. A policeman accompanied them. Their grim expressions signified they were in search of the dastardly crime's perpetrators. Taking cover in a back alley filled with discarded metal barrels and wooden boxes, Hesh prayed they wouldn't discover his hiding place or where he lived. He rightly surmised one of the Jewish boys recognized him from school and knew he lived in one of the Irish river ward sections of South Philadelphia. As he watched the men go from shop to shop on the avenue and periodically inquire about the boys in question, his imagination exploded with ugly possibilities of his arrest, separation from his parents, and being sent to a reform school for juvenile delinquents.

At one point the men were so close to his alley hideout that he overheard one of them ask a store owner in Yiddish-inflected English, "We're looking for a boy named Heshel. He's about twelve and lives in this area." Fortunately, the working-class neighborhood's code of silence—especially when the questions were coming from outsiders, and in this case Jews accompanied by police—resulted in no one divulging any information about the neighborhood's lone Jewish boy.

For the rest of the day and the many that followed that summer, Heshel would be wary and constantly on the lookout for police and his Jewish pursuers. Though he would escape retribution or a visit by police on that occasion, the incident unnerved him. It also underscored his dilemma. He was trapped: a Jew in a Gentile world.

However, even when amongst his own people Heshel often felt ill at ease; he didn't fit in. For example, a couple of years later when sent into the Jewish Quarter several days a week to attend Hebrew School and learn his Bar Mitzvah Haggadah, he fought his parents' wishes vigorously. The language, customs, and people at the shul were foreign to him, and he could count few of the children his age as acquaintances, much less friends. He sat in the back of his classes, disinterested and resentful that such a travesty had befallen him. Hebrew School made regular school seem a walk in the park. And though he tried not to draw attention to himself, several students knew him or knew of him.

A few even feared him. Herbie Levin, for instance, the pint-sized school bully who could usually be found walking the halls, barking orders and issuing threats to most boys and girls, was deferential to Heshel. In fact, he was scared to death of him. "Whatever you want or need, just let me know," said Levin on Glass's arrival. "This place is a joke. Nobody will bother you; they'll never challenge us. We can run the entire joint."

Levin's admiration of his new classmate had little to do with Glass's reputation as a local tough guy and neighborhood ruffian. Hesh wasn't either of those things, really, but he did have some renown. It had to do with the fact that Hesh lived among the dreaded Irish. Known for their drunken, menacing, thuggish ways, just living in that violent dog-eat-dog world earned one recognition, if not respect. He not only lived with them, he fought with them, played a rugged style of sports with them, and was known to travel, socialize, and commit crimes with them. For poseurs like Herbie Levin, Heshel Glass was the real deal. He was someone you didn't mess with.

Herbie did all he could to ingratiate himself with Hesh, but the latter had no interest in bullying anybody or running anything, especially in a religious institution. His only interest was getting out of the stupid school and the entire religious ceremony his family had planned for him. The traditional Bar Mitzvah ritual—a rite of passage insisted on by his parents—was one he'd quickly come to loathe. Considering his Irish-Catholic surroundings, solidifying his affiliation and fealty to his Jewish heritage was the last thing he wanted to do.

Gradually, Heshel would become one of the guys in the local gentile gang, but that would prove a dubious honor on occasion. Fights with other gangs, provoking general mayhem, and assorted criminal mischief including break-ins and instances of commercial theft could have resulted in severe injury, not to mention arrest and reform school. But that was the price he had to pay if the goal was acceptance. He had learned early how to be alone, but it had not been his choice. He wanted to be one of the guys, one of the gang.

All the kids in his neighborhood, especially the tough, more athletic ones, hated school. An average student, Heshel recoiled at the entire experience. Most of each class day would be spent looking out the window and imagining the many fun, athletic endeavors he could be doing. School was like a prison; few subjects interested him and he particularly dreaded being called on in the classroom. He spent much time keeping his head down and contemplating how he could avoid being asked questions by the teacher. As he watched the clock on the wall slowly move toward dismissal each day, each hour, each minute, seemed endless. The school system's saving grace proved to be its athletic teams, where Hesh repeatedly showcased his mettle and athleticism. Though only occasionally the star player, he usually acquitted himself well and was recognized by all as a good athlete and serious competitor.

He was just fine with the notion of quitting school early and getting a job like most of his friends, but his parents would have none of it. Though they had little formal schooling themselves, they valued education and insisted their only child complete high school. He did as they wished, earned a diploma, and then knocked about with a series of low-paying menial jobs. He could have qualified for less-physical, more-rewarding positions as a transportation dispatcher or bookkeeper, but the neighborhood ethic had imprinted him with a distaste for pencils, desk work, and numbers.

Life took a cruel twist when, just a year after graduation, Heshel's father was killed in a shipyard accident. Just nineteen and now the main wage earner for the household, Heshel had to grow up quickly. Initially, he and his mother received aid from family and friends as well as assistance from the Jewish Federation and Jewish Family Services. Even some Irish neighbors and store owners offered food, clothing, and money to Molly Glass in the aftermath of her loss. One of the more unusual offers of help at the time would come from a neighbor named Marcus McLaughlin. A low-level but rising ward politician with a city job, he needed assistance for his many party functions and campaign duties. McLaughlin supplied groceries and occasionally a few dollars in return for Heshel's help.

The requests were sporadic, diverse in nature, and though not physically taxing, they did require his time. Handing out handbills on election day, hanging colorful bunting and building stages for campaign rallies, and providing assistance to local officeholders at campaign stops took him away from athletic contests and occasions with his friends, but Mr. McLaughlin could be counted on when Hesh or his mother were in need.

Thought by most a good-natured, optimistic sort, McLaughlin habitually passed on advice to Glass and the other young recruits. Party fealty was a recurring theme. One of his favorite aphorisms was "Don't ever forget, loyalty to the party will one day pay dividends." As McLaughlin often cautioned his young assistants, "You never know when you'll get into a jackpot or have a beef with somebody and be in need. It's always good to have a friend." Like most others his age, Glass gave little weight to the advice at the time.

As the years passed, Heshel would try his hand at a number of occupations. He worked for a short period at the Navy Yard, spent time as an electric trolley conductor, shoveled coal at a utility plant, and delivered ice on a horse and wagon. He even considered a career as a policeman. Ever so slowly, however, McLaughlin's counsel and connections proved influential and financially rewarding. One of the more significant was McLaughlin's tie to the city's printing department. "Sure, it's not much to start with," argued the seasoned pol to his young aide regarding the job's low status and meager pay, "but in time, you'll see, there will be advancement and other opportunities. Many men have started at your level and gradually done okay for themselves. It's a big operation, and loyal party workers with a nickel of ambition and some ability get promoted."

Though Glass would remain unexcited about the ink trade, he did learn the nuances of the print forms business, earn a steady wage, and pick up a few valuable nuggets about the courts and the legal system. In the political arena, Glass moved from division inspector and judge of elections to committeeman, becoming an expert in ward mechanics. When his mentor grew too old to carry out his functions as ward leader and said, "Son, how about you taking my place on City Committee?" Glass inherited the position. His willingness to do what was necessary and follow McLaughlin's directives were paying off.

Glass would recount over the years, "I used to work hard at being a committeeman. At election time, most of the other committeemen and ward leaders took a vacation and spent the day in bed. They knew there wasn't any use in getting excited in a Republican town, but I worked. My hardest job was getting 200 names on petitions so we could fulfill legal requirements to nominate candidates. It meant canvassing every house in the ward. And on election nights I'd go around myself to polling places to get the Democratic total. Nobody else was interested in collecting the figures."

Hesh's occupational and political promotions weren't only due to his work ethic, his patron's advice, or connections. His own athletic notoriety played a role. Although he excelled at both baseball and football, many of the friends and acquaintances he had made over the years in the Jewish community were increasingly attracted to the game of basketball. Growing in popularity, especially in South Philly's Hebrew ghetto, Jewish spectators and players were some of early basketball's most avid fans and recognizable stars. The sport's first dominant team, the SPHA (South Philadelphia Hebrew Association) became renowned for their skill, knowledge of the game, and success. Their games regularly drew sizable crowds at venues like the Broadwood Hotel, and their star players like Morty Soloman, Gussie Leibman, and Hymie Kurtz became household names in Jewish enclaves throughout Pennsylvania, New Jersey, New York, and Delaware.

Though a few years older than most on his team, and not the most gifted shooter or dribbler on the court, Hesh Glass proved a valuable asset. He could run, play defense, and grab rebounds with the best of them. And he often proved a steady hand—someone who couldn't be intimidated—when playing against the more physical Catholic, industrial, and upstate anthracite mining teams on the schedule.

"We were a tough outfit," Glass would recount for inquiring minds when the greatest SPHA triumphs came up for discussion. "We didn't take any crap. We battled with the best of them." It was often at this point that Glass would pull out an old photograph of himself in his basketball uniform, his hair combed low over his forehead almost covering his eyes. It wasn't his attempt at a new fashion statement but Glass's way of preventing his mother from seeing the bruises on his forehead. He got them from opponents' overly aggressive elbows and from caroming off the walls of assorted gymnasiums.

And he'd boast as to how the hometown team was shrewd as well as tough. One savvy tactic according to Glass was waxing the floor before a game. "We'd then put little piles of sawdust in the corners," recounted Glass. "We knew about the sawdust, but our opponents didn't. We rubbed our shoes in it and managed to keep our feet during the game while out-of-town teams slid around as if on ice skates."

Accounts of SPHA's games were regularly covered in the sports section of local newspapers, and Hesh Glass was periodically mentioned as an "important contributor," "stalwart defender," and "imposing force under the basket." Even those outside the local Jewish community took note. At meetings and social gatherings, Democratic Party politicians made favorable comments as to his athletic prowess, and officeholders would extend encouragement, congratulations, and the occasional offer, "Hey, Hesh, let's get together for lunch sometime."

That recognition along with the political guidance of Marc McLaughlin propelled Glass through a series of increasingly important and better-paying municipal staff assignments. Though Glass would never earn a reputation for managerial creativity or programmatic originality, neither would he be viewed as incompetent, lazy, or corrupt. Maybe most shocking, considering his growing list of patrons and steady climb in Democratic Party circles, was his restrained ambition. Surrounded by a bevy of politicians seeking fame, fortune, and higher office, Glass was rather subdued in his personal aspirations.

It was all the more surprising then that his name was put forth by party leaders as their candidate for coroner of the city and county of Philadelphia in the election of 1935. The coroner's office had come under severe criticism; one scandal after another seemed to plague the office. Party elders agreed new blood was needed; that became apparent to all when the incumbent was indicted. Competing factions championed the candidacies of prominent individuals for the position of county coroner, but they neutralized each other.

It was not that unusual a scenario. And even though more well-known, accomplished, and ambitious political operatives were seeking the position— almost all possessing a medical or legal degree—party elders tended to use their own arcane calculus, incorporating ethnicity, religion, and neighborhood geography to designate a slate of candidates for public office. Ironically, it was Hesh's identity as a Jew—and the prospect of a former Jewish basketball player attracting Jewish votes—that played a pivotal role in securing his position as the Party's endorsed candidate. In that election cycle, Glass would be the only candidate for the coroner's office who never attended college, and the only one seeking the office unable to write "Dr." before his name.

Chapter 11

Seeking the Truth

Arriving home in South Philadelphia physically and emotionally exhausted around one-thirty in the morning, Glass was fast asleep as soon as he discarded his rumpled, sweat-stained clothes and placed his head on the pillow. To his great regret, however, he awoke less than two hours later. Restless and filled with anxiety, he was consumed with the investigative demands and political threats now facing his office.

Glass began reading an assortment of recent news articles on the Holmesburg food strike that Miss Renwick had collected and had delivered to his home the previous evening. The articles, some of which he had read a couple of days earlier, now had much greater import. The *Philadelphia Evening Bulletin's* front-page story on Saturday, August 20, was typical of the initial local news coverage as it announced, "Prisoners Strike at Holmesburg." Estimates had nearly "700 prisoners participating in the strike," and inmates demanding an "end to a steady diet of hamburgers, spaghetti and cheese, bologna, fried eggplant, and soup." Their call for "ice cream and cake every other Sunday," and their demand "to elect an inmate committee of control" with a "voice in setting prison regulations" seemed less preposterous to him. Of special interest, however, was the superintendent's reaction as quoted in the various articles.

"There is only one committee running this prison," snapped Superintendent Davis in the *Bulletin* article. "It's a committee of one and that's me."

The superintendent would go on to inform the press that the inmates were "delusional" if they thought their strike was going to accomplish anything, and their effort to gain control of prison operations was communist-inspired. "They would have been the most astonished men in the world if I had given the slightest sign of acceding," Davis was quoted as saying. "Their demands were deliberately framed to be unacceptable. There really wasn't dissatisfaction. The movement was so well planned that there is no doubt in my mind that underlying communistic influences among the prisoners possibly directed by letters or visitors from outside were responsible."

Similarly, the *Philadelphia Inquirer's* August 20 front-page story alerted readers that "650 Holmesburg Prisoners Were on Strike" and contained more of Davis's bluster. "Who ever heard of men in their right minds protesting against the articles of diet that they are kicking about." There was also his bold prediction: "We haven't had any trouble and we aren't going to have any trouble. The situation is under complete control and not a violent hand has been laid on any man."

Most articles in other newspapers contained the same information about a "deep-laid and well-organized, non-violent penal insurrection" at Holmesburg, but one article stood out. Not so much for its quotes or analysis, but for its prestigious standing in the journalistic community—the *New York Times*. Similar to the *Inquirer's* headline, the *Times* article titled, "650 Prisoners Out on Hunger Strike," announced in the nation's most prominent broadsheet that things were amiss in Philadelphia. Superintendent Davis was quoted as giving a cold shoulder to the cellblock malcontents. "The strikers could go hungry as long as they like," he proclaimed. "We're not going to force food on them. If they want to starve, so be it."

Davis further let it be known that their willingness to end the strike wasn't going to impact relations between the keepers and the kept. "When they want to start eating again they'll have to say so," the *Times* quoted Davis as saying. "And when they do, all they'll get for a while is bread and water. Then they'll realize the food they've been complaining about isn't so bad." The article also underscored the situation's severity as "all guards were summoned to duty and quarantined at Holmesburg for the period of the emergency."

For city officials, trouble in the city prison system was practically routine. However, having it exposed publicly for all to see—and in the *New York Times,* no less—was not only embarrassing, it was unacceptable. Now, several days on, Glass better understood the elements leading to the unprecedented cruelty and loss of life. He imagined prison officials under intense pressure; the mayor was known to be a tyrant with underlings who attracted embarrassing headlines.

As he continued to peruse coverage of the prison protest, Glass was surprised to learn news accounts had the inmate strike ending quickly and peacefully. For example, just three days after it began on August 22, newspaper headlines were reporting, "All Except 51 End Prison Food Strike" and "Bread-Water Bait Breaks Food Strike at Holmesburg Jail." The *Inquirer* article gave the clear impression "all was over but the growling," regarding the protest over "monotonous prison fare." And Davis, obviously feeling triumphant, was quoted as saying, "It's a hundred to one shot they won't pass up breakfast, even if it is only bread and water for the time being."

News accounts of a peaceful end to the inmate protest had proven inaccurate. Glass was left wondering what had occurred between the publication of newspaper headlines Monday morning and the discovery of eight disfigured bodies that same morning. Had reporters been hoodwinked into believing a company line while the roof was falling in behind prison walls?

As Glass read on, he was pleased his secretary had included the criminal records of several of the deceased. The oldest and most dangerous proved to be John Webster, a career criminal new to Philadelphia. One of his earliest convictions was for drug addiction back in 1913, and his criminal ways continued uninterrupted for the next two decades with multiple convictions for drug peddling, burglary, shoplifting, larceny, assault, and carrying a concealed deadly weapon. Shooting a South Philadelphia pharmacist during the course of an armed robbery finally took him off the streets. Webster, who was also known by a host of aliases over the years, had served time in county and state institutions stretching from Blackwell's Island in New York to Stateville in Illinois.

Webster's criminal capers turned increasingly violent over time, and he was convicted of shooting two gamblers in Youngstown, Ohio, in 1928. Given the inmate's ten-to-twenty-year sentence, Glass was stunned to see that Webster had somehow earned parole only five years later in 1933. Numerous arrests would follow, but his sentences were usually relatively brief. Coming to Philadelphia proved a fatal mistake as Webster was arrested and convicted of shooting a popular neighborhood druggist at Broad and Catherine Streets during a botched hold-up. His new sentence of ten to twenty years, combined with the back time he owed the state, now had him behind bars until at least 1957. His involvement in a prison protest managed to extricate him from prison, but only as far as the city morgue.

Tim O'Shea was much like the others who lost their lives in Klondike, a Philadelphia native and relative novice in the criminal arena. Just twenty-seven, he augmented his income as a welder at a locomotive yard by burglarizing upscale homes along the Delaware River. Eventually nabbed and convicted of several after-dark burglaries in the Frankford, Tacony, and Torresdale sections of the city, he had been given a three-to-ten-year sentence by a law-and-order judge who lectured O'Shea at his sentencing. "I hope your time isolated from society," the judge soberly told him, "will cause you to reflect on whether you want to become a productive and respected member of the community or a perennial miscreant deserving of our scorn and constant vigilance."

One could argue O'Shea's premature death short-circuited that decision. Others may argue his participation in a prison strike showed a continuing inclination toward troublesome behavior. Regardless, he was clearly of concern no longer, except to the coroner as a victim of a particularly heinous crime.

As Glass familiarized himself with the arrest records of the deceased—all of whom, except Webster, seemed insignificant and unknown to the general public—he continued to ponder the same questions. Why did eight men have to die in the Klondike punishment unit? What else must have occurred to necessitate the loss of eight lives and under such extreme circumstances?

By the time he exited his home and slid into the seat behind the steering wheel of his city automobile, Glass was still undecided if he should drive directly to Holmesburg or stop first at his office in City Hall. A long list of overdue phone calls was in order, as well as myriad assignments related to the Holmesburg matter. Local politicians, as well as news reporters from near and far, had sought his comment on the case. He was just about to start the vehicle when he spied something odd on the hood.

Just beyond the windshield were several small objects he couldn't quite distinguish due to the sun's early morning glare. Confused, Glass stepped out of the vehicle for a better look only to be met with three copper-jacketed bullets standing upright on the hood. There was no accompanying note, but one was not needed; a chilling message had been delivered. The strategically placed .44-caliber slugs were confirmation that someone thought he had crossed a line.

Glass quickly grabbed the bullets and examined the car then the street for any signs of potential trouble. He couldn't help but feel he was being watched. Scanning the doors and windows of the row houses for leering neighbors or more foreign threats, Glass felt small, vulnerable. He understood that his popularity in some quarters was in rapid decline. He had not only taken on the city's political establishment and some entrenched interests, but he was doing so on behalf of the least-popular segment of Philadelphia society—incarcerated criminals.

Reentering the vehicle, Glass sat motionless for a minute. It crossed his mind that it might be prudent to have one of his deputies chauffeur him around, but he fought the urge to exit his automobile and call the office. He didn't want to appear weak and afraid. Bracing himself, he held his breath and grasped the ignition key. The coroner took a deep breath, preparing to turn the key, when a horn blared and a large black city vehicle pulled alongside him. He recognized the two men inside as detectives who normally traveled with the mayor. "The mayor wants to see you," said one detective, holding the door open. "Get in."

Chapter 12

Mayor Clarke & Coroner Glass

As the city vehicle pulled onto the expansive cement apron that surrounded the northeast corner of City Hall, Glass noticed a disturbance occurring close by the entrance to the building. Several uniformed police officers holding batons were trying to control over three dozen argumentative protesters who were being blocked from entering the building. It was only when Glass and his plainclothes escorts exited the vehicle and neared the entrance that he heard cursing, anguished cries, and the demands for justice.

"You allowed them to kill my son," wailed one distraught woman who appeared to be in her fifties. "You took my boy from me. You killed him, for what? You're all a bunch of killers, murderers all. You should all be tried for murder." Her gray hair blew in the warm breeze and tears ran down her cheeks as friends and family members tried to restrain the woman and the others who seemed intent on entering the building. Then a raving, wild-eyed man in his thirties screamed, "They killed my brother. Those prison guards killed my brother. What are you goin' to do about it?" Others shouted similar messages and threats. They were determined to register their moral outrage with the mayor and any other elected officials they could find regarding the deaths at Holmesburg.

Others in the group made similarly emotional charges and demands for justice. Glass, who was quickly ushered into the building, did not believe any of the angry protesters recognized him, but he was struck by the level of pain and the cries for justice by relatives of the deceased.

"Don't mind them," said one plainclothes detective who aggressively prodded Glass through the building's doors. "If they were really concerned about their kids, they would have made sure they never went to prison in the first place." Glass knew there was an element of truth to the officer's comment, but he wasn't ready to concede the city had no responsibility in the untimely and brutal deaths of eight men remanded to the county lock-up.

Ushered into the second-floor City Hall office of Mayor G. Thomas Clarke, Glass was met with a half-dozen unsmiling men including mayoral adviser Jennings, Police Commissioner Gleason, District Attorney Campbell, and several of their top deputies. The customary practice of a pleasant "hello" or "good morning" greeting along with a congenial handshake with governmental colleagues was dispensed with.

"I'll say this, Glass. You got a lot of fuckin' guts," bellowed Clarke as he rose from behind an impressive dark-mahogany desk covered with an array of local and out-of-town newspapers. "You think you caught a wave and are just gonna ride it to shore . . ."

"Mr. Mayor, I just want to—"

"Let me tell you something, Glass. You fucked up big time. These newspapers," said the mayor waving his arm at the front-page accounts of the Holmesburg tragedy, "are gonna line your political coffin. You're through in this town. I'm gonna—"

"But, Mayor—"

"Forget it, Glass," said Clarke raising his voice. "You're history."

Clarke's face turned crimson, the pronounced bags under his eyes seemed to momentarily vanish, and he appeared on the verge of exploding. Of average height, with a slight paunch, receding hairline, and double chin, Gavin Thomas Clarke wasn't much to look at, but he was a consummate politician who had not only survived Philadelphia's brutal political infighting but had risen to the top of the electoral heap. A natural opportunist, he'd banked time as both a Democrat and Republican over the years; just a few months earlier, he was on the verge of switching his allegiance once again from Republican to Democrat in an effort to win the nomination for either the US Senate or governor of the state. He increasingly urged followers to discard their party affiliations and remain loyal to him. His ascent, he would argue, would be best for all concerned.

Clarke not only knew the players and political landscape but was also intimate with the city's neighborhoods, the nasty ethnic rivalries, and the myriad social and economic concerns that consumed constituents. Possession of the municipal playbook, however, didn't always translate into smooth managerial sailing.

"Hardly a week passes that doesn't witness some dramatic gesture, bold overture, or indefensible gaff by our mayor," wrote one news reporter of Clarke's amazing ability to provoke controversy and stoke partisan animus. His many courtroom battles, recurring disputes with utility companies, and preposterous comments in defense of a beleaguered and corrupt police force were headline-grabbing events. But Clarke could also make positive news by selling the city as a site for presidential conventions, Army-Navy football games, and theatrical tryouts for Broadway plays. Each of these, however, could also explode into name-calling, partisan rancor, and embarrassment for the city.

Clarke precipitated an artistic and racial furor, for example, when he vowed to block *Mullato*, a Langston Hughes play with an all-black cast, from opening in Philadelphia. Though the play, a "melodrama about miscegenation in the deep South," had garnered favorable reviews in both New York and Chicago, Mayor Clarke found the production offensive and promised, "the play won't go on here." The play's storyline, he declared, was "an outrageous affront to decency and traditional values. As long as I am mayor, I will not permit such shows in Philadelphia."

Though such obstinate rants may have only impacted theater-goers and African-Americans, many more citizens took notice of the mayor's penchant for having his name plastered all over town. Within a year or two of assuming office, every signpost, sewer, traffic light, and trash can in the city seemed to have Clarke's name on it. He even broached with a friendly city councilman the notion of his name being affixed to the city's municipal airport. Though he may have delighted in such widespread recognition, newspaper columnists, and then fellow citizens, started referring to the mayor as "Ashcan Clarke."

At the moment, however, Mayor Clarke was neither the brunt nor instigator of friendly, light-hearted humor. He was a thoroughly outraged government official seeking to end an event causing widespread embarrassment orchestrated by a misguided underling who had wandered off the reservation. And the press gave no sign of losing interest in the story. Broadsheets already devoting front-page, above-the-fold coverage, and tabloids giving full-page attention to the grisly Holmesburg murders, allowed their reporters dramatic license to embellish their accounts of new developments in the story. From early on, normally staid, just-the-facts newspaper scribes were crafting attention-grabbing opening lines like, "The volcano that is Holmesburg Prison blew its top off early yesterday, not only leaving eight hunger-striking prisoners dead, but their lifeless, discolored bodies resembling visitors from a distant planet."

As the investigation proceeded, literary license only increased. For example, a *Philadelphia Inquirer* banner headline read, "Guards Taunted Dying in Torture Chamber, 3 Survivors Tell Investigators." One reporter took dramatic flight, informing readers the prisoners were forced to endure "Heat that squeezed the life from men as they babbled prayers in their parched throats. Heat that drove men to their knees, to the slimy, water-slopped floor, and then to unconsciousness or death. Heat that drove men mad in the pit-like blackness of Holmesburg Klondike. Heat that wrung broken prayers from lips of hardened convicts who had forgotten how to pray. Heat that coated the iron grillwork of cell doors. Heat that caused men to go mad, to attempt suicide, to cry out incoherently for their mothers and wives . . ."

Philadelphia had become the focus of national attention, but the morbid narrative was nothing to be proud of, and the mayor was beyond livid. The enormity of the story, and in particular its grisly aspects, were too great an attraction for even the press-savvy mayor to squelch.

"When I'm done with you, the only job you'll be able to get is selling peanuts at the Palestra and Franklin Field," Clarke shouted at Glass. "That's where you belong, you punch-drunk idiot. You've taken too many shots to the head." It was then that Clarke's tirade was interrupted by a coughing fit. With his health in decline recently, it was not unusual for the mayor—especially when emotionally taxed—to become a red-faced, profane, and spittle-spewing avatar.

Not used to being spoken to in this manner, especially in front of high-ranking city colleagues, Glass struggled to maintain his composure. Combined with the .44-caliber slugs he discovered on the hood of his car less than an hour earlier, the last thing Glass needed was the mayor's irrational lecture. As the mayor continued his tirade, Glass didn't know whether to walk out, shout the mayor down, or punch him in the face.

Finally, after listening to more verbal abuse, Glass erupted. "Eight men are dead," he practically yelled out, startling everyone.

Suddenly, the mayor was mute.

"Yes, you heard me. Eight men roasted alive as if they were sausages in a hot fryer," he continued angrily. "I don't care what you think of me, but you're not going to do business as usual with a bunch of disfigured bodies lying around. Sure, you can make some problems and people disappear. Cops on the pad, no-show civil servants, and constables paid to look the other way . . . all of them can be hidden or explained away. But eight men stuffed in a charnel house so hot they come out looking like Amos 'n' Andy is more than a run-of-the-mill inconvenience. As the police officers in this room will tell you, not very many of them have experience getting rid of a bunch of Martian-looking cadavers."

"Listen, Glass, don't lecture me," the mayor replied, his assertiveness returning after a moment of stunned silence. "You're in this alone. No one is going to help you blacken the name of this city. Where do you get off comparing us to Calcutta? Keep this in mind: the police department, the district attorney's office, everyone will be aligned against you."

"But I believe the evidence will show—"

"Evidence my ass, what evidence?" barked the mayor. "Yours or what experienced homicide detectives discovered? The deceased—all of 'em convicted criminals—fought among themselves. They were notorious malcontents. First, they got arrested for committing a crime, then they disrupted prison operations, and they finally got on each others' nerves. Once they had seen what their conniving and their food strike had gotten them into, they turned on each other."

"No, it's not true," replied Glass. "I think I can prove these men were targeted by guards and administrators for retribution. The public will see—"

"The public will see nothing," said Clarke. "Don't think I'm going to be fooled by this political reformer act of yours," said the mayor angrily. "Ever since we gave you that job you've made a nuisance of yourself. You don't know the complaints I've received over the years about your management and plans for that office. Hell, I had a revolt on my hands from party leaders when you took office and they heard of your comments at that legislative hearing in Harrisburg. Who do you think you are talking about, turning certain functions of the office over to other municipal entities? You don't decide that. You don't recommend that. Christ, one would think you got that position on your own merit."

Clarke was referring to a legislative hearing in Harrisburg three years earlier, shortly after Glass became Philadelphia's new coroner. Critics claimed the office was a "corrupt and useless appendage" and should be taken over by the district attorney's office or the city's health department. "You can't abolish the functions of the coroner's office," Glass had fired back, "any more than you can abolish murder and sudden death. I believe that an independent agency such as the coroner's office is necessary for the protection of the public and the efficient conduct of the city government. Experience in other cities has shown that where the coroner's office has been transferred to some other department it has doubled the expense and lessened the efficiency."

Party loyalists, however, especially in Philadelphia, were stunned that Glass admitted some office functions could be taken over by other municipal agencies. After stating he would be supportive of such initiatives "if any consolidation could be effected whereby the taxpayers can save money," he further surprised everyone when he admitted there were "phantoms on the payroll." When questioned by lawmakers regarding the discovery of ghost employees, Glass came right out and testified, "There were two employees on the payroll I never was able to catch up with. They were supposedly high-ranking deputies. Their names were there, and apparently the money had been paid to them, but I never saw them."

The revelation, especially coming from the coroner himself, caught onlookers at the capitol off guard. It was unusual, to say the least, for an officeholder—and one who was brought up in Philadelphia's ethically challenged political system—to blow the whistle on himself. Glass went on at that time to testify that when he took office in 1935, he quickly discovered "the books for a period of several years had been destroyed. Turns out the office accountant, a former chief deputy coroner, cooked the books. I don't know how long the charade was going on, but when news of the missing monies was discovered, a warrant was issued for his arrest. He short-circuited the process, however, by committing suicide."

When legislators followed up with questions as to how Glass would improve the coroner's office, he replied, "I've reduced the cost of running the office from $96,000 to $83,000 annually, and taken a $354 reduction in my own salary in order to not reduce our workforce further."

The admissions of past incidents of corruption and Glass's willingness to sacrifice his own salary to maintain the coroner's office pleased governmental reformers. In addition to his candor, they also appreciated his folksiness. "I guess I'm a bit funny," admitted Glass at one point, "because I won't let the boys in my office take graft, and I won't take it myself."

Old-line party operatives back home, however, were less enthused. The new Philadelphia coroner had shown himself to be an odd duck, and one whose political career was now thought to be both problematic and of short duration. Mayor Clarke was convinced the latter scenario couldn't come soon enough.

"You're done," Clarke told Glass. "This Holmesburg nonsense is the nail in your political coffin. Your incompetent career as coroner is over."

"That's not your call," Glass fired back. "I'm not one of your appointees. I was elected by the people."

"And they'll un-elect you if I tell them."

"Maybe so," said Glass, "but until then I'm going to do my job. And maybe you should consider doing your own."

"Why, you impudent son-of-a-bitch," Clarke angrily replied before erupting in a rage-fueled coughing spell.

Rather than continue the bitter dialogue, the coroner turned and briskly walked out of the room.

Glass was immediately confronted by a handful of reporters and photographers who had been tipped off that the mayor and city coroner were meeting.

"We're looking for answers. We're looking for full and complete responsibility for what appears to be the murder of eight Holmesburg Prison inmates," said a red-faced Glass at what had become an impromptu news conference in a City Hall corridor. Reporters were anxious to learn of the latest Holmesburg developments, his relationship with the mayor, as well as the prospect of an unusual investigative procedure—a coroner's inquest. Additional questions, leveled in rapid-fire succession, concerned the mayor's silence, the DA's invisibility, unsupported claims by the police, and increasing talk of a high-level governmental cover-up.

After what would be described in the press as a "short and frank meeting" with Mayor Clarke, Glass informed reporters, "I'm leaving for Holmesburg immediately. I will spend the day there, more if necessary, in order to determine what really happened. Everyone, guards and inmates, will be interviewed. We're making headway and I would hope an inquest by my office will not be needed, but if circumstances demand such, then one will be initiated. If the jury feels that by reason of the evidence and testimony certain individuals should be held responsible, and that includes Superintendent Davis, Warden Stryker, and anyone else in a position of authority, I will abide by what they recommend. Preliminary interviews suggest at least seven or eight arrests could be made at the conclusion of our investigation. There may be more, and some may be high-ranking officials."

In rather blunt terms—and no doubt in response to reporters' questions regarding mayoral indifference to the crime and opposition to a thorough criminal investigation—the coroner went on to say, "I and my office are going through with this case—let the chips fall where they may. Yes, I have been accused by some of stirring up this case, and I will continue to pursue it. And I'm not going to stop halfway, no matter who or what group is concerned.

After talking with survivors and witnessing the scene for myself, I can say with certainty something happened at Holmesburg of unimaginable savagery. The guilty persons must be brought to justice and punished appropriately. Rest assured, there will not be a whitewash."

As the coroner departed for the corner stairwell, several reporters ran after him continuing to shout questions. When one inquired about the report turned in by police investigators, Glass stopped and fired back. "Very suspect. Mostly rubbish, that's all it is," Glass told them. "Something else took place up there. There's something wrong about that building, that so-called punishment unit."

When pressed further by reporters, Glass replied, "By my estimate, the building is no more than fifty feet long, fifteen feet wide, and ten feet high. Yet it has a heating system strong enough to warm a good-sized hotel. You combine radiators that can heat an area up to 190 degrees, then shut windows and air vents on a hot, humid day, turn off the water in the cells, and then have the gall to question the fatal results. And worse yet, manufacture a fantastic story about inmates on the verge of baking to death, attacking and killing each other. Please . . . Any reasonable person witnessing that scene would know that something truly horrific happened up there."

"But the police report—"

"But nothing," Glass shot back. "Maybe the real question is why more didn't die. To be frank, it's amazing anyone survived."

Chapter 13

Factions Target the Coroner's Office

Before traveling back up to Holmesburg for additional interviews, the coroner made what he expected to be a quick stop at his office on the sixth floor. Unfortunately, as soon as he entered the outer office, Miss Renwick cornered him.

"The State welfare secretary has called again. He said the governor is very interested in what is happening." She handed him a list of nearly three dozen names consisting of mostly news reporters and ward leaders who said it was urgent he return their call. The reporters and news editors on the list made sense; he was at the center of what was looking more and more like an urban catastrophe.

"What do all these ward leaders on the list want of me?" As the county coroner, whose primary mission pertained to the deceased, telephone calls from ward leaders were a rarity. Now he had over a dozen key party activists on a callback list.

"Call them back and find out," Miss Renwick said, shrugging as she ran off toward the sound of a ringing telephone.

When he entered his private office, there to greet him was another surprise. Sitting on his desk was a stack of local newspapers whose front pages trumpeted news of the Holmesburg horror. The newspaper stories had been referenced by the mayor just minutes earlier, but now the coroner had a few moments to digest the full depth and scope of the coverage. He was amazed by the number of articles, the banner headlines, and the many photographs of himself.

During his three years in office, he had rarely been quoted. Photographs of him appearing in one of the city's major newspapers were a rarity. Now his image permeated the news like a celebrity.

The *Philadelphia Record*'s front page read, "8 Convicts Roasted to Death; 8 Others Nearly Lost Lives." Pictured beneath the headline were two photos, one of himself and the other of Superintendent Davis. Related stories on the front page were entitled, "Horror at Holmesburg" and "Guards Will Be Held Responsible by Coroner."

Turning the page of the broadsheet, Glass was further shocked to see both pages filled with stories related to the deadly debacle. The top of one page read, "Coroner Charges 8 Convicts Were Roasted to Death in Cells." Articles below the headline read, "8 Others Nearly Succumb in 'Black Hole of Calcutta,'" "Former Convicts Disagree on Cause But All Interviewed Agree Steaming Is Not Uncommon," and most bizarre of all, "Corn Flakes, Prunes, Corn Flakes," which presented a daily chart of what inmates were served for breakfast, dinner, and supper in the Philadelphia County Prison system. Smaller sidebar articles offered profiles of the story's major players like the superintendent, grim reminders of Holmesburg's dark history, and even a column on Calcutta's infamous "Black Hole."

Other newspapers like the *Philadelphia Evening Bulletin* and *Philadelphia Daily News* were equally consumed with the story. For example, the *Philadelphia Inquirer*'s Tuesday morning edition had a banner headline reading, "Shocking: Dead Bodies Discovered at Holmesburg Prison." Articles on the front page and several additional pages detailed past grand jury investigations of the prison system, prison riots over the years, criminal histories of the deceased, reactions of distraught parents, speculation on cause of death, and illustrations of Holmesburg's physical layout. In addition to photos of the prison were numerous photographs of Superintendent Davis, police detectives, and the inmates who had lost their lives.

Many papers had statements of concern from Governor Everton, who was on vacation in Central America. "This is terrible news," Everton was quoted as saying from his hotel in Ancon, in the Canal Zone. "Naturally, I shall have my administration assist investigators in any way possible, and I will be leaving for Harrisburg as soon as flight arrangements can be made."

Several newspapers devoted prominent coverage to the widely differing explanations of the Holmesburg event. The two versions—one by police detectives, the other by the coroner's office—were so different in description and motive that one could easily understand discerning readers coming to the conclusion they were reading about two entirely distinct events. In fact, differences between the stories were so stark, several newspapers pitched the competing scenarios right next to each other in an unusual dueling column format. The *Philadelphia Daily News,* for example, devoted an entire page to "Death Versions; Over-Exhaustion or Roasted." The *Philadelphia Record* gave its readers similar side-by-side accounts of the Klondike deaths in an article entitled, "Two Versions of Jail Killings: Detectives; 'Over-Exertion' – Coroner; 'Death Roasting.'"

On the left was the investigative report submitted by Detective Sergeant Brian Hennessey and Detective Richard Wilson, which emphasized "nothing suspicious" had occurred. Blame was placed on inmate leaders who overestimated their ability to effect change in the jail and fomented a food strike. When they were isolated in a punishment block and placed on bread and water rations, however, they quickly tried to get fellow strikers to abandon the campaign and submit to authorities.

It was Myles McCabe, according to their report, a "widely known thug hired by prominent bootleggers to protect their inventory and customers," who "formed a committee a week or so ago to protest against the food at the penitentiary. McCabe, along with the rest of them, was sick and tired of having nothing but bread, coffee, and prunes for breakfast, a mediocre lunch, and a lousy supper. They also wanted something to eat before going to bed; they got tired of going to bed hungry."

Their report went on to say Myles McCabe had formed the committee that served notice to prison authorities that unless the prison diet was changed, the inmates would go on a hunger strike. The prison officials just laughed at them and slapped them in the punishment unit. "John Webster raised hell about it, and so did James McBride in another cell. With their endless complaints, and constant yelling and screaming, their cellmates were unable to get any rest or sleep." According to their investigation, "Webster blew his top off, started raving around his cell and banging his head on the bars and walls. He cursed and knocked down cellmates, stepped on their heads, and created havoc in other cells till there was hell there for a little while. Finally, everything got quiet."

The article on the right, however, presented an entirely different picture of that terrible weekend. The coroner's report began with the words, "The deaths of the prisoners were due to suffocation applied by an outside agency." In fact, the coroner's account would directly attribute the inmate deaths to retribution; the indifference—if not outright callousness—of prison guards who were quoted as saying, "Let's give those bastards the treatment," and "Let's turn on the heat."

The coroner's report disputed the detectives' account and went on to describe "crowded cells," the "absence of food and water," and most troubling of all, "the purposeful application of intense, unbearable heat." For hours on end, inmates considered to be leaders of the food strike were "victims of inhuman conditions" in the form of "oppressive steam heat." When the cell doors were opened on Monday morning, authorities were met with the "frightful specter" of a "literal death chamber." Those lucky enough to survive—"the sick, the retching, and those out of their minds from the agony they endured"—were permanently scarred.

The article's concluding paragraph—a quote from Glass himself—must have angered the mayor and given prison leadership a collective chill as it read, "I am determined to establish who is responsible for the deaths of these eight men. An investigation, one that will be open and not behind closed doors, will be undertaken. There will be no cover-up if I have my way."

Glass realized that such varied accounts of the Holmesburg tragedy only confirmed for most newspaper readers that the city's penchant for hiding and excusing criminal activity was as strong as ever. However, he also knew this event raised the stakes considerably. The large loss of life was significantly different than the city's normal level of corruption and political intrigue. The Holmesburg Prison story had resonated nationally; people outside of Philadelphia were not only aghast, they were watching closely.

⟞⟝

Stunned by the extent of the coverage, Glass could not recall another local event in the city during his lifetime drawing as much newspaper copy. And this was one in which he was likely to become a center of attention.

"Congrats," said Miss Renwick as she walked in and tossed another newspaper on his desk. "It's not every day someone around here makes the front page of the *New York Times*." As his secretary walked back to her office, Glass picked up the newspaper. There, right on the front page, was an article entitled, "8 Die in Mysterious Prison Revolt in Philadelphia." The article's subtitle, "Four Pair of Prison Hunger Strikers Pictured Battling to the Death," only underscored the brutality of the incident.

It did not take Glass long to discover his name and key role in the investigation. The column's second paragraph began, "City Coroner Heshel Glass called the circumstances surrounding the prison deaths very suspicious," and went on to illuminate his "doubts" regarding the account put forward by "city detectives that eight men had gone berserk and killed one another."

The coroner now understood why the mayor was so worked up and had threatened to end his political career. The Holmesburg story had achieved national recognition. Moreover, the *Times* article questioned police competence and generally cast a dark cloud over the city. And Glass knew there was every indication that things would only grow worse.

Better attuned to the story's prominence now, Glass decided to delay his trip to the prison and take some time to return phone calls to various news agencies. In the course of answering reporters' questions, he tried not to cast blame or speculate on issues yet to be determined. He repeatedly emphasized the need for additional interviews and the importance of autopsy results.

After conversing with a few local and out-of-state newsmen, he decided to return one of the many phone calls Secretary of Welfare Phillip Enteen had made to his office, seeking updates on the investigation. When he got through, the secretary was in a meeting and unavailable, but Glass was pleased at least one state official was supportive and interested in the progress of his investigation. Access to the governor was crucial, and the welfare secretary would be key to that connection.

Glass then looked over the list of ward leaders who had called. With the mayor threatening to terminate his political career, he couldn't afford to be cavalier about his interactions with key party operatives. His first call was to Abe Siegel, the leader of the 23rd ward in the Feltonville section of North Philadelphia. "Hello, Abe, it's Hesh Glass returning your call. Pretty busy now, but what can I do for you?"

"I know you're busy, Hesh," said Siegel. "You got yourself in quite a jam."

"Yeah, I guess you could call it that. What can I do for you, Abe?"

"I guess it looks pretty bad up there . . . at Holmesburg, I mean."

"Yeah, it's a real mess," replied Glass, imagining Siegel with his ever-present cigar protruding from his mouth and ashes on his chest. "I'm going back up there once I get off the phone."

"I heard the prisoners went at each other pretty good."

"Where'd you hear that?" said Glass after a brief delay.

"Well that's what people are saying, and some of the newspapers—"

"Since when do you believe everything you read in the papers?"

"Hesh, if that's what happened," said Siegel, "that's what happened, right?"

Glass did not respond. He was growing annoyed. He couldn't recall the last time Abe Siegel had called him but was sure it was about one of the ward leader's committee people getting a job in the coroner's office. Now Siegel and a bunch of other ward leaders wanted to talk to him. Something was up.

"What do you want, Abe?"

"Hesh, I think you should consider what you're doing. You got a good job and you don't wanna jeopardize it by—"

"Did someone tell you to call me?"

"You know, Hesh, I supported you in the primary."

After a brief pause, the coroner inquired again. "Who got to you?"

"No one's said anything . . ." Siegel claimed, but the coroner wasn't buying it. He suspected the mayor or one of his henchmen had instructed party leaders like Siegel to encourage him to back off and not challenge the official police version of the Holmesburg incident.

"Tell me, Abe," said Glass calmly, "since when did you become interested in prison matters?"

"Hesh, I'm just saying it's not worth losing your position over. No one cares about that prison stuff. They're all murderers and rapists and—"

"Listen," interjected Glass, "I gotta go. Thanks for the call." The coroner abruptly hung up on the long-time neighborhood politician.

His anger growing, Glass was certain the mayor was telling party workers to lean on him to back off the Holmesburg investigation. He knew he shouldn't be surprised; such hardball tactics were not uncommon for those in the political arena, but Glass had never been subject to such treatment, at least while he was in the coroner's office.

Glass was anxious to get back up to the prison and continue the inmate and guard interviews, but the phone call with Abe Siegel nagged at him. Were all the local pols on the list going to urge him to cease his investigation of what he suspected was one of the most brutal crimes in Philadelphia history? He looked over the list Miss Renwick had given him and selected Edward Houser, a Chestnut Hill florist who was the leader of the 9th ward. Though he had few dealings with him, he considered Houser a decent, thoughtful guy. He would be a good indicator as to whether Glass was imagining things or if his worst fears were being realized.

"Hello, Ed," said Glass after Houser answered his phone. "Just returning your call. You wanted to speak to me?"

"Yes, I did," replied the Chestnut Hill ward leader. "I don't want you to repeat this, but I was told to give you a call. The folks downtown are anxious for you to drop this investigative crusade of yours. That's their term, not mine. I told them I was reluctant to get involved in such matters and that I hardly knew you, but they were insistent. In fact, I told Harold Jennings the Holmesburg deaths were a blight on the city's reputation and deserved a thorough investigation. He said the police believe it's a simple case of prisoners killing each other. I said it well may be, but wouldn't it be good if all possible explanations were explored?"

"What did he say?" asked Glass.

"He got all huffy. He said you were out to get headlines and make a name for yourself at the city's expense."

"Do you believe that?"

"Doesn't make any difference what I believe," replied Houser, "but I have other concerns. I told Jennings I wasn't interested in bothering you. He got upset and sort of leaned on me. Well, not me so much as I don't have a city job, but I do have some committee people on the city payroll. And I've been trying to help some constituents get jobs and one young fellow get into Penn. I was given the clear impression those requests would be shelved if I didn't give you a call. I'd hate to see any of my people lose jobs over this thing."

"Goddamn it," barked Glass as he began penciling lines through the names of ward leaders who had contacted his office. "Really goddamn unbelievable."

"Listen, Hesh," said Houser, "you gotta do what you have to do. I did what I had to do. I called you. But don't tell anyone downtown what I told you. I don't need Clarke or his people giving me grief or any of my people getting laid off."

"Well, I thank you for your honesty. Hopefully, we get answers soon and this mess will be over."

Glass ended the conversation discouraged. He decided there would be no more phone calls—at least not to any Philadelphia ward leaders or party activists. The last thing he needed now was the knowledge that innocent party workers may lose their jobs over his attempt to investigate a brutal crime.

Just as Glass rose from behind his desk to begin the fourteen-mile journey up to Holmesburg Prison, his secretary walked in to tell him Rabbi Mordecai Levitt was on the line.

"What's he want?" asked Glass, who was not interested in making or receiving any more phone calls.

"He didn't say," replied Miss Renwick. "You want to take it, or should I just say you're out and take a message?"

"Okay, put him through," said the coroner reluctantly. "I'll try to keep it brief. I want to get outta here."

He picked up the phone receiver. "Shalom, Rabbi," said Glass, trying his best to sound pleasant and unburdened. "How are you doing?"

"As well as can be expected for an old man," replied Rabbi Levitt with a slight chuckle. "I see you're all over the news, Heshel. You've got quite a meshugas on your hands."

"Yes, I guess you could say that."

"That Holmesburg business, everyone is talking about it," said the rabbi. "All of these deaths, it's terrible."

"You can say that again. I'm leaving now to go back up there to conduct additional interviews. I'm trying to figure out what happened. It's still a mystery. And don't believe everything you hear or read. I'm afraid only half the truth is coming out."

"Heshel, I'm an old man. I've been around for a long time. I'm well aware of the old Jewish saying, 'A half-truth is a whole lie.'"

"Well put, Rabbi."

"You're doing God's work, Heshel."

"You may be the only one who thinks so."

"Well, don't let an old man interrupt you," said Levitt. "It's very important work you're doing. As a great rabbi once said of the search for justice, 'Truth is heavy, so few of us can carry it.' Shalom, Heshel, good luck with your investigation and be well."

How odd was that? Glass thought to himself when he ended the conversation. He hadn't spoken to the leader of one of South Philadelphia's largest Jewish congregations for many months, and now he should call. It was yet another mystery, but the coroner had no time to explore it. He had more important things to ponder.

As he rose from his desk and prepared to leave for Holmesburg, Miss Renwick walked into his office again. She was holding several pieces of mail and closed the door behind her. "There were a few phone calls," she commented soberly, "I didn't put on the list."

The coroner did not reply, but she had his undivided attention.

"We've gotten a few calls . . ." repeated his secretary hesitantly.

"Go ahead, I'm listening."

"Well, I guess you could call them warnings," said Miss Renwick. "The girls out front are calling them death threats. Basically, the messages have been the same. 'Tell your boss to back off or else.'"

"Damn," was the coroner's only response, though his shoulders slumped and his expression turned dour.

"I'm not sure what to do," she said. "The girls answering the phones are getting a little nervous."

"How many have there been?"

"Three so far," replied Miss Renwick with a look of concern. "I answered one, and two others were answered by other office staff."

"Well," said Glass, trying to put a positive spin on things, "maybe three isn't too bad considering the magnitude of this thing."

"Don't get too comfortable. There are also these," said Miss Renwick, handing him several envelopes.

Glass opened a letter that read in bold block letters, "Listen glASS, You are a disgrace. You've got no business in that office. I won't be happy till your body is fished out of the Delaware River." The next letter he opened was worse. It read, in red ink, "I wish you were over there in Germany. They know how to deal with dirty commie Jews like you. Prosecute prison guards at your own peril." More troubling was the drawn image of a hooked-nosed, menacing-looking Jew at the bottom of the page. A third had an equally nasty message along with a drawing of the Star of David being defecated upon by a horse. None of the letters had the senders' names, nor return addresses.

"There are more like that," said Miss Renwick. "It's pretty disgusting stuff."

Speechless, the coroner continued to thumb through the letters.

"It's also . . . well . . . the other women in the office are wondering if a police officer might need to be stationed here as extra security—just to be on the safe side."

Glass initially said "Okay," thinking the suggestion prudent under the circumstances, but then he recanted. "Wait a second," he said, realizing the police and the mayor were in cahoots. They were no friends of his or his investigation; their sympathies were in line with those issuing the threats. Clarke and the police commissioner would no doubt place someone in the office loyal to them. The last thing Glass needed was a spy in his camp. "Let me think about it. Now, if that's all, I'll get up to the prison. Can you get me a car and someone to drive me there?"

"Of course . . . but where's your city vehicle?"

He didn't want to instill additional fear in his office staff, so he simply said, "It's at my house. Can you have it towed to a private garage and checked out?"

"What's wrong with it?" Miss Renwick asked.

"Just have it checked out," Glass snapped. "Top to bottom. Now, I've got to get going."

"I don't know how you put in so much time at that place, but you better not leave yet," warned Miss Renwick.

As they left his private office, Glass heard shouting coming from the corridor.

"There's a group of protesters out there," she cautioned him. "Friends and relatives of those who died at the prison. Sheriff deputies are holding them at bay, so you may wanna wait until they leave."

Glass remembered seeing them outside City Hall when he entered the building. "No, I'm already late getting up to the prison," the coroner replied. "No more delays, and I need to do these interviews. I'll deal with it."

"Okay," said Miss Renwick as the coroner walked out the door, "your funeral."

In the corridor stood nearly two dozen emotional men and women calling for justice and demanding the prosecution of the prison officials involved in the deaths of their loved ones. Two uniformed sheriff's deputies stood between the protesters and the front door of the coroner's office.

"When the hell is the city gonna do something about this?" shouted one man upon seeing the county coroner. "My boy is dead, and the killers are walking free," shouted another. "Eight people are dead, and no one gives a damn," yelled a third. "How do you get any justice around here?"

As Glass attempted to inch his way through the raucous crowd, a middle-aged woman in a dark print dress pushed her way up to Glass and grabbed his arm. "My boy, Timothy O'Shea, was one of those tortured up there at Holmesburg," said the obviously grief-stricken woman as she shoved a photograph of her son in the coroner's face. Gaunt, her salt-and-pepper hair askew, and her eyes ablaze, Mrs. O'Shea wasn't about to let pass the only public official she had been able to confront about her son's gruesome death. "Look, look at him. He was handsome, but I didn't even recognize him when I saw him at the morgue," said Mrs. O'Shea, who maintained a firm grip on the coroner's forearm. "They murdered him, and for what? Yeah, he done some things he shouldn't. But he never hurt no one. He was a thief, an' he was doin' his time. Did they really have to kill him?" Glass tried to wrench free of the woman's hold, but despite her thin arms and bony fingers, her grip was firm.

Others—some who were parents like Shirley O'Shea—expressed similar outrage. As the grieving families closed in upon Glass, the deputies tried to maintain order and push the demonstrators back, but with little effect. "I'm going up to the prison right now," said the coroner. "I'm determined to get to the bottom of this. Like you, I want some answers. I want to know what happened."

As he spoke, others in the crowd yelled, "Why aren't the police tellin' the real story?" "Why doesn't the mayor do something?" "You're all corrupt! You're all guilty of a cover-up!"

Glass tried to pull away as others in the crowd attempted to grasp his jacket, make a point, or just ensure he understood the depth of their anger. As one man shouted in his ear, "You're all crooks—you should be ashamed to be an elected official," the coroner broke free and pushed his way forward.

Glass was eventually able to pull away from the crowd and gain entrance to an elevator while deputies ensured none of the protesters boarded the car. As the vehicle descended, Glass couldn't help but dwell on his day so far. Live bullets were placed on the hood of his city car, the mayor promised to end his political career, and ward leaders had confirmed the threat was real. To add insult to injury, though he was the only public official to show interest in the Holmesburg tragedy, relatives of the deceased had targeted him with their moral outrage and demands for justice. And the day was only just beginning.

Chapter 14

Interviews with Klondike Survivors

On his return to Holmesburg, Glass went immediately to the prison hospital on C Block. As he removed his jacket and took a seat next to the bed of Anton Scheinbach, the coroner was not unaware of the reaction of others in the makeshift dispensary. Nurses, inmate orderlies, and guards all kept their distance but still managed to convey a sense of disapproval, if not outright hostility, to the coroner's presence in the modest infirmary.

Hooked up to an intravenous tube and oxygen mask, and bathed in the cooling air of a large fan, the inmate was said to be on the road to recovery. His appearance, however, argued his condition was still precarious.

"Mr. Scheinbach, I'm the county coroner. I want to know what happened to you. Why were you in the punishment unit?"

The inmate remained silent.

"Mr. Scheinbach, when were you placed in Klondike, was it Friday, Saturday, or Sunday?"

The inmate, breathing through an electric respirator, made no attempt to answer.

"I know this is difficult for you," said the coroner, "but we have to know what happened in that building. Justice demands it."

Glass wasn't even sure the man understood what he was saying. It was clear, however, what was in the inmate's eyes—terror. But was it fear of a city official, being thrown back in the hole, or testifying against those who put him in Klondike in the first place?

Carl Ferencz called out to Glass, directing him to another nearby hospital bed where a recovering prisoner suspiciously eyed him. "Max Teague was one of the early strike leaders," said Ferencz. "He was pulled out of his cell on J Block and placed in Klondike on Saturday night."

Glass sighed, withdrew from Scheinbach, and turned his attention toward Teague. "Hello," the coroner said and extended his hand, but the inmate made no effort to grasp it. The coroner explained the purpose for his visit, but Teague, unshaven and skeletal, showed little interest. "Those who did this to you, Mr. Teague, need to be punished," said Glass. "We can't let them get away with this."

The inmate turned his head away. Increasingly frustrated, the coroner grasped the man's arm and leaned over the prisoner. "Look, you're in this prison for some violation, some law you broke," said Glass. "You were given a trial, found guilty, and sent to prison. Don't tell me the men who put you in this condition, and killed eight others, don't deserve the same. Are you gonna tell me you believe they deserve a pass?"

Teague opened his mouth but could barely speak an audible word. The coroner leaned closer and heard the inmate say in almost a whisper, "Not here. Can't talk here."

"I understand," said Glass, patting the man's shoulder. "I understand. We'll do it another time."

Glass walked toward another recovering prisoner when his deputy said, "No, forget it. I've tried already. He's adamant. He won't talk."

The coroner and his chief deputy then stepped into the corridor. While Ferencz named other Klondike survivors to be visited and interviewed, Glass couldn't help but ponder the power of working-class customs and neighborhood traditions. Incredible, he thought to himself, how individuals who were tortured and nearly roasted to death remained unwilling to name their tormentors. Though brought up in a similar working-class environment and schooled early on that one never become an informer—a "rat," "stoolie," "fink," or "snitch," in neighborhood parlance—Glass had matured. He was baffled by the pull of such working-class prohibitions as keeping silent, especially in criminal matters. More experienced and wiser with the passage of time, Glass was now the county coroner and an extension of the criminal justice system. He was infuriated by the backward practice of keeping mum and thereby allowing criminals to beat justice. How had such attitudes captured the allegiance of so many people, particularly those who had suffered so grievously as in the Klondike tragedy?

Fortunately, there were those like Wesley Hickok and Patrick Palumbo who had opened up to Ferencz about what had transpired inside the walls of

Holmesburg Prison. But Glass feared that even those who had spoken up could be silenced. He had to get the survivors out of Holmesburg, especially those brave enough to describe what really occurred over the weekend. At the moment, however, he needed to interview additional Klondike survivors; he needed to be sure of what really happened on that brutally hot August weekend. He decided to take another crack at the tough Kensington truck driver, Hank Luzinski.

Appearing much improved but still confined to a prison hospital bed, the inmate suspiciously eyed his visitor. "You again," said Luzinski dismissively.

"Yeah, guess you're just lucky," Glass glibly replied.

"I've never been so lucky," the prisoner shot back. "Whattaya want this time, my endorsement for mayor?"

"Thanks for the vote of confidence, but what I really want is help in putting on trial the fellows who did this to you."

"Who you kiddin'?" said Luzinski. "Those guys run this fucking place. You ain't touchin' 'em."

"If you and the others dummy up that's just what will happen," said Glass. "You comfortable with that? Webster, Oteri, O'Shea, and the others can't talk, but you can. I figured you for more moxie than that."

Luzinski was angered by the comment. "How do I know you're on the level?" asked the inmate. "I bet you're like all the rest, bought and paid for by the guys downtown."

"Well, I'm back here again, aren't I? And I'll be back tomorrow, and the day after that. I'm after the real story. If what I'm hearing is correct, if you guys are telling the truth, what happened inside that punishment unit is a crime."

"And so is spittin' on the sidewalk."

"Listen, Luzinski," said the coroner angrily, "the families of eight men are looking for justice. They gave me hell this morning, and they're probably still camped outside my City Hall office right now demanding I do something. They want justice. Do you want me to tell them what the cops said is true? That you dumb mutts fought among yourselves? That it was you who killed Oteri and O'Shea? It's your choice. Do you wanna help the mothers and wives of Oteri, Palumbo, Smyzak, and the others get justice, or do you wanna help the guys that killed them and nearly killed you? It's that simple."

Luzinski was silent for a moment.

"Well?"

The inmate looked Glass in the eyes and asked, "How do I know I can trust you?"

"I'm all you got, mister."

"That ain't much," said Luzinski, with a contemptuous sneer.

"At least we agree on something."

Nearly ten seconds went by. Growing tired of waiting for an answer, the coroner spoke up. "You have something to say?" After another few seconds, Glass shook his head in disgust and said, "Have it your way," and began to walk out of the room.

"Wait," replied Luzinski as Glass approached the corridor. Grimacing as if in pain, he looked at his inquisitor and said, "What do you want to know?"

Glass considered the inmate's change of heart a major victory. He hoped the tough-talking prisoner would not only have the nerve to identify the perpetrators of the Klondike murders but also the guts to testify against them in court if it came to that. "Tell me about yourself," said Glass. "What got you in here, where are you from, and what did you do before you got locked up?"

In what amounted to little more than a hazy whisper, the inmate said he came from a good Polish family on Emerald Street in Kensington and said he was a driver for a local trucking company when there was work to be had. He mostly delivered heavy steel pipes and high-pressure valves to the Cramp Shipyard and other naval concerns along the river. When Glass stated such work wouldn't put someone in Holmesburg, the inmate admitted to hanging out with a neighborhood gang called the Blue Dragons. They did some commercial burglaries and provided muscle for a few Kensington Avenue speakeasies. When one of his buddies got caught last fall, Luzinski discovered he and a few others in the gang had been ratted out. Police didn't waste any time putting them behind bars.

"Tough luck," Glass replied. "Tell me again what led to this mess?"

"I been in this hellhole for nine months when McCabe, one of the big shots in here, started stirring things up about the quality of food we're gettin'. You know, the same lousy meals being served day after day."

As the coroner listened, he was pleased he had finally gotten the inmate to talk. He thought there was something special about this one. He wasn't sure if it was Luzinski's surly attitude or physical resilience, but both qualities would prove useful in what Glass expected to be a difficult campaign.

"We got prunes, bread, and coffee every morning," said Luzinski, describing their dissatisfaction with the menu at Holmesburg. "Every day, prunes and coffee and bread. The bread was the worst. Either wet and soggy or hard as a brick; guys often lost teeth tryin' to bite into it. Too soft, too hard, after a while you just chucked it. Some mornings they'd give us corn flakes, but not often. For lunch, we'd get hamburger, spinach, and potatoes, sometimes pork and beans, and cabbage. Couldn't ever be sure, it all looked and smelled the same. Bologna sandwiches were a big thing too. But the meat was bad; more like rubber and it smelled like shit. You'd never give that stuff to your wife and kids. Dinner wasn't much better. Lotta guys couldn't eat it. Smelled awful. Made you sick before you even got it near your mouth. Some guys just stopped goin' to chow hall. Once in a while, we'd get roast beef, but when you cut into it, it would be green on the inside. It tasted all right, but I wasn't keen on green beef."

"So you're telling me it was the quality and the monotony of the meals that united the men and caused them to go on strike?" asked Glass, now convinced the deaths of eight men had started in the prison's kitchen. He pulled up a chair next to the inmate's hospital bed, shed his suit jacket, and encouraged the inmate to relate all he could remember about the food strike. He wanted Luzinski comfortable and talking openly before he brought up his time in the punishment unit.

"Yeah, that was it, the lousy food, nothin' else," replied Luzinski, who had become surprisingly talkative. "The guards weren't that bad. They weren't brutal or anything, at least not with me. It was the little things that got people pissed off. The place was packed. You know, just too many fuckin' guys jammed in one place. The joint was way overcrowded, and the heat this month was fuckin' crazy. The temperature on the cellblocks musta been over a hundred degrees. Day after day, even at night. You couldn't sleep. You'd sweat your ass off. It wore you the fuck down. In the winter you froze your nuts off and in the summer you fuckin' boil. You couldn't escape it. With four, five guys in a cell . . . Christ, even the walls were sweating."

"But according to you, it was really the food that started the strike?"

"Yeah, like I told ya before, when you know just what you're going to get at every meal, every day, and every week, and every month, you start goin' crazy. I remember they once gave us ham and all the prisoners felt like celebrating. It was a real treat.

"People on the outside don't understand. When you're locked up and you have the same food over and over you get so disgusted you just don't care. That's why prisoners go on hunger strikes. They know it's stupid and they can't possibly win, but they have to do something. And it wouldn't cost much for the prison officials to change the food a little. What's wrong with a real apple or orange or grapes once in a while? All of us hated that canned crap they dish out, and all of us were constipated. We were all dying to take a good shit. Christ, the line for Epsom salt was as long as the dinner line."

It was at that point that Warden Stryker entered the dispensary. Luzinski as well as others—including doctors—immediately grew quiet and self-conscious, the coroner noted. He feared Luzinski would become permanently mute but soon realized the intense expression on the prisoner's face wasn't fear but hatred. When Stryker walked back to the corridor, Luzinski let it be known he wouldn't be intimidated. "I been through hell because of that cocksucker," sneered Luzinski. "That asshole and his goon squad, they tried to kill me. Nearly did, too . . . and I don't put it past him to take another crack at it."

"If I can get you out of here," said Glass leaning closer to the inmate, "would you be willing to testify against Stryker and the superintendent?"

Luzinski glared at the coroner. "Shit, I'll testify against that bastard even if I'm stuck in here," the prisoner replied. "You just gotta make sure they don't kill me first. A dead man ain't gonna answer all your damn questions."

Glass appreciated the prisoner's moxie. His unwillingness to be intimidated only encouraged Glass to continue trying to get the Klondike survivors out of Holmesburg. Undeterred by the warden's sudden appearance, Luzinski continued to explain how McCabe, a well-known enforcer for the city's biggest bootleggers during the Depression, organized a group of prisoners to spread dissension throughout the prison. He then demanded a meeting with the superintendent about the quality and variety of food they were receiving.

"McCabe set things up pretty good," said Luzinski. "He had a crew of well-connected guys who backed him. He picked six of 'em and added one guy from every cellblock to form a committee of sixteen. Some guys he knew; others seemed to be grabbed, you know, at random. I don't know why, but I was picked to represent J Block. McCabe told Stryker and Davis he wanted a meeting. We was all amazed when he got one.

"When we met in the gym last Wednesday," Luzinski recalled, "McCabe did all the talking. He told Davis there should be changes in the prison menu. He said the food was terrible and we all backed him. He said no more hamburger, no more spaghetti and cheese. No more smelly bologna, lousy eggplant, and watery soup. We was tired of that crap. He also asked for ice cream and cake every other Sunday."

Glass remembered reading about those demands in the newspaper just days earlier, but his reaction now was less dismissive. A catastrophe had taken place, and he couldn't afford to be cavalier about any of the details. As the city coroner, it was his job to unravel the mystery surrounding the eight bodies now undergoing postmortems in the city morgue.

Luzinski said McCabe added another demand that the inmates hadn't even discussed. "He told the superintendent we wanted an inmate council. You know, a committee made up of two men from each cellblock, which would be consulted whenever Davis and Stryker wanted to change rules and regulations affecting prisoners. McCabe said we should have some say when punishments were handed out for infractions and what duties prisoners had to perform."

"I can't imagine they reacted well to that," said the coroner.

"You got that right," recalled Luzinski. "Stryker's face turned bloodred. I thought he'd explode, but he kept his mouth shut. He let the superintendent do the talking. Davis got all huffy at that point. He said, 'What do you want, a goddamn union like automobile workers? You guys must all be crazy. You're letting this heatwave get to you. There's only one committee running this prison—a committee of one, and that's me.' And then he sarcastically says, 'The warden and I are really sorry you're not happy with your meals. We'll have to talk to the chef about some changes. How would lobster bisque, roast duck, and Alaskan salmon sound to you?'

"He and Stryker had a good laugh over that. Davis then stops laughing, starts grittin' on us, and finally barks, 'Now let me inform you mutts of something. This ain't the goddamn Waldorf-Astoria, it's a county jail. And last I looked you're not paying customers. You're damn lucky we feed you at all.'"

"What happened then?" asked the coroner, anticipating something dramatic.

"Nothing," said Luzinski. "Davis walked out. He and Stryker just walked out."

"And after that?"

"That's when we decided to call a strike," said Luzinski. "We went back to our blocks and spread the word. Guys went from cell to cell telling everyone nobody was to go to chow. We were on strike, we were goin' to shut the joint down."

"As I recall," said the coroner, "the newspapers said over six hundred men refused to go to the dining hall that night."

Luzinski admitted he didn't know the exact number, but it seemed like well over half the prisoners remained in their cells. "I think that sort of reaction frightened the hell out of 'em," said Luzinski. "They weren't laughing no more. They didn't expect we'd be so united, that we'd have so much support for a jail-wide strike."

"Were any guards physically hurt or attacked?"

"What?"

"You heard me," said Glass. "Did any inmates take it out on a guard or officer?"

"Nah, like I told you before, we didn't touch nobody."

"So, there were no attacks on staff?"

"You deaf or something? Like I said, there was no physical stuff. We just didn't go to chow."

The coroner had a hard time believing the loss of so many lives was due to inmates choosing not to eat their meals. But the inmate was insistent it was a peaceful protest.

"The screws immediately locked the joint up," said Luzinski. "All the programs were shut down. No family visits, no outdoor exercise. They even called in the guards who were off duty and put 'em on twelve-hour shifts. They musta figured a riot was coming, but we never had any such notion. No one talked about a riot or taking over the jail. Davis and Stryker panicked. They ordered a lockdown, no movement. The tactic helped divide us. The inmates, for the most part, had never signed on to support a protest. Bread and water was placed before each cell door twice a day. Some inmates refused it, while others took it. Some assholes even asked for their regular meals."

Even though the strikers were pleased to learn newspapers—a few as far as New York and Washington—had given front-page coverage to the prison protest in Philadelphia, Luzinski said that inside Holmesburg's high walls, inmate resolve was crumbling. By Saturday morning inmates were requesting to go to chow hall—they wanted their regular meals. "We were losing guys all day Saturday," said Luzinski. "Guys were hungry and thirsty. It was so damn hot on those cellblocks. The sweat just poured off you. There was no relief, you couldn't sleep. Some guys were expecting a visit, you know, from a wife or girlfriend. Others just wanted to get out of a hot cell and walk around a little. You know, get some exercise and fresh air in the yard."

"Hank, tell me about the Klondike," said Glass, leaning closer. "What happened in there?"

Lying on his back, his head resting on a sweat-stained pillow, the inmate's bloodshot eyes focused on the pale-green paint peeling on the prison hospital ceiling. Luzinski didn't reply.

"Hank," said Glass, squeezing the inmate's arm, "I need to know what happened in there. Eight men are dead, and I need to know what killed them. What happened in there?"

The prisoner groaned, and Glass could see him clench his fists. The coroner was about to make another verbal pitch when Luzinski began to speak.

"Sometime Sunday morning they came and pulled me out of my cell," replied Luzinski, still fixated on something only he could see on the prison ceiling. "It must have been close to a hundred degrees on the cellblock, so gettin' taken off was no big loss. I thought they were transferring me to another block because I'm one of the few still supporting the protest, but I start wondering why it takes a captain, a sergeant, and two screws to move me. I figure they're gonna give me an ass-kickin', so I prepare myself for an old-fashioned thumpin'. I plan on gettin' in a few shots myself, but instead, they take me outside. As we walked across the prison yard between D and E Blocks the sun was hot, but I could feel a slight breeze. I really needed some fresh air, you know. It was stifling on the cellblock.

"Then they push me into this little brick building. I had never seen it; I'd never been in that yard before. The building was dark, no lights, and stunk like a pigsty. But the main thing was the heat. It was incredibly hot . . . like a fuckin' oven. I couldn't tell for sure what was goin' on 'cause it was so dark. They then tell me to take off my pants and shirt and shove me in a cell. On the way out one of the guards, I think it was Smoot, says, 'Okay, smart ass, let's see how you like the accommodations now.'"

Luzinski grew silent and began to grind his teeth. Glass feared forcing him to relive the terrible ordeal might result in losing him, so instead he encouraged the prisoner to take a drink of water. When the inmate declined any more liquid, the coroner gently urged him to continue. "Go ahead, Hank. What happened next?"

"They threw me in a cell. Two guys were already in there," said Luzinski, his voice barely above a whisper. "The older guy was Webster, and the other guy, I think his name was Oliveri or Oliva or something like that."

"Oteri?"

"Yeah, that's it," said Luzinski. "I recognized both of 'em from the group that met with the warden and superintendent a couple days earlier. But they . . . they looked really bad now. You know, like a couple sailors shipwrecked on a deserted island. They told me they had only been in there a day, but they were a mess. You know, really wasted, sweating like crazy . . . lookin' desperate. Their eyes, even in the dark . . . Christ, they reminded me . . . they looked like inmates in a lunatic asylum. God, they looked awful." He paused.

"Go ahead, Hank," said the coroner. "What happened then?"

"They were wearing shorts, that's all. Now I knew why they took my shirt and pants; it was too damn hot to wear any clothes. All the windows and air vents were closed. Everything was shut tight, and it was hard to breathe. It was dark and hot as hell. They told me what to do. One of 'em said . . ."

The inmate paused and the coroner gently grabbed his arm.

"What'd he say, Hank?"

"This is Klondike. Get ready for hell on earth."

The inmate stopped again and took a deep breath. A nurse appeared to check his pulse and temperature. "I think you better go," the nurse told Glass. "He should get some sleep."

Glass smiled politely and waited for the nurse to attend to her next patient. "Go ahead, Hank," urged the coroner after the nurse departed. "I'm listening."

The inmate remained mute. Glass knew he should probably leave and let the prisoner rest, but he was so close. He had to know.

"Hank, please . . . What happened next?"

"All there was in the cell was a spigot and a hopper," said Luzinski in a soft monotone. "The spigot was shut off, so we had to use the hopper for water. We soaked our undershirts in it and then wrapped 'em around our head, shoulders, and feet. The toilet got dry real quick. If you took a piss or a shit it just sat there. It only flushed from the outside. Guards were supposed to flush it three times a day, but that even stopped. We had no control of it. The crap and piss just sat there stinkin' up the place. We had no control over nothin.' Soon after they locked me in the cell, I hear one of the guards leave the building, slam the steel door shut, and turn up the heat. You could hear him turning the valve. Then you could hear the steam hissing through the pipes and feel the heat even more. After a while it felt like you were suffocating; like you were drowning in a volcano."

Sweating, his jacket folded over his arm, Glass was on the edge of his seat. "Sunday night," said the coroner. "What happened that night?"

"Everything was so fuckin' hot," said Luzinski. "You couldn't touch nothin.' Even the mattress on the floor was hot, so hot you couldn't sit on it. Forget about laying on it. Sunday night the heat got worse. I was only in there about ten hours at that point, but it felt much longer, and the heat was terrible. It felt like you were in a broiler. You couldn't breathe . . . constantly gulping air. But there's no oxygen in the air, and your lungs are burning. Felt like they're on fire. After a while, I'd put my nose by the crack in the door hoping to get some air from the corridor, but the metal door was as hot as a branding iron. The whole time my heart was pounding. I thought I was having a heart attack."

Glass nodded, finally understanding how the tip of the inmate's nose became discolored; it was burned. The coroner listened carefully to every word of Luzinski's saga and found himself becoming increasingly horrified.

"You could hear guys in the other cells yelling, screaming, begging for someone to open the windows and turn off the heat," said Luzinski. "They were out of their minds. Some guys started calling for their mothers, their wives . . . praying to God. I remember one guy screaming, 'Shoot me, shoot me, why don't you just get it the fuck over with?'"

Luzinski paused and closed his eyes for a few seconds.

Glass stood up and patted the inmate on the shoulder. "It's over now, Hank," said the coroner. "You made it out."

"It was the worst thing I've ever gone through," replied Luzinski. "I don't know how more of us didn't end up like those other poor bastards you got in your morgue."

The coroner had little doubt; an hour longer in the punishment unit and Luzinski and the others probably would be in the morgue as well. About to exit the infirmary, Glass turned back. "One last question, Hank. Why wasn't McCabe in Klondike with you guys?"

"Beats me."

"But you and others have said Myles McCabe was the original leader of the food strike," said Glass. "How the hell does the guy who comes up with the idea, the guy who calls for a food strike, and organizes it, not get tossed in that inferno as well?"

"Luck, I guess," offered the inmate. "Why don't you ask him?"

"I'd like to, but he's gone. He's been transferred."

"Where to?" asked Luzinski looking puzzled.

"They won't tell me," the coroner replied. "Interesting, huh?"

"Yeah, real interesting . . ."

Chapter 15

Additional Inmate Interviews

The tough-talking Polish truck driver's account of his ordeal inside the red brick broiler known as Klondike was a significant milestone in the coroner's search for answers. But Glass and his team knew there were other witnesses in addition to Luzinski, Palumbo, and Hickok out there.

Ferencz took his boss to G Block, a colored block, to meet a Negro named John Armstrong. Nicknamed "Cannonball" by his cellmates, the bald, dark-complexioned inmate was built like a football player and was obviously someone who did heavy labor for a living. He had nearly killed a man in a bar fight over a woman and was serving a ten-year sentence. During his three years at Holmesburg, he had twice been taken to the punishment unit. Both occasions were due to insubordination and threatening guards. White inmates committing the same offense, he claimed, would be transferred to the hole on C Block, but the colored prisoners were often taken straight to Klondike, where a few other guards would work them over. They were put on bread and water rations and every fifth day received a regular meal.

"Ain't no big deal," Cannonball said of his time in Klondike when the coroner inquired about his treatment. "Hartzell, Bridges, and Smoot didn't do me like they just done those white boys. Shit, they just locked my black ass up, give me a beatin', and put me on bread and water for a few days. Damn sure coulda been worse."

"You mean the steam? They didn't turn on the radiators?" asked Glass.

"Yep, lucky I guess," replied the inmate. "They don't always be tryin' to roast your ass. Guess you gotta be a special case."

The coroner appeared puzzled, and the inmate went on to explain, "When inmates get in a fight or cause a disturbance, they be taken to C Rear where they're locked up for a while. Usually ten days to two weeks. Something real big, like striking a guard, could result in a trip to the punishment unit between D and E Blocks. Now Klondike, that damn sure can be a cold stop," said Cannonball, shaking his head to emphasize the potential severity of the move. "The man decide to turn the heat up on you, you can find your ass cooked. You know, just like those white boys the other day. But they really wanted to get them strikers," said the inmate with a knowing nod. "They wanted to punish their asses."

"What do you mean?" said Glass.

"Don't take no Einstein to figure it out. Those white boys started something. Told everyone in the jail to stop eatin'. They be saying don't go down to the chow hall, we're on strike. Got more support than anyone thought, but what really pissed off the man was all that stuff they wrote in the papers and on the radio. That really pulled their tail. That's what got 'em to fire up the oven. They was gonna teach 'em a lesson. And they did. Don't think we be havin' no more food strikes for a long time now."

Glass turned to Ferencz and said, "We need to find out more about the punishment unit, when it was built, its purpose, and how often heat was employed." Overhearing their conversation, the inmate interrupted. "You know, you got one of those guys that got roasted working for you."

The coroner and his deputy turned to each other with a look of confusion.

"That's right," Armstrong added, "he be workin' with you."

"What are you talking about?" said Glass.

"He be workin' in City Hall," said the now-smiling inmate. "Bill Roberson got a job down there in City Hall. He did eleven years here for manslaughter some time ago. I met him comin' in when he be on his way out. Heard guys say he be one of those fellas that got toasted in Klondike back some time ago. Heard he got a job in City Hall. That's where you guys are at, right?"

The coroner and his deputy looked at each other in amazement. Both tried to visualize who Armstrong could be talking about; they were intent on discovering the accuracy of the inmate's statement.

It was while the coroner and his deputy were just completing another inmate interview when David Sandler walked into the cell. "Here, this is for you," said the young intern as he handed a sealed envelope to his boss.

"What is it?" asked Glass, who was busy checking off names of inmates to be interviewed.

"I don't know," replied Sandler. "One of the police detectives gave it to me. He just said, 'Give it to your boss.'"

The coroner opened the envelope and quickly read what was on a thin sheet of paper. "How 'bout that." He snickered. "This explains a few things."

"What is it?" inquired Ferencz skeptically. "An account as to what happened here?"

"Just the opposite, actually," replied Glass with an air of satisfaction.

"What are you talking about?" asked Ferencz.

The coroner turned to his deputy with a broad smile. "Turns out Detective Sergeant Brian Hennessey and Detective Richard Wilson were protégées of Superintendent Davis when he was in charge of the police department nearly a decade ago. In fact, both men were promoted to their current positions by Davis."

"Wow, that's interesting," said Sandler.

"Indeed," said Ferencz, "just one cozy family looking out for each other."

"Who gave you this?" asked the coroner, turning to the intern.

Sandler explained it was one of the many police officials still walking around the prison grounds gathering information. The coroner suggested it was more likely the police investigators were there to keep an eye on them. The mayor and his people were no doubt keeping track of what they were doing and who was being interviewed. Hoping there was more to learn, the coroner sent his intern to locate the man who had passed them the information.

Now that they were alone, Ferencz coyly mentioned to his boss, "You know some of these reporters are convinced the police version of what happened here is bogus. They're already writing stories questioning it. I'm sure one or two of them are chomping at the bit to expose the dishonesty of it all. Think we should drop this little nugget on one of them?"

"And let them dig up and expose the connection between the superintendent and the police?"

"Exactly."

"It would certainly put the mayor and the police on their heels," said Glass.

"And help undercut their bullshit account of this mess," added Ferencz.

For the next several hours, Glass, Ferencz, and Sandler would interview as many inmates and guards as were willing to talk. Not all of the interviews were helpful, as many had no direct knowledge of what occurred inside Klondike over the weekend. Others had some personal scores to settle; their tales were unreliable.

But there seemed to be unanimity of agreement that turning up the heat on prisoners being held in Klondike was not an unusual event. A number of men recalled the August 1932 inmate uprising that precipitated widespread use of the heat treatment. In that event—almost to the day six years earlier—200 inmates and 150 guards and police fought each other on cellblocks and in the prison yard for control of the institution. Once again, the initial protest was over the quality and variety of food prisoners were offered. Eventually, their decision to refuse the food culminated in a full-scale riot. After authorities regained control, numerous strike leaders and inmate combatants faced time in the Klondike "hot box," but there was no loss of life.

Two years later there was another food strike, this one initiated by prisoners who had recently been transferred over to Holmesburg from Eastern State Penitentiary. Accustomed to far greater portions and variety of fare at "Cherry Hill"—Eastern's nickname—nineteen men went on a two-week hunger strike at the county institution. The demonstration of inmate resolve from state prisoners resulted in several strike leaders going to Klondike. That would prove the end of that hunger strike. There was talk of earlier protests over food and riots, but inmate recollections of those events were sketchy and unreliable.

The coroner was still set on discovering the date of the building's construction, its original purpose, and why the need for so many radiators. Who determined when inmates received the heat treatment was also of keen interest to him. Glass gave his young intern the specific assignment of discovering the answers to these questions and whatever else he could come up with concerning Klondike's history. Sandler was also tasked with discovering the City Hall Negro worker by the name of Roberson who may have done time in the county jail.

The research assignment would keep Sandler in the city archives, architectural repositories, and newspaper morgues. His absence temporarily resolved what Ferencz had described to his boss as the "nasty abuse" the young man was receiving from both inmates and prison guards. Whistles, foul snickers, and vile comments attacking the college student's manhood were all too frequent. "Princess," "fairy," "sissy," and "faggot," were some of the names Sandler had been pelted with. Glass himself had witnessed some of the bigoted epithets showered on his young aide. On one occasion he heard an inmate call Sandler a "queer punk" from his cell. But Glass was reluctant to become protective and sequester Sandler to the City Hall office. Neither did he choose to discuss the issue with him personally; he found the subject too uncomfortable. He had wondered about Sandler, but there was little time to deal with personnel matters; the Klondike investigation was paramount, and Sandler was a conscientious worker.

As the coroner and his deputy traveled from cell to cell and cellblock to cellblock seeking out inmates and guards willing to be interviewed, more of the Holmesburg story started to come together. Most of the men were in agreement that the food they were served was the initial motivation for the protest and the reason for the eventual eight deaths. But inmates suggested other reasons as well. Monotony was voiced by numerous prisoners. As one inmate said, "The boredom of sitting in your cell all day was terrible. Most of the men would be willing to break rocks just to get something to do."

And for many prisoners, going to chow hall three times a day became the most anticipated activity of the day. As one elderly prisoner told the coroner, "You have to remember when you sit in prison all day, with not a damn thing to do but eat, meals become very important to you. You think about them all day long."

Many inmates groused about the bland, repetitive nature of the menu. "A few prunes, soggy bread, and cold coffee for breakfast," hamburgers for lunch that were "green inside," and "roast beef for dinner that tasted and smelled so bad you couldn't eat it," was a recurring theme sparking resentment. The oppressive monotony—in both life on the cellblock and the meals they were given—contributed to a contentious if not explosive environment.

"When you know just what you are going to get at every meal, every day, every week, and every year, you get half crazy," admitted Harry Warner, a Klondike survivor. "What I'm trying to say is, you know . . . just a little thing that most people never think of becomes important. But when you have the same stuff to look forward to all the time, you get so disgusted you just don't care. That's why the prisoners go on a hunger strike. The heat and overcrowding this summer only further riled guys up. Besides, everybody in here would give his left arm to take a good crap. Skipping a few meals would probably do us some good."

"But doesn't the likelihood of organizing a protest only result in severe punishment?" asked the coroner.

Warner replied, "Sure, they know it's foolish. They know they can't possibly win, but they have to do something. Guys get so angry and frustrated." The inmate went on to say, "Why can't the administration do something to relieve the tension, relieve the crowding? It wouldn't cost much for the prison officials to change the meals a little. They ought to give some fresh vegetables once in a while instead of that canned mush. But they're as likely to give that as they are the keys to the front door."

In confirming what Hank Luzinski had first told him, Glass was now convinced the food was at the heart of the inmate protest at Holmesburg. But he was less successful in getting information about the events occurring inside the Klondike punishment unit over that deadly weekend. Many were afraid to give up the names of officers who patrolled the building, though there was now little doubt that intolerable heat was an integral part of Holmesburg's punishment options. And, the coroner learned, Klondike's robust heating apparatus was connected to the main prison boilers and that the master valve controlling steam pressure was situated beneath another cellblock and out of the reach of guards, though they had the capacity to adjust it once turned on. In fact, the mechanism was controlled by a city engineer and not a member of custody. George Rediker was the man's name, and Glass was intent on talking to him. Until then, however, he busied himself interviewing additional prisoners.

"Let me give you some inside dope so they don't put some smoke up your ass," said one wrinkled, heavily whiskered inmate who Glass presumed was well into his seventies. "They got a beat-up squad here," said the inmate. "About five or six tough screws who'll take a man to C Block and beat his ass with blackjacks. If they're really pissed, they'll take him out to that chicken yard where they got that hot box, that Klondike shack, and fry his ass. Yep, the guards will just lock his ass up and turn on the heat. I heard 'em once say to a guy, 'That'll take the starch out of him.'"

When he crossed paths with Officer Bridges, the coroner was slightly taken aback. The officer's resemblance to Bronko Nagurski, the rugged professional football player who had recently retired, was uncanny. Described by numerous inmates as a "tough bull" who "enjoyed thumping guys," Officer Bridges was a thick-bodied, grim-faced physical specimen, the type Glass recalled from his days on neighborhood football fields. Sturdily built with dirty-blonde hair and pale-blue eyes, the officer sported a nose that veered both left and right along its short trajectory. It was clear the broken proboscis had seen its fair share of violent confrontations on both cellblocks and athletic fields.

"Could I have a moment of your time?" the coroner cordially asked as they passed each other in the C Block corridor.

"I'm pretty busy now," said Bridges as he kept walking. "Maybe some other time."

"Mr. Bridges," said Glass more assertively, "I think the time is good now. You should know that a number of Klondike survivors have mentioned you as one of the guards who placed them in that brick furnace and oversaw their physical deterioration."

Bridges stopped, turned, and angrily looked back at the coroner. "Who told you that?"

"I think we should talk, Mr. Bridges."

"I have nothing to say."

"Are you sure?" asked Glass.

"You have questions about this place," said the officer, "you should talk to Warden Stryker. I'm busy." He then turned and assertively walked down the cellblock corridor.

Though the exchange was brief, there was enough for the coroner to measure the man. Glass took notice of how inmates gave Albert Bridges a wide berth when they walked past. Their eyes never met his. The thick-necked, linebacker-sized prison guard definitely had a physical presence.

There was one other thing Glass took note of—Bridges mentioned Warden Stryker but not Superintendent Davis.

Leaving the prison after another long day of pressing inmates to talk, the coroner was intercepted by newsmen besieging him with questions. He did not respond except to state, "My investigation is making headway." In fact, they were very near issuing arrest warrants for several prison staffers. Dozens of inmates had been interviewed as well as a good number of guards, and what had occurred in the Klondike punishment unit was becoming horribly clear. Men were being punished for their roles in the food strike. "Certain guards and administrators had taken it upon themselves to not only isolate the strike supporters but also torture them," Glass told the reporters. "Guards apparently shut all the windows and air vents and then turned on the radiators to approximate a blast furnace-like environment. We have a number of names, and we're focusing our investigation on them. We're pretty sure who is responsible, but we want to know if there was an order to do this thing from a higher-up. We're searching for those at the top."

When asked when his investigation would be complete, the coroner said, "We'd be further along if prison guards and officials had chosen to cooperate. To be candid, there's been a conspiracy of silence and a willingness by guards to agree on their stories and refuse to implicate anyone. I may have to move interviews to City Hall if we can't get to the bottom of this at Holmesburg." He then added, "We'll get prison employees in my office. And if we can't get it there, we'll get it in a City Hall courtroom at an official inquest."

The coroner voiced his firm belief that Klondike survivors had to be relocated with all deliberate speed. "Some of these men are near death and still in need of proper treatment," said Glass. "They need to be cared for in a real hospital, not a makeshift prison infirmary." Glass wanted to add that the men were constantly under threat of reprisal, and to address the difficulty of getting witnesses to talk who were still under the thumbs of the men who put them in an oven roaster. But, he feared he was already too frank and didn't want to generate any more negative commentary than was necessary.

His fears would prove accurate as the next day's newspapers would heighten expectations that indictments, if not actual arrests, were coming. The *Philadelphia Daily News,* for example, ran an eye-catching, front-page headline that read, "Coroner to Jail Two Guards for Boiling 8 Cons."

But the coroner's candid and forthright stance was already paying dividends. On his return to City Hall after a long day at Holmesburg, Glass was surprised to learn the mayor had taken action and shelved Detective Sergeant Brian Hennessey and Detective Richard Wilson. As evening newspapers were reporting under headlines, "Clarke Maps Cop Shakeup in Whitewash," "Detectives Busted for Homicide Story," and "Mayor to Question Two Sleuths on False Holmesburg Story," the officers were paying the price for creating a captivating tale the facts couldn't support.

Their account, according to one newspaper article, of "malnutrition, overexertion, and communist influence" as the reasons for the prison tragedy rang "hollow from its inception," and the coroner's explanation, though chilling, was viewed as the more credible line of inquiry. Clarke had supported the police version until the effort proved increasingly embarrassing, as newspapers either totally dismissed the homicide squad's report or printed allegations of another City Hall "whitewash" and "cover-up."

"This step," the mayor told newsmen, "is because of the discrepancies between the preliminary reports by the homicide squad and the actual evidence secured and presented to me by the police commissioner yesterday. The preliminary reports of the homicide were of such a character as to make necessary the reassigning of the two investigators."

"Detectives Hennessy and Wilson will be given a hearing," the mayor declared after demoting both men, "and if the charges are proven they will be proceeded against. I will undertake a personal investigation of the conditions at the prison. I have only remained out of the matter as the Ruth Commission criticized me for interfering in police matters. But I promise the people of Philadelphia that I will not permit a whitewash of the circumstances behind these prison deaths."

The mayor cloaked his action as part of a campaign to "shake-up the City Hall homicide squad" and talked of hiring Federal Bureau of Investigation forensic scientists to beef up and modernize the department's investigatory capabilities. Most newspaper editorial boards, however, were having none of it. Editorials in usually mayor-friendly newspapers either politely implied or directly lambasted the police detectives for describing the Holmesburg deaths as "nothing suspicious," and the mayor for supporting such an outlandish finding. Clarke, an accomplished survivor, quickly discovered the Klondike debacle was unlike any obstacle he had ever confronted. Even when he did the right thing, he was the target of criticism.

Sandler walked into the coroner's sixth-floor office escorting a colored man who appeared to be in his late sixties and attired in a City Hall janitorial uniform. Nursing a discolored right eye and slight limp, the gray-haired old man seemed nervous and on the verge of bolting from the office.

"This is Bill Roberson," said Sandler proudly. "He's been employed here as a lavatory cleaner and building custodian for almost three years."

"Well, Mr. Roberson," said the coroner, somewhat surprised, "I can't remember ever seeing you in City Hall."

"They keep me kind of busy," replied the unshaven man, trying to hide his unease. "I don't be hangin' around much. They don't pay me to stand around gabbin'."

"I guess not," said Glass, eyeing the man with interest. "Please have a seat. I'm sure you're wondering why I wanted to see you."

"Yeah, it crossed my mind."

Glass leaned back in his chair. "Would you like to take a guess?"

"Not really."

"Try."

"Don't know, but you been in the papers a lot lately," said Roberson, unhappy he was pressed to give an answer. "May be 'bout that Holmesburg stuff. You know, those killins up at the jail."

"Very good. Why do you assume that?"

"I don't know, you never sent for me before. Besides, everybody been talkin' about it. People say it's the worst thing that happened in this town in a while, right?"

"It just might be," said the coroner, turning more serious and looking the former inmate directly in the eye. "Mr. Roberson, maybe you can help me. Can you tell me about your time in Klondike? It's come to our attention you've spent some time in that building and managed to walk out alive. That makes you of special interest to me."

Roberson, growing tenser, did not respond. He warily gazed at Glass, then Sandler, and back at Glass again. "I ain't done nothin' wrong," he said.

"I didn't say you did," the coroner replied. "I'd just like some information. You can help me."

"I ain't gonna lose my job, am I?"

"No, I don't want your job," Glass assured the man. "I'm not interested in harming you in any way, but I do desire some information about Holmesburg and what went on inside the now-infamous brick building between D and E Blocks.

"Who told you I been in Klondike?" asked Roberson.

"We're interviewing everyone who can help us understand what occurred at the prison last weekend. We've talked to scores of inmates. Your name came up. We'd just like some information. We think you can be of help to us."

"I ain't so sure," said Roberson. "I been outta there awhile. What do you wanna know?"

"Tell me about the punishment unit," said Glass. "Who put you in there? How many days did you endure the heat treatment? And I want to know what officers had authority over Klondike while you were locked up there."

"You'll make sure nothin' happen to me? You know, throw me back in there again?"

"I promise," replied Glass. "We'll put the full weight of my office behind you—as long as you're honest with me."

The former inmate looked wary, unsure whether he should comply, but finally spoke up.

"Back in the day it be damn rough in the jail," Roberson began. "The blocks be either white or colored, the food was bad, and there was a whole lot of craziness goin' on. Beatings were a regular thing. And they had a gang of tough colored prisoners who broke heads for the man. We called 'em 'the wrecking crew,' and 'the Black Musketeers.' All of 'em were over six foot and could fight like Jack Johnson. The boss man used 'em to keep order in the jail and get revenge on those be causin' problems. McSorley, the warden, was finally charged with brutality and having guys beat to death. But don't think they ever got him in a courtroom. They said he went crazy and they put him in the nuthouse."

"Yeah, I remember a little of that," said the coroner. "It was about ten years ago. I think you're right; McSorley never saw the inside of a courtroom. So, it was pretty bad up there?"

"You better believe it," the former inmate replied. "I seen guys get beat up pretty bad. Anybody step outta line, they'd put him on G Block, the colored block, and turn the Musketeers on 'em. White or brown, tore 'em up pretty bad. One time I seen 'em beat up prisoners comin' from court. Yep, just as soon as they got off the bus from City Hall. McSorley had 'em do it just to show newbies who was boss, who ran the jail. No joke, kicked their fuckin' ass soon as they stepped inside the jail. The goon squad got paid off in cigarettes and other commissary privileges."

"As time went on," said Roberson, "complaints be comin' in and politicians, judges, and newspapers writin' about it. People didn't like colored prisoners beatin' up white boys, so they kicked the warden out and stopped using the Musketeers to maintain order and punish guys."

"Tell me about the Big Mob," Glass prompted. "I've heard a few old-timers talk about them."

Roberson sneered and said, "They just like the Musketeers, but they wore guard uniforms. They were tough prison guards and went around enforcing discipline in the jail. Only about eight or ten of 'em, but they did what they wanted. Cracked heads, beat up guys accused of being disorderly and gettin' out of line. They ran roughshod over the joint; anyone challenge 'em got a beatin'. Don't let no one tell you different—Holmesburg was a cold stop back then."

"Tell me, who made up the Big Mob? What were their names?"

Roberson shook his head. Despite the former inmate's reluctance, Glass pressed on and mentioned officers Hartzell, Bridges, Smoot, Trent, Crawley, and a few others. "I heard they were key members of the Big Mob," the coroner coyly remarked.

"Maybe."

"I bet Albert Bridges could do some damage," said Glass.

"Shit, you better believe it," said Roberson enthusiastically, apparently unaware he had been tricked. "I seen Bridges hit a man with a blackjack so hard, it broke right in half. He and that crew, that's a bad bunch. They don't mess around. They fuck you up big time and don't think a second about it. They's enjoy it. I seen Smoot once stand on a man's head while they were tryin' stuff him down a toilet. Nearly drowned the son of a bitch. They fucked up a few guys so bad, I heard they went nuts. Had to send them over to Byberry. I seen one guy on my block go a little nuts and start runnin' around naked. He was scaring the hell out of people. Instead of sending him to Byberry or some other nuthouse, they threw him in Klondike and cooked his ass. They brought him out like a pile of fertilizer in a big wheel-barrow."

When Glass voiced his skepticism about some of the inmate's claims, Roberson became annoyed and replied, "You see this here eye?" He pointed to his discolored and deformed eye socket. "Can't see a damn thing out of it. Got this up at the Burg. Trent kicked me right in the face with his boot after they tackled me and pinned me on the ground. I was bleeding like a stuck pig. Ain't nothin' happen to Trent or any others. They do what they want up there."

While Sandler sat rapt, listening to Roberson recount his time at Holmesburg, Glass contemplated how to approach the former inmate with some of his more sensitive questions concerning the culpability of top prison officials.

"You mean a doctor was never brought in to take care of you?" asked Glass.

"Not until the next day," said Roberson. "By then I was soaked in blood and blind in one eye."

"Did the doctor report it to anyone in authority?"

"Man, you crazy . . . Nothin' happenin' up there gets reported. An inmate start complainin' about guards and they throw his ass in Klondike as sure as I'm sittin' here. They turn the steam on, then you got an even worser problem."

"And Davis, what about Superintendent Davis?" asked Glass. "What role did he have in all this?"

"Hardly ever seen the man," said Roberson, shaking his head dismissively. "When he first got the job, you'd see him around Center, talking to the captains and walking the block once in a while. But as time went on he disappeared. Only times I saw him before I made parole he'd be walking his dog in the yard.

One time I remember exercise bein' cut short so the superintendent could walk his dog in there. Damn dog got more exercise than the prisoners."

"How about Warden Stryker?" said Glass. "What is he like?"

"Mean, don't bend at all. Man don't give an inch," replied Roberson. "He don't play around. He was only a captain when I went in there, but the captains controlled the joint, and Stryker was the most serious of the bunch. I never seen that guy when he wasn't grittin' on somebody. Never smiled, not once. Don't think he can. Hell, he probably thought the mayor should have made him superintendent and not Davis. Stryker was the warden when I made parole. Davis, you know, was a cop. He ran the police and was brought up to the Burg to clean things up. Always havin' problems up there so they brought Davis in. But he didn't know about prisons. Runnin' the police and runnin' prisons is two different things. Now, Stryker, he spent all his time in prisons. I think, between you and me, he probably told Davis what to do. I guess they're okay though; Davis walks his dog and Stryker runs the jail."

"Tell me about Klondike," said Glass.

"Shit, that hotbox nearly killed me."

"What happened?"

"I nearly ended up like those poor fellas over the weekend," said Roberson. "They really caught it."

"And you?"

"Spent almost two weeks in Klondike, but only a couple days when they tried to cook my ass. Like bein' thrown in a tank of boilin' soup. Only reason I survived is dumb luck and Dr. Moretti. Usually they just threw me in there and kept me on bread and water, but one time they decided to fuck with me and turned the heat on. Turned it on around noontime and by early evening I thought I was dying. By midnight you couldn't breathe, couldn't touch a thing . . . you almost wanted to die just to end the agony you was in."

The former inmate shook his head in wonderment, his one good eye drifting off, absorbed in dark visions only he could see. He mumbled a few words, but the coroner and his young aide were unable to make sense of it.

"Go ahead," Glass urged, trying to regain Roberson's attention. "What happened, how'd you survive?"

"I managed to squeeze my hand through the iron mesh latticework," said Roberson as he showed a scar on top of his hand. "Cut myself pretty good, and with the heel of my shoe, I knocked the bolt out of the lock on the door. It was broke and I finally got it to open. Pushed the cell door open, fell out of my cell, and crawled to the control gauge for the radiators. I turned it down as much as I could. Then I crawled to the far end of the corridor where it wasn't so hot and must have fell out. Next morning a guard found me hiding there but never told on me. I figured he never wrote me up cause he woulda been blamed for not knowing the lock was broke and allowing me to get outta the cell. But he did me no favors. He threw me in another cell and turned the heat back on."

"How'd you get out that time?" asked Glass.

"Guess the good Lord was lookin' down on me cause later that day Dr. Moretti came in and examined me. After lookin' me over and seein' how bad a shape I was in, he told the guard to get me outta there. When the guard didn't obey him, Dr. Moretti went to Stryker and told him to get that man outta there. I know one thing—I woulda been cooked for sure if I'd stayed in that damn hotbox."

Glass and Sandler were both impressed by Roberson's near-death experience. While the intern imagined trying to survive in such conditions, the coroner's curiosity was piqued by Dr. Samuel Moretti. More and more it seemed the good doctor had dual loyalties: one to his craft—the medical profession—and the other to the prison system's punitive culture. Glass was increasingly convinced that Moretti knew more than he was letting on about prison operations and the treatment of prisoners over the years.

When the coroner told Roberson that some of those interviewed denied knowing anything about Klondike and the heat treatment, the former inmate laughed.

"Shit, that's a bunch of baloney," said Roberson. "Any prisoner who hasn't heard of guys bein' cooked in Klondike must be one of those deaf, dumb, and blind folks. It's one of the first things a con learns when he hits Holmesburg. Hell, guys talk about it all the time. And if you wanna stay out of trouble, you do as you're told. Don't be fuckin' wit no guards. Guys comin' in just off the street are told don't be lookin' funny at no guard or you'll get fucked up. They drop you in the box and turn on the heat, you're cooked. You'll be begging for mercy."

"So everyone knows of it?" asked the coroner.

"Hell yeah," said Roberson. "People say they don't be knowin' about Klondike is a bunch of horseshit. They know, and it's used all the time. Only time they stop is when there's a Grand Jury investigation or the prison inspectors come around, which ain't often."

When Roberson mentioned that he had been in Holmesburg when Klondike was built, the coroner asked the inmate to describe what he knew of the building's history.

"Put it up in '29—I remember it well. I know 'cause it was right after the riot in '29 and right before everybody's money got taken in the crash. Back then the riot was over the lousy food too. Guys got violent that time though. Tore up the dining hall, flooded some cellblocks. Police came in like they was General Pershing and the army. You know, dogs, shotguns, smoke bombs. It was a damn mess. Took forever to clean the place up. Soon after that, they started building out in the yard. Figured they were building more cellblocks, but one of 'em was this little joint. Turned out to be a punishment block. It was built to tighten up on guys, you know, keep 'em in line. Instead of throwing guys in the hole on C Rear, they started taking some out to this new joint. You know, to make an example of 'em, teach 'em a lesson. Guys were soon calling it Klondike. They'd freeze your ass off in the winter and then turn the heat on in summer. Yeah, turn the heat on when it was a hundred degrees outside. Freeze in the winter, boil in the summer. You was fucked whatever time of year it was. And nobody out here on the street be knowin' about it."

"Were the colored treated worse than white prisoners?"

"What do you think?" Roberson replied.

"Could all the guards throw someone in Klondike or just certain ones like the warden and captains?"

"Ain't sure. Seemed like they all could. They'd just grab you and throw your ass in there. Ain't like there was a vote or something."

Glass leaned forward and asked, "Who were the guards that ran Klondike?"

"Can't remember," Roberson said. "I ain't been up there in a while. Guys probably left, you know, moved on."

"How about I mention some names," suggested Glass, undeterred. "All you have to do is nod if they had anything to do with putting men in Klondike or knew of their treatment while confined there."

Roberson didn't agree, but neither did he verbally oppose the ruse. The coroner mentioned the names of ten guards and officers, but the former inmate did not budge. Showing his irritation, Glass said authoritatively, "Let's do it for real this time. You ready?" He mentioned the names again. The former inmate nodded five times. Glass thanked the City Hall custodian for his cooperation and expressed his hope he would continue to assist them with their investigation.

After Coroner Glass completed his interview with former inmate Rober-son, Deputy Ferencz escorted his boss two blocks south on Broad Street to the Bellevue Stratford Hotel, one of the city's most fashionable hotels. When they entered a small room on the seventeenth floor, Glass was introduced to Frank Conroy.

"I told your man, Mr. Ferencz, I wouldn't testify," said Conroy, as the deputy coroner quietly exited the room and closed the door behind him. "I won't go into a public courtroom. No way."

The Holmesburg guard was adamant. He had informed Carl Ferencz he was willing to talk, to be interviewed, but not behind Holmesburg's walls. And only in front of Coroner Glass; no one else. Because of the prospect of get-ting some valuable information about the Klondike deaths, Glass agreed to the meeting. Others expressed similar concerns about their safety. The coroner's office had taken a room at the hotel to interview Conroy and other Holmesburg guards and officers who did not want to be seen conversing with investigators. It was understood that those perceived as cooperating would pay dearly.

Coroner Glass crossed the room, took a seat, and immediately inquired, "What can you tell me about what happened in Klondike last weekend?"

Now seated alone with the coroner in the hotel room, the forty-five-year-old cellblock guard was visibly nervous. Of average height and weight, Conroy blinked often and his foot and leg vibrated at a dizzying pace. His comments were rushed, as if his auto were double-parked on Broad Street and about to be towed. Giving up information about coworkers that may lead to their arrest and prosecution was not something to be taken lightly. Prison inmates were not the only ones with contempt for snitches. For both the cons and their keepers, a rat was universally despised.

With a concerned expression on his face, Conroy looked the coroner in the eye. "I want out," he said. "Get me out of Holmesburg."

Appearing confused, Glass replied, "What do you mean?"

"You heard me—I want out. I don't wanna go back to that hellhole. You've got connections. Get me on the police force."

"First, let's talk about this past weekend. What do you know about what happened inside Klondike?"

The guard shook his head. "No, no, no, I ain't saying nothing till I know I ain't going back there," said Conroy. "You know what happens to me they find out I'm talking to you?"

"But you're not talking to me," Glass replied. "What happened last weekend? Who directed the heat be turned on inside the punishment unit?"

"You know as well as I do," said the guard leaning forward. "Ain't no secret who runs that place."

"How often do they use the heat treatment on prisoners they place in the hole?"

"As often as they like."

"Does Davis give the orders?"

The guard remained silent.

"Does Stryker?" asked the coroner. "Or does the order come from the captains?"

The guard leaned back against his chair. A slight smile crossed his lips. "I ain't saying nothing until I know I'm not going back there. You've got some juice—can you get me on the police force?"

Growing frustrated, Glass replied, "Why should I help you? You haven't told me a thing."

"Listen, you don't know what that place is like," said Conroy. "It's worse than Byberry. It's a nuthouse for killers. Yeah, a damn mental asylum, but way more dangerous. You're liable to get shanked or severely fucked up at any moment. Hell, there's nearly 1,500 animals in there and no more than a hundred of us. Christ, at night a shift may have only twenty-some guys, thirty tops. How'd you like to be the only guard on a cellblock of 150 vicious assholes who'd just love to put a shank in your back or a rod up your ass?"

"I know it isn't easy, Mr. Conroy," said Glass, "but you took the job. Nobody forced you into that line of work."

"Hey, I ain't blaming no one," said Conroy. "I needed a job. You know what the last few years been like, the Depression and all. They been rough. Work was tough to come by. I used to work in a Kensington mill. Wasn't bad, but then I got laid off with a hundred other guys. Thought I'd become a cop, but you gotta know somebody. I couldn't even get a spot in the sheriff's office. The only thing my ward leader could pull off was a screw at Moyamensing. Didn't really want it, but I got a wife and two kids. Had to take it. I did three months at Moko and was then shipped to Holmesburg with some other guards. The worst assholes in America are locked up there. The joint is far worse than Moko or the House of Correction. I wasn't there two weeks when some shit jumped off on a cellblock and all hell broke loose. I got fucked up pretty good. Got hit on the head with a piece of iron, broke a bone in my back, and dislocated my elbow. Still can't straighten the damn thing. Now look at me. I went in there three years ago. Within one year my hair turned gray. My wife couldn't believe it. Now my nerves are shot. I'm tellin' you, I'm in a bad way."

"Tell me," inquired Glass, undeterred, "was it usually the same crew of guards who staffed the punishment unit?"

"Know what it's like spending ten, twelve hours a day on a cellblock with the fucked-up guys locked in those cells?" asked Conroy, completely disregarding the coroner's question. "They spit and piss on you, throw food, shit, and homemade matchstick-and-gasoline bombs at you . . . You can't imagine what goes on in that place. The queers runnin' around, the gangs. Just the constant yelling, name-calling, and screaming can drive you nuts. Lotta guards end up with mental problems, get drunk every night, beat their wives. Just yesterday I had beef with a con who was cursing me for not letting him out of his cell. For hours he raised hell and wouldn't shut up. And this is a guy who slit his wife's throat and killed his two kids."

"Frank, did you ever work in Klondike?" asked Glass, who remained focused on the information he hoped to gain. "Did you ever work in the punishment unit?"

"No, I was never assigned there," said Conroy, his leg twitching even more rapidly. "They got a special squad that deals with that place."

"Can you name the guards?"

"Not really."

"How 'bout Albert Bridges, Joseph Smoot, Robert Trent, Thomas Burnley, and Alex Crawley?"

Conroy looked surprised and said, "Maybe."

"What's it like in Klondike?" asked Glass.

"Never been in there," replied Conroy. "Just heard about it."

"What have you heard, Frank?"

"You know, guys fuck up, cause a problem, they get put in Klondike."

"And what happens in there?"

Conroy shook his head but remained silent.

Beginning to display some exasperation, the coroner leaned forward and asked the nervous guard, "Have you ever heard of the 'Big Mob' and whether the heat treatment is regularly used on prisoners in Klondike?"

Conroy remained silent.

"Frank, does Superintendent Davis give the order to turn on the heat?"

"That guy?" the guard said with a dismissive sneer and shoulder shrug. "Christ, I see him about as often as I see you."

"How 'bout Stryker? Does the warden give the order?"

"Forget it," replied Conroy. "I'm not saying nothing about him . . . or anyone else."

Frustrated by the inability to acquire useful information, and resentful that he was being leveraged for a job on the police force, Glass rose from his chair, thanked the guard for meeting with him, and ushered the bewildered man out the door. The coroner was not in the mood to trade jobs for information. Some individuals were talking, and as long as there was a chance the full story of the Klondike murders could be gleaned from actual participants, there wasn't going to be monetary or occupational rewards for information.

Some guards—off prison grounds and away from their colleagues—were actually admitting that the heat treatment had been used more or less as standard practice for years. A few guards voiced their surprise the practice lasted as long as it did considering how brutal it was. "Everyone," said one confused guard, "from prison bosses to city politicians must have sanctioned it. How else could it have been in use for so long?"

More and more, the coroner heard the name Sergeant Hartzell being mentioned. He was said to be in charge of Klondike, and guards like Bridges, Smoot, Trent, Crawley, and others directly answered to him. The sergeant, however, made himself unavailable to investigators, at least those from the coroner's office. The more Glass learned from those willing to talk, the more critical Hartzell became—for he was that crucial link between the guards who mistreated the Klondike captives and the upper echelon that ran the prison. But how to get the sergeant to talk remained a mystery.

There were other puzzles to ponder. For example, Glass was fixated on why doctors were to make daily visits to Klondike when inmates were housed there. It had to be the effects of the heat treatment. Why else would daily medical inspections be necessary? Fifteen hundred men were incarcerated at Holmesburg, and the cells in Klondike were no different than those in the main jail—except for the debilitating bake-oven effect. The coroner was left pondering just how complicit the prison doctors actually were.

Another question he pursued with guards was why the original organizer of the food strike, Myles McCabe, was not tossed in Klondike with the other strikers. "Explain to me," Glass asked one corridor guard, "how McCabe, the strike leader, doesn't get baked with the others. How the hell did that happen?"

"The guy's got some serious connections," one guard replied. "He's been in the system off and on a long time. Think he was first arrested in the early twenties, earlier. He does a stretch, says he's reformed, gets out, and goes back to committing crimes. He's got some friends in the church who always stand up for him. But he's no choir boy. He's broken out of various prisons, stuck up legit and illegal businesses, had numerous gunfights with cops and guards, and yet he's still treated like a big shot. You tell me how he does it?"

Glass chalked it up to another yet-to-be solved aspect of prison culture. Logic and free-world rationalizations only got one so far when trying to understand what went on behind Holmesburg's thirty-foot walls.

Chapter 16

Mayoral Mischievousness

It was well into the evening of August 24 while Glass, Ferencz, and Sandler hurried from cellblock to cellblock, interviewing prisoners, that they noticed some sudden gossip being shared among concerned-looking guards. Though curious, the coroner kept busy; his fear something might terminate his ability to gather evidence and question potential witnesses never waned. His deputy, however, was more inquisitive and eventually asked a guard what all the quiet conversations were about.

Ferencz immediately sought out his boss and found him on one of the segregated cellblocks, interviewing four colored inmates. "C'mon," he interrupted, grabbing Glass by the arm, "we have to go. You won't believe this."

"What is it?"

"Apparently the mayor just arrested Bridges and Smoot."

"What?" blurted Glass. "You have to be kidding!"

"It's true," said Ferencz. "It happened a few minutes ago. Clarke's personal security detail just took Bridges and Smoot out of here in handcuffs. They were taken down to City Hall and are being charged with homicide."

"I don't believe it," said Glass.

"Check out the guards," said Ferencz. "They wouldn't look so concerned if it wasn't true."

The shocking news struck the coroner hard, but the inmates overhearing the conversation were jubilant. They had known Bridges and Smoot as two of the most ruthless and feared guards in the institution, and the fact that they were going to be charged with murder was worthy of celebration. Only inmates learning a judge had granted them parole would have been more joyous.

But Glass was in no mood for celebration. He was caught by surprise and thrown off balance tactically. He planned to interrogate both men, lean on them for the truth, and dangle reduced charges in exchange for their cooperation. The coroner knew both men were involved up to their eyeballs in the deaths of the Klondike captives, but who was it at the top of the command structure that ordered or allowed the guards to torture the men in such a barbarous fashion? There was still much to learn, but now that Bridges and Smoot were charged with murder, their willingness to cooperate was probably gone. Their lawyers would never let them be interviewed. But why, Glass kept asking himself, would the mayor act in such an outlandish and extra-legal fashion? Who was he protecting?

When Glass and Ferencz reached City Hall they learned both officers were being held without bail on homicide charges. To their further chagrin, they also learned from the press that Mayor Clarke was now patting himself on the back for sending police detectives up to Holmesburg to arrest "the perpetrators of a vicious crime," and telling reporters he was "personally committed to removing the black mark recently placed upon the city's escutcheon."

The coroner was furious and told newsmen before storming out, "Bridges and Smoot were made valueless as witnesses unless they choose to talk voluntarily. Being defendants, they have constitutional immunity from further questioning. The mayor butted in here and has given us a big legal mess to straighten out."

Knowing he wouldn't get anywhere with Mayor Clarke, Glass immediately went to the district attorney's office on the sixth floor, where he discovered that First Assistant District Attorney Vincent Doyle was equally flabbergasted by the unexpected development. "Did you know about this?" demanded Glass. "Is this another effort by Clarke and Campbell to sabotage this investigation?"

"Hell no," replied Doyle. "We had no warning. I was at home when I got a call from an *Inquirer* reporter. The district attorney is furious."

"Sure, I believe that."

"Listen to me," Doyle shouted. "We were blindsided as well. The mayor tells Campbell he doesn't want the district attorney's office to get involved. He says, 'We'll wait till it blows over.' Then we get slammed by the press for doing nothing. And now the mayor goes out on his own and pulls a stunt like this."

The coroner sneered and shook his head in disgust.

"I'm telling you the truth," said Doyle. "Campbell is livid. He says it makes him and the entire office look like a bunch of goddamn idiots. Neither of us can recall the last time the chief executive of the city tried such a maneuver. I'm not even sure it's legal. Maybe a couple generations ago the mayor could control the police like this, but not today. It makes a mockery of the entire criminal justice system."

Like others in government, Glass knew Doyle as a competent, no-nonsense lifer in the DA's office who had risen to the position of Campbell's top deputy. Once described in a news article as "the legal wheelhouse of the city's prosecution department," Doyle was a veteran of many homicide trials and grand jury investigations. Without bluster or theatrical pyrotechnics, he had built an impressive record prosecuting liquor violators, numbers racketeers, and Center City pimps. The one time he ran for public office, a judgeship, he lost. It was that defeat, and Doyle's loyalty to Campbell, a Clarke lieutenant, that made Glass nervous. If Doyle still had electoral aspirations, it was unlikely he'd vigorously oppose the mayor's unprecedented attempt to hijack the criminal justice system.

"The entire thing is just incredible," sighed Glass. "We're involved in a major investigation of an outrageous crime, and the mayor wants to suddenly take over. He's gone from being a complete obstructionist to lead investigator and circus ringmaster."

"Circus is right," said Doyle. "Clarke has the two Holmesburg guards in the Mayor's Reception Room under police guard. He's waiting for a magistrate to arrive and then he's going to file additional charges. And all in front of the press. A big show, that's what he wants, but how much of it will be legal is anybody's guess."

"I can't believe the mayor would do something like this," said Ferencz. "We'll never be able to get the real instigators of the Klondike murders with this sideshow dominating the courts."

"Can anything be done?" asked Glass. "Is there any precedent for this?"

"I don't think anyone's around today who ever experienced anything like this, but Campbell believes the Board of Judges will be equally concerned when they learn the mayor is now taking it upon himself to arrest, charge, and incarcerate people. That's a bit too far even for them. The judges read newspapers; they know a lot of people around the country are watching this case. He thinks we'll be granted the authority to intervene. I'm leaving now to file a habeas corpus appeal with Judge Fleetwood in Quarter Sessions Court. It's possible Fleetwood, knowing how unusual this all is, will allow us to intercede. Maybe he'll allow us to void or at least re-charge the defendants. We'll ask for bail, try to get the mayor to keep his nose out of the judiciary's business, and hopefully get your investigation back on track."

"What a goddamn mess," said Glass, voicing his frustration, "just when we were getting closer to nailing this thing down."

"I think we both know why this happened," Doyle replied. "Clarke looks like a dunce in the papers for hiding out and not responding earlier. And then when he does get involved, he goes and backs his detectives' suspect claim that the inmates went nuts and killed each other."

"The DA's office wasn't much better," added the coroner, regarding District Attorney Campbell's silence and not pushing for a real investigation. "Your office and the police were far from helpful. There's been opposition every step of the way. And let me tell you, prison guards got the message. They knew you guys weren't serious about this thing."

"Don't get me started," Doyle replied. "We weren't all on board with that decision." Glass could see that the fifty-one-year-old first assistant was embarrassed by the coroner's accusation. Short, thick-set, and normally soft-spoken, Doyle shied away from publicity and enjoyed a serious, by-the-book reputation. "Campbell felt he had to go along with the mayor," explained Doyle. "Remember, he needs the mayor for reelection. Something I'm sure you're aware of. But a lot of us in the office weren't thrilled with the order to keep out of it. It really angered a few of us. And now, well . . . I guess Clarke figured he had to do something dramatic to get ahead of the story. He's trying to restore his good name."

"Good luck with that," offered Ferencz.

Doyle left to argue his case in front of Judge Fleetwood. The unusual plea would be held in the judge's chambers as all the courtrooms were locked at that late hour of the night. In addition to denouncing the absurdity of the county's chief elected official interfering in a serious criminal matter, Doyle was equally set on preserving any evidence the coroner had gathered and preventing public exposure.

Only a handful of court personnel and Mayor Clarke's legal representatives were in Judge Fleetwood's chambers when the assistant district attorney began his argument. "The arrests earlier this evening," Doyle informed the judge, "grew out of a situation at the county prison where eight inmates of the institution met their deaths in rather gruesome fashion. The coroner immediately initiated an investigation, an investigation that is supported by the State Department of Welfare and the District Attorney's office. We are working together to establish the manner in which these men died, and to fix responsibility for the deaths on any person or persons who may be responsible. This does not mean that we do not welcome the cooperation of the mayor and the police, but actions such as those this evening definitely thwart that effort.

"We ask that the premature arrests conducted earlier this evening by the mayor's detectives be struck, bail of $2,500 be imposed on both men, and further request that the Commonwealth not be required to disclose any evidence pertaining to the investigation currently underway."

To the assistant district attorney's great satisfaction, Judge Fleetwood, an old codger with a distinctive handlebar mustache and crusty disposition, was in total agreement. The judge, whose initial appointment to the bench went back to 1913, laid down the law as to who would conduct the investigation, and who would prosecute any charges brought against the prison officials. "Precedent and common sense support you, Mr. Doyle," said Judge Fleetwood. "The investigation by the three agencies apparently has been stopped completely for the moment, but that shall change. I'll allow no one to interfere with the investigation being made by the coroner, the district attorney, and the State Welfare Department into the prison deaths until their investigation is completed. In short, I'll not tolerate another miscarriage of justice in a matter of such high public importance. If any further interference occurs, I can assure you proper steps will be taken."

"Does that include other official branches of government, Your Honor?" Doyle's inquiry was a coy attempt to provoke the judge and thereby ensure that the jurist's decision captured Clarke's attention.

"That's exactly what I mean, Counselor," replied Fleetwood, emphatically. "So let me underscore this order so no one can say they misunderstood. The mayor's office has a full panoply of powers, but that does not include unilaterally arresting and incarcerating people. Anyone, individual or agency—and that includes the mayor—who interferes with my order will be hit with a citation for contempt. And be assured, I'll see that their incarceration follows shortly thereafter."

Just past midnight, and with his last-minute intervention rewarded, Doyle informed newsmen waiting outside the judge's chambers that the mayor's actions were "premature and destructive to a sound and thorough investigation" of the deaths, and it was time Philadelphia "stop impersonating a lawless dictatorship bent on disregarding traditional judicial procedure, and replacing it with personal fiat in the so-called pursuit of justice."

With Hitler's controversial Nazi governmental strictures, racist policies, and threatening behavior prominent in the news, Doyle's acerbic comments were probably more critical than his boss, the district attorney, would have preferred. And though much aggrieved at the mayor's unilateral takeover of the criminal justice system as well as his own embarrassment at not getting involved earlier, Campbell was still dependent on the mayor's political control of party apparatus for reelection. But there was little doubt the mayor's unprecedented, self-serving actions involving a case of national notoriety required a swift response.

The aging jurist's emphatic statement did as both he and Assistant District Attorney Doyle had hoped: Mayor Clarke was put on his heels. By sun-up, the mayor had a statement ready for distribution. It read, "I have the statements by witnesses taken by detectives, that these two prison guards turned the steam on. It was clearly my duty, in any police matter, when there was such evidence, to direct the police department, to make the arrests. If I had failed to order the police to arrest these men with such evidence before me, I would be open to the most serious criticism."

The mayor's statement went on to explain, "There may be others involved, but the evidence submitted to me was very definite as to the two guilty participants. As this evidence was brought to me, I had police captains make the arrests and continue their investigation. If the court takes this action, it relieves me of responsibility. I did my duty under the law. As far as I am concerned, I shall do nothing more. From now on our city police will cooperate only to such an extent as may be requested."

The mayor's concession statement was a noteworthy departure from his normal vain, self-congratulatory comments. It was another sign that the Klondike tragedy was truly extraordinary, and the mayor's talent for steamrolling his opponents and twisting events to his advantage had hit a wall. To further ensure his compliance was an early morning visit to Holmesburg Prison by Judge Fleetwood and a half-dozen members of the Board of Judges. After surveying the institution and its infamous Klondike punishment unit, the jurists held a private discussion in one of the exercise yards. When they exited the institution, they were met by a small contingent of reporters. Speaking for the group, Judge Fleetwood said, "The wanton cruelty practiced on the prisoners who died last Monday morning and upon the other prisoners who were with them, indicates that there is on the part of at least some of those in authority a cruel and inhuman point of view with regard to the management and control of the prison. It is an alarming menace, which must be promptly eradicated.

"The Board of Judges is studying all phases of the case in order to place the responsibility for the matter where it properly belongs. It appears to us that the investigation by the coroner has been prompt, thorough, and painstaking. The Board is disposed to have the district attorney impanel a Grand Jury for a careful review of the incident, but we will not slow up the course of justice in the matter until we receive the findings of the coroner's investigation. The matter is currently in competent hands, and I do not propose to interfere with it."

Glass appreciated the support of Fleetwood and the Board of Judges. For the moment, at least, it was proving a judicial restraining order or legal straitjacket on the city's mischief-making chief executive. But the Klondike's massive press coverage had awakened city judges of their responsibility and role in the matter. Until now, they had taken cover like the Prison Board and other city departments. One jurist, however, a known ally of the mayor, trekked up to Holmesburg the evening the deceased were discovered and shockingly informed the press, "There is little doubt the prisoners turned on each other, broke steam pipes, and battled through the night, resulting in a penal tragedy."

The tide was definitely turning, however, and Glass knew that much of the credit was due to the press. Yes, they had played up the most grisly and horrifying aspects of the story, but several of the papers had also sought answers, questioned authorities, and pushed responsible parties to act. As one newspaper editorial succinctly stated early on concerning the indifferent reaction of the mayor, district attorney, prison board, and local judiciary, "If Superintendent Davis and his subordinates responsible for this dastardly crime aren't punished, if this outrage goes unaddressed, Philadelphia justice will be a stench in the nostrils of the nation."

Going a step further was another tabloid that advocated "complicit or negligent prison officials belong in one of two places; outside the prison, or inside—in cells." And some were taking note of the one elected official who seemed determined to discover the truth. Comparing Glass to the intrepid British general who pursued the perpetrators of the infamous abomination known as the Black Hole of Calcutta, the *Philadelphia Record* observed, "The only one who has shown real action so far is Coroner Glass. He is the Lord Clive of Holmesburg."

The series of sudden investigative turnabouts left not only average citizens but also civic and religious leaders bewildered and depressed. What, they wondered, had become of the city's criminal justice system? Already under suspicion for its periodic spasms of confusion, bias, and outright corruption, pursuit of the truth in the Holmesburg debacle had become little more than an embarrassing charade. The whiplash turn of events provoked many newspaper editorial boards to print scathing denouncements of police incompetence, mayoral interference, and growing support for a thorough, non-political investigation of the Klondike murders.

The *Philadelphia Daily News,* for example, published a column-long editorial denouncing any form of "factionalism," "political grandstanding," or "crony favoritism" in a sleazy effort to bury "one of the worst crimes in the city's history."

Entitled, "This Is No Time for Horseplay," the editorial began with the line, "Here in Philadelphia we turned back the pages of history to the Dark Ages and took a chapter in torture as a guide to modern prison management." After recounting aspects of the tragic saga—from the inmate "hunger strike" and "breakdown of prison management" to the "super-heated Klondike" and "half-mad prisoners shrieking for their lives"—the editorial demanded "the righteous hand of the law be placed upon the shoulders of the men who engaged in a modern-day inquisition."

Calling the Klondike episode a "crime against civilization," it was deemed imperative that "any dispute between the coroner's office and the mayor's detective force be subordinated to accurately fixing the blame and punishing the guilty." The editorial concluded with a capital-letter call-to-arms, informing readers, "This Offense is Not so Much Against a Few Desperate and Vicious Crooks as it is a Crime Against the Decent Citizens of Philadelphia. We Cannot Allow it to be Used for Political Advantage or Horseplay."

Glass was pleasantly surprised by the *Daily News* editorial and the others that staked out similar positions. Not only did such endorsements provide a semblance of institutional support for his investigation, they were also a welcome reprieve from the occasional editorial shots he was forced to endure. For example, the last two times he was mentioned in a *Daily News* editorial, the tabloid took note of his lack of academic and medical credentials. No longer, however, did his modest educational record seem newsworthy.

After another physically taxing day filled with frustration and occasional success in the pursuit of prisoners and guards willing to talk about their experience with Holmesburg's super-heated punishment block, Carl Ferencz couldn't wait to lay his head on a pillow and shut his eyes. He was so exhausted he thought he'd dispense with the cold shower that had become a nightly ritual since that terrible Monday. The refreshing waters not only rid him of the sweat and institutional mire but also the odor that came with being around 1,400 foul-smelling men and grime-filled cellblocks for twelve hours at a time.

As he parked his city auto on the 6200 block of Ogontz Avenue, he knew his children would be asleep, and probably his wife as well. It was the third straight night he was arriving home just before midnight, and the long hours combined with the pressure of a high-profile investigation were taking their toll.

As he exited his vehicle, he was blinded by the headlights of another car that came upon him from behind. Even though he waved the driver on and there was ample room for the driver to proceed around him, the vehicle remained motionless. Once again, he waved his arm, but the car did not move. Finally, the driver-side door opened, and the outline of a tall man appeared. "Mr. Ferencz," he called out, "could we have a few seconds of your time?"

Stunned, Ferencz raised his arm in front of his eyes to ward off the glare from the blinding headlights. The deputy coroner wasn't sure what to do when a passenger door opened and a man exited and said, "Carl, it's me, Felix Heisler. Please come join us for a moment."

"Felix, what are you doing here this time of night?" said Ferencz as he extended his hand.

After shaking hands with the former ward leader and his one-time political patron, Ferencz asked again what Heisler was doing in his neighborhood at such a late hour.

"I'll explain it all," replied Heisler, "but please get in the car."

Ferencz moved cautiously as his friend opened the rear door of the large city auto. Another man sat on the far side of the back seat, but the dim streetlight provided too little light to allow Ferencz to see who it was. The deputy coroner had just taken a seat when the shadowy image across from him extended a hand and said, "Good evening, Carl. Tom Clarke. Pleased to meet you once again." The surprising midnight meeting with the mayor of Philadelphia was a shock, to say the least.

"Sorry to come upon you like that, but we recognized your car," said the mayor. "I'd appreciate your giving us a few minutes of your time. I know it's late, but I'd like to talk to you."

Ferencz was startled by the unexpected late-night rendezvous with the city's controversial leader. His surprise became concern when the vehicle proceeded to make a swift U-turn and then at the traffic light headed east on Godfrey Avenue. A million thoughts ran through the deputy coroner's head as the vehicle drove off and quickly distanced itself from the bed he so desired to collapse into. What did the mayor want of him? Where were they going at this time of night? And most eerily, was he in any danger?

Oddly, no one said a word for a half-dozen blocks. Surely, being picked up outside his home by the mayor and then driven to some unknown destination was worthy of inquiry. Just as he was about to ask where they were going, Clarke said, "Carl, how long have you worked in the coroner's office?"

"About twelve years," replied Ferencz.

"That's what I thought," said Clarke, looking out the window. "And you started as?"

"I started as a staffer at the morgue on 13th Street, then worked my way up to the front office and then the main office in City Hall."

"Smart boy. Did it the old-fashioned way, from the ground up. Very good."

As the car crossed Broad Street and slowly drove along the well-maintained grounds of the Philadelphia College of Ophthalmology, conversation ceased. The driver, a city detective Ferencz presumed, turned into a ritzy residential neighborhood. First north on to 12th Street and after two blocks, on to 65th Avenue, and then back down 11th Street to the plush ophthalmology campus.

"Nice neighborhood, isn't it?" remarked the mayor of the upscale East Oak Lane section of the city.

"This is where you should be living, Carl," contributed Mr. Heisler. "Only a mile or so from Ogontz Avenue and the 17th ward, but a world of difference. Big, beautiful homes, with a lot of land, trees, and shrubs."

As the car glided past homes with ornate light standards, pools, and shrubbery expertly hewed to represent bears, whales, and other animals, Ferencz continued to wonder when the anvil would fall. As the chief deputy of the office pursuing the Holmesburg matter, he expected a barrage of threats, requests, and demands. The mayor wasn't known for collegial, late-night tours of city real estate.

"Must be tough in a row house with a wife and kids," commented the mayor. "How many children do you have, Carl?"

"Two girls," Ferencz replied. "Four and six."

"I think Councilman Shoyer lives in one of these homes," said Clarke.

"You're right, Mr. Mayor. The councilman lives one street over," said Heisler.

"You know, Carl," offered Clarke, "you could be here in East Oak Lane too."

It was then that Ferencz recognized what was happening. There was a distinct prospect he was about to be offered something. It was now obvious the mayor had either followed him home from the prison or was lying in wait. Any claim of a chance meeting in front of his home was bogus. Uncomfortable with the notion of being asked to do something in exchange for more attractive residential accommodations, but unsure how to act as they perused East Oak Lane housing stock, he finally blurted out, "Mr. Mayor, how can I help you? What do you want of me?"

"This Holmesburg business, Carl—it's become quite a problem."

"I know," said Ferencz. "We all realize it doesn't put the city in a favorable light."

"It's an ugly story, Carl. It never should have gotten this bad. If handled properly, all this unpleasantness could have been avoided."

Ferencz knew what the mayor was getting at—the coroner's decision to conduct a serious investigation of the Holmesburg murders. He wondered if he was going to receive a tongue lashing from the mayor; a common experience to which many of the mayor's subordinates had become accustomed.

"How serious is Glass about this inquest, this blue ribbon investigation of his?" asked Clarke, never once looking at the deputy coroner.

Ferencz was hesitant to share office information with a potential target of the investigation sitting next to him. He knew the mayor was a master of police cover-ups and political skullduggery. "I think he's very serious," said Ferencz, eventually. "He hasn't empaneled a jury yet, but he intends to."

Clarke groaned. "That's unfortunate, Carl. All the press hoopla, all the questions, damage to the city's reputation. And further investiture in an unorthodox medical inquest by a high school graduate would permanently cripple the city's image. We'll become a laughingstock," said the mayor. "I think you can see how embarrassing and detrimental that would be."

Ferencz made no comment as the car slowly meandered through the quiet neighborhood with the mayor and former ward leader periodically commenting on statuary, fancy bird feeders, and other front lawn decorations. Practically holding his breath in anticipation of what he might be asked or ordered to do, Ferencz contemplated how best to request he be driven home.

"I think the party made a big mistake," said Clarke, looking out the window, "when it chose a layman—a damn basketball player—for city coroner."

Ferencz remained silent, annoyed by the comment. Ferencz was especially irritated because he had been pushed aside at the time. He had a college degree and actual experience working in the office. He knew Heisler was perturbed, too, as the ward leader had urged Ferencz's selection, but party leaders—including the mayor—went with Heshel Glass as the party's choice for coroner. Both men had heard the rumors. When campaigning against his Democratic mayoral opponent, a former Olympic athlete, four years earlier, Clarke had charged him with being a pawn of Jewish interests and "a willing hostage of Hebrew bankers." Hoping to tamp down allegations of anti-Semitism, Clarke helped engineer a Jew for the position of county coroner. A little-known South Philadelphia ward leader better known for his basketball play than his political acumen was the beneficiary.

Being shoved aside for a novice without academic degrees stung, but Ferencz knew the nature of electoral politics in Philadelphia. Academic credentials, experience, and other attributes bolstered a candidate's prospects but weren't necessarily critical to the arcane calculus party elders used in fielding candidates for the ticket. Nailing down a row office took some serious plotting and gamesmanship.

"I know this is not your doing, Carl," said the mayor, "so I'm hoping you can see your way to helping us correct this thing?"

"Carl, the mayor can make things happen for you," said Heisler. "This is what we both wanted. That office would be yours; you'd be the one calling the shots. And you could afford living here in East Oak Lane or Chestnut Hill or anywhere else in the city you desired. I'm sure your wife and girls would love that."

Clarke continued talking about Glass as if the Klondike deaths were the coroner's fault, and that he was the one solely responsible for doing damage to the city's reputation. The mayor said he needed to "end this insanity as soon as possible." Heisler occasionally interjected comments about how much Ferencz's wife and children would enjoy living in a home with a swimming pool and a neighborhood with better schools, parks, and other social amenities.

Ferencz, however, was increasingly uncomfortable. He didn't like what was happening and was beginning to feel more and more guilty. He hadn't been asked to do anything specific yet but knew it was coming. Moving to a bigger home in a more fashionable neighborhood had been his and his wife's dream, but the thought of stabbing his boss in the back, and terminating the Holmesburg investigation, turned his stomach. Sure, he wanted the coroner's job; it would have been a crowning achievement to his career. But Glass had treated him well, had come to trust his judgment, and had given him considerable leeway in running the office. He was reminded of their first meeting, when he expected Glass to fire him and appoint his own choice as deputy coroner.

"Listen, Carl," said Glass at that initial sit-down after he had won the election, "I know we were both vying for this position, but that's settled now. I've been watching you and asking around about you. The reports are all good. I need someone I can trust here, somebody who knows the office. I could bring my own guy in as deputy, but they'd know as little as me. Yeah, eventually we would both learn the history and intricacies of the coroner's job, but you know it now. If you think you can set aside your own disappointment at not getting the office, be loyal, and always do the right thing, I'd like it if you stayed on as the deputy coroner."

The offer had come as a shock to Ferencz. Tradition was for new occupants to clean house, but here he was being asked to stay on. Sure, there was resentment that a novice—a Jewish former basketball player, no less—was given the job, but that was politics. More importantly, he had a wife and two children to support. Good jobs weren't that easy to come by, even for loyal party workers. Ferencz agreed, and as it turned out, both men worked well together. Disagreements occurred, but dialogue between them remained cordial, and the office functioned smoothly.

But now an opportunity was being presented to him that would end all that. If he understood the mayor correctly, he would become the next city coroner, and his family could abandon cluttered, row-house Philadelphia for a more spacious and fashionable section of the city.

By the time he was dropped off at his home, Ferencz was adrift in alternating waves of expectation, dread, and indecision—even though an actual request hadn't yet been made. Ferencz poured himself a couple of shots of rye whiskey, took a shower, and went to bed. But he would remain awake the entire night.

Chapter 17

A Young Man's Folly

Late for his lunch meeting at the restaurant on Mole Street, Glass was moving at a rapid clip. After entering the crowded establishment that had become a well-known midday hangout for both City Hall politicians and Center City businessmen, the coroner was forced to greet a number of patrons and well-wishers. "Hello, Hesh, good to see you. That's certainly an ugly business you got yourself involved with up at Holmesburg," "You're all over the papers," and, "Boy, that's a real mess you're dealing with concerning those prison murders," were typical of the fleeting comments he heard.

While shaking hands and uttering a brief "Hello" and "Good to see you" to an array of acquaintances and glad-handers, he spotted his party of five well-dressed labor and civic leaders at the rear of the restaurant. As he moved in their direction, he caught a glimpse of his summer intern, David Sandler, seated by a secluded table along the wall. Glass had never known the young man to frequent the popular watering hole for local movers and shakers, but here he was, and obviously engrossed in conversation with his lunch guest. Sandler was practically leaning over the table relating something of intense interest.

Glass didn't immediately recognize the other man. Thin, bespectacled, and clean shaven except for chin stubble, the fellow appeared only slightly older than the intern, and much intrigued by the topic under discussion. But there was something about the fellow that caused the coroner to believe he had seen him before. Was he a denizen of City Hall? Maybe a staffer for one of the councilmen or possibly tipstaff to one of the many judges who held court in the massive building? As Glass continued to his table, he pondered the man's likeness until it suddenly dawned on him; the person seated with Sandler was

153

one of the many newspaper reporters he had observed standing outside the wall of Holmesburg Prison. He couldn't recall from which paper, but he was now certain the stranger was a journalist. Glass now recalled the young man had a Southern accent and had proffered the question, "How did the police come to the conclusion communists were behind the prison uprising?" The coroner never replied at the time, but the reporter's youth and Southern drawl obviously stuck with him.

The realization that an out-of-town newspaperman was now having private conversations with young Sandler sparked concern. Did he have a leak in his office? Could someone close to him—someone involved in the Klondike investigation—be providing critical information to the press?

Throughout lunch and discussion of his reelection chances with a group of business, religious, and labor leaders, Glass furtively glanced at the two young men across the room. He brooded over the nature of their relationship and what, if anything, his young aide might be relating to the news reporter about the Holmesburg investigation.

⊸⊷⊶⊷⊶

Judson Henry Jones was from Asheville, North Carolina, a small town in the southwestern part of the state that was closer to Georgia than Raleigh, the state capital. Though his parents were of modest income—his father, a traveling shoe salesman with an attraction for loose women and cheap alcohol—young Jud, a somewhat shy, sickly child as a youth, had overcome a variety of family and economic impediments to develop a love of books, poetry, and short stories. His strong academic record and gift for language earned him a scholarship to Davidson College, where his intellectual interests meandered from one major to another but always seemed to gravitate back to literature.

Desiring to hone his skills as a poet and playwright after graduation, Jones matriculated at the University of North Carolina for its respected graduate writing program. Economic constraints during the Depression forced him to withdraw and begin earning a living as a freelance reporter for a series of small-town newspapers. Covering an array of mundane events from local weddings and divorces to government construction projects and the occasional bank robbery did not impede his artistic inclination. He continued to write short stories, a few earning publication in rather small, relatively unknown academic journals.

When he was hired as a general assignment reporter for the *Washington Star* in 1937, he was delighted not only to be relocating to a big city but one that

154

also had a vibrant theatrical community. His love of the dramatic arts was only encouraged by the move, and he continually pitched storylines to his editor that captured the impact of the economic depression enveloping the nation. Though assignments regarding the despair and turmoil visited upon struggling families in the district during the Depression were occasionally granted, many were adopted as themes for his personal writing projects. Jones was attracted to the darker side of humanity, the lives of vagrants, prostitutes, and skid-row bums who lived hand to mouth and were shunned by polite society.

Most of these late-night literary efforts—which increasingly emphasized playwriting—went unrewarded. However, his dream of writing an important, critically-praised work remained undiminished. He told friends, "If only I could find a subject—a person or event—that could spark my artistic breakthrough."

That discovery was made one warm Monday morning when an account of a deadly prison incident in Philadelphia came across the news wire. The number of victims along with several competing explanations of the tragedy captivated Jones's imagination. The specter of over a dozen imprisoned criminals being roasted to death was a storyline so far afield from his normal news assignments and article submissions that he immediately knew he had to cover it. Initially rejected by his editors, young Jones remained undeterred. At first, he threatened to quit, and then he came up with a less dramatic alternative. He would go up to Philadelphia on his own dime and file a couple of stories on the incident. If they resonated with readers, the paper would pay for his trip and lodging. If the story proved of little interest, he'd return to Washington properly chastened. His deal was accepted, and editors—albeit begrudgingly—now had him stationed in the City of Brotherly Love covering an event of untold brutality and public fascination.

<hr>

Herman Rosen was retained by guards Bridges and Smoot shortly after their arrest. Rosen was a surprising choice—not that he didn't have the proper credentials, as he was one of the most prominent defense attorneys in the city. But he was usually associated with well-heeled individuals of some celebrity or influential corporate clients. Many wondered how lowly prison guards could afford such high-priced legal talent.

Consistent with his tactical style, Rosen was quick to defend his newest clients. Attired as usual in an immaculate brown pinstriped three-piece suit with a crisp, pale-yellow shirt and expensive dark bowtie, Rosen told the press that his clients had nothing to do with the deaths of the eight prisoners. He informed all who would listen that an examination of the punishment unit would disclose that an accident or defect in the machinery or design of the heating system was responsible for the tragedy.

"Both of my clients, Mr. Bridges and Mr. Smoot, are sure there was nothing deliberate, nothing regarding omission or commission," said Rosen, "that caused the deaths of these men. In fact, my clients, along with several others, were the first to discover the deceased prisoners. If it had not been for their quick response more may have died and a human catastrophe made that much worse. They have told me that they were in the cellblock at five o'clock Sunday afternoon and made sure the heat was turned off. They assure me the men were in good condition at that time."

Rosen would go on to add, "The building was heated by rule," but shed little light on what that actually meant, and that prison procedures were in a state of flux at the time due to the inmate strike, the threat of violence, and the extraordinary situation that existed at the time.

Under pressure by a host of newspapers and radio stations for a response, the Board of Prison Inspectors—the six-member body designated by the city charter to determine prison and personnel policy for the county—finally issued a long-awaited statement. The board had been the recipient of severe criticism for shirking their duty. Reports from various sources seemed to indicate that individual members rarely did inspections, knew little of what was occurring inside individual institutions, and were generally ill-informed about the day-to-day operations of the county prison system.

Reporters from different city newspapers had done some digging and discovered that mayoral appointees rarely visited a prison and knew little about key issues such as overcrowding, funding, and personnel shortages. When one member was tracked down and confronted about his duty to inspect one facility a month, he lamely replied, "I don't recall whether I did or not."

Superintendent Davis was asked by the press about prison inspectors' visits; he wasn't much help. "I'm busy." Davis shrugged. "I haven't had time to look into it."

As Glass would learn from his interviews with guards, the lack of interest by prison inspectors was par for the course—and perfectly fine with penal administrators. The less involvement by outsiders the better. Davis, Stryker, and other prison officials would be the last ones to blow the whistle on an oversight commission neglecting its job.

Now, however, the prison inspectors were under scrutiny and forced to take action. After declaring their "deep regrets regarding the tragic occurrence that transpired at Holmesburg Prison," and claiming "unrest and riot are to be expected from time to time when dealing with desperate criminals in large numbers," the board stated its emphatic "opposition to cruelty and lack of humanity in controlling such outbreaks," and went on to officially bless the personnel changes made by the mayor's office. "Superintendent Davis, Warden Stryker, two captains, and all of the guards concerned with the unfortunate event," read the statement, "are relieved from duty."

It was while addressing the Citizens Committee for Criminal Justice Reform at the Palmer House in Chicago, on the subject of constructing houses of detention for untried prisoners in order to separate them from the convicted, that James V. Bennett, director of the Federal Bureau of Prisons, was asked to comment on the alarming prison catastrophe that had taken place in Philadelphia.

Closing the booklet containing his prepared remarks, Bennett reflected for a moment and then soberly said, "If the reports are accurate, it would appear a coolly calculated cruelty took place at a prison in the nation's third-largest city. By any stretch, it's a tremendous setback for those seeking a more scientific approach to prison management. Discipline is a key principle of penal operations," Bennett went on to say, "but what occurred in Philadelphia is an entirely useless demonstration of ineptitude, if not outright sadism. We must get the problem out into the light where we can see it, deal with it, and make the necessary changes. Reform will not come easy or quickly, but it must come."

Though Bennett tried to return to the subject at hand, the separation of the convicted from the untried in America's penal institutions, many attendees still preoccupied with the gruesome tragedy in Philadelphia continued to inquire as to how such a horrible thing could occur in a modern, sophisticated city.

"The young and the old, the sick and the well, and the innocent and the guilty, are often forgotten and neglected under the present system," said the federal prison director. "Sometimes barbarous incidents occur, maybe not as vile as took place at Holmesburg Prison last week, but they occur, and we are left to dwell on our humanity or the lack of it. I believe all of the deceased in Philadelphia were tried and convicted, but consider how much worse if an untried, and presumably innocent, detainee had been amongst the victims. And it could have easily happened," concluded Bennett in an attempt to return to his original point of his presentation.

"We need a better standard and understanding of punishment," he went on to say. "A better system must be found. This need not be soft, maudlin, or sentimental. It can be firm and bring to bear a discipline that is realistic, yet humane. Philadelphia should have the intelligence and scientific appreciation to accomplish this. Above all, however, it must have the direction of skilled, interested, and non-political personnel."

Though the head of the federal prison system, Bennett wasn't the only one in the penal community to criticize what had happened in Philadelphia. Meeting in New York City at the same moment was the American Prison Association, and the Holmesburg event was proving a particular embarrassment. Both academics and prison practitioners attending the annual conference were hard-pressed to understand what had occurred in the City of Brotherly Love. Shaken by the allegations of incompetence, if not outright torture orchestrated by penal overseers, plans for the construction of a "new Alcatraz-like super prison" in Pennsylvania were put on hold. By a voice vote of the conference delegates, the new facility to be known as Mount Gretna Prison was tabled. Conference officials informed the press they "frowned upon rewarding the Keystone State for allowing such a devastating display of inmate abuse." It was now likely, they suggested, that another state would be chosen for the expensive project.

Not far away, at another midtown hotel, Congressman Vito Lucibello, president of the International Labor Defense Committee, was telling delegates at their annual convention that the death of so many prisoners in Philadelphia was "nothing short of ghastly." He urged his members to "fight for nationwide prison reform and work to ensure that never again will defenseless prisoners be tortured and murdered in America."

⊷⊷⊷

Back in Pennsylvania, a group of state legislators was pushing for immediate penal reforms including the prompt removal of Warren Davis as superintendent of the Philadelphia Prison System. Led by William B. Pike, a state senator from Montgomery County, and member of the Ruth Commission's investigation into political corruption in Philadelphia, the lawmakers were frustrated that such a large loss of life could occur and business seemingly go on as usual. They couldn't understand how the head of the prison system could continue to function and remain on the public payroll. What's wrong with Philadelphia? They wanted to know.

"Any official in Mr. Davis's position," argued Senator Pike, "should at the very least be better informed than the superintendent apparently was of what was going on inside the walls of Holmesburg Prison."

Pike and his colleagues were so aggrieved by the disaster that they looked into Philadelphia's almost intractable corruption problem, including the part that impacted the criminal justice system and prisons, and made what they thought were prudent and appropriate recommendations. However, all of their policy and programmatic recommendations were rejected by a county grand jury designed to look into the very same problems. Now a major tragedy had occurred, and city leaders were proffering a line that smelled of chicanery, if not a complete cover-up. State lawmakers had come to agree with Lincoln Steffens, that Philadelphia was corrupt and quite content to remain that way. Hence, they were now calling for heads to roll, and Superintendent Davis was first on their list.

"The building was constructed in 1929 by Winthrop & Company," said David Sandler as he shuffled papers disclosing the results of his various research assignments. "Nobody seems to know its exact purpose, but news articles mention other construction at the time at Holmesburg. There was a major riot in '29. It came after another food strike by the inmates. Must have been a big deal, as it got front-page coverage in the *New York Times*. The headline said 600 inmates rioted over unfit food. I found another article that mentioned two new cellblocks, which were built later that year, making a total of ten inside the walls. Apparently, when the prison opened in 1896, there were only six cellblocks. Two more were added later, and then, in 1929, they built the last two along with the smaller cellblock—the one inmates now call Klondike."

As the coroner and his deputy listened to the office intern present his findings, both men tried to shake off the exhaustion from another long day of interviews at the prison. The late-night session at the coroner's City Hall office was necessary, however. Both men understood nothing could be overlooked; information was critical to their effort.

"Anything about the number of radiators they put in Klondike?" inquired Glass. It was obvious to him that the new punishment unit was constructed exactly for the purpose of putting an end to the recurring hassle of inmate protests over food.

"Nothing about the radiators," said Sandler. "And no mention of the building's purpose or size. I don't think the heating system was ever of interest to anyone. But I found one newspaper article from 1934 where a grand jury actually praised the use of Klondike by prison administrators for punishing rioters and malcontents."

Glass was pleased with the discovery, though Ferencz mused aloud, "Odd not one reporter or newspaper ever took note of a special building on prison grounds with a heating system five times the size of what would normally be needed."

"Not really," replied the coroner. "We rarely know what goes on behind those walls. And, quite frankly, I don't think the public wants to know. It's a world unto itself. Look how long they've probably been turning on the boiler, sweating men, torturing them, and only now are we finding out about it."

Ferencz did not disagree with his boss; he had investigated enough mysterious deaths at Holmesburg over the years to know the place had its own unique culture and medieval operating procedures. The coroner's office was often left holding the bag—a body bag—and forced to grapple with determining the cause of a decedent's sudden demise. Suicides were common, but Ferencz wasn't the only one in the office who thought many of Holmesburg's "accidental" deaths were actually homicides. But the former coroner had almost always taken the word of prison authorities. Some puzzles were more difficult to solve than others; the fact that there were now multiple bodies made it no easier.

"There's a lot more on Davis, however," said Sandler, eager to show the fruits of his labor. "He really has had some career. Didn't realize he was a hero during the Spanish-American War, a pretty good football player in his day, and he apparently did some really innovative things regarding traffic control and schooling for detectives in the police department."

As Sandler spoke of the prison superintendent's many accomplishments over the years—including his record as a cavalry officer, his pioneering work with police teletype and radio transmission, and his simple adage that "keeping prisoners occupied will allow them to earn a living when they step out of jail"—neither Glass nor Ferencz commented. Both men were familiar with Davis's well-documented career stretching from his military and athletic achievements to his highly publicized terms as police chief and head of the county prison system. As Sandler went on enumerating various aspects of Davis's public career, the coroner was increasingly preoccupied with finding a viable explanation for the superintendent's involvement in the Klondike tragedy.

Sandler said that Davis, according to news accounts, never mistreated prisoners—wasn't a "thumper," in the coroner's lexicon—and wasn't known for abusing those he arrested or had under his watch as a prison superintendent. Some considered him an enlightened reformer, a rarity in Philly law enforcement. For example, just two weeks prior to the food strike, according to Sandler, "Davis fired two prison guards who had punched and kicked an inmate who escaped from the prison farm in Northeast Philadelphia." Both guards had worked many years in the prison system, and their abrupt firing, in the coroner's mind, was significant. Reading from an *Inquirer* article, Sandler quoted Davis as saying, "It was one of those things we don't allow. Guards must not strike a prisoner except in self-defense. In this case, the two officers disobeyed orders and abused a prisoner."

Glass was unable to reconcile the superintendent who barred the pummeling of prisoners with the superintendent who allowed men to be roasted to death. What had caused such a dramatic shift in attitude and practice? Was it the number of men involved? Or the fact that the strike had garnered front-page coverage in the *New York Times*? It was a riddle he was desperate to solve.

❧

"What now?" exclaimed Glass when informed by his deputy the following day, "We've got a problem."

"The *Washington Star* has a page-one story today," said Ferencz, looking exasperated. "You're not gonna like it."

"Go ahead," said Glass. "I'm listening."

"It states the Holmesburg prisoners died of asphyxiation," said Ferencz. "The article says the eight men were victims of thermal death, and physicians for the coroner's office will present their findings in twenty-four-hours."

"Jesus Christ," barked Glass. "How the hell did they get that?"

"I don't know, but every other newspaper is now crying foul. Local reporters and editors for the *Inquirer, Bulletin, Record,* and *Daily News* are all in a fit we'd give out such information to an out-of-town paper before them."

"I didn't," said Glass. "Did you—"

"Absolutely not," replied Ferencz. "I told them a press conference was imminent, but nothing about the doctors' conclusions. And we can be sure Dr. Mattingly didn't do it."

"I knew the *Washington Post* had a reporter here," said Glass, "but I never ran into anyone from the *Star*. Who the hell are they?"

"They've had a reporter here almost from the beginning," said Ferencz. "It's that young guy with the odd manner and a wisp of hair on his chin. You must have seen him—he often wears a white suit and one of those ancient shirt collars from yesteryear. He looks like a Southern dandy. Very mannerly but intense; always asking questions. I'm sure you've seen him. He's been up here at the prison, down at City Hall, always talking to people, trying to get information . . . Like some others, he's quite taken by the story."

"Now that you describe him . . ."

"Strange little guy," replied Ferencz. "Sticks out in a crowd with his Southern accent and manner."

While Ferencz continued describing the young *Washington Star* reporter who had just presented the coroner's office with a serious credibility problem, the coroner recalled witnessing his intern having lunch with just such a fellow at Kelly's Restaurant. It had to be the same person. Glass's suspicions had been confirmed. He now wondered if Sandler had compromised the investigation. What else besides the autopsy results had he passed on?

Originally scheduled to be delivered to the press in the coroner's office, the unexpected interest and resulting tumult dictated a last-minute shift to hold the press conference in the much larger Mayor's Reception Room on the second floor of City Hall. It was agreed by all that the much-anticipated autopsy results of the Klondike cadavers would be a significant milestone in establishing just what—or who—killed the eight inmates.

Without any fanfare, Coroner Glass introduced Dr. Mattingly who, along with Dr. William Harvey, had performed the autopsies on the deceased Holmesburg prisoners. To the side stood Carl Ferencz and David Sandler. They were holding abbreviated one-page copies of the doctors' medical findings for distribution to members of the press.

"As we originally theorized," began Dr. Mattingly, "the men confined to the Holmesburg punishment unit died of heatstroke of the asphyctic type. Their deaths were directly due to their prolonged exposure to a large bank of steam radiators situated along one wall of the building. In laymen's terms," said the coroner's chief medical officer, "the prisoners' respiratory and circulatory systems, taxed to their limit in an effort to keep their bodies at a normal temperature, were overcome finally and no longer able to utilize oxygen. The upshot being the blood failed to secure oxygen and asphyxiation resulted."

Reporters scribbled notes frantically as Mattingly continued his presentation. "As you may know," said the youthful-looking, bespectacled physician, "when the body temperature reaches 108 or 110 degrees, the protein contents of the millions of cells in the body begin to coagulate. Normal chemical activities necessary for life start to bake. The result is initially congestion and, soon after, poisoning of the body by its own waste."

A medical school lecturer, the doctor noticed confusion on the faces of some reporters and took time to educate them as to what the human body is forced to endure when taxed by unusually high temperatures. "When cells can't take up oxygen and can't get rid of carbon dioxide," explained Dr. Mattingly, "the body's wastes, which are normally carried off through the blood and lungs, remain. The body then begins to poison itself. As the toxemia or poisoning increases, the victim can pass out or become delirious. This condition, as you can imagine, only worsens with a lack of water and ventilation. Moisture in the air decreases the resistance of the body to high temperatures. The body normally cools itself by sweating. But with no ventilation and too much moisture in the air, the sweat would not evaporate.

"How long the prisoners could stand excessive heat and lack of water would depend on the constitutions and physical condition of the men. It might be a short time; it might be a matter of hours. Plus, the breathing of steam would cause death by burning of the lungs—a death that I can assure you is quite painful. Intense heat turns the air into a fiery vapor that irritates the bronchioles, the small, pinpoint-sized tubes leading from the windpipe to the lungs. Spasm occurs in the muscles of the tubes, closing them, and shutting off the air.

"An individual forced to endure such a state would either slip into a coma or, if still conscious, become irrational, even hysterical. Throwing oneself about would not be unusual, as some prisoners evidently did in their cells, with resulting injuries."

While Mattingly presented his findings, Glass peered through the crowd and quickly spotted J. Henry Jones of the *Washington Star*. Like the other three dozen newsmen in the room, Jones rarely looked up. He busily wrote down every word coming out of the doctor's mouth, though the coroner suspected that the youthful-looking pressman in his distinctive off-white suit was already privy to the autopsy results. Young Sandler listening across the room was also fully engrossed in Mattingly's presentation, but when he caught the coroner's eye, he quickly looked away. A telltale sign, Glass believed, that the young man was the source of the *Star's* scoop on the inmates' cause of death. How else would a newspaper based hours away in the nation's capital discover what had been known to only a few people in his office? But how would Glass prove it, and how should he deal with his loose-lipped intern? They were questions he would continue to ponder. The nature of the relationship between the college student and the reporter proved to be yet another vexing distraction as he sought to steer his Holmesburg investigation through a dense thicket of legal, political, and social obstacles.

Mattingly, in the meantime, had begun fielding reporters' questions and was explaining—sometimes for a second and third time—how the lack of water and ventilation would cause "excessive sweating, thereby depleting the body of its salt content and adding to the trouble." He pointed out that "the high humidity of the prison cells, caused by lack of ventilation and excessive heat, would help raise the body temperature by preventing evaporation of perspiration from the men's bodies, just as high humidity in the outdoor atmosphere increases our discomfort by hampering this natural cooling system."

Glass was pleased as he listened to the doctor's thorough presentation. He believed the less he spoke at this important, quasi-scientific session, the better. He understood he had become something of a lightning rod in the city and was happy to step back and gain some much-needed support through the introduction of concrete medical evidence.

Reporters—most never interested in the subject of heatstroke—were now engrossed by the topic and appreciative of the detailed tutorial they were receiving. The coroner's chief physician was peppered with a host of questions. Mattingly, understanding the importance of the moment, was more than willing to explain just what had occurred behind Klondike's red brick walls. "Blood turns black as the oxygen is literally boiled out by the heat," said the doctor of the deadly process. "The sweat glands stop functioning, and the body of the individual may continue increasing in temperature for an hour or so after life has expired. The body temperature may go as high as 112 degrees. As you know, normal body temperature is 98.6 degrees. When it goes ten, twelve degrees above that, the brain starts to disintegrate, and death ensues. It causes death as surely and in much the same manner as choking a man until he ceases to breathe."

Mattingly explained, "In cases resulting from thermal death, human tissue becomes unusually hard and rigor mortis sets in much more rapidly than after other types of death. This is the reason," he argued, "that when the bodies were first discovered, they seemed to have been dead a considerable time, hours earlier than they probably did."

Seated behind his newspaper-strewn desk, Coroner Glass read with interest an article on how the Holmesburg story and the Klondike deaths were impacting prison operations around the country. Apparently, prison strikes regarding the quality or variety of food inmates were fed were not unique to Philadelphia. In fact, there were numerous instances of such culinary friction. Officials at Clinton Penitentiary in Dannemora, New York, for example, ignored an inmate's demand for different potatoes to be served in the chow hall, which resulted in a riot and the death of a prisoner. As one injured inmate told reporters, "We're told you must eat this for days, weeks, months, and years. At some point, you can't take it anymore and rebel."

At Auburn, another New York state institution, inmates demanding better food had their rations cut back substantially resulting in what was described as a "wild orgy of indiscipline" in which two were killed, dozens injured, and prosecutors called for the "riot organizers to receive the death penalty."

In Kansas, guards at Leavenworth Federal Penitentiary were forced to put down an inmate uprising over what newspapers called "Mexican rice being served day in and day out," and the administration's "resistance to providing ice for their glasses of water." The disturbance resulted in four inmates getting shot and one dying of his wounds.

And in Illinois, inmates at the state prison in Joliet rioted when rumors circulated that the meat they were being fed was of low quality and alleged to be "originally intended for animals in the Chicago zoo." The inmate revolt culminated in much destruction and the death of four prisoners.

The coroner had not yet finished the article when Miss Renwick walked in and informed him that J. Henry Jones of the *Washington Star* had arrived. When the reporter he had requested to see walked into his office, Glass was taken by the man's youth, slight stature, and distinctive manner of dress.

"I was just reading your article about Holmesburg's impact around the nation and the number of copycat food strikes it had spawned," said Glass, motioning to the reporter to take a seat. "Quite a piece of reporting. And all from a city you're just a visitor in. Impressive."

"Why thank you," replied Jones. "We at the *Star* try to be resourceful, and our editor insists we should always strive to do a thorough job. You know, go the extra mile on a story if you want to be the best."

"And so you do."

"Thank you."

"Is that what you did on your recent story regarding the autopsy results of the Holmesburg decedents?" asked the coroner, his demeanor changing drastically. "The one that came out prior to our official release of the autopsy results?"

Blood drained from the young reporter's face, and he grew more rigid. His visage registered that this would not be the friendly get-together he was hoping for, and he almost unconsciously slipped his notepad into his jacket pocket. Nor would this be the opportunity to obtain some additional information about the coroner's forthcoming special inquest.

When Jones did not reply, Glass inquired, "So, how did you manage to acquire information only doctors who did the autopsy and we in the coroner's office had knowledge of?"

"As I said," Jones replied, trying to hide his nervousness, "we at the *Star* can be resourceful when necessary."

"Too resourceful, if you ask me," said Glass, forcefully. "In fact, reporters much more experienced than you, and working at significantly larger papers, have asked why we would share such important information with a relatively minor out-of-town newspaper. How does Henry Jones of the *Star* acquire inside information that Sel Rossman of the *New York Times* and reporters at the *Record*, *Inquirer*, and *Bulletin* had been unable to get? When I tell them we didn't slip you anything, they don't believe me. And you know what, I wouldn't believe it either."

Jones remained silent and tried to conceal his unease.

"Care to tell me who it was?" the coroner soberly inquired.

Jones replied hesitantly, "Journalists are not required to divulge the names of their sources."

Glass leaned back in his chair and said, "So you say, but from my side of the fence I'm a little sketchy on that law. Besides, I believe I already know your source. And you may have served your own interests, and those of your editors, but you've done a great disservice to a young man who's just starting out in the world."

Jones tried to hide his concern, expressed ignorance, but his nervousness and flushed face revealed his true feelings. "I don't know what you mean," Jones replied. "Who are you referring to?"

"We're not country bumpkins up here, Mr. Jones," said the coroner. "I think you know as well as I."

The reporter was silent, searching for an appropriate response when he quickly gushed, "I can have my editor call you if you'd like . . ."

Glass smiled, stood up, and said, "That won't be necessary. We'll handle this ourselves. In the future, however, give some thought to those you use to acquire information and then discard. Not all share in the bounty that comes with a good story."

The young reporter tried to talk his way out of the uncomfortable situation, but the coroner was already escorting him out the door. Though the name of his source had gone unmentioned, Glass wondered if Jones cared that his confidential source of office information was in for a rough time. The prospect that the summer intern was headed for an official grilling, and would possibly lose his job, unsettled the coroner, but he could not afford critical information being leaked to newsmen.

Later that day as the coroner drove west from the prison and then north to the outer limits of the city on Roosevelt Boulevard, Glass pondered broaching issues such as professionalism, honesty, and office loyalty with David Sandler, but he realized the discussion would take some time and leave them both uncomfortable for their business at Philadelphia State Hospital. Glass was hesitant; he knew a frank discussion of Sandler's egregious act would most likely lead to his firing the young man. The prospect of such an action bothered him, for he liked the intern. Sandler was earnest, hardworking, and trustworthy—at least until he crossed paths with the equally young but conniving white-suited reporter from the *Washington Star*. The stakes were too high for Glass to give the office intern a second chance. With his blue ribbon inquest about to start, and the *Star* reporter anxiously anticipating it, the college student was a liability he couldn't afford. But, business first: the hospital visit.

Known by most area residents as Byberry, the sprawling multi-building institution may have had a worse reputation and more troubling history than Holmesburg Prison, if that was possible. Situated at the northern end of the city in a vast complex of scattered two-and three-story brick buildings straddling the boulevard, the overcrowded and underfunded mental asylum was home to several thousand of the city's most troubled souls.

From "feebleminded defectives" to the "congenitally mangled" and just plain insane, all were thrown into one large and stomach-turning repository. The campus even had a couple of units for the criminally insane—and that's where they were headed.

During interviews, numerous inmates and even a couple of guards had mentioned that some prisoners had been beaten up and steamed so bad they went crazy and eventually passed on to Byberry. Roberson, the colored City Hall custodian, had even supplied a name of one such unfortunate soul: Willie Anthony. Unable to break the cell door lock and turn down the radiator pressure as Roberson had, Anthony felt the full effect of Klondike's heat treatment for three days.

When they dragged Anthony out of Klondike, according to Roberson, he had been sweated to the point that he neither knew his name nor why he was in prison. He never quite recovered, became catatonic, and just rocked back in forth in his cell. "They done pulled him out of Holmesburg and dropped him off at Byberry," said Roberson. "No one's ever heard from him again so he may still be up there. Not sure it be worth the trip, but old Willie was one of those that got roasted."

When the coroner and Sanders met with Byberry's director, Glass was surprised to learn that Anthony wasn't in the more secure criminal section but in a regular housing unit. When the coroner asked why a Holmesburg prisoner would not be kept in one of the hospital's two buildings for the criminally insane, the director replied, "Come with me. You'll see for yourself."

As they left the administration building and walked to Building #6, Glass observed his intern carefully taking in the movement of doctors in white lab coats and nurses crisscrossing the expansive mental hospital campus. The young man was preparing for medical school; his matriculation at the University of Pittsburgh Medical School was to start in September. Being in such an environment seemed to pique his interest. But Glass knew the interiors of these buildings were some of the most depressing places on earth. He was curious how the young man would react to them.

On entering the building, they were met with the repugnant odor that came with such institutions for society's flotsam and jetsam. When told Anthony was currently in a day room with other patients, Glass prepared himself for the dark human menagerie he was about to see. Patients, some only partially clothed, wandered around in a stupor, talked to themselves, or sprawled on the tile floor, consumed by thoughts the coroner couldn't begin to fathom. When Willie Anthony was pointed out near a window, they saw the back of a colored man in a dirty white shirt, grimy shawl, and soiled pants rocking back and forth in a wooden chair, mumbling to himself.

As they approached the man, however, they realized he wasn't mumbling incoherently like the others, but singing. "The Lord has promised good to me,

His word my hope secures; He will my shield and portion be, as long as life endures," sang Anthony in a gravelly murmur while staring at the sky through the window. The dark-skinned, heavily whiskered, broad-nosed man with yellowish-brown eyes remained oblivious to his visitors.

"Mr. Anthony, my name is Heshel Glass. I'm the county coroner, and I'd like to talk to you about your time in Holmesburg."

The colored man continued to sing as if he had never been approached or asked a question. "Through many dangers, toils, and snares, I have already come. 'Tis grace hath brought me safe thus far, and grace will lead me home."

Glass and Sanders watched and listened as the man recited his poem, song, or prayer. For the coroner, there was the disappointing realization that this was another Holmesburg inmate who would be taking his story of prison abuse to the grave.

Though he tried a second time to get through to Anthony, the former Holmesburg inmate was unreachable.

"He's been like this for several years," said a hospital orderly overseeing the dayroom. "You may recognize that song he's singing. It's an old Christian hymn, 'Amazing Grace.' Heard we got Willie from Holmesburg Prison some years back. Don't know if he came into the prison this way or he went nuts there, but this is Willie now. His mind is gone; that song is all he says."

As Glass and Sandler watched the old man rock in place and chant, "I once was lost, but now am found; was blind, but now I see," the coroner couldn't help but wonder if the spiritual's lyrics were the last desperate words the former inmate gasped before the Klondike's radiators fried his brain.

Just as they were about to depart, the blue shawl around the patient's shoulders slipped off and fell to the floor. The coroner made no effort to retrieve the old, heavily stained shawl, but Sandler did. He then gently placed it on Anthony's shoulders. The incident was of no great importance, but the coroner continued to dwell on his intern's act of kindness as they walked to the parking lot.

As they drove south on Roosevelt Boulevard, Glass was undecided whether to return to the prison or just head back to City Hall. Before making up his mind he found himself asking, "What did you give Jones besides the autopsy report?"

"Who?"

"Judson Jones of the *Washington Star,*" said Glass authoritatively. "What did you give him?"

After a brief delay, Sandler replied, "I didn't give him anything."

"Oh, how I wish that were true. But neither you nor your reporter friend are very good liars."

"But I didn't give him anything," said Sandler, "I swear."

"Watch it, boy. Don't make matters worse than they already are."

They drove without speaking for a while. "Did he pay you," the coroner finally asked, "or offer you something in return for the report?"

"No, he didn't give me anything."

"Then why would you give him something of such importance? Newsmen at every broadsheet and tabloid in the area have complained. You've damaged the office's reputation and credibility."

"But I didn't—"

"Did that Jones fella promise you something? Does he have something on you?"

Sandler remained mute but shook his head, his face twisted in a look of disgust at the situation in which he found himself. Glass never pressed for an answer, but eventually he inquired, "September is just a couple of days off, don't your classes start soon?"

"I was leaning toward delaying my start," Sandler replied. "Classes at Pitt begin in a few days, and my father wants me to go. But I thought I'd wait till after the inquest. I'd like to see the thing through and be around for anything else that comes up like the grand jury investigation or a criminal trial. I could start a new term in January."

"I don't think you should wait," said Glass. "It's probably best you start now."

Sandler looked like he'd been thrown into a tub of ice water. Coroner Glass had given him an order to leave, and the sooner the better.

"I won't say anything to your father, and it's probably best you don't either," said Glass, matter-of-factly. "You're young, you made a serious mistake. But that's no excuse. You're smart enough to know what you were doing was wrong. Ferencz and I would have a hard time trusting you after this. Hopefully, you'll learn something from this incident."

The coroner was inclined to commend Sandler's contributions to the Holmesburg investigation, but he could not get the words out. This was not the right time. The coroner and college intern drove on to City Hall in silence.

Chapter 18

A Young Man's Loss

Nearly a full page in length, the article was capped off with a dark, mesmerizing sketch of a skeletal head rising out of smoke and ashes spelling the word "Barbarism" above a walled-prison facility. The prominent *New York Times* article was entitled, "Prison Deaths Stir Storm of Protest." Selwyn Rossman's commentary in the important Sunday "Opinion" section of the paper began with the words, "The steaming to death of eight convicts in the Philadelphia county prison this week as an aftermath of a hunger strike not only added another chapter to a long story of major and minor riots at the Holmesburg institution but centered attention anew upon the set-up of the Pennsylvania prison system."

Recounting the institution's troubled history—the periodic riots, the familiar I-told-you-so attitude of prison reformers, and comparisons to the Black Hole of Calcutta—left investigators in a maze of cover-up stories, contradictions, and official denials.

As the national paper of record, Rossman's embarrassing piece illuminated the long-standing tension between "mollycoddlers" and "strict disciplinarians." Moreover, those in charge of penal operations, and the fickle elected city officials they answered to, showed little interest in the subject. Keeping costs down and providing jobs to loyal party workers appeared to be their only focus.

Glass was both stunned and pleased by the *Times* article. He knew the mayor would be furious, but the spotlight shed on the Klondike murders and Philadelphia's historically troubled prison system would hopefully provide further investigatory protection and safeguard his intention of instituting a blue ribbon inquest. All too familiar with Clarke's bullying, dictatorial ways, Glass desired that the scathing editorials and national focus would act like a muzzle on a vicious dog.

Mayor Clarke had been uncommonly quiet, but Glass worried it was the proverbial quiet before the storm. The mayor controlled enough levers of power to interfere with if not totally disrupt any attempt at a reasonable and well-thought examination on the Holmesburg deaths. There was considerably more talk, however, of the mayor undermining the coroner's bid for reelection.

Just as Glass was finishing a series of telephone conversations with inquisitive reporters in his office, Miss Renwick walked in dragging a heavy canvas United States postal bag. To the coroner's alarm, she struggled to lift and spill much of the bag's contents on his already cluttered, paper-strewn desk.

"What the hell is this?" Glass demanded.

"Your fan club," replied Miss Renwick as she walked out the door. "There's another bag as well."

Confused by the scores of letters addressed to the "Coroner of Philadelphia" now littering his desk, Glass tried to push them aside when he realized they had originated from cities and towns across America. He pulled out one official-looking envelope from the pile with the postmark "US Attorney's Office of the Western District of Louisiana." Wondering if it was official business, Glass opened it only to discover the federal prosecutor was lauding him for his Klondike investigation. "The Holmesburg murder saga," wrote the government official, "out-rivals anything that was ever done in the days of the Spanish Inquisition. Every officer of the prison, trusty and guard, who had anything to do with it, ought to be tried, convicted, and executed if the act was willfully or maliciously done."

Glass grabbed another piece of mail from Amarillo, Texas. "Thousands of people in the Panhandle of Texas," wrote the sender, "can't imagine anything so uncivilized. Here's hoping the entire prison staff will be tried and get prison sentences in Holmesburg."

Another letter, from Atlanta, Georgia, was from a widow who voiced her concern about Philadelphia's ability to parcel out justice. "The ones responsible are the worst murderers, but will they pay?" she asked. "Don't let them mar your wonderful, straightforward record. Thank you for your efforts to do the right thing for the families of the deceased."

As he randomly thumbed through the pile of letters, Glass was awed by the outpouring of interest. Spokane, Washington; Detroit, Michigan; Topeka,

Kansas; Independence, Missouri; Burlington, Vermont; and dozens of other cities, big and small, were represented in scores of personal missives that now covered his desk. He couldn't quite grasp the distance news of the Holmesburg story had traveled or the depth of its emotional appeal.

Just then, his secretary walked in lugging the second canvas bag. "Gotta give you credit," commented Miss Renwick, who had not lost the irony of the moment. "Who else could have managed to become a national hero while working so diligently to join the nation's unemployed?"

Glass was mystified by his newfound celebrity status. Though generally pleasing, he was on-guard not to let all the ink go to his head. To further ensure he did not develop an ego and remained properly grounded were not only the legal and electoral challenges that confronted him but also real threats to his life and property. In fact, shortly thereafter, Miss Renwick entered his office again with a more ominous message. Glass's neighbor had just called the office to relay that a brick or rock had been thrown through the coroner's front window. Shards of glass now littered the pavement and police had just arrived. The neighbor said she was afraid they'd kick the door down in order to check the premises. Glass left immediately to examine the extent of the damage. As he quickly descended the six flights of City Hall stairs to a waiting automobile, he couldn't get over how he'd become something of a heroic figure in cities and towns across America and a pariah in his own backyard.

When he arrived at his home on Morris Street, there were a number of people milling about, including a few policemen. They escorted the coroner into his house, surveyed the damage, and picked up a brick that had a message tied to it with string. Glass quickly read the three-word message, "No Holmesburg Inquest."

An officer grabbed the note from the coroner and read it. He smiled. Another officer then read it and asked, "Have you received any threats? Have you noticed any other suspicious activity lately? Any idea who would do this?"

Glass remained silent and just shook his head.

"I know you're involved in a big case," said Officer O'Bannon, "so we'll file this and try to keep a watch on your place. I'd be surprised if this was the end of it, however."

The coroner thanked the policeman, righted a fallen table light, and picked up pieces of glass as the officers departed. It was then that he noticed the broken picture frame and damaged photograph lying beside a table. It was a photo of him and his wife shortly after they were married in 1917. Holding the broken frame and creased photograph, Glass sat on a chair and wondered if the photo could be repaired. He didn't often think of Helen and those relatively few months of marriage. The memories too painful to ponder, he'd immediately jettison the images of long ago and force himself to think of something less depressing. But with photo in hand and its repair questionable, he began to dwell on that deadly season that took his wife and the lives of 20,000 other Philadelphians.

Ever since America entered the war in the spring of '17, Glass felt the urge to fight the Hun, defend democracy, and join his friends in the great adventure taking place on the other side of the Atlantic. But competing with his desire to enlist in the military was his attraction to a beguiling neighborhood girl. Though he displayed little interest initially, over time, Helen would become more alluring; and as his interest grew, she began showing up at his basketball games. Their mutual attraction intensified, and once they started dating there was talk of marriage, but the conversation was always cut short. Helen wouldn't consider the subject until Heshel committed to remaining in America. She insisted he forgo his desire to take part in the Great War and restrict his appetite for manly challenges to local athletic arenas. Like other Americans, Helen knew of the thousands of soldiers dying in bloody trenches in France and Belgium and had no interest in losing a husband to the never-ending human carnage occurring in distant lands.

Though Glass would never regret his marriage to Helen, the decision to skip the military and the chance to display bravery on the battlefield would often nag at him. No enlistee knew for sure how he would respond to trench warfare, mustard gas, and endless bombardment, but the lost opportunity often made Heshel feel inferior around those who answered the call. It was the feeling of inferiority—or at least a lost opportunity—that would ultimately result in the tragic death of his wife and a lifetime of guilt and regret.

In mid-September 1918, Philadelphia began witnessing the first deaths from the influenza outbreak that had arisen in Europe and various locales across America. The few cases and even fewer deaths drew little notice, though some prescient doctors feared a coming deluge of sickness and death. They argued for greater preparatory measures. Philadelphia's public health director, however, would accept none of it and proclaimed all was well. There was no reason for alarm, he repeatedly argued. Within weeks, in fact, just days, cases mounted quickly, and influenza deaths were spiking well into the hundreds. Military bases and the nearby Philadelphia Naval Yard were widely viewed as vectors of contraction and contagion, but the flu had already invaded the city's heavily populated neighborhoods.

By mid-October, there were so many dead, and so few city employees and health workers to collect the deceased from row house neighborhoods throughout the city, that a call went out for volunteers. Able-bodied men were encouraged to step forward, collect the bodies, and bury them in mass grave sites. Police, soldiers, and others were recruited for the noxious sanitary campaign; even young seminarians were conscripted by their monsignor to help dispose of the cadavers.

Having walked away from the chance to demonstrate his bravery on the battlefield, Glass felt obliged to participate in the battle against an even more insidious foreign invader, influenza. His young wife cautioned him in the dangers of entering homes filled with germs, sickness, and death, but Glass couldn't be talked out of it. "The sooner we burn or bury the dead," he boldly told her, "the sooner we rid our streets and neighborhoods of this deadly scourge."

Leaving his printing job at noon, he'd work well into the evening with other volunteers wearing handkerchiefs, face masks, and work gloves, taking out the dead from flu-ravaged homes throughout the city. Occasionally they'd do additional mercy missions and convey the sick with raging fevers to already overburdened hospitals and clinics. Not surprisingly, many of those handling the dead and entering flu-ridden homes contracted the disease. Heshel Glass was one of them.

Waking up one morning feeling exceptionally tired, he attributed the ill sensation to the long hours and strain of lifting literal dead weight day after day. He went to work as normal that morning, and then to the many depressing sanitation assignments later that day. By the time he returned home he had the chills, an escalating fever, and the sickening realization he was now one of the pandemic's victims. Helen nursed him as best she could; she made him eat soup and kept him warm, but there was little else that could be done. There was no vaccine, antibiotic, or effective treatment to combat the ever-mutating strains of the disease.

For three days, Glass shivered in bed and fought the bug that was killing millions around the world. His constitution, strong until now, he was able to endure a high fever, severe aches and pains, and periodic bouts of diarrhea. By the morning of the fourth day, his temperature returned to normal, and he was seemingly on the road to recovery when his wife began complaining of headaches and chills. By noon, she was sharing the bed with her husband; by late afternoon, she had grown pale and feverish.

As history would record, the influenza pandemic of 1918 would prove particularly lethal and be characterized by some unusual traits, such as its greatest impact on those in their twenties and thirties. Normally, the young and old were most likely to fall victim to disease, but the influenza strains of 1918 appeared to be targeting society's heartiest members.

Now administering to his wife, and her condition worsening, Heshel took her to an overburdened South Philadelphia hospital where she languished on a gurney in a crowded corridor with other influenza patients. Many died within hours of their arrival, the disease so lethal an individual could acquire symptoms before noon and be dead by six. Heshel stayed by her side, encouraged her to rally as he had done, and fought the overwhelming dread that came with knowing he had brought the deadly germ into their home. As she grew wan and more ghostlike in appearance, she was occasionally delusional and other times non-communicative. Heshel feared the worst. He applied cool compresses to her forehead, wiped a pasty mucous from her nose and lips, and encouraged her to drink liquids and eat fruit the hospital provided. And like many others accompanying the sick, he pleaded with doctors to do something, anything. And all the time he knew it was he, and he alone, who had caused her to arrive at death's door.

As he held her hand, Helen took her last breath only minutes after telling her husband, "I'm sorry, Heshel. Please take care of yourself."

Glass would bury his wife of just fourteen months at Har Nebo Cemetery in Northeast Philadelphia. There would be little comfort that similar services were occurring in other sections of the Jewish cemetery that morning. Over the course of just a few months, influenza had wreaked havoc around the world. Philadelphia would be hit particularly hard, with some families losing several members. Heshel Glass would physically survive his bout with the flu and go on to compete in sports at a high level, but he would never be quite the same. Friends and colleagues noticed the change. His young wife's death would leave a permanent mark on his soul, an invisible scar that comes from guilt, sadness, and resignation.

Chapter 19

Inquest Preparations

The reactions of newsmen ran from chagrin to rage when they learned a film crew shooting footage inside Holmesburg had been detained and their cameras and film equipment confiscated by the police. Allowed by Secretary Enteen and his state investigators to film the interior and exterior of Klondike, the exercise had not been given the okay by the district attorney's office. Assistant District Attorney Doyle had been keeping newsmen on a short leash and had granted reporters and photographers access on just two occasions, and for a very brief period of time. The hush-hush attitude of prosecutors rankled newsmen and reminded them of similar efforts by the mayor and police to embargo access and shift blame for the tragedy onto the victims themselves.

Learning that the state welfare secretary had allowed a film crew to enter the walls of the facility caught Doyle by surprise, and he'd acted quickly. Cameras and audio equipment worth $18,000 were confiscated and held for hours while lawyers negotiated with authorities for their release. News agencies demanded, then pleaded for their equipment as the Davis Cup competition was being held at nearby Germantown Cricket Club, and it was imperative the international tennis event be recorded for sports fans throughout the country.

Consumed by the Klondike deaths after he and his boss, District Attorney Campbell, initially showed little interest in the mass murder, Doyle wasn't about to release the cameramen's gear until they turned over the 665 feet of film they had taken inside Holmesburg's walls. The standoff resulted in an appearance before Common Pleas Judge Curtis Fleetwood, who ordered the district attorney's office to return the audio and film equipment to its rightful owner. However, he would retain ownership of the Klondike film footage until he decided who deserved possession of it.

Coroner Glass did not involve himself in the debate. Though he could have easily enumerated the many news articles that either got facts wrong or highly exaggerated aspects of the Klondike story, the press was generally more reliable than what was coming out of the mouths of police and prison officials, not to mention top administrators in City Hall. He had no doubt that if it had not been for the many newsmen camped outside Holmesburg's immense front doors the day the inmates' bodies had been discovered, he never would have been able to conduct his investigation. Their interest, their focus on the gory details and who took part in the deadly crime was invaluable in a city that too often shoved criminal acts under the rug.

If the district attorney's office wanted to continue to restrict newsmen's and photographers' access to Klondike, that was their choice—Glass had other more important issues of concern.

Arriving back at the state capitol with a faint sunburn after abruptly ending his tour of Central America, Governor Everton met with his welfare secretary concerning the Holmesburg matter. He then held a brief press conference outside his office.

"The manner in which the prisoners in Philadelphia met their death is the most horrible thing I have heard of," said the governor, underscoring the seriousness of the issue. "It is worse than the torture chambers of the Middle Ages. If what I hear is correct, the Klondike punishment unit was built as exactly that, a torture chamber where live steam could be injected into the cells. What happened there could not have been an accident, but directly due to inhuman degenerates or sadists. I shall personally visit the institution shortly, and I also propose to see to it that there is no repetition of this most awful tragedy in Pennsylvania.

"And yes, I am fully aware Holmesburg Prison is a Philadelphia County institution. However, the state has the right to inspect it. Whether that right carries any other jurisdiction I am not now prepared to say. But regardless of legal technicalities, as governor of this Commonwealth, I am determined to make impossible a recurrence of such a shame on the name of the state and city.

"Consistent with that, I have communicated with both Coroner Heshel Glass of Philadelphia and Phillip Enteen, state secretary of welfare, to report to my office at the capitol at three o'clock tomorrow afternoon."

It was while Coroner Glass was meeting with the governor in Harrisburg that his deputy, Carl Ferencz, was notified Mayor Clarke wanted to see him.

The messenger, an undercover police officer, informed Ferencz of the time and location of the meeting. Since Mayor Clarke's midnight ambush just a couple of days earlier, Ferencz had tried to jettison the prospect that the mayor would be requesting something of him.

He could not deny there were occasions when flights of fancy had him sitting in the coroner's rich leather chair, making key office decisions, and frequenting high-level corporate and municipal meetings alongside the region's major players. Invariably, however, cracks in that attractive scenario would arise. Ferencz would begin to feel guilty about stabbing his boss in the back and sabotaging the most important investigation of his career. The power, influence, and recognition he'd receive as coroner excited him, but the thought of becoming a willing cog in an ethically challenged if not totally corrupt administration nauseated him. Abandoning what few principles he had left was disheartening.

Maybe the deciding factor had come from his wife, Andrea. That morning on the way out the door, his wife suggested that when the pressure and turmoil of the investigation and inquest were completed, he'd invite Coroner Glass over for a relaxing Hungarian dinner she'd prepare at their home. "I'll cook a grand meal," his wife said, "so we can celebrate the successful end of your prison investigation." He had not told her about his late-night travels with the mayor. Nor the possibility of his advancement and their new economic fortunes. He wondered how Andrea would react if he agreed to become one of the mayor's legion of subordinate yes-men? And even if she did support his decision, would she still respect him?

Those questions and his own doubts prompted Ferencz to call his political mentor, Felix Heisler, and inform him he had decided to remain the deputy coroner; he would not be taking advantage of the mayor's offer. "Please tell Mayor Clarke," said Ferencz, "I appreciate him thinking of me, but I am content where I am."

"But, Carl, you may never get an opportunity like this again. This is your chance, please don't blow it."

"Listen, Mr. Heisler, I want to thank you for your support now and in the past," Ferencz replied, "but I don't think I could do what Clarke is going to ask of me."

"But he hasn't asked you for anything yet," said Heisler.

"You know he will. And I'm afraid I'd do what he asked. I don't want to live that way. Please inform him I won't be meeting with him." Ferencz then hung up the phone, took a deep breath, and tried not to think of the opportunity he just threw away.

On his return from meeting with the governor in the state capital, Glass was approached by his deputy. "They want some names," said Ferencz. "They're anxious for news. Reporters keep asking when you're going to select people for the jury."

"I know," replied Glass wearily. "I keep putting it off. Every time I begin choosing a person or two, I start doubting myself."

"It's gotta be done, Hesh. The jurors need to know. They need to plan for the inquest."

"Yeah, I know," said the coroner. "I'm going to do it."

Ever since the coroner shocked the Philadelphia criminal justice community—not to mention the city's political establishment—by threatening to initiate a coroner's inquest to investigate the Holmesburg deaths, news agencies as well as citizens were fixated on the potential impact of the unusual legal procedure. It was just another curious act—a high-stakes courtroom drama—in what was being viewed as one of the nation's most chilling murder mysteries. Challenging the mayor and legal tradition with an independent inquiry, then upping the ante by allowing the voting public to suggest jurors for the blue ribbon panel added further interest to the process.

Newspapers were all too willing to cover this unexpected aspect of an already riveting story. In just forty-eight hours, hundreds of letters, postcards, and phone calls poured into the coroner's office. The cast of prospective characters ran the gamut from newly retired members of the Philadelphia Athletics and prominent local businessmen to heads of law schools and retired military personnel. With the scheduled special inquest just a few short days away, it was now time for Coroner Glass to act.

His first call was to Gilbert Hendricks, owner of the Bromley Knitting Mill in Kensington. In addition to being a successful businessman and resident of the exclusive Alden Park Manor in Germantown, Hendricks was also a well-regarded civic leader who took on numerous assignments with various religious and educational groups in the city. His role as vice-chairman of the Board of Education was one of the more notable. Though not a personal friend or political ally of Heshel Glass, and fully aware of the controversy now enveloping the coroner's office, he didn't hesitate to accept the call when his secretary announced the city coroner was on the line.

"Hello, Hesh, what can I do for you this morning?"

"Mr. Hendricks, I need you to do me a favor," said the coroner without mincing words. "I'd like you to chair the panel I'm setting up to investigate the Holmesburg matter."

After a short pause, Hendricks replied, "I don't know. I don't think I want to get involved in something like that."

"I know exactly how you feel. I'm not happy about it myself. But we have to do the right thing here. The city has to deal with this—"

"Hesh, I've never even served on a jury. I wouldn't know what to do, especially something of this magnitude. Hell, it's being written about daily in the *New York Times* and most other papers across the country. One of my customers in San Francisco even quizzed me about it yesterday, even though I knew little more than he did."

"I know," said Glass. "That's why I need your help. I need someone of impeccable credentials and sound character to guide this—"

"Don't sweet talk me," interrupted Hendricks. "I'm too old for that. And if you don't know already, I try not to get involved with things I know little about. Pardon my bluntness, but this appears to be a no-win situation. Even with the little I know about this tragedy, doing the right thing could cause problems. For example, taking a position on an investigative panel won't endear me with the mayor's office."

"I know I'm asking a lot, Mr. Hendricks, but eight men were found dead up at Holmesburg last week, and the parents, wives, and children of those men are looking to me and my office for justice. They have nowhere else to turn. You know what's happening. You're smart enough to recognize that the city's criminal justice system has closed ranks and shut down any proper investigation. The whole thing stinks, and if I don't do it, well . . ." After a short pause, the coroner continued. "I'm selecting people for the jury now. They're all going to be good people. People you'd feel comfortable with."

"Why me?" Hendricks asked. "You've never reached out to me before. We've never really spent time on any political or municipal projects before. There are other good men to choose from."

"Philadelphia is under a microscope. Never before has our . . . our style of governing been exposed as it is now. We both know how things work, how things get done in this town. But now the whole world is watching. Eight people lost their lives in a human bake-oven, a prison crematorium. Do you really believe we can do business as usual?"

"I don't know, Hesh," said Hendricks, his voice disclosing his reticence. "This is outside my experience. I don't know anything about prisons, and truth be told, I'm not anxious to learn."

"I understand," replied the coroner. "But you don't need a PhD in penology. Common sense will do."

"And the mayor? He's likely to come down on me like a ton of bricks."

"You've seen his reaction since the governor lectured him and the newspapers revealed his handiwork. I'm hoping he's been properly sensitized and his shenanigans are at an end."

"That doesn't mean he won't take me aside and create some mischief for my business or the groups I'm involved with. Do I need to make an enemy out of him?"

"With all due respect, Mr. Hendricks, you do a lot for this city. I realize your commitment and contributions. But I'd argue this town has never needed you more. Philadelphia is being tested. People are watching. I'd hate for us to fail."

"Let me think about it, Hesh. I'll get back to you shortly."

By the time Hendricks got back to Glass later that afternoon, the coroner had received commitments from five individuals who represented a cross-section of Philadelphia citizenry. The Rev. John Billington, a Methodist minister at St. Stephen's Church, an active and growing congregation on Germantown Avenue. Paul Dedman, a Fairmount resident and former chief financial officer of the Philadelphia Rapid Transit Company who was known for his civic work. Miss Anna Giovanni of South Philadelphia, a Democratic member of the General Assembly and president of the Women's Democratic Luncheon Club. Miss Crystal Reed Walker, a Chestnut Hill socialite, member of the Philadelphia Charter Commission, and coordinator of the city's annual Christmas fundraiser for children. And Henry Perkins, a Fox Chase resident and Frankford hardware store owner who was active with neighborhood youth organizations.

Not every call and request for participation by the coroner had proven successful—several people expressed their fear of such an assignment and refused—but with Gilbert Hendricks's acceptance as jury foreman, Heshel Glass had his six-member blue ribbon panel. The jurors, all of whom voiced some level of trepidation, would receive a dollar a day for their services.

⊷◈⊶

Speculated upon for days on the front pages of various newspapers, the "human guinea pig experiment" inside Holmesburg's now-infamous Klondike punishment unit finally commenced shortly after four P.M. on Monday, August 29. As the much-anticipated event was suggested by Secretary of State Enteen and coordinated by state agencies, an exception was made for the media. Radio and print journalists were allowed to observe the proceedings from the small grass plot between D and E Blocks, the same patch of land that just days earlier was littered with eight lifeless bodies and an equal number of physically and mentally scarred survivors.

Attired in just slacks and sneakers, five bare-chested representatives of the Bureau of Industrial Hygiene, the State Department of Health, Carnegie-Mellon University, and the city's Department of Health entered the much-written-about building. They would take with them an array of scientific monitoring instruments including thermometers, barometers, wind detectors, pressure gauges, and respiratory devices. All the instruments were designed to discern and document atmospheric conditions inside the cellblock.

From the very first, Enteen took umbrage with the scientists being referred to as "test animals" and "human guinea pigs." He fired back that "such an outrage as occurred inside Holmesburg demands a thorough investigation," and that "determining what exactly the conditions were inside that building when the men succumbed" should be a crucial part of the investigation. As to any threat of a nasty reoccurrence, Enteen assured citizens, "each engineer will be given a rigid physical examination that would include blood pressure and heart rate before going in and during their time in the cells." He also made mention that "outside the wall, temperatures had cooled a bit in recent days." The volunteer test subjects would also take with them 1,500 salt tablets to ward off the effects of heat prostration, and professional state engineers would closely monitor the level of heat pumped into the building's seven radiators. Moreover, he would note, "there will only be five men taking part in the test, and they will be in the structure for hours, not days."

In reply, newsmen mentioned in their articles that conditions would still be eerily similar to those of the deadly weekend with windows and air vents shuttered, little or no water provided, and depending on radiator pressure, the volunteer engineers would be forced to endure potentially unbearable heat.

After just one hour, the temperature inside the cellblock had risen to 97 degrees.

At about nine-thirty—after five hours in the cellblock—banging and shouting could be heard from inside the cell. When outside scientists entered the cellblock to see what was wrong, one subject looking dehydrated and nauseated weakly pleaded, "I've had enough. Get me out of here." The others expressed their intent to continue but requested additional water. They said it was their goal to withstand the oppressive heat and discomfort until at least midnight. Temperatures had reportedly reached 112 degrees and were continuing to climb.

When asked questions about his confinement, the heavily sweating, pale-faced chemical engineer who had exited Klondike opened his mouth but could barely be heard. "Could I have some more water, please," he whispered. Unsteady, he was given a chair to sit on but was eventually encouraged to lie down on the grass until he regained his strength. To the dismay of reporters, Secretary Enteen suddenly intervened, stating the scientist was in no condition to take questions, and comments of the participants would come after the scientific data was collected and analyzed. Little more than an hour later, doctors making periodic visits to check on the men advised that another engineer whose vital signs exhibited a noticeable decline should be removed from the study for his own protection.

The following day, newspapers would describe the unusual "super-charged sauna," "fireless cooker," and "hotbox" study for their readers. Under the headline "Officials Baking in Scientific Re-creation of Holmesburg Roasting," The *Philadelphia Record*, told of "sweat pouring down the backs of dazed, throat-parched participants," and in "Five Men Sizzle In Eight Hour Test of Prison Oven," the *Philadelphia Inquirer* described a "hellish experiment" where "heat rolled out in waves, and steam saturated the fetid air of semi-dark cells where men had been roasted to death just days earlier."

Though more prudent observers considered the scientific re-creation an ill-advised sideshow, it confirmed what most had already thought: the treatment of prisoners locked in a furnace-like tomb between August 19 and August 22 was as unconscionable an act as had ever been perpetrated on American soil. Secretary Enteen may have had the professional training and poise to refrain from uttering controversial remarks at the time, but his boss—the highest-elected official in the state—had no such intention. Just a day later, Governor Everton would visit Holmesburg Prison. It would prove a heart-searing experience.

As he exited the prison through Holmesburg's huge wooden and iron doors with Coroner Glass, Secretary Enteen, Superintendent Davis, and several other elected and appointed officials, Governor Everton appeared pale and shaken.

Overwhelmed would not be too strong a characterization. Perspiring and requesting a glass of water, the governor walked up to a quickly improvised lectern, and after taking a sip of water and a deep breath he stated, "First, let me say it is imperative that steps be taken to see that there is no recurrence of anything like this horror in Pennsylvania ever again. Secondly, those responsible for the actual cooking to death of eight men and the torturing of eight others must be punished."

Wiping his brow with a handkerchief and looking over a crowd consisting of both news reporters and neighborhood residents, the governor recounted that he had first heard of the Holmesburg Prison incident while on a vacation tour of Central America with his wife. He admitted to being dubious about certain claims made by his secretary of welfare concerning the affair. "Regardless," he said, "I thought it imperative I get back to the Commonwealth and see how I could be of assistance."

Taking a couple of seconds to organize his thoughts, Governor Everton started again, saying, "You know, we Americans are apt to exaggerate, but in this case, after having gone through the matter and now visiting the actual site, I found the press has, if anything, understated the horror of the deaths of the eight men.

"I have heard references to the barbarity of the Black Hole of Calcutta, but those who died suffocated more quickly, while those at Holmesburg were cooked alive slowly, and over many hours. In some cases, the torture went on for days. The bruises on the men's bodies, I am informed by the coroner's physician, were due to their delirium as they rushed about in a mad frenzy in search for oxygen, and in a desperate effort to escape the oppressive heat."

After a slight shake of his head in wonderment, the governor went on to say, "I just returned from Guatemala, Nicaragua, and Panama. Countries that are not nearly as fortunate as ours in regard to natural resources, scientific advancement, and public education. And yet, to know that with all these advantages and accomplishments something like this abomination could happen here, in America, in Philadelphia, is just unbelievable. Truly appalling.

"This looks to me like the work of one, two, three, or four very cruel sadists, and not part of the general prison routine. If we do find the inhuman degenerates who did this, no punishment is bad enough for them. Let me state clearly, I do not believe these deaths could have been accidental. I've been told live steam can be shot into the cells through the toilets simply by turning off the water valves and turning on the steam valve. Superintendent Davis has testified very feelingly to me that he knew nothing about the heat. Whether that is true or not should be established at the coroner's inquest."

As photographers angled for better shots and reporters began firing questions at the Commonwealth's highest elected official, Everton remained fixated on the deadly landscape he had just toured. "What I particularly criticize about the Klondike punishment unit," added the governor responding to a question, "is that sixteen desperate men, three to a cell, were practically hermetically sealed in the building for hours on end. In fact, some for several days. The cruelty of such an act is astounding."

In reply to a reporter's question about the accuracy of the information he was receiving, the governor said he was being educated on the matter by numerous sources. He pulled an envelope from his jacket pocket. "This is from a former Holmesburg prisoner," said the governor, opening a hand-written letter. "Like the coroner and other officials investigating these murders, I, too, have received mail from average citizens as well as former prisoners. This one begins, 'May I inform you of some of the guards who have the reputation of being killers and who, I personally know, brag of their power to do what they want. My knowledge comes of having served several years at Holmesburg and hearing them talk and seeing the result of their handiwork.'

"The writer includes the names of a half-dozen or more guards," said the governor, "but it would be inappropriate for me to release them here. I have shared them with the coroner and district attorney. The writer goes on to state, 'These men in 1933 delighted in blackjacking defenseless prisoners who were then put into punishment cells and given a sweating. Most ended up either in the prison hospital or Byberry.'"

When pressed for his prescription, the governor would go on to admit that Holmesburg was a county institution and not a state penal facility, but he insisted the state had the right to inspect county institutions and make recommendations. "And if they refuse to follow our heed," said the governor, "we can cut out their appropriations. In the case of Holmesburg, however, there is no state money involved."

"But let me be clear," the governor added, "what happened here a week ago is not only abominable morally but also criminal. I am asking the attorney general to study existing legislation to find out just what the state powers are, for my inclination is to take over absolute control of Holmesburg."

The governor's statement caused a ripple of applause and favorable comment throughout the crowd. Holding up his hand to silence the assembly, the governor enumerated a series of initiatives the state planned on taking immediately, including, "The state police will be making weekly inspections of the 60 county prisons and 500 local lock-ups in the commonwealth; they will also take over operations of Holmesburg if Coroner Glass thinks it appropriate; and I will have legislation introduced that will put teeth in the state's ability to have greater oversight of county jails in the Commonwealth."

When asked if he had faith in Philadelphia's ethically challenged political leaders and much-criticized criminal justice system to get to the bottom of the Holmesburg tragedy and prosecute those guilty of such a horror, the governor replied, "Normally, I'd be somewhat dubious, but I get the sense city leaders recognize the importance of resolving this matter as quickly and judiciously as possible. The district attorney's office and the coroner's office have pledged to do the right thing. I take them at their word. But be assured, I will monitor the coroner's inquest closely. If he should be in need of anything from my office, all he need do is ask."

While most Philadelphia broadsheets and tabloids were having a field day with the Klondike story—and anticipating additional storylines with the commencement of the coroner's "Blue Ribbon Inquest"—there were a few writers and papers attempting to restrain their journalistic juices. Whether they were allies of the mayor or sympathetic to the daily challenges of prison guards and administrators, some columnists and editorial writers tried to explain the actions of those who earned their living working behind prison walls. "The torture killings at Holmesburg have lifted the lid from a situation citizens must consider," wrote one *Philadelphia Bulletin* columnist. "Somebody was to blame. When we have found and hounded the responsible officials, the public will probably heave a sigh of satisfaction, and relax with a feeling of, 'Well, that's settled.' But will it be?"

The writer went on to ask, "What makes a guard cruel?" He suggested it was fear. "They are cruel when they are frightened; when they feel themselves inadequate to deal with their tough charges; when they have a job to do that they don't know how to do or are put in a position where their lives are in jeopardy. Panic may then enter the equation, and then their worst natures come to the surface and they resort to cruelty.

"Let's face it," the editorial went on to state, "most prison officials, high and low, and guards are appointed for political reasons and because they are useful to some politician. It is not an easy job to handle criminals, the worst elements of society. Even proper training can't prepare for all of the violence and degradation with which one will be forced to contend.

"The public is horrified and rightly so by the cruel deaths of the eight convicts and the tortured sufferings of the others. But it is very likely no one is really more distressed and haunted by nightmares, the suffering, than the very men who are responsible for turning on the steam. I can find it in my heart to be sorry, not only for the victims but for their torturers. They are the victims of a system that has given them a different and dangerous job."

⥊⬤⬤⥋

The ringing phone startled Glass. He had just fallen asleep after another exhausting day. "Hello, who is it?" he inquired crankily.

"It's me, Ferencz."

"What is it? What now?"

"Some good news, actually."

"What time is it?"

"Around twelve-thirty or so," said Ferencz. "Sorry if I woke you, but I just got a call. They're finally moving the men, the survivors, out of Holmesburg. They're doing it right now. They're taking them down to Moyamensing Prison. Can you believe it? They're doing it in the dead of night!"

"Christ, it took them long enough," replied Glass. "How many days has it taken them to move eight men fourteen miles? I asked to have it done a week ago."

"I know," said Ferencz, "but at least they're doing it. And after midnight no less. Guess they're getting nervous about the inquest."

"More the governor's visit today," said Glass. "I'm sure the mayor got a chill when he heard the governor's remarks. He'll feel even worse when he sees the morning newspapers."

"And on top of the *Times* article yesterday he must really be in a foul mood," replied Ferencz. "I heard he's not looking well."

"Hasn't for a while. He's watching his dream of running for governor get flushed down the sewer. Serves the dumb son of a bitch right."

"But why do the move after midnight?" asked Ferencz. "They could have done it earlier in the day."

"No reporters out there now," said Glass. "He probably thinks no one will notice and there won't be any news copy on the transfer. The guy hates to be viewed as buckling under pressure."

The coroner knew the mayor well. During his many years as a minor party operative, he had witnessed a variety of mighty egos, out-sized personalities, and managerial types claim ownership of the spacious second-floor office in City Hall. Some mayors were competent, others less so, but G. Thomas Clarke was a breed unto himself. Headstrong, obsessed with dominating the political arena, and impressed with his own powers of observation and problem-solving, the mayor didn't brook disobedience and disdained opposition. Those who opposed him were generally steamrolled. Retaliation was common, but Clarke now recognized he had miscalculated.

Containing the Holmesburg Prison affair was more complicated than he had originally anticipated. It wasn't like the typical police corruption, public housing, or financial kick-back scandal he routinely quashed. Public interest in the Klondike story and the dead prisoners, along with demand for a thorough investigation by a minor but determined elected official, had proven disastrous. Clarke had his eye on statewide office, but the clamor over the prison debacle was proving an impediment he couldn't hurdle. Newspapers, some of national repute, had savaged him. He'd have to be more prudent in the future, maybe even let the coroner's investigation play out. But that did not mean he'd have to acquiesce to the coroner's newfound acclaim. Clarke would get his revenge; Glass would get turned-out in the next party primary.

Summonses were served by sheriff's deputies to a lengthy list of potential witnesses. No one, it appeared, escaped the coroner's wide net, as everyone from the superintendent on down had been ordered to appear for the special blue ribbon inquest. In addition to Davis, others receiving summonses included Warden Victor Stryker, Captain of the Guard Richard Brennan, Dr. Samuel Moretti, Dr. Oliver Hankins, and guards Albert Bridges, Joseph Smoot, Robert Trent, Alex Crawley, and Joseph Barnwell.

Only Sergeant of the Guard James Hartzell had managed to avoid being handed a subpoena. He hadn't shown up for work in recent days and there was talk he had gone into hiding to avoid testifying in open court about his role in the Klondike deaths. Glass sent court officers to find him, but their efforts proved futile. Subpoenas were also served on five prisoners including, Patrick Palumbo, Wesley Hickok, Henry Luzinski, Anton Scheinbach, and Harry Warner.

When asked by reporters why so many prison employees were ordered to appear, Coroner Glass replied, "No one is free from suspicion and they all face the possibility of arrest. Our interviews show they all had contact with the Klondike prisoners. And I have been assured by the district attorney's office that arrests will be made at the conclusion of the inquiry. Their complicity and level of involvement will be based on the recommendations of the jury."

When questioned by the press regarding his preparation for such a widely speculated upon and controversial maneuver, Glass replied, "I feel we're ready. We have questioned every witness; some individuals have been interviewed multiple times. I believe we have prepared thoroughly. The inquest will probably take two or three days, include the testimony of nearly two dozen witnesses, and hopefully resolve one of the most heinous riddles in recent Philadelphia history."

Additional questions led the coroner to state, "I will probably open the session by explaining why I became so interested in this case. I'm referring to the early reports that eight men were suicides, and the equally bizarre story that they died of exhaustion fighting each other. I wanted to know what really happened and to bring the guilty to justice. I have also requested an extra complement of police to assist deputy sheriffs as I am concerned about the safety of witnesses in both the courtroom and the corridors leading to the courtroom on the sixth floor. It has been suggested that relatives and friends of the deceased may be unable to control themselves when in the presence of prison employees who directly contributed to their relatives' death. I hope that is not the case."

The coroner did not mention that precautionary measures had been instituted at Holmesburg Prison as well. Inmates would be locked in their cells for the duration of the inquest. All leave for staff was canceled, and due to the number of prison personnel subpoenaed, two dozen state police officers from surrounding counties were now assigned to oversee prison cellblocks and to man tower observation posts. And not only were family visits canceled but newspapers were prohibited and radio service was silenced.

The information lockdown was all in a well-orchestrated effort to ensure inmates remained uninformed of developments in the City Hall courtroom. The threat of a major riot was near unanimous by penal authorities fearful of a jury verdict in favor of Davis, Stryker, and the other prison guards. "Regardless whether it be by radio announcement or newspaper headline," said Don Ohlmire, the former warden of Moko now running Holmesburg, "if the 1,400 inmates learn the superintendent and warden got off scot-free, I'm afraid this place will blow like a torch thrown in a munitions dump." The lockdown secured and news embargoed, prisoners would only hear the constant replaying of "Rose Marie, I Love You," on the prison loudspeaker system.

PART III

Chapter 20

Blue Ribbon Inquest

"Hear ye, hear ye, hear ye!" trumpeted the baritone-voiced court crier, signifying the start of the rare and much-anticipated quasi-judicial medical proceeding. With three rapid swats of his gavel on a small wooden block, Coroner Heshel Glass announced a special inquest of the coroner's office of the city and county of Philadelphia into the recent deaths of eight inmates at Holmesburg Prison.

It was ten forty-five A.M., August 30, 1938, the last Wednesday of the month, and though the height of vacation season, when everything in the city usually comes to a standstill—especially judicial activity—every seat in the courtroom was taken. Many of the county's top lawyers who would normally be bathed in sunshine at their Long Beach Island, Atlantic City, and Wildwood beachside retreats, were now either seated or standing along the walls of City Hall Courtroom 653. Everyone focused their attention on the three grim-faced men on the elevated rostrum: Coroner Glass, Chief Deputy Coroner Carl Ferencz, and First Deputy of the District Attorney's Office Vincent Doyle.

Though the nation was still technically mired in a terrible economic depression, the courtroom's interior was the embodiment of opulence. Both its size and ornamental accouterments were eye-catching. Nearly two stories in height and adorned with lavish mahogany and Italian marble, the expansive and richly detailed chamber reminded one more of the palaces of the great pharaohs than a normally austere municipal hall of justice.

The building itself was something to be reckoned with, and more than a few out-of-towners were in awe of City Hall's magnitude and artistic flamboyance. A vast and imposing edifice advertised as the largest building in America, and viewed by many an architectural connoisseur as both a sculptural and structural masterpiece, Philadelphia's City Hall was considered one of the most majestic government buildings in the world. Three decades in the making and modeled on the Palais des Tuileries and the Louvre in Paris with mansard-roofed pavilions, deeply sculpted columns, segmental arches, and tautly drawn tiers of dormers, the 700-room structure with an exterior adorned with some 250 sculptured figures was a marvel of design, creative masonry, and public will. And all topped off above the building's imposing clock tower with the 37-foot, 27-ton bronze statue of Pennsylvania's founder, William Penn. At 538-feet above Broad and Market Streets, the unique landmark was visible for miles around and proclaimed by experts of such things to be the largest statue on top of a building in the world.

Home to the county's executive, legislative, and judicial offices, the building's many courtrooms were paragons of conspicuous grandeur. Courtroom 653 was a particularly large and lavish affair, usually reserved for the most important or controversial criminal trials on the calendar. The judge's bench, a colossal hunk of rich mahogany, stood like an imposing rampart at the head of a room seemingly large enough to hold two full-sized basketball courts. The over four hundred now in attendance sat on long rows of wooden chairs or stood along walls that displayed more than a dozen large oil portraits of long-forgotten bearded jurists. A large jury box with a three-step rise was on the left; the seals of Philadelphia and Pennsylvania along with the flags of the city, state, and nation were prominently set on a raised platform along the front wall. A clock, three feet in diameter, hung on the wall above the flags.

Spectators were becoming anxious, and reporters representing a cross-section of local and national newspapers speculated amongst themselves as to what new facts the coroner's rarely used gambit would deliver. The much-anticipated inquiry was already forty minutes late getting started due to the large numbers desirous of attending the event, as well as the time-consuming process of searching everyone entering the courtroom. Also contributing to the delay was the unexplained requirement that everyone walk through a small side room where Bill Roberson, the elderly Negro and former Holmesburg inmate, visually inspected them.

The line entering the courtroom grew so long additional police were needed to patrol the corridor where nearly two hundred unlucky people unable to gain entry expressed their disappointment. The case had not only sparked widespread interest but also deep divisions in the city. An unprecedented number of death threats had been reported to authorities. Initially targeting Coroner

Glass, a growing number of threats were now aimed at Superintendent Davis and Warden Stryker. Even the mayor had received mail wishing him ill.

Coroner Glass requested that the many photographers from various news agencies busily taking photos find a seat. He then nodded toward a side door. Out walked four sheriff's office deputies escorting Holmesburg Prison guards Albert Bridges and Joseph Smoot into the courtroom. The two guards had been held in the sheriff's seventh-floor cell room for safekeeping, as no prison in the city was thought able to guarantee their safety. Bridges, a strongly built man with sandy hair, pale blue eyes, and a nose that had seen more than its fair share of physical contact, and Smoot, a short, stocky man with dark hair and a heavy bulldog face, took seats alongside Superintendent Davis and Warden Stryker. The eight others receiving subpoenas—six guards, one physician, and one city engineer—sat next to and behind them. Whispers echoed throughout the courtroom, and many strained their necks to get a better view of the proceeding's key players. After making eye contact with the jury foreman, Gilbert Hendricks, the coroner once again struck his gavel.

"Ladies and gentlemen, this is an important case," began Coroner Glass, looking out on the largest audience he had ever appeared before, with the exception of the large crowds that attended basketball games during his former athletic career. "Terribly important would not be an exaggeration," Glass added. "The event that sparked this inquiry was initially reported to me as a case of eight suicides. You can imagine my shock at such a determination. After further investigation by the police, I was informed that prisoners in custody had fought among themselves and dropped dead from exhaustion. There was even mention of a communist aspect to the case. Again, an account difficult to envision.

"At this point, and after my own personal observation of the setting, circumstances, and fatalities, I decided to make a formal investigation of the matter. I want you members of the jury to pay strict attention to all the evidence. It is our duty, in fact, it is our responsibility that this matter be fully examined. It is your job to ensure justice is done. Those guilty of this outrageous crime must be identified, tried, and punished.

"In recent days, the district attorney's office, and particularly Mr. Doyle, who is seated alongside me, has shown interest in solving this case. We must lay our trust in his office that any determination made by our inquiry will be honored and followed through on. It is our expectation that the District Attorney's Office of Philadelphia will put the responsible parties for this tragedy on trial."

The coroner paused briefly, then announced, "Our first order of business will be the identification of decedents in this case. Mr. Ferencz, will you call your first witness?"

Carl Ferencz called Mrs. Shirley O'Shea to the stand. Attired in a white blouse, dark-green skirt, and black jacket, the witness unsteadily walked toward the stand. After taking a seat, she held her handbag tightly on her lap as if it provided some form of protection. She glanced nervously at the hundreds of spectators who had now given her their undivided attention. After she took the oath to tell the truth, the deputy coroner asked the witness to describe the events of Monday, August 22, when she learned of her son's death.

"It was a hot day," said Mrs. O'Shea. "Very humid, as it had been for weeks. But household chores had to be done so I had just cleaned the kitchen and washed a load of clothing and was hanging it in the backyard when I heard the phone ringing."

Mrs. O'Shea abruptly stopped, rocked slightly in her chair, and her eyes began to tear up. She took a hanky from her handbag and wiped her cheek; the deputy coroner gently encouraged her to continue. She apologized and said, "I answered the phone, and it was some woman from the coroner's office or the morgue, I forget which now, and she said I should come down to 13th and Wood Streets to identify the body. She said my son was there and the body needed to be identified by a family member before an autopsy could be done. I told her she must be mistaken. It couldn't be my son. But she was insistent, and it was then that I told her my son was in prison . . . he couldn't be dead."

The witness stopped, took a deep breath, and gathered herself. "The lady on the phone told me there had been an incident at Holmesburg Prison and a number of prisoners had been killed. I can't recall much after that. I think I screamed. I must have called my daughter and brother. I really don't remember."

"But they took you down to the city morgue at 13th and Wood Streets, didn't they?" said Deputy Ferencz.

"Yes, we went downtown and there were all these reporters and photographers there, and they were all asking questions and taking pictures. But we didn't know anything . . . nobody told us anything."

"And what happened then?"

"We were taken into the morgue, to a large room, like a hospital or laboratory, where they had . . . where they had a row of . . ."

"Go ahead, please," said Ferencz. "I know this is difficult."

"There were a lot of metal tables and hospital gurneys with dead people and white sheets over them," said Mrs. O'Shea. "It was terrible; I had never seen anything like that before. A doctor took us over to one of them, pulled the sheet back, and asked, 'Is this your son, Timothy O'Shea?'"

Her voice now breaking and tears flowing freely, Mrs. O'Shea, repeatedly squeezing her hanky, turned to Superintendent Davis, Warden Stryker, and the other men in the rows reserved for prison personnel. "You killed my son," she shouted. "You treated him no better than you'd treat a rabid dog. He was just a thief . . . you don't kill somebody cause they're a thief. He was in prison, doing his time. He didn't hurt nobody—why'd you have to kill him?"

Cyrus Black, Superintendent Davis's attorney, quickly jumped to his feet and yelled, "Objection, objection," as Coroner Glass repeatedly brought down his gavel. He ordered Black to sit down and instructed Mrs. O'Shea to not call out or attack anyone from the witness stand. "Please, just answer the questions put to you by Mr. Ferencz."

With tears running down her cheeks, Mrs. O'Shea apologized for her outburst but quickly lost her composure again. Overcome with grief and anger, she bemoaned her only son having been killed by prison authorities. "He was only twenty-five years old," cried O'Shea, her voice occasionally cracking. "He had a job . . . he was a welder and worked at the train yard. He had his whole life to live. Yeah, I know he wasn't perfect; he took stuff that wasn't his. But he was doin' his time. He promised me he'd never do it again, he'd never get arrested again. But they didn't give him the chance. They threw him in that Klondike oven and tortured him. Oh, what they did to him," she wailed. "It didn't even look like him at the morgue. All puffy and blue and deformed . . ."

Mrs. O'Shea then leaned to her left, her eyes fluttered, and she collapsed against the wooden side rail of the witness stand. Gasps and shouts could be heard throughout the room as bailiffs and tipstaff raced to help the distraught woman to her feet and out of the courtroom.

After asking for quiet and lecturing the audience about courtroom decorum and warning about what was expected to be some graphic testimony, Coroner Glass instructed his deputy to call his next witness. Ferencz asked Dante Oteri, brother of deceased inmate Paul Oteri, to come to the stand. Wearing a brown suit, black tie, and a look of consternation, Oteri said his younger brother still lived with his parents in Tacony when he was arrested for burglarizing a couple of residences in Frankford. When the dark-haired Mayfair auto mechanic was asked by the deputy coroner to describe how he learned of his brother's death, Oteri replied, "I was at work when my mother called in a panic. She said something happened to Pauly. She said someone had told her Pauly was dead and she had to go down to the city morgue. I told her someone was pulling her leg. I said Pauly's in jail and to forget about it. But she was a mess and insisted I come over. I called a friend of mine who lives near the prison, and he told me he had been hearing police sirens all morning. He said something big musta happened up there. So I got my mother and drove to 13th and Wood, still expectin' it to be a waste of time, but then . . . but you know, when we saw all the people outside, all the reporters, cameramen, and others, I knew something was up. I got a little scared."

"What happened then, Mr. Oteri?" asked Ferencz.

"We went inside, and they took us to a big back room," Oteri replied. "It was like a medical operating room. There was a lot of equipment, you know, medical stuff, but there were also these metal tables and hospital gurneys. And there were these white sheets covering . . . you know, on top of dead people."

The witness started to choke up, and Ferencz encouraged him to continue. Oteri said his mother became hysterical as a doctor took them over to a gurney. "I was holding her up," said Oteri, "but I was gettin' a little wobbly myself. I kept on prayin' it was a mistake, it wasn't my brother, it wasn't Pauly. But when they pulled the sheet back . . ."

"Go ahead, Mr. Oteri."

"When the doctor pulled the sheet back I kinda felt relief," said Oteri. "'That ain't my brother,' I said to myself. 'That don't look like Pauly.' It looked like a monster. I mean, a bulging eye, scaly blue skin, swollen head. But my mother was about to pass out . . . she had her mouth open like she wanted to scream, but nothin' came out. And I turned back to the body on the gurney and took another look. The face and head were . . . the head was big and bloated, and the face was blue, almost black. I said to myself this can't be my brother . . ." Overcome, Oteri stared at the floor and gripped his chair tightly.

Encouraged to continue, the witness finally said, "I couldn't understand what happened to him. What the hell did they do to him? I mean, your brother goes to prison. He's a normal guy, a good-looking guy, and then you get him back and he looks like Frankenstein's monster. Hell, I wouldn't blame anybody who took his own life if he knew he was goin' to that jail. I mean, gettin' fried in the chair is a picnic compared to Holmesburg. At least you die quick in an electric chair or at the end of a rope."

For the next hour, relatives of the deceased were called to the stand to formally identify the dead for the record. One by one, fathers, brothers, and a couple of wives emotionally described their journeys to the city morgue to identify and pay their last respects to a loved one. Several faltered, overcome with grief. Others concluded their comments by denouncing the city and its penal system for wantonly taking the lives of family members.

"I never would've believed it," said a distraught Captain Fergus McBride, father of the late James McBride and longtime Philadelphia Fire Department employee. "I worked for the city for thirty-four years, and for them to do this to my boy, to roast him like a pig . . . for what, for not eating his meals? I ask you, is that a crime worthy of the death penalty? Do we kill people now for not eating their breakfast and supper?"

McBride, like several others, had to be helped from the stand and escorted to an anteroom. No one had the heart to ask further questions of the family members, and numerous women in the gallery were seen pulling out tissues and handkerchiefs and dabbing tears from their cheeks. Due to the emotionally jarring testimony and a late start, at well-past the normal lunch hour, Coroner Glass announced there would be a short recess. First up in the afternoon session, announced the coroner, would be testimony from the first doctors to arrive on the scene that fateful Monday morning.

As soon as he entered his office, Miss Renwick apprised Coroner Glass of several phone calls threatening serious consequences if the coroner continued with his inquest. She said a few secretaries had voiced concern for their safety. "If they feel unsafe," Glass replied, "send them home. I'm not going to shutter the office." Unable to trust the police, the mayor, or anyone else on the city payroll, Glass had requested the help of some of his former SPHA teammates. Could they, he asked, donate some time and sit in his office? Just in case. Their presence wasn't as reassuring as uniformed police officers, but for several nervous secretaries, it was better than nothing. Now that the inquest was underway, Glass was determined to plow ahead. Nothing was going to impede his search for the truth.

After returning from lunch, it was obvious that many in the courtroom were still unnerved from the morning's gut-wrenching testimony. Some observers had departed and not returned. Still, every seat in the courtroom was taken, and many remained in line along the sixth-floor corridor wall. Chilling word-of-mouth accounts from the morning session did little to dampen spectators' enthusiasm. After calling for order, Coroner Glass quickly moved to the Holmesburg doctors who were the first to treat Klondike survivors.

Dr. Oliver F. Hankins, a subpoena recipient, was the first Holmesburg Prison physician called to testify. Approximately fifty years in age, gray-haired with a heavy gray mustache and eyeglasses, Hankins was frequently inaudible, and he often hesitated when answering questions. Chief Deputy Coroner Ferencz opened by asking Dr. Hankins about his educational background and experience as a prison doctor. He said he had degrees from Bucknell University and Hahnemann Medical School and had been employed as a visiting physician at Holmesburg for eight years.

"Doctor, what did your days at the prison usually look like?" asked Ferencz.

"I was usually at the prison by nine A.M. and stayed till noon, Monday to Friday," said Hankins. "I spent most of my time in the prison hospital and would inquire if any inmates required treatment in their cells."

"Did that include Klondike?"

"Yes."

"Was there a written rule," asked Ferencz, "that made it necessary for doctors to visit Klondike?"

"No. There was no written rule that I know of," Hankins replied, "but it was generally understood that when there were any prisoners at Klondike we should visit them at least once every twenty-four hours."

"What was the reason for those visits?"

"We would examine them and see if they were in fit condition to remain in the Klondike."

"Why would they not be fit?" inquired Ferencz. "Or better yet, why would they need to be fit to be kept in the punishment unit? Was there anything special about Klondike?"

Dr. Hankins warily looked around the room. Jurors, reporters, and the several hundred in the courtroom observed the doctor's hesitance.

Deputy Ferencz asked, "Would you like me to repeat the question?"

"Isolation," Dr. Hankins answered. "Isolation and . . . well, not everyone can handle isolation. You know, being celled alone."

Glass found the doctor's reaction and answer of interest. He suspected prison doctors and other medical personnel knew of Klondike's heat treatment but did little to oppose it. He was familiar with city employees, even professionals, deferring to the law enforcement community.

Deputy Ferencz continued the questioning and asked, "Did you ever examine men before they went into Klondike to see if they were fit?"

"No."

"But there have been occasions where you determined men were unfit for Klondike and you had them removed?"

"Yes," said Hankins. "On several occasions, I have requested the removal of prisoners because I felt they were no longer in fit condition to remain in solitary confinement. They received limited rations, so some could fall ill during their time there. And we also checked on the building's general sanitary conditions."

At this point, Coroner Glass, showing his impatience, interrupted his deputy. "Doctor, since we've established you and your medical colleagues had the authority to remove ill and unfit prisoners from Klondike," said Glass, "let's move to the weekend in question. On August 20 and 21, a Saturday and Sunday, you were on duty at the prison, right?"

"Yes."

"And when were you there," asked the coroner, "what time did you arrive and when did you leave?"

"I was there from approximately nine A.M. till twelve-thirty P.M. Both days."

Coroner Glass leaned forward in his chair and asked, "And during that time, did anyone request . . . that is, did any official or guard request you visit Klondike?"

When the doctor replied, "No," Glass immediately asked, "But you did learn that morning there were men in Klondike?"

"Yes."

"Did a guard or prison official inform you?"

"No," said Hankins. "A hospital aide, an inmate named Greeley, told me early Saturday morning there were men in Klondike. He said I should go check on them."

"And why was it not a prison official or guard who informed you?" Glass replied.

"I don't know," said the doctor. "They just didn't notify me."

"Okay," said Glass, "so once you learned Klondike was occupied, what did you do?"

"I then mentioned the fact to Warden Stryker and asked him if I was needed," Hankins replied. "I asked if I should go to the punishment unit. He said, 'No, there is no need to go over there at this time.' He said he would let me know when he was ready for me to make the visit. But I never received any calls from him."

"So, you left the prison and went home?"

"Yes, I went home."

Grumbling and murmurs of disapproval raced throughout the courtroom.

"So, over the weekend, that Saturday and Sunday, you did not inspect the prisoners in the punishment unit?"

Looking embarrassed and answering meekly, Dr. Hankins replied, "No, I did not."

"And why not?" asked Glass.

"I was told it would not be necessary."

"And how unusual was this?"

"It was the first time in almost nine years of service as visiting physician that the standing order of checking on the men in Klondike was not adhered to."

"And the reason you were given for breaking with prison custom?"

"I was never given one," said Dr. Hankins. "I still don't know . . ."

After a stern glance at the prison employees seated to his right, the coroner quickly followed with the question, "So when did you finally visit Klondike?"

"I was called to the prison Monday morning," said Dr. Hankins. "It was my day off since I had worked the weekend shift. When I arrived, I was directed to Klondike. It was terrible. I found six men dead in their cells. Outside the building on the ground were a dozen or more men. They were in bad shape. Dr. Moretti, Superintendent Davis, and Warden Stryker were also there, overseeing things. There were just a lot of dead and desperately ill men around. They were lying on the lawn or on cots in various states of physical distress. Some seemed burned, others dehydrated, and some were delirious or comatose. They were all in bad shape."

"Isn't it a fact," interjected Assistant District Attorney Doyle, "two more inmates would die later that day?"

"Yes."

"Of the survivors," said Doyle, "isn't it true they were all terribly dehydrated? In fact, nearly bled white?"

"Yes."

"And what did you do at that time in the prison yard?"

"We treated the men as best we could," Hankins replied. "They were badly dehydrated, as you say. Some were very disoriented, others uncommunicative. We injected them with glucose and saline, got them in the shade, and generally tried to revive them. We tried to cool and rehydrate them as quickly as we could. All I can say is, things were pretty hectic at the time. I had never seen . . . it was certainly out of the ordinary. Initially, I didn't even think they had come from Klondike. During my years as prison physician, I had never seen that many men in there before."

"Doctor, have you ever treated any prisoners for the same condition as these men you treated last Monday? Isn't a fact that heat was the regular punishment in the isolation cells?"

Looking anxious, the doctor replied, "I do not know that heat was used as a regular form of punishment, although it was warm on several occasions when I visited the Klondike."

Snickers and incredulous gasps could be heard in the courtroom. The doctor quickly attempted to clarify his statement. "I never saw anyone in such dire condition before, much less a group of them," said Hankins. "It was a first for me. I've taken sick men out of there before, but I've never experienced anything like it. I'm not sure anyone has. It might be the most calamitous thing that ever happened in a penal institution."

"And what do you say about your role in this ugly affair?" said Doyle.

The doctor did not reply and looked sheepishly around the courtroom. He would be met with facial expressions running the gamut from mild disapproval to rage.

After Dr. Hankins was excused, Dr. Samuel B. Moretti, Holmesburg's chief physician, was called to the stand, which he approached with a serious demeanor. The compact, balding fifty-two-year-old physician was from a prominent South Philadelphia Italian family. Two of his brothers currently served in the state legislature. Though some would argue Samuel was as skilled a politician as his brothers, he had chosen medicine instead of politics as a career. After graduating from the University of Pennsylvania Medical School, he would serve as a medical lieutenant in the Marine Corps during World War I and return home to start his own medical practice. Initially taken on as a part-time medical assignment, his prison work would gradually become full time and develop into a quarter-century relationship.

After being sworn in, the heavily-jowled physician glanced quickly at the men who were now thought to be involved in the deaths of eight prisoners. He had spent years in their company and knew many of them intimately. The hundreds in attendance tried to discern the import of his glance. When asked by Deputy Ferencz to recount his initial involvement with the deadly Klondike episode, Dr. Moretti said he had just returned from a weekend in Wildwood at the Jersey Shore and was sitting in Superintendent Davis's office when Warden Stryker entered and said, "There are four or five dead in Klondike. You had better get out there."

"What did you do then?" asked Ferencz.

"We ran out to the isolation ward and found six bodies," said Dr. Moretti. "When I found two apparently dead men in Number Six cell and two in Number Seven cell, and more in other cells, I obviously thought of resuscitation but quickly decided it would be useless and pronounced them dead. Due to the intense heat, my first concern was to get those still alive out of their cells. I told Superintendent Davis to issue an order to take those men still alive out of their cells, which he did. It was unbearably hot in there, and I directed that all the windows should be opened. I kept yelling that those still alive had to be taken out immediately. We got them out on the grass and told the guards to bring cots, cold water, and medical supplies. There was much happening, it was very hectic, but I focused my attention on the living after determining six were dead and nothing could be done for them. I said the dead should be left as they were and the coroner's office should be contacted."

"Anything else about the scene?" asked Assistant District Attorney Doyle.

"It was devastating," Moretti responded. "Men were strewn across the cell floors, some dead, some near dead. Smyzak and Palumbo were lying across the floor with their feet toward the door. Their heads and shoulders were bowed back against the cell door, and in the next cell, Oteri's head was bent over resting on Webster's leg. It was like that cell after cell. We got those still alive out as quickly as we could."

As the doctor went on, everyone in the large courtroom listened in horror to the portly physician's dramatic account. His description of the deceased at the time of their discovery and his recollection of events both captivated and repulsed listeners. When asked about the treatment survivors received, Moretti described a combination of "cold water bath, salt, nourishment, and medication," with most requiring "coramine hypodermic injections, glucose intravenous, phenol and glycerine tablets, and triple bromide solution."

"And those who didn't survive?" asked Doyle.

"As for the dead, we left them as we found them. They were now the preserve of the coroner and police investigators."

When asked by Doyle to describe the condition of the deceased inside Klondike and his determination as to the inmates' cause of death, Moretti replied, "It was very unusual. 'Unnatural' may be a better term. The bodies in Number Six cell were livid, purplish-and-bluish discolorations on the thorax, abdomen, and extremities. The feet and hands were blanched and shriveled. Rigor mortis had set in, but there were apparent bruises and lacerations along with burn marks.

"On the bodies in Number Seven cell, both were strange. One was so dark he appeared to be a Negro, while the hands and feet of the other were blanched and shriveled. Rigor mortis had set in on both bodies. I did not disturb the position of these bodies but left them for the coroner's office. All six were dead, and I did not wish to destroy the relationship of the surroundings. It was a horrendous scene that I knew would require an investigation. It was obvious the coroner and the police would be involved. I made no diagnosis nor gave any cause of death. I determined that was the coroner's duty."

"Considering your many years at Holmesburg," inquired ADA Doyle, "what is your understanding regarding the medical care of prisoners locked in Klondike?"

"It is the general rule," Dr. Moretti explained, "that a prison physician visit and examine prisoners in the punishment unit once every twenty-four hours, and if in his opinion a prisoner's physical condition is such that the individual cannot continue punishment he must be taken out of the punishment unit."

"Will you agree," asked Doyle, "that someone should have gone in at regular intervals to inspect Klondike?"

"Definitely."

"Would you then not consider it your duty or that of Dr. Hankins to visit Klondike when it was occupied, regardless of whether the warden or guards authorized it or not?"

"No, absolutely not," replied Dr. Moretti, surprising many in the courtroom. "Holmesburg is a prison, not a hospital, and the prison head is supreme. He has the final word. And, yes, this is by far the worst situation in my lengthy career in prison work, but doctors have only so much freedom in a prison environment. Let me underscore the fact that a guard escorts a physician to Klondike, and the key to the building is held at Center by the warden, deputy warden, or captain of the guard. A physician cannot take it upon himself to visit Klondike. It is my firm conviction that had the warden, deputy warden, captain, or sergeant obeyed the regulations and allowed a physician to see these men on Saturday or Sunday, these casualties might have been prevented."

"Doctor, have you ever seen anything like this in your experience as a physician?"

"Only during my time along Belleau Wood in France during the Great War," said Dr. Moretti. "Nothing comes close to this during my prison experience of nearly a quarter-century. Quite frankly, it's unprecedented. I don't suspect that I or anyone else who was there that hellish day will ever forget it."

"And your thoughts on the conditions inside Klondike?" asked Doyle.

"If the cells had been properly ventilated, the heat not turned on, and the men given access to water, they'd still be alive," said Moretti. "They'd have never died. I believe the men died from heat exhaustion with contributory causes of carbon dioxide."

"And Klondike?" asked Doyle. "Have you ever seen or heard of the heat treatment as part of the punishment procedure in Klondike?"

"No."

"But, Doctor," inquired Doyle, appearing confused, "you just said that Klondike was hot, unbearably hot. Why does there have to be heat in a building on an already searing August day? Could you explain that?"

"The building known as Klondike," said Moretti, "is made of cement and brick. It is, therefore, necessary to turn some heat on to dry out the building, otherwise, it would be possible for the men confined there to become ill and contract pneumonia."

"But tell me, Doctor," Coroner Glass quickly interjected, "is it necessary to roast the men in order to protect them?"

"No, of course not," replied Dr. Moretti. "It should not take four hours or six hours or two days to dry out the building. There is no need for additional heat in Klondike in hot weather, except to dry it out, and then it could be turned off and kept off. But that was not the case here. It was damnably hot. The cells remained hot long after the radiators had been shut and the doors opened on Monday morning. It was so hot you couldn't touch any piece of metal."

"Then you agree," said the coroner, "something untoward happened here? Something unusual, if not evil?"

"Yes, I guess you could say that," the doctor replied. "I never saw anything as terrible as this in the twenty-five years I have been at the prison. I could never have imagined such a thing. I'll never forget what I saw that morning. But please understand, Klondike itself, the building, is a necessary adjunct to any prison. Troublemakers, dangerous men, occasionally need to be isolated. In my opinion, Klondike should be considered an instrument of precision, and if used as such is a very valuable and important adjunct to any prison. However, men incarcerated there should be examined every twenty-four hours. If they are found to be ill, they should be taken out and punished later."

After excusing Dr. Moretti, the coroner said, "I would like to take a few minutes to explain an unfortunate development that no doubt confused many citizens, especially newspaper readers very early on in the case." He was referring to initial statements by certain members of law enforcement that inmates had fought among themselves over ending the food strike, resulting in numerous casualties and eight deaths. To accomplish that, Glass said he needed his deputy to take the witness stand. He explained that Mr. Ferencz was the first one from his office to witness the carnage. After leaving the bench for a chair in the witness stand and taking the oath, Carl Ferencz was asked to recount what he found when he entered Holmesburg Prison on the morning of Monday, August 22.

After describing a battlefield-like scene with bodies littering a grass plot alongside an unremarkable single-story brick building, Ferencz told of entering a dark, foul-smelling cell house. The putrid air and sweltering atmosphere only grew more revolting when he was shown four cells containing the bodies of dead inmates. "Everything was damp, dark, and still very hot," said Ferencz. "The bodies lay tangled on the hot cement floor, and the air was vile with the pervasive odor of urine and feces."

"What did prison officials know or speculate had caused the death of so many prisoners?" asked the coroner.

"Superintendent Davis told me he didn't know how the men died," Ferencz replied, "but he believed they had fought among themselves."

"What happened then?"

"I asked the superintendent what the men had been convicted of, but he was unsure. He stepped away to ask the warden."

"Did someone then approach you and ask you to do something?" the coroner inquired.

"Yes, Detective Hennessey of the police department came up to me and said that our reports should be alike."

"His exact words were?"

"He said, 'It would be best if our reports were similar.'"

"And your reaction?" replied Glass.

"I was taken aback by the request," said Ferencz. "I told him I would make my own report. I then cut off any further discussion with him."

"And what happened then?"

"I was surprised to learn a little while later Detective Hennessey and the police were postulating a cause of death completely unsupportable by the facts," said Ferencz. "They were telling newsmen that inmates had fought among themselves. They never once mentioned the heat, the intense steam heat the inmates were exposed to over a sustained period of time. There was no mention of windows and vents being shuttered, no mention of water being denied to the prisoners. I was stunned . . . their version was completely unsupportable."

Grim-faced and occasionally glancing at certain spectators in the court-room, Coroner Glass expressed his dismay that the investigation into such a terrible catastrophe began in such a dishonest manner. "Not only did such an outlandish story hinder a proper investigation," said Glass, "but it misled citizens and ultimately caused city residents to justifiably doubt the veracity of their government officials. In addition, it provided to those around the country an even darker picture of the challenging task of pursuing justice in Philadelphia. As you are well aware," Glass informed the jury, "Detectives Hennessey and Wilson were eventually demoted in rank and removed from the homicide squad. I believe their story is one future investigators should take to heart before fashioning completely untrue criminal scenarios."

As courtroom spectators whispered among themselves, Glass thanked Ferencz for his testimony and asked him to retake his place on the panel. The coroner waited for the large audience to grow quiet.

"In an effort to frame the cause of deaths in a more scientific and exact manner," Glass told the audience, "I'd now like to call to the stand Dr. Philip Mattingly, chief coroner's physician of Philadelphia." After citing his academic and medical background and current university affiliations, the forensic pathologist was asked what he determined to be the cause of death for the eight prisoners housed in the Klondike punishment unit.

"After performing autopsies on the eight convicts who died inside the Holmesburg punishment unit," said Dr. Mattingly, "we determined their deaths were caused by heatstroke resulting from exposure to abnormally high temperatures."

When the coroner asked if the doctor cared to elaborate, Mattingly pulled out a few sheets of paper from his suit pocket. "When we examined the bodies at the site," said Dr. Mattingly, "the skin of each of the deceased was warm and dry. Each of the decedents presented evidence of external congested phenomena, which in laymen's terms is the localization of the blood, or the blood trying to cool itself off. For example, John Webster had contusions on his arms and knees, nostril burns, congestion of the lungs and heart muscles, and also hemorrhages of the eyes. Bruno Palumbo had abrasions of the left cheek and chin, multiple contusions on both knees, burns of the right hip, left shoulder, and right upper arm, and congestion of the lungs, and hemorrhaging of the heart muscles, brain, and other viscera. Jake Smyzak had burns on the right shoulder, abrasions of the wrists, and contusions of the right upper arm. The internal examination was the same as the others. James McBride had hemorrhages of the eyes and nose, burns on both knees and feet. His internal condition was the same as the others, however, he also showed evidence of tuberculosis. By the way, I should mention that all of the deceased were severely discolored."

The city pathologist acknowledged that "Steamfitters sometimes have to work in temperatures of 140 to 150 degrees near boilers, but they only stay on the job a half-hour at a time, and someone is always watching to rescue them in case of collapse. It's been estimated by engineers that the Holmesburg punishment unit—a building 50 feet long, 15 feet wide, and 10 feet high—only required 165 square feet of radiation to keep the temperature at 70 degrees on a zero-degree day. Inexplicably, the small brick building had 300 to 400 feet of radiation installed, making for a furnace-like environment capable of exceeding 200 degrees on a humid day when the windows were closed."

Asked to explain the impact of such temperatures on the human body, Mattingly said, "The proteins of human cells begin to coagulate at 108 degrees, hampering normal chemical activity, preventing the absorption of oxygen and the throwing off of carbon dioxide and other wastes. In short, the body would be poisoned by its own waste products. The excessive loss of salt through perspiration would only add to the trouble."

"And the result, Doctor?" asked Ferencz.

"Thermal death," Mattingly replied.

When the city pathologist completed his testimony, Jack H. K. Ryan, attorney for Warden Stryker, raised his hand and inquired if he could ask the witness a question. Granted permission, Ryan asked Dr. Mattingly, "It struck me that some of these symptoms might be produced by a man being choked to death. In other words, Doctor, it may not have been asphyxiation but strangulation?"

Muttering could be heard in different parts of the courtroom, but the coroner quickly brought down his gavel. "I'll remind you that we must have silence from the observers in the gallery," Glass admonished the audience. Then to Mattingly, "Doctor, would you please respond?"

"Counselor, it's true, some signs could be mistaken for strangulation," said Dr. Mattingly, "but an experienced pathologist would recognize the symptoms weren't that of strangulation. Asphyxia is one of the results of prolonged proximity to excessive heat. In milder forms, it's commonly known as shortness of breath. Over lengthy periods, higher temperatures, and with no water, exposure can quickly prove fatal. The hemorrhaging of the eyes, heavy congestion of the nasal passage, and striation of the lungs all indicate intense heat, not strangulation."

"But, Doctor," argued Ryan, "there were also bruises and wounds of the arms and legs of the deceased that lead one to believe a struggle ensued."

"A struggle did occur," said Mattingly, "but it was one of survival in an oven-like environment, an artificially heated sweatbox. Subjected to extreme heat over long periods without relief or water will tax even the fittest person."

"And the extensive bruising and wounds on the bodies?" the lawyer continued. "Could they not have come from fighting among themselves?"

"Perhaps, if you are not aware or purposely shun knowledge of the conditions in which the men were confined. Yes, the skin had been rubbed off the arms and legs of the prisoners, but that was not from conflict with each other. For a trained eye, it's clear the surface tissue had coagulated as a result of close contact to some extremely hot surface. The marks on the arms, shoulders, legs, buttocks, and soles of the feet were actually burns. The walls, mattresses, and floors of Klondike were extremely hot and could easily cause burns. And as for strangulation, there were no choke marks of any kind on the necks of the victims. The men suffocated internally, not from any external blunt force trauma."

After the warden's attorney took his seat, Glass asked the witness, "In conclusion, Doctor, did you find any evidence the deceased inmates turned on one another and died from some sort of physical brawl among themselves?"

"No, absolutely not," said Mattingly. "The inmates died from heatstroke of the asphyctic type. In other words, prolonged exposure to extreme heat."

Chapter 21

Testimony of Klondike Survivors

"Dr. Mattingly, thank you for your testimony. You're excused," said Coroner Glass. "I'd like to now call to the stand several inmate survivors to recount the deadly events of the weekend in question."

Many in the jury and gallery straightened up and reporters shuffled their notes, preparing themselves for what was expected to be one of the more emotional high points of the inquest. The coroner asked his deputy to open the questioning of the next witness.

Patrick Palumbo was called to the stand. A slight man with bushy dark hair, Palumbo was attired in a beige suit and light-brown tie. The 28-year-old Klondike survivor displayed obvious evidence of his recent injuries, most noticeably a pronounced facial tic. In addition, his skin appeared unusually pale and waxy, as if it had been stretched over his nose and cheekbones. His nervousness was evident as he took his seat in the witness box. He glared at the prison officials and guards seated in front of him while being sworn in—a fact that was likely not lost on the spectators in the courtroom.

Deputy Coroner Ferencz opened by asking the otherwise youthful-looking man how long he had been incarcerated at Holmesburg. "I've served four years and four months of a sentence that has twenty-one more months to go," Palumbo replied in a low monotone. "Another go-around like this," the inmate added, "and I probably won't make it."

There were a few nervous snickers from a gallery that anticipated a first-hand account from someone who had escaped death.

"Why were you sent to Klondike?" Deputy Coroner Ferencz continued.

"I was put into Klondike early evening of August 19," said Palumbo. "I don't know why. I hadn't done anything. I just refused to eat with the rest of the boys. I didn't think it was such a big deal, but Sergeant Hartzell, along with Bridges, Smoot, Trent, and a couple of other guards, pulled me out of my cell early Friday evening and took me to Klondike with a few other guys on strike."

"And your prison record up till then?" asked Ferencz.

"Good," Palumbo replied. "Never a mark against me. I even worked in the prison hospital as an orderly. There were no complaints."

"And on August 19, how many of you were placed in Klondike?"

"That first night there were five of us. Joe Moffett was there, I was there, my brother, and Tim O'Shea, and Jimmy McBride was there. We each had our own cell."

"What did a cell in Klondike look like? What did it contain?"

"The cells were small, smaller than a regular Holmesburg cell," Palumbo replied. "There was a mattress, a hopper, and a spigot."

"Was water in the toilet, and did the spigot work?"

"No, sir. The water was turned on through a valve outside each cell, and the toilets were flushed once or twice a day when the guards came to give us water. They could only be flushed from outside the building."

"How were you clothed when you entered the punishment unit?" Ferencz asked.

"I wore pants, shorts, top shirt, and undershirt," Palumbo replied.

"Was any of that taken away from you?"

"Yes, my top shirt and pants," said Palumbo. "Mr. Bridges told me to take 'em off. He musta known I wouldn't be needin' 'em where I was going."

"Who came the next day, if you can recall?"

"On Saturday, they brought in a bunch of guys; Teague, Oteri, Webster, Hickok, Smyzak, and a few other guys."

"When you went in on Friday night was the heat on?"

"Yes, but it wasn't that bad," said Palumbo. "It was warm, warmer than the air outside, and warmer than a regular Holmesburg cell. But you could live with it."

"Were the windows open?"

"At first, but not for long," said Palumbo as he glanced at the group of prison guards. "Soon after we were thrown in there the windows and ceiling vents were shut tight. It was dark; there are no lights in the cells. Just the corridor had a light bulb or two. They were put on when the guards came in and then turned off when they left. It was always dark."

"Tell the jury," said Ferencz, "what happened after you were locked in your cell."

"Officer Bridges turned the heat up," said Palumbo. "All those radiators can be adjusted from the corridor. I heard one of the guards say, 'Have fun, boys. Got a feelin' it's gonna be a hot night.' He then slammed the doors shut; both the steel door and the outside wooden door."

"Could you hear the steam in the radiators?"

"Yes, sir," said Palumbo. "It kind of made a hissing sound. Heard that sound all through the night. It went on all night and into Saturday morning. And then all day until Saturday night when it was turned up stronger."

"When did the guards next enter the Klondike?"

"Saturday morning, about nine o'clock," said Palumbo. "Bridges and Smoot and some other guards came in. They flushed the toilets and brought each of us a slice of crusty bread and a cup of warm water. We begged them for more water, we were dying of thirst. We asked for the spigot to be turned on. And we pleaded with them to turn off the heat."

"And their reply?" asked Ferencz.

Palumbo glared at Bridges and Smoot. "'Don't worry, you guys won't die,' Bridges told me. He said, 'This ain't so bad. You'll get over it.'"

Ferencz turned toward the guards and asked the witness, "And they never opened the windows despite the heat and your pleas for some air?"

"No, sir. They just turned the heat up."

"Are you sure you saw them turn the heat up?"

"Yes, sir. I could see them from the cell door turning the handle."

"And what happened then?"

"It just kept getting hotter and hotter," said Palumbo. "They came back around noon and gave us a slice of bread and a small cup of water. We kept asking them to turn off the heat. Bridges said it couldn't be done."

Coroner Glass leaned forward and asked, "Mr. Palumbo, did Superintendent Davis or Warden Stryker come in to check on you?"

"No, they never came over."

"Did Dr. Moretti or Dr. Hankins come in to check on your condition?"

"No," said Palumbo. "No, none of 'em ever came around."

"Did you ask to see them?" inquired Deputy Ferencz. "Did you tell the guards you wanted to see the warden or the doctors?"

"Sure we did. Every time a guard came in, we asked to see the warden, a doctor, anyone who could get us outta there or at least turn off the heat. Even opening the windows would have helped. It was getting hotter all the time. We were sweating like crazy and it was getting tough to breathe. There was no air; we were suffocating."

"And who did you make the requests to?"

"Bridges, Smoot, Trent, and the other guards that came in," Palumbo replied. "We told 'em we were feelin' pretty bad. We got on our hands and knees and begged them to turn the heat off. We all had headaches, pains in our chest, and couldn't breathe. We told 'em we were all sick and wanted to speak to the warden. We asked to see a doctor."

"And what answer, if any, did you get from the guards?"

"Smoot just laughed at us," said Palumbo. "He said 'You fellows are on a picnic and don't know it. This ain't so bad. You won't die.' Then he turned the valves even farther to the right, causing the radiators to hiss even louder. They were steaming us to death. I screamed, 'You're killing us,' and pleaded with Bridges to bring the warden down. He said, 'I'll see.'"

"Did they come?" asked Ferencz. "Did anyone come?"

"No. No one came."

As the Klondike survivor fielded the deputy's questions, Glass observed the jury members. The male members wore serious expressions, listened intently, and appeared to be moved by the testimony. Miss Giovanni occasionally put her hand to her mouth as if to blunt comment, while Miss Walker appeared to be grinding her teeth and shaking her head in dismay as the witness recounted his near-death experience. Many in the gallery were similarly affected. Even news reporters—an unusually cynical lot, in the coroner's experience—seemed aghast at the inmate's testimony. More seasoned newsmen like Sel Rossman of the *Times* were as engrossed as trial neophytes like the young Judson Jones. Glass knew, however, there was more to come; the accounts would only become more horrid. Emotions would run even higher as his deputy moved the questioning toward the appalling events of Sunday night and early Monday morning.

Palumbo was holding up well, though his facial tic was becoming more pronounced and his grip on his chair grew tighter. The several hundred in attendance, not to mention the dozen prison personnel seated just a few feet in front of him, seemed to have little impact on his memory. He was determined to get justice for his brother. The coroner had convinced him an honest accounting of his ordeal was the best way to accomplish it.

"I hollered to Bruno, down in cell nine, to ask how he was doing, how he felt. He said, 'Pretty sick. I don't think I'm gonna make it.' He sounded pretty bad. That got me really worried."

"Did you relate your concerns about your brother to any guards?" Ferencz asked.

"Yes, sir. I told Bridges and Smoot my brother was sick. I told them he was in bad shape and needed a doctor."

"What did they say?"

"Bridges answered. He said, 'Your brother is a pretty mouthy son of a bitch. He don't need a doctor.'"

Deputy Coroner Ferencz glanced at Bridges. The guard appeared unmoved. "I'd like to move the questioning to the events of Saturday night," Ferencz said to Palumbo. "What were the conditions like inside Klondike at that time?"

"The boys were moaning and hollering for air," Palumbo replied, "and they kept that up until they couldn't talk anymore. The floor was really hot. The metal doors were so hot you'd burn your skin if you even touched them for a second."

"Was there water to drink?"

"Only what little there was in the hopper," said Palumbo. "We splashed some on our faces. Soaked our clothes in it and wrung out what we could over our heads and shoulders."

Muffled groans of revulsion could be heard in the courtroom. Many visibly winced and others were increasingly nauseated by Palumbo's testimony. Suddenly, there was a loud bang from the middle of the room, which startled everyone. It was the sound of a middle-aged woman fainting, her head hitting the back of a chair and her body crashing to the floor. There were gasps and an immediate rustling among courtroom observers near the woman. Cries for help and calls for a doctor could be heard. Coroner Glass banged his gavel in an attempt to restore order. Herman Rosen, the attorney for Officer Bridges, rose and yelled, "I move for a brief recess."

"No," replied Glass angrily. "There will be no adjournment. The inquest will continue."

As the attorney objected and commotion filled the courtroom, Glass tried again to restore order. Determined to move forward with the grim Holmesburg story, Glass feared any suspension of his inquest would encourage opponents and successfully thwart what little chance there was of discovering the guilty parties and prosecuting them.

"Everyone will take their seats," Glass shouted as he stood and directed bailiffs and sheriff deputies who were now attending to the ill woman. He ordered that she be removed from the courtroom. "Have her taken to my office or a hospital if need be. Please, everyone else, be seated. This official inquest will continue. Those discomforted by witness testimony should leave the courtroom immediately. This is a serious investigative hearing and one that will not be delayed, postponed, or derailed by those nauseated or enraged by witness testimony."

Several news reporters took note of the coroner's heavy-handed approach while courtroom observers commented to each other about the ill woman's condition and the brutality Klondike prisoners had to endure. Attorneys for Bridges and Smoot once again requested a short recess. The coroner shouted them down, struck his gavel, and ordered them to take their seats. The Holmesburg contingent, from prison superintendent to cellblock guards, finally seemed to recognize that someone else was now in charge and giving the orders.

After the sick woman was assisted from the courtroom and order was restored, the coroner asked Assistant District Attorney Doyle if he had any additional questions for the witness. Doyle followed with a question as to whether the guards brought any water to the Klondike prisoners during the day on Saturday.

"Not much," Palumbo answered. "One cup in the morning and one cup around noon."

"Is that all?"

"Yes," Palumbo replied, "except for what little we got out of the hopper."

"Did you complain to the guards? Did you tell them you needed water and to turn off the heat?"

"Yes, sir. We begged them to turn off the heat, to give us some water, and open the windows. I told them about my brother. I said he was sick; this heat was killing him. But they didn't do anything."

When asked what happened then, Palumbo replied, "Things just got worse. With the sun beating down on the roof and the radiators turned up, it just got hotter. You felt like you were in a broiler. It was terrible, like we were thrown in an oven. I heard some of the boys in other cells shouting. They seemed to be out of their heads. They were calling for their wives, calling for their mothers. They were going mad. I don't know how more of us didn't die. One of the boys kept shouting, 'Shoot us and get it over with. Don't let us suffer like this.'"

"When was the first time," Doyle asked, "that someone responded to your cries for help?"

"Not until sometime Sunday," said Palumbo. "Probably late afternoon or Sunday evening, Captain Brennan came in with several guards. Soon as he came in, we heard him say, 'Christ, it's too damned hot in here. Turn off the heat and open the windows.'"

"So, things improved?" interjected Deputy Ferencz.

"Only for about ten minutes," said Palumbo. "Soon as Captain Brennan left, they closed the windows again and turned the heat back on."

"Who closed the windows?"

"Bridges and Smoot," said the witness, pointing to the two guards.

"And the heat? How could you tell it was turned on again?"

"You could hear the hissing as plain as day," said Palumbo. "It was even louder this time. When we started complaining, we heard Smoot say, 'Forget it. The party's over, fellas.'"

"What did he mean by that?" asked Ferencz.

"I guess he meant the heat being off for a few minutes, but it really wasn't. It was still hot as hell."

"Did he always respond that way to your requests?" asked Ferencz.

"Yeah, he always had a snide line like that," said Palumbo. "When I asked him for salts one time 'cause I was sweating so much and passing out, he said, 'Hell no, no salt for you guys. I give you salt you'll then be asking me for steak and potatoes to go with it.' Then he laughed."

Ferencz gave Smoot an angry gaze and then turned back to the witness. "What happened next?" asked the deputy. "What were conditions like?"

"Well, it just kept getting hot," said Palumbo. "Hotter than Saturday night. The doors were steaming hot. You couldn't get near them. And the floors were too hot to sit or lie on. It just got hotter and hotter. That's how we got burned, all these burn marks we now got. And we were squeezed in like sardines. We couldn't take it. Webster hollered he was going to commit suicide, and he began banging his head against the wall, but one of the boys finally stopped him. O'Shea was moaning for his mother and screaming he was going to die."

"How did you deal with the conditions?"

"I'd stand for as long as I could before I started to faint again, then I'd lie on the floor . . . till the floor got too hot, then I'd try standing again. There was nothing you could do to cool off though. You were at the guards' mercy. I tried to get the boys to keep quiet and save their energy. I told them to get on the floor 'cause it was easier breathing down there. But the floor was real hot, and you'd end up burning your hands, knees, and backside. Whatever part of you touched the cement floor started to burn. I still got burn marks on me."

"So you were in bad shape whatever you did?"

Palumbo nodded and then glared at Davis and Stryker as well as the contingent of prison guards in the first three rows of the gallery. They appeared unaffected.

Coroner Glass, however, was more interested in the reactions of jury members and the large group of newspaper and radio personnel busy capturing the inquiry for their respective news agencies. The gallery was quiet but fascinated. It was an account of human depravity that few had ever heard before.

When the coroner encouraged Doyle to proceed with the questioning, the assistant district attorney inquired about the initial accounts of police investigators.

"Initially, there were reports of fighting amongst the inmates," said Doyle. "Was there any disorder during the night?"

"Disorder?" said Palumbo, obviously puzzled. "I don't know what you mean. We were dying. How were we supposed to act? They were trying to kill us. We were being roasted alive."

"Objection, objection," shouted Rosen, standing up and vigorously waving his arm.

"Objection denied," barked Glass. "Sit down, Counselor. This is not a trial. Let's hear what Mr. Palumbo has to say."

Palumbo remained confused. "We were all in bad shape. How is somebody supposed to act when they're dying? Yeah, all of us in Klondike were shouting, screaming, and crying at one time or another. What were we supposed to do, just sit there and bake like sausages on a grill? Yeah, we complained, we were crying out, begging for help. We couldn't breathe; the heat was terrible. Our lungs were on fire, our throats were burning. We were slowly baking to death—" Palumbo suddenly stopped, looked down, and appeared to be on the verge of crying.

Coroner Glass told a bailiff to get the witness some water.

After he took a gulp, Palumbo was encouraged to continue. "Sometime Monday morning, maybe two or three o'clock," said Palumbo, "Hickok hollered down from his cell that his two cellmates were dead. He said, 'I think they're gone.' Then, later, he hollered that they were cold and getting stiff."

"What did you do when you heard that?" asked Ferencz.

Palumbo shrugged and said, "I just thought that would be me soon. I wondered how my brother was doing. I was concerned about him 'cause of what he said earlier. I didn't hear from him after that. And I thought about Webster and O'Shea lying next to me. They hadn't moved in a while, and their breathing stopped. I know 'cause they were taking big gulps of air for a while, you know, trying to breathe, and then they started to cough and gag. It was like something had got caught in their throats. And then it got quiet, except for the hissing of the steam. Yeah, I think they stopped breathing. I wanted to check on 'em but was afraid to. I guess I knew; I figured they were dead. I was gonna be next. It frightened the hell out of me. You can't imagine how it feels when everybody is dyin' around you."

"Did anyone check on you or bring you water during the night?" asked Ferencz.

"No, no one came," said Palumbo. "Not the guards, not the warden, not the doctors. We were dying of thirst. The water in the hopper was nearly gone. There wasn't enough to scoop up and splash on our faces. We dipped our shirts in it and squeezed drops into our mouths. But then that was gone."

After hearing gasps of revulsion from some in the gallery, the inmate grew silent and appeared embarrassed. "Sure, I know it sounds bad when you think about all the crap and piss in the hopper," Palumbo explained. "I know it don't sound so good, but we were being cooked alive. If you wanted to live, you had no choice. You'll do anything to survive."

It was at that point that several women rose from their seats and quickly exited the courtroom. A couple had their hands near their mouths as if to prevent an embarrassing accident. Unprepared for such stomach-churning testimony, even a few men in the gallery thought it better to leave before they vomited or fainted like the poor woman earlier.

After many in the courtroom took a moment to absorb what they were hearing, Assistant District Attorney Doyle spoke up and said he'd like to turn to Monday morning. "Is it true," asked Doyle, "that sometime Monday morning guards came into the cellblock?"

"Yes, the guards came in Monday morning," said Palumbo. "I guess around eight or nine. I can't be sure. I heard Hickok tell Bridges that the other two in his cell were out. Hickok told 'em, 'They're gone and I'll soon be joining 'em.' I heard Bridges reply, 'That's your tough luck. You shoulda stayed in Virginia.'"

Glass carefully examined the horror-stricken faces of jury members. A few shook their heads in disbelief. Reporters busily took down every word.

"Go ahead," said Doyle. "What happened next?"

"Smoot came into my cell and gave me a cup of water," said Palumbo. "He asked if Webster and O'Shea wanted any. I told him I thought they were dead. I said they hadn't moved or said a word all night. Smoot just said, 'Then I guess they won't be wantin' any water,' and left."

Even Assistant District Attorney Doyle, a stern, seasoned criminal prosecutor who had handled dozens of homicide cases, shook his head in disgust. He then gave a dismissive glance at Davis, Stryker, and the other members of the prison staff seated before him. Turning back to the witness, he said, "Go ahead, what happened then?"

"They left," said Palumbo, "and I figured it was only a matter of time and I'd be dead like the others. But a few minutes later I heard the door open again. I heard someone curse and say, 'Jesus Christ, it's hot as hell in here. Open these goddamn windows and get the men out of here. And shut off those damn radiators. For Christ's sake, turn the heat off.'"

"Who made those comments?" said Doyle.

"It was Dr. Moretti."

"And that's when you were you carried out?"

"Yeah," said Palumbo. "I was dragged out by the guards. I was weak as hell and could barely breathe. They dropped me on the grass. Some of the other guys were in worse shape—they were put on stretchers and carried out. I couldn't really see. My eyes couldn't get used to the light. We had been in the dark for three days. I think I saw Hickok, Scheinbach, Walters, and Teague. I looked for my brother, but he wasn't one of 'em. I waited to see him, but he was never brought out. He was one of those left inside on the cell floor. He was just a kid . . . he was only twenty-three."

Recognizing the emotional impact of the inmate's story and the need for a break, Coroner Glass called for a brief recess. Reporters quickly scrambled toward the phones to call in their stories. Jury members seemed shaken and discussed among themselves the incredible horrors they had just heard. Those in the large gallery stood and stretched their legs. Many could be seen taking deep breaths. Spectators began recounting those pieces of testimony that most resonated with them, but they did not dare leave their seats. They were too hard to come by; leaving the courtroom meant giving up a seat for the best show in town. While Glass and Doyle whispered between themselves, the Holmesburg contingent displayed either grim or defeatist expressions.

When everyone returned and the jury and press gallery were seated, Coroner Glass banged his gavel several times to silence the large chamber. With order restored, he then called Henry Luzinski to the stand.

The well-built, dark-haired Klondike survivor wearing a snug, light-gray suit entered the witness box. Asked to raise his right hand and be sworn in, he did as told but remained mute and never verbally affirmed to tell the truth. Distracted, he concentrated on the Holmesburg Prison officers seated before him. It was the first time in over a week he had been in the presence of Warden Stryker and Officers Bridges, Smoot, Trent, and the others who had placed him in Klondike. His tormentors glared back at him. The coroner was forced to bang his gavel to gain the witness's attention, and his affirmation to tell the truth.

"Tell us," asked Assistant District Attorney Doyle "when were you taken to Holmesburg's punishment unit and for what infraction?

"Sunday morning," said Luzinski. "I was taken to Klondike on Sunday, August 21. I guess it was like the rest of the guys. I was on the strike and refused to eat."

"What was your prison record like?" asked Assistant District Attorney Doyle.

"My record's been good," said Luzinski. "I have never had a mark against me, and I had a job cleaning the officers' mess hall."

"Tell us what you found in the punishment unit."

"It was bad. I never felt such heat before. Imagine somebody putting you in a large brick oven. That's what Klondike is, a large oven. They use it to roast people."

Several attorneys for the defendants immediately stood up and voiced their objections to the comments. The coroner banged his gavel, told the attorneys to sit down, and instructed the witness, "Please answer the questions you're asked, Mr. Luzinski. No personal editorial comment needed. Just describe the general atmosphere of the building."

"It was dark, hot, and stunk like hell," Luzinski replied. "The heat was so strong it was like walking into a blast furnace. I don't know, try to imagine jumping into a pool of water that's two hundred degrees and you can't get out. That's what it was like, drowning in a pool of burning water."

"Who was in the cell you were placed in?" asked Deputy Coroner Ferencz.

"Smyzak and Bruno Palumbo were already in the cell," said Luzinski. "They looked like hell. Palumbo was a real mess. Smyzak was gaspin' for air; he couldn't breathe. He was holding his chest like he was having a heart attack."

Ferencz asked, "What, if anything, did the inmates have to say?"

"They were begging the guards for water and to turn the heat off," Luzinski replied. "The guards didn't say much. I heard Smoot tell one guy, 'I want you to know, and never forget, that I'm the guy who put you in here.'"

Ferencz leaned forward and asked, "What was your reaction to that?"

"Me, all the guys, were furious," said Luzinski, "but what could we do? We were helpless. Guys were afraid they weren't gonna make it. Palumbo was goin' nuts. He got up but was wobbly and toppled over a couple of times. I tried to keep him still and help him as best I could. I talked to him and said we'd get out of it, but I really didn't believe it. He asked me to keep talking to him and make sure he didn't shut his eyes and fall asleep. We all felt that if we fell asleep, we'd never wake up again. I don't know, somewhere around eight or nine o'clock Sunday night, he fell over from where he was sitting. His head fell on the floor and he didn't say anything after that."

"Do you believe Palumbo died at that point?" asked Ferencz.

"I don't know. He may have," said Luzinski. "A few hours later, I'm just about gone myself, and I crawl on my hands and knees to another corner of the cell looking for a cooler place, and my hand hits his leg. He didn't move, and his leg was cold. I guess he died sometime before that. I figured my time was comin' . . ."

"When did you see the guards again?"

"I guess it was sometime Sunday evening," the inmate replied with a shrug. "We heard the outside door open and someone enter and call out, 'Christ, it's hot as hell in here. Open the damn windows, and turn off the heat.' It was Captain Brennan along with Smoot, Bridges, and a few others. They brought us a cup of water, some stale bread. Brennan told 'em what to do. We pleaded, we told 'em we were boiling and needed a doctor."

"What happened then?"

"They left," Luzinski replied. "They were only there for five or ten minutes at most. Brennan went first and then the others. After the captain walked out, I heard one of the guards curse him and close the windows again. Then they turned the heat back on. It was just like before, maybe worse. The steam pipes were hissing again, and all through the night. You couldn't breathe. We were slowly dyin', roasting to death."

"And then?"

"I crawled around looking for a cooler spot but couldn't find one," said Luzinski. "You couldn't stand or sit.

Deputy Coroner Ferencz then asked about his cellmates.

"Smyzak was moaning off and on," said Luzinski. "Kept saying he wasn't goin' to make it. Then he'd be quiet for a while. I never knew if he was dead or unconscious. A couple times I shook him, and he'd come around. I told him Palumbo was dead but don't think he heard me."

"And after that?"

"Around one or two in the morning, Smyzak got a bad coughing spell," said Luzinski. "I think he was coughing up blood. I didn't know for sure cause it was pitch black in there, but some of it got on me. It was thick and hot, more like blood than spit. I thought maybe his lungs burst or something."

Groans could be heard from different parts of the courtroom. Glass noticed that Miss Giovanni and Miss Walker both appeared pale and reached for their hankies, as if they were about to lose control and bring up some of their last meal.

Ferencz encouraged the witness to continue.

"Smyzak started moaning and calling for his mother, his wife, and then his kid," said Luzinski. "He kept moaning, 'What's gonna happen to my baby? What's gonna happen to my baby?' After that, he sorta sank back and his head just rolled to the side. He got quiet. I tried talkin' to him, but he didn't answer. Sometime later I tried talkin' to him again. He didn't answer so I shoved him with my leg, but he didn't move. I reached out and grabbed a leg, but it was cold. He was dead. I thought it was Palumbo, so I felt around for Smyzak and I found an arm, but it was cold also. Both of 'em were dead. They had been in there longer than me."

"Go ahead," asked Ferencz. "What happened then?"

"What could I do?" said Luzinski. "The rest of the night I just lay on my back or belly trying to breathe. All I could hear was the radiators steaming away and my heart pounding. Thought I was gonna have a heart attack at any moment. Worst night of my life. I was surprised I lasted till sun-up. When morning came, I heard the outside door open and some guards enter the hallway. I told 'em I was dying and the two guys with me were already dead."

"What did the guards do?"

"Nothing," said Luzinski.

"Did they say anything?"

"Yeah. 'Too bad, that's what they get for acting like assholes.'"

Ferencz grimaced, his disgust obvious. "But they eventually got you out of there, right?"

"Yeah, about ten minutes later," said Luzinski. "Took 'em a while. They were in no big hurry. They finally opened the cell door, looked inside, and then threw some water on 'em as if they expected them to wake up. But they were both gone. They had been dead a while. Then they dragged me out and dropped me on the grass outside Klondike. They probably wouldn't have done anything if Dr. Moretti hadn't been with 'em. Another hour or two with the sun coming up we all woulda been dead."

The coroner turned to his colleagues on the panel and then to the jury to see if anyone had a question for the witness. Seeing no hands rise, Glass thanked the witness for his testimony.

After Henry Luzinski was excused, Gregory Corso was called to the stand. Attired in a drab, ill-fitting brown suit, the dark-haired man took his seat in the witness box, held up his right hand, and swore to tell the truth. He gazed at the prison officials seated in the first several rows to his right and quickly turned away, his discomfort obvious.

"How old are you and where do you reside?" asked Deputy Ferencz.

"I'm thirty-four years old and currently in Holmesburg Prison."

"How long have you been a prisoner there?" asked Ferencz.

"Eighteen months," Corso replied. "I have nine more months to go, but I hope to get out sooner."

"On the weekend of August 19, Mr. Corso, where were you celled in the prison?"

"I was on E Block. Cell 34 on E Block."

"Were you alone?"

"No, nobody has their own cell at the Burg," said Corso. "It's way too crowded. There were three other guys in there with me. Every cell is like that; four guys to a cell."

"And what do you know of the tragic events that resulted in the deaths of eight prisoners over that same weekend?"

Corso recalled the food strike, his willing participation early on, and his gradual disgruntlement. "We was locked in our cells all day," said the inmate.

"The administration decided no yard, no exercise, no fresh air, no visits. It was hot as hell in our cells; we couldn't even walk the block. To make matters worse, there was no food or water. It was bad . . . you just sat around and sweated."

Asked to describe what followed over those few days, Corso said, "Little by little, guys started to fold. They started goin' down to the dining hall for meals. By Sunday morning, I joined 'em—I had enough of the protest."

"Did you know some strikers were being placed in Klondike, the punishment unit?" asked Ferencz.

"Yeah, we knew," Corso replied. "Klondike is right next to E block. Our cell was real close and we could hear 'em screaming from Friday night on. By Saturday morning, you could hear 'em pleadin' for water. Pleadin' for the heat to be turned off. It was really bad. You knew they were sufferin'."

"But how could you have heard them?" asked Ferencz. "It's been claimed all the windows and ventilators in Klondike were shut tight."

"E Block is only a few feet from Klondike," said Corso. "And our vents, the air vents at the top of our cells, were open in order to get some air. Yeah, the sound was muffled, but we heard 'em. We couldn't see 'em, but we knew they were in bad shape."

"What did you do?" Ferencz asked.

"What could we do?" said Corso. "We were locked up too. Word got around the guards were throwin' strike leaders in Klondike and givin' 'em steam. You know, tryin' to roast 'em."

"Objection," bellowed Cyrus Black, attorney for Superintendent Davis. "I object to this entire line of—"

Glass banged his gavel, shouted Black down, and told the witness to continue.

"My cellies said it's good we went down to chow and gave up the strike or we might've been thrown in there too," Corso told the panel. "Guys were scared. We called the block guards and told 'em the guys in Klondike were crying out for help, but they didn't care."

"What did the block guards say?"

"The guards told us to mind our own business," said Corso. "They said if anyone stayed on strike they could be joining 'em in Klondike."

"Go ahead," said Ferencz. "What happened then?"

"Nothing really," said Corso. "Guys in Klondike just kept on crying for water, pleadin' for the heat to be turned off, askin' for a doctor. Heard one guy callin' for Helen. Guess it was his wife or daughter. I don't know. Went on around the clock, day and night. Hearing guys crying out for help. Wished I had a cell on G or H Block over on the other side of the jail so I didn't have to hear 'em."

"And then?" Ferencz inquired.

"Well, it went on for a long time," Corso replied. "But then it finally stopped . . . there was no more cryin' and pleadin'. Must have been late Sunday night, early Monday morning. I was hopin' it meant they had gotten them to turn the heat off and given 'em some water. But I didn't really believe it. Wasn't that shocked when we heard they found a bunch of 'em dead Monday morning. Guess I was more surprised how many got out alive."

With many in the room emotionally exhausted from a long day of testimony that included family members of victims and Klondike survivors, it would have been an appropriate time to end the session, but Glass was intent on getting one last inmate account on the record. Excusing Corso after thanking him for his testimony, Glass called Harold Warner to the stand.

Of average height and weight, Warner was attired in tan slacks, a navy jacket, and light-blue tie. Despite a slight limp, the Klondike survivor moved rapidly. It was as if he were hoping to complete an unpleasant chore as quickly as possible. Nervous, he leaned forward in his chair and anxiously scanned the large gallery now focused on him. Close observers could spy discoloration around his neck that appeared just above his shirt collar. After confirming that he was thirty-five years old and serving a five-year sentence for a Roxborough grocery store robbery, Warner was asked when he was sent to the prison's punishment unit.

"They pulled me outta my cell Saturday morning and took me out to Klondike," said Warner. "They never said anything, never told me it was because of the strike, but I figured that's what it musta been. I didn't do anything else, so it musta been the strike."

"Were you in a cell by yourself," inquired Deputy Coroner Ferencz, "or were others in the cell?"

"They tossed me in a cell with Max Teague," said Warner. "It was dark so I couldn't see too good, but he looked bad . . . you know, sick. It was hot, the whole place smelled bad, and Max looked real strung out, like he was dying."

"Did he say anything to you?"

"Yeah, he said, 'They got the cooker fired up. They're gonna fuck us up good this time.'"

"Did you know what he meant?" asked Ferencz.

"Sure," Warner replied, "I had been in the jail three years. You get to hear things. People talk about Klondike and what goes on in there. But I thought you really had to do something serious, you know, like punch a guard or try and break out of the place. I never thought they'd throw you in Klondike for not going down to chow. I thought that was a bit rough. Pretty soon I was in bad shape as well. During the night I started callin' out for help. I wasn't the only one. You could hear guys in the other cells doing the same. Some guys were crying . . . we thought it was over."

"Go ahead," said Ferencz, "what happened then?"

"Well, it just got worse," said Warner. "The sun by midday was beating down on the roof and the radiators were turned all the way up. You could hear the radiators whistlin' and feel the temperature goin' up. Must have been over 150 degrees in there. The spigot was shut so the only water we had was in the toilet. They never flushed it, so the shit and piss just sat there and the water dried up. We just sat there, sweatin', prayin', and cryin'. Wasn't long before the floor, the mattress, the walls got so hot you couldn't bear touchin' 'em."

"Is it true," asked Ferencz, "they put another inmate in your cell?"

"Yeah, sometime Sunday morning Cal Crouse was brung in. I think he got scared as soon as he felt the heat and saw us. We musta looked like a couple of sewer rats."

"So there were three of you in a cell designed for one man and with one mattress?"

"Yeah, three of us shoved in one little cell. Only one mattress, but nobody wanted it. It was too damn hot, so I put it up against the door to try and keep the heat out. Max thought the mattress would catch on fire and we'd burn to death, so after a while, we took it down."

"Is it true," asked Ferencz, "that later that day you suffered a serious burn?"

"Yeah, I got burned pretty bad," Warner admitted. "I musta passed out from the heat and bein' unable to breathe. Guess I fell against the metal door and knocked myself out. Musta banged my head pretty good and just laid against the door. I don't know for how long. Guess it was the pain that revived me. My back was on fire. The pain was terrible. I was moanin' and screamin'. The guys tried to hold me down. There was no water or anything to put on it, so I asked them to spit on me. It burnt like hell; still hurts pretty bad. Doctor says it's a third-degree burn and it's gonna leave a nasty scar."

"Mr. Warner," said the deputy coroner, "would you mind showing it to the jury?"

Warner was surprised by the request. He had clearly not expected to be asked to undress in front of hundreds of strangers. He glanced at the jury, the press contingent, and then back at Coroner Glass for guidance. The coroner nodded in the affirmative, giving the witness the impression he had no choice. As soon as the prisoner stood up to take off his jacket, Jack Ryan, Warden Stryker's attorney, called out an objection. He argued that such a display was not only unusual but highly prejudicial. Glass ruled the inquest wasn't a criminal trial and the wound would document the level of heat inmates endured during their confinement. When Ryan continued to oppose such a demonstration, arguing there was no way to determine whether the wound came from the inmate's incarceration in Klondike, the coroner smiled.

"Well, Counselor," Glass replied, "I guess we could ask Dr. Moretti to return and testify to whether he saw the burn mark on the witness when he was removed from Klondike on the morning of August 22."

Frustrated and murmuring expletives under his breath, Ryan sat down.

"Mr. Warner, if you don't mind," said Coroner Glass, "please take off your jacket and shirt and show the jury your wounds?"

Warner took off his jacket, then his tie and shirt. When he turned around so the jury and gallery could see his back, there were a few gasps. A large surgical pad with adhesive tape covered a good portion of the inmate's back. Warner was about to put his shirt back on when Glass asked, "Could you remove the bandage, please? We'd like to see the actual wound."

Unhappy, the inmate hesitated and replied, "I can't really do it myself." The coroner then asked a deputy sheriff to assist the witness. Jack Ryan immediately rose and voiced his objection. "No, you can't do this. This is highly prejudicial—"

"Counselor," said Glass firmly, "would you prefer we have the doctors return, assist the witness, and testify to the extent of Mr. Warner's injuries?"

Ryan once again sat down while giving the coroner a menacing look. The deputy sheriff then approached the witness and gently began removing strips of adhesive tape. When he was done and laid the large bandage on a table, he turned the witness around, allowing all to see his back. Gasps, muffled sighs, and several "Oh my God" comments were heard from different sections of the courtroom. On Warner's back was an ugly blotch of dead and burned skin about a foot in diameter, covered with a mix of blood, leaking body fluids, and various medicinal lotions. The raw wound appeared to be oozing pus, and many in the room could be seen turning away to hide their discomfort. Others shook their heads in abhorrence, some visibly fighting back a tinge of nausea. Miss Crystal Lee Walker and Miss Anna Giovanni were not the only members of the jury to wince in horror this time.

"Thank you, Mr. Warner," said the coroner. "The panel appreciates you showing us your injury, but one cannot help noticing several other bruises on your arms and especially your neck. Were they from your internment in Klondike as well?"

"Yes, sir," Warner answered.

Suddenly, Cyrus Black, attorney for Superintendent Davis, rose and asked, "May I proffer a question to the witness?"

Granted permission, the attorney asked, "Mr. Warner, are the black-and-blue bruises around your neck due to one of your cellmates trying to strangle you?"

Warner, now seated and holding his shirt and jacket on his lap, appeared hesitant, undecided. He looked down at his feet and then turned back to Coroner Glass, apparently hoping to avoid addressing the question.

"You can answer the question, Mr. Warner," said Glass.

Warner bit his lip, gently rubbed his neck with his hand, and then looked at Mr. Black. "I'm Catholic," said Warner. "I know it's a sin, but I . . . I tried to end my life. I tried to kill myself." Mouths of many in the gallery as well as several jury members were agape, and a number of reporters stopped taking notes. They were already transfixed by the inmate's disturbing wounds, and now by this further admission. "I was in such pain and the heat was so terrible on Sunday night that rather than suffer any more, I tried to hang myself," said Warner. "I know I shouldn't have, but I was going crazy. The heat was bearing down on us, crushing us. My heart was pounding so hard I didn't know if I was gonna die of a heart attack or roast to death."

Embarrassed, ashamed, and still unclothed above the waist, the Klondike survivor squeezed his shirt and jacket tightly as hundreds of onlookers digested his painful confession.

"How could you have accomplished such an endeavor in a small cell with two other inmates present?" Coroner Glass asked.

"It wasn't that hard."

"Could you explain?"

"We were all struggling to survive. The heat was so intense, no air, no water, we were all passing out at different times. I was going crazy, so I got some rags and scraps of clothes from the floor, twisted them into a noose, and tied it to a crossbar above the door. With the little strength I had left, I then lifted myself up, stuck my head through it, and . . ."

Though the courtroom was filled to capacity, not a sound was heard. When Warner regained his composure, he went on to explain he started to gag, groan, and thrash around, thereby rousing his cellmates, who stumbled around in the dark and eventually got him down.

"I know it was wrong," said the tearful inmate as he rubbed his throat, "but we were gonna die anyway. I just wanted to get it over with."

Again, there was complete silence.

Coroner Glass glanced at his colleagues on the bench and then at the jury. Everyone appeared exhausted, beaten down. It had been a long day. Much was learned, but it seemed to come at great emotional cost. Even the news reporters appeared drained. Glass believed he, Carl Ferencz, and David Sandler had done a good job. They had presented a good case for what really happened.

Glass momentarily reflected on his former intern and how unfortunate it was the young man couldn't be there to witness the culmination of his efforts. Sandler was a good worker, well intentioned, and understood the importance of their investigation. But for whatever reason, he displayed a terrible lapse in judgment. His partner in crime, the beige-suited reporter from a Southern newspaper, looked at Glass like everyone else in the courtroom waiting for direction. The reporter's one and only scoop—news of the autopsy results— was the end of his access to inside information. Glass hoped Sandler had learned a valuable lesson from the experience; he was less confident the young journalist had.

The coroner finally asked if there were any questions for the witness. When no one raised their hand, he dismissed the witness, banged his gavel, and said the inquest would reconvene at ten the next morning.

Chapter 22

Ward Meeting

As the car traveled up Broad Street and approached the intersection of Broad and Rockland, Glass examined the list of talking points he had scribbled for his presentation. He was physically drained, but now nervousness was setting in, and rightly so. His appearance before the 49th Ward Democratic City Committee was an unusual and hastily scheduled affair. Though summer meetings were unusual—and one conceived and held in just a couple of days—this one was designed to shore up his support with party loyalists from the vote-rich Logan section of the city. The incumbent coroner was fighting for his political life, and he believed such appearances were mandatory.

His anger overflowing, Mayor Clarke had sworn to teach Heshel Glass a lesson. He'd find an opponent for a primary run at Glass and ensure every ward leader and committeeman in the city got the message; the coroner was being cut loose for being an incompetent, press-obsessed, political ingrate. The fact that the leader of the 49th ward, a former childhood friend of Glass's and a fellow Southern High classmate, was willing to buck Clarke's orders and stick by the coroner was gratifying. He and any others across the city Glass could convince to rally around his banner would be worth their weight in gold during the coming election campaign.

The timing of the ward meeting—less than an hour after his blue ribbon inquest's first day of highly emotional testimony—wasn't ideal, but the coroner was still much appreciative that a ward leader and his committee people were willing to stick their necks out and come hear a recently excommunicated member of the flock.

Adjoining Mosconi's, a popular pool hall, on the second floor of a wallpapering establishment, the meeting room was packed, a testament to the coroner's newfound celebrity status rather than any sort of civic duty by neighborhood residents on a sultry summer evening. The gruesome deaths at Holmesburg Prison had captivated the newspaper-reading public for more than a week, and Glass was the eye of the storm. Granted, many had come to see and hear the suddenly controversial elected official, but not all were Glass loyalists. Mayor Clarke and the party still had their troops in the room. Tempers could easily flare and violence erupt between opposing camps. With that undesired prospect in mind, Glass and the ward leader agreed that the coroner would not discuss the explosive inquest going on in the City Hall courtroom.

The plan was just to stick to the basics. Glass would address the historical role of a city coroner, never comment on the mayor's heavy-handed and buffoonish involvement in the investigation, and thank committee people for their past support. And if asked questions about the much-talked-about hearing, he was to answer in the most innocuous way possible.

"I've never voted for any other than a Democratic ticket," said Glass, after he was introduced to the audience. "I'm a Democrat; have been and will continue to be. After many years of loyalty, I still say I was right in my lifelong party allegiance and see no reason to change now. I have never traded, nor compromised, nor evaded the issue. I never voted for or worked for anyone but a Democrat. I am proud to have been one of the 'Old Guard' who remained true to the creed of democracy, no matter what the temptation."

The admission drew applause and smiles, but Glass recognized there were many in the room with their arms crossed, wearing stony expressions. He had his work cut out for him. Hoping a history lesson may win over those who considered him a lightweight for having neither a college nor medical degree, Glass illuminated the role of the "crowner" in protecting the king's person and revenue in medieval England. "Charged with investigating all violent crimes, such as arson, rape, murder, and prison breach," said Glass, "the crowner also dealt with feudal rates, levies, and other issues of finance."

Glass described the start and evolution of the office in America and its nineteenth-century permutations in Pennsylvania and Philadelphia. He appreciated the chance to show off his knowledge about the office's origin and varied functions, though it was increasingly clear not all in the room were equally captivated by British history. Glass told the ward committee, "When I entered the coroner's office a few years earlier, I found a cesspool of iniquity and obscenely offensive behavior, and all at the taxpayer's expense. It was a rendezvous of all the harpies and buzzards of unclean trade, an unspeakably foul crew that fattened themselves on the city's dead."

Glass would go on to describe the shock of confronting suborners of perjury, connivers at manslaughter, panderers of abortionists, shysters, and vice-tricksters; all unjust men who plied their evil traffic in chiseling relatives of persons killed in accidents out of indemnities bought and paid for in insurance contracts. "It was just such a corrupt and pervasive culture," he explained, "that led to the scandal that forced out my predecessor and enabled myself and the Democratic Party to establish new standards and operating procedures.

"I was carried into office," Glass reminded his audience, "on a wave of public indignation at the callous, brutal, and improper handling of bodies and the effects of the dead. I promised the people of Philadelphia honesty, courtesy, economy, and efficiency. My four years in office have demonstrated my sincerity.

"I immediately tried to spark a new spirit of service and kindly treatment. Families were shown the utmost consideration. We released bodies earlier to families, kept the office open twenty-four hours a day, seven days a week, and deputies worked longer hours and more days a week."

Signaled by the ward leader that he should sum up, Glass told the group, "I have reduced expenses in my office by twenty percent, never exceeded my budget, and added extra duties while decreasing office staff. When I took office there were forty-two employees, some who never even showed up for work. Now we have thirty-six employees, from doctors to secretaries, and all put in an honest day's work. Yes, we're doing more with less.

"And if you grant me a second term," said Glass, "I will continue to campaign against uninsured drivers, against unsafe and careless industrial conditions, and against illegal drugs and liquors." Receiving a good hand from attendees, Glass was pleased he never had to mention the controversial Holmesburg tragedy, though he did cite his office's role in assisting the district attorney's office in apprehending more than six hundred murderers.

When the ward leader announced there was time for one or two questions, numerous hands went up in the audience, but before one could be called a man shouted out, "What about the guards you're prosecuting? What about them? My brother-in-law works in Holmesburg and there's a lot of good, decent fellows working in that hellhole. What about them? You're just a politician trying to make a name for yourself and—"

Suddenly, shouts of "Shut up," "Sit down," and "Keep your mouth shut," burst from different corners of the room. Several men and women started approaching each other in a menacing fashion, and Glass, the ward leader, and others tried to lower tensions and keep opposing parties apart. As the shouting, accusations, and verbal threats gradually declined, the coroner offered to explain his position and the importance of his controversial blue ribbon inquest. The ward leader, however, approached him and vigorously argued it was best he leave and not become embroiled in an ugly name-calling session.

"You did a good job, Hesh; no need to burden yourself further," said his friend. "Between the mayor's people and those who hate criminals, you're never going to win them over. But the rest of the ward committee saw you, and I think they were pleased."

It was a disappointing ending for Glass but not totally unexpected. He'd have to live with such turmoil if he had any chance of being reelected. It was that prospect he pondered when he noticed his driver frequently looking at his rearview mirror and suddenly speeding up and slowing down as they traveled on Broad Street back toward City Hall.

"What's wrong?" Glass asked.

"I think we're being followed," his driver replied. "They've been with us since Rockland Street. They do whatever I do, and they seem in no hurry. Too dark to see who's driving or how many are in the car."

Concerned, Glass told his driver, "Take a left at Vine. Let's see what they do."

The driver did as ordered, and as they both feared, the vehicle in question kept on their tail. "It looks like a city auto," said the driver, who was able to get a better view of the vehicle as it turned the corner.

"Probably the mayor's deputies," Glass replied, relieved that it was not a more ruthless faction opposed to his investigation of the Holmesburg tragedy. He knew they could not have been pleased with the inquest earlier in the day.

As they traveled through the city's Tenderloin district toward the Ben Franklin Bridge and New Jersey, Glass told his driver, "Turn right when you can and come back to City Hall by way of Market Street. If they're the mayor's people, they've been assigned to keep an eye on me. He'd wanna know who I'm talking to, who I'm meeting with. Let's see if they park at City Hall."

"And if they're not?" replied the concerned driver.

Glass did not reply. They were followed back to City Hall, but their pursuers had an unexpected surprise. The coroner's vehicle took off again, dangerously weaved through some traffic as they circled City Hall, and shot down Broad

Street at a rapid rate of speed. They did not stop until they were deep into South Philadelphia and parked at the intersection of Broad and Wolf Streets, the site of Temple Shalom Synagogue. The late-night meeting with Rabbi Mordecai Levitt was not unexpected as the coroner had communicated with the rabbi early that morning about his desire to meet with him. Though his inquest was his central focus, he needed to tend to his reelection campaign as well. His presentation at the 49th ward and his meeting with a prominent South Philly rabbi were confirmation of his dual interests.

Most astute party workers paying attention to recent developments had consigned the coroner to the city's political graveyard. Glass, however, wasn't about to give up without a fight. His meeting now with Rabbi Levitt—someone outside the political arena but still influential with a segment of South Philadelphia residents—was integral to his reelection effort. The rabbi's congregation sat in the heart of South Philadelphia, an area still abundant in Jewish voters and home to thousands of potentially friendly election-day supporters. Glass apologized for arriving at such a late hour. Rabbi Levitt, a short, white-bearded gentleman in his late seventies, explained there was no inconvenience as the congregation's men's club and sisterhood had just departed. Events overseas, he explained, were getting worse by the day, and there was much to do.

As the rabbi poured the coroner a glass of red wine he inquired about the special inquest. "What did you find out, Heshel?" the rabbi asked. "Did you learn anything important?"

Glass gave him a brief summary of the day's events and then said, "I'm really here to ask your help in the forthcoming primary election. I can deal with the Holmesburg investigation myself, but reelection is a different kind of problem. I could really use some help."

"I don't know what I can do for you, Heshel," said the rabbi as he gathered papers and rearranged some files on his desk. "You know you have my vote, and I already told the mayor I thought you should be allowed to do your work."

"You talked to the mayor?" said the coroner, surprised by the admission. "When did that happen?"

"The mayor called me a few days ago. He was very upset. Said you were causing problems. He said you were giving the city a bad name on this prison business. He wanted me to talk you out of doing the investigation. I told him the deaths of all those prisoners weren't your fault. You had the responsibility to look into the matter."

"And what did he say?"

"Oh, he got very angry," replied the rabbi. "You know he's a little bit meshuggah. He started yelling and screaming and coughing like someone with pleurisy. He kept telling me what people were saying, what the newspapers were writing. Then he started calling you names—I won't repeat them. I really wanted to hang up on him."

"You should have."

"I wanted to, but I couldn't," said the rabbi. "Can't afford to make an enemy of him, you know; he's the mayor. We're trying to get the city to agree to let us expand the synagogue by building on the parking lot. It's some kind of zoning issue. And some of the local schools have maintenance problems, and there's a bar in the area that has become a real nuisance. They're all important causes to us, so I let him scream and did what he asked—I called you."

"So that's why you phoned me the other day."

"Yes, I called you, but I would never tell you what to do," the rabbi said. "Heshel, that's important work you're doing. It's a mitzvah if you can figure the whole thing out. What happened up there at the prison is a shanda, just terrible. I read people were baked to death or something like that. He told me to phone you, so I called and asked how you were. That's all. But please, don't tell that putz in City Hall what I told you."

Glass chuckled at the request. He then explained that the mayor was now sworn to defeat him at the Democratic Party primary, and his chances of reelection looked dim. He had been advised to either call off his inquiry into the Holmesburg deaths or end his reelection campaign. Glass said neither were going to happen. "I won't be intimidated," said Glass. "Nothing may come of the inquest, and I may lose my job at the coroner's office, but I won't be threatened out of either."

Glass never mentioned the bullets found on his vehicle's front hood, the threats he was receiving, or the brick thrown through his living room window.

"But, Heshel," said the rabbi, "the newspapers and radio have said good things about you and your investigation. They said your inquest was necessary, and maybe the only way to get at the truth. I read the papers. They said with the police and the district attorney showing little interest, your investigation was the only way to discover who did this terrible crime."

"That may be true, Rabbi, but the papers and radio don't vote. Most of the ward leaders will follow the mayor's orders. I'll be shut out of meetings, ward events, and party dinners. That's why I was hoping you could help arrange some meetings for me where I could talk to voters and explain to them why I deserve a second term."

Rabbi Levitt agreed that he would like to help, and would definitely organize an event at the shul, but that the timing was very bad and all of the synagogue's members were preoccupied with the horrid events taking place in Europe.

"Hitler and these Nazis are an abomination," said Levitt. "People are being arrested, thrown in prison, some have gone missing—possibly forever. They've taken away businesses, family possessions; the best universities and medical schools have fired and chased out all who are Jewish. And Germany keeps threatening its neighbors, placing armed troops on the border as if they're preparing to invade. I discounted such talk early on, but I've now come to see it for what it is; I feel war is inevitable. Look what they've done with Austria, Czechoslovakia. Hitler won't be happy until Germany stretches from Russia to the sea . . . the entire world will be involved."

"I don't know, Rabbi," said Glass. "No one wants another war."

"Heshel, don't be so naïve. If you keep up with current events, there's no way one can be optimistic. The whole world is going meshuggah. Do you see what's happening in Austria, Spain, in China? It's all so depressing."

The rabbi opened a file cabinet, pulled out a stack of newspaper clippings, and handed them to the coroner. "Look at the articles, Heshel," said the rabbi. The headlines read: "Germany's War Moves Alarm Europe," "Germans Blame Foes for War Scare," "Hitler Lauds Armed Troops During Field Maneuvers," "Europe Drifts Towards Another War," "Roosevelt Pledges Defense of Canada," "Germany Tightens Pressure On Jews," and "Anti-Semitism Hits New High as Nazis Push Persecution."

The coroner admitted he was not as familiar with all the conflicts around the world as he should be but promised to pay greater attention to events overseas. He then went back to his original concern, requesting assistance for his reelection campaign. Rabbi Levitt explained that many area synagogues were currently organizing a trip to the Capitol to lobby President Roosevelt and Congress for help in assisting displaced German Jews and a more aggressive stance toward Hitler and the Nazis. Additional efforts were being planned.

When Glass respectfully stated that a few neighborhood and synagogue meetings regarding his candidacy would not take much time away from this work, the elderly rabbi shook his head. "Heshel, you have your work to do and we have ours," said Levitt. "My congregants have hundreds, maybe thousands of family members and friends still in Germany, Poland, the Ukraine, and other places in Europe. They have very few, if any, relatives in that prison of yours. Our thoughts, prayers, and actions must be for those Jews in harm's way. I will try to schedule a meeting at the men's club for you, but any more than that I cannot commit. Good luck in your investigation, Heshel. *Z'ai Guzint.*"

After a night of little sleep, the coroner was in his office early the next morning reading the many banner headline stories of the previous day's testimony. Newspapers printed full-page accounts of the controversial inquest ranging from the testimony of victims' relatives and prison doctors to the unsettling recollections of Klondike survivors. Editors knew from the beginning they had a goldmine with the Klondike story. The survivors' chilling accounts of "suffocating" and being "roasted alive" were powerful nuggets for a readership that couldn't get enough of a home-grown horror story.

Glass was pleased with the newspaper accounts; everything from the phony police reports to the emotionally jarring accounts of Klondike victims was just as the coroner desired. But now was the hard part, identifying the perpetrators and especially the higher-ups who orchestrated the deadly event. As he and Carl Ferencz walked the long corridor to Courtroom 653, he noticed people who stopped and paid attention to him. His inquest had become front-page news, and he was no longer an unrecognized City Hall bureaucrat. In fact, just his walking into the large, capacity-filled courtroom was enough to quiet the crowd.

When everyone was seated, the coroner began the session by calling city engineer George Rediker to the stand. In his mid-fifties, with sandy hair and a slight paunch, Rediker claimed to have worked for the city for thirteen years; nine years as a prison engineer, and four years before that as a plumber at Philadelphia General Hospital.

Coroner Glass wasted little time in getting to the heart of the matter. "Mr. Rediker," asked Glass, "who ordered you to turn the heat on in Klondike?"

"Hartzell," Rediker replied. "Sergeant Hartzell told me to turn the heat on."

Many in the courtroom, from jury members and news reporters to average citizens, perked up, recognizing the importance of the statement. Glass quickly asked, "Tell me, does Sergeant Hartzell have the right to issue those orders?"

"As far as I know," Rediker replied.

"Did you ever turn steam on in Klondike prior to this?" Glass asked.

"Yes, sir, a number of times," answered Rediker. "It was done to take the dampness out of the building. There's no basement and the place would get damp, so we warm up the building to get the dampness out."

Looking dubious Glass shot back, "You really expect us to believe that?"

The Holmesburg engineer shrugged his shoulders but remained silent. "Friday, the nineteenth, was a warm day," said Glass. "In fact, according to meteorological records, the temperature reached ninety-five degrees that day."

The witness remained silent. Irritated, the coroner quickly followed up by asking, "What was the temperature of the boiler room?"

"Sixty-four degrees," said Rediker.

Glass chuckled and appeared amused. Then his smile suddenly disappeared. "You're telling this panel the temperature in the boiler room was thirty degrees below the temperature on the street," said the coroner angrily. "It had been in the nineties for at least a week, one of the most sustained hot spells in recent memory. Witnesses have told us the temperature and humidity on Holmesburg's cellblocks were even warmer. Now you're gonna tell me the temperature was a cool sixty-four degrees next to steaming boilers generating all that heat?"

Once again, the witness just shrugged his shoulders.

"Weren't you a bit warm?" asked the coroner.

"Yes, I was perspiring," Rediker admitted.

"And yet you want us to believe the temperature in the boiler room was sixty-four degrees?"

"Yes," Rediker replied.

"Tell us the truth," demanded Glass. "You really don't know what the temperature was inside the boiler room or Klondike, do you?"

After warily looking around the room, the witness replied, "Well . . . no, not really."

As members of the bench displayed their distrust in the witness's forthrightness, head juryman Gilbert Hendricks raised his hand and inquired if he could ask a question. Given permission, Hendricks asked the witness, "How long was the heat on in Klondike?"

"From five o'clock Friday afternoon till some time Monday morning."

Many in the courtroom gasped. Coroner Glass quickly fired back, "And that was to take out the dampness from the building, right?"

Appearing embarrassed, Rediker gave no reply.

After Rediker was dismissed, Emil Morris was called to the stand. Tall with light-brown hair and wearing an ill-fitting suit, Morris said he had been a guard at Holmesburg for three years and had only limited exposure to the isolation unit. He claimed to have never received any particular instruction or guidance concerning the prisoners housed there. However, he did admit to being one of the guards who brought a slice of bread and a cup of water to each of the prisoners on Sunday evening.

"Did you talk to any of the prisoners inside Klondike?" asked Ferencz.

"Yes," said Morris, "one man told me he was just sent in there earlier that morning and that he couldn't stand the heat."

"Did he say anything else?" Ferencz inquired.

The guard warily glanced at his fellow officers but did not answer. Ferencz pressed him once again and issued a warning if he did not respond to the question.

"Yes," Morris replied. "He said one of the other prisoners in his cell was dying. He said the guy had been in there for a day or two and looked in bad shape. He said the guy had gone through some convulsions or something and was now almost dead."

Ferencz asked, "Did you tell anyone?"

"No," Morris replied.

Appearing shocked, Ferencz asked, "Couldn't you conceive it to be your duty to report that there was a sick man in Klondike?"

"No," said Morris.

Members of both the panel and jury shook their heads in amazement, but the witness only glanced at the small contingent of Holmesburg guards. Continuing to press the issue, the deputy coroner inquired if the witness found the interior of Klondike to be hot that evening.

"Yes, it was hot," he replied.

Ferencz, growing increasingly frustrated, asked, "Mr. Morris, did you get orders to open the windows?"

"Yes," said Morris. "The captain said it was damn hot in here. He said open the windows and turn off the heat."

"Then who closed them?" asked Ferencz. "Tell us who turned on the heat."

"I'm not sure."

"But it's clear from all reports," said Ferencz, "that when you all left the windows were closed and the heat was turned on again and remained that way until eight men were found dead the next morning, correct?"

"Yes."

Gilbert Hendricks raised his hand and asked the witness, "Who was the last guard or officer out the door?"

Morris looked concerned and peered over to his fellow prison staff members.

"They cannot help you now, Mr. Morris," declared Coroner Glass. "Answer the foreman's question. Who was the last person out of Klondike Sunday evening?"

"I think Mr. Smoot and Mr. Bridges. They came out together."

"And who locked the door?" asked Glass.

"Mr. Bridges always had the key," Morris replied.

The next witness called to the stand was Holmesburg guard Thomas Burnley. The tall, strapping guard was attired in a gray three-piece suit. Burnley repeatedly glanced at the press section; the many reporters with notepads and pens in hand ready to memorialize his every word appeared to make him nervous. Burnley said he had been a guard at Holmesburg for five years and had worked every assignment from cellblock and chow hall guard to the wall tower and the prison farm.

Assistant District Attorney Doyle asked if he was assigned to the punishment unit during the weekend in question. Burnley replied that he had made two inspections, one on Friday night and one on Sunday night.

"What did you do Sunday night?" asked Doyle.

"I was assigned to take bread and water to the men in Klondike."

"Did any of the men locked up in Klondike tell you they needed help?" said Doyle. "Did any cry out for some type of aid?"

Like Morris before him, Burnley shifted his gaze from the assistant district attorney to his stone-faced colleagues, particularly Superintendent Davis and Warden Stryker. "They're unable to help you now," declared Doyle, echoing Glass and growing agitated. "Answer the question. Did any of the men in Klondike tell you they were sick and needed help?"

"Yes," said Burnley, "one man told me he was sick. I think it was one of the Palumbo brothers."

"Who else was with you?" asked Doyle. "Who else would have heard Palumbo say he was sick?"

"I don't recall," said Burnley.

"Wait a second," said Doyle, raising his voice. "You told us during an interview a few days ago that Albert Bridges, Joe Smoot, Emil Morris, and one or two others were with you at the time. Do you recall that conversation?"

"No."

"C'mon, Mr. Burnley," interrupted Coroner Glass. "You don't remember that conversation?"

"I guess I forgot."

"Who have you been talking to about this case since you were interviewed?" Glass demanded.

"No one," Burnley replied. "I just forgot, that's all."

"He's lying," yelled a man in the middle of the courtroom. "They're all lying. They know what they did." Others began to shout, and photographers jumped up to take pictures of the courtroom disruption.

Glass banged his gavel and called for silence. Many were now on their feet to see who had called out. The coroner instructed deputy sheriffs to remove anyone who disrupted the proceedings. After a man was escorted from the room, the coroner asked Doyle to continue his interrogation of the witness. The assistant district attorney inquired if Captain Brennan was in Klondike with them when one of the Palumbo brothers said he needed help.

"Yes," said Burnley, "he was there. That's why I never reported that an inmate claimed to be sick. A captain was there to hear it for himself."

After the witness was dismissed, Joseph Barnwell was called to the stand. Slim, of average height, but significantly younger than the other guards, Barnwell clearly showed his unease. He spoke in a whisper, and when asked his age and experience as a prison guard, Barnwell was immediately urged to speak louder so the jury could hear his answers. He then repeated that he was twenty-three and had been a guard for just over a month.

When asked by Ferencz if he was one of the Holmesburg guards who entered Klondike between Friday, August 19 and Monday, August 22, Barnwell said, "Yeah, I guess you could say I was there."

"What does that mean?" Ferencz fired back. "Were you or were you not in Klondike during the weekend in question?"

The witness hesitated. When he finally answered, few could hear his response.

"I'm sure prison guards must have voices on occasion," snapped Ferencz. "I've been in that jail. The cellblocks are two hundred feet long and you have a large number of prisoners in your charge. You have voices for them. Use some of that lung power now. Did you enter Klondike over the weekend in question, yes or no?"

"Yes," Barnwell replied.

"Mr. Barnwell," interjected Assistant District Attorney Doyle, "had you ever been in there before?"

"No."

"Well," said Doyle, "what caused you to go in on this occasion?"

240

"I guess I was curious to see Klondike," said Barnwell. "I had heard talk about it."

Surprised by the young guard's response, Doyle said, "You mean you had never seen the interior of the Klondike unit before, and you just went down to satisfy your curiosity?"

"Yeah, something like that. But I just looked in the door. I . . . I didn't really go in."

"What put such a sudden stop to your curiosity?" Doyle asked.

Barnwell sheepishly looked over to his fellow colleagues and then at the many newsmen on the other side of the courtroom. He remained mute and seemed to be searching for an appropriate answer.

"I'm waiting, Mr. Barnwell," said Doyle, his patience clearly being tested. Still with no response, Doyle suggested, "Could it just be that it felt too damn hot? That it smelled to high heaven and was dark as a coal mine? It was someplace you'd rather not be, correct, Mr. Barnwell?"

"Well, it was pretty hot and dark in there."

"Thank you for that," said Doyle. "Could you now tell me if you left with the other guards?"

Once again, the witness hesitated. The young guard's discomfort was apparent. "Listen, Mr. Barnwell," said Doyle, "please answer my question. I'll tell you when the question is dangerous."

Many in the courtroom chuckled, though the subpoenaed guards found little humor in the exchange.

Deputy Ferencz now asked, "What did you hear the prisoners tell the guards?"

"I heard them talking to the guard, but I couldn't hear what they were saying."

"How interesting," said Ferencz. "Inmates locked on E Block could plainly hear them crying for water, for the heat to be turned off, for the windows to be opened. They even heard them call out for their wives and children. But you, right at the front door of Klondike, heard not a word."

"Well," said Barnwell nervously, "I might have heard something like that, someone asking for water."

"Something like that, indeed," said Ferencz with a sneer.

Coroner Glass dismissed the witness and then announced a brief recess. While many in the courtroom took a breather and discussed the most salient aspects of the day's testimony, the coroner and the assistant district attorney debated whether to charge ahead and call prison leadership to the stand. After weighing the pros and cons of the issue, they both returned to the panel and the coroner announced the inquest would be in recess until the following morning.

Chapter 23

Prison Officials Face Scrutiny

Superintendent Warren B. Davis was called to take the stand at ten forty-five A.M. Friday morning. Tall, with a full head of white hair, and no longer the strapping Spanish-American War cavalryman he once was, Davis moved to the witness box unable to hide his concern. His career—one that stretched from soldier and athlete to police chief and prison official—had, according to some political pundits, come to a sudden and ignominious end.

Assistant District Attorney Doyle began the questioning by inquiring, "Superintendent Davis, what is your understanding of this case?"

The surprising question was met by an equally odd reply as Superintendent Davis pulled out a sheet of paper from his jacket pocket and began reading the names and prison numbers of the eight deceased inmates. He also provided the times they had been placed in the "isolation ward."

"Why were prisoners placed in what you call the isolation ward?" Assistant District Attorney Doyle immediately asked him.

"They were placed in the isolation ward before they could create any further disturbance in the prison," Davis replied.

"Why was Bruno Palumbo placed in the isolation unit?"

"I didn't see him placed there," said Davis. "If I recall correctly, it was Warden Stryker who assigned Palumbo to the isolation unit."

"Did Warden Stryker tell you Palumbo was a consumptive?"

"No."

Realizing the impact of sending a sick man with a modest criminal history to a punishment unit where he would be baked alive, Davis quickly argued they weren't all like Palumbo. "Take Webster, for example," said Davis. "I told the guards to take him to the isolation block because I knew Webster was a bad egg, a desperate criminal. They had him out at Western State Penitentiary in Pittsburgh and weren't able to handle him. He was then sent to Eastern State Penitentiary, and they couldn't handle him there. He was a ringleader of the rioting there, and at that time state officials called me and said, 'For God sakes, take this son of a bitch out of this prison or they are going to wreak havoc and escape from here.'"

Disregarding the superintendent's comment, Doyle asked, "Did you go to Klondike yourself to check on the men?"

"No."

On hearing the superintendent's answer, Coroner Glass suddenly intervened. "Do the men sent to the punishment unit receive any medical check-ups?"

"When I took charge of the prison," Davis replied, "the practice was that when a man was sent into the block he would be visited by a prison physician every twenty-four hours."

"Since in this case the man was one you sent there yourself," said Glass, "did you apply the rule to see that this man was looked after?"

"No," Davis replied. "I did not personally because in the management of the prison there are rules and regulations and practices, which I presumed would be carried out. With the prison in such a state—the potential of a riot—I could not be everywhere."

"Do you have any printed rules and regulations that the guards may learn from and study?" asked Glass.

"No. There were no printed rules and regulations. They were all verbal orders."

"At any time over the course of the weekend in question did you visit Klondike to inspect the condition of the men?"

"No, I did not," Davis replied.

"Did Warden Stryker go there?"

"No, not that I know of."

"Did you instruct anyone to look after the men in Klondike after they were placed in there?"

"I did not," said Davis. "I did not feel it was necessary."

Turning the questioning over to ADA Doyle, the superintendent was asked if doctors were permitted to make an inspection of Klondike without permission of the superintendent, warden, or at least a sergeant.

"No," Davis replied, "the practice is that when a doctor goes to Klondike he gets the key from Center, the command unit at the center of the prison. The key is in the custody of the sergeant."

Doyle momentarily pondered Davis's reply and then asked, "Could a doctor visit Klondike and examine the men without your okay, or that of Warden Stryker, or one of the other officers?"

"No," said Davis. "For the doctors' own protection, we have them escorted by a guard because they are dealing with dangerous men and their safety could be at stake."

"So that I am clear on this," said Doyle, "neither you, nor Warden Stryker, nor any of the physicians checked on the men in Klondike from Friday night till Monday morning?"

"On Sunday night about a quarter of eleven, the prison was quiet," answered Davis. "I thought we had succeeded in addressing a serious attempt to break down the morals of the prison, without the use of clubs or tear gas, simply by removing the leaders. I believe we had settled what might have been a dangerous condition without injury to any of the 1,400 men confined there. Mr. Stryker and I left Center and started up to my office. We were both very tired. We had gone without sleep since Wednesday. I figured that a good job had been done. When I got into the office, I saw that the deputy had not followed me. He had taken his car back inside the wall and while passing Klondike heard the inmates talking. We assumed the men were okay."

"So that is a long-winded explanation that no one of rank or medical authority checked on the men celled in Klondike. In a building," added Doyle, "where the water had been turned off and all the windows and air vents had been closed on a brutally hot weekend."

Davis tried to reply, but Doyle continued to press his case. "But isn't it true that information you have gotten since then would clearly enable you to conclude that Klondike was shut tight? There was no air entering or escaping, making breathing near impossible. And you want us to believe that inmates interned in that brick oven were perfectly fine over the course of the twenty to sixty hours they were locked in there?"

Flustered, the superintendent tried to explain. "I only learned the condition of the men when we took them out of there," said Davis. "It was then I learned that some of the windows and vents had been closed."

"Then you did not know from your own knowledge that the windows and ventilators had been purposely closed?"

"No, I did not know."

"So you never heard from anyone on your staff over the course of three days," continued Doyle, "that Klondike windows and ventilators were closed?"

"Correct."

"But we've had testimony that guards were going and coming from Klondike over the three days in question," Doyle replied. "None seemed troubled by the conditions. What would you have done if you were a guard, aware of brutal heat and its effects on prisoners, and your superior continued to ignore the situation?"

"I'd have gone over his head to the warden," said Davis. "I would have reported such conditions because I would have considered it my duty."

"But your duty as superintendent," Coroner Glass interrupted, "did not include a visit to Klondike during that weekend?"

Put on the defensive, Davis paused for a few seconds to consider an appropriate answer. "As superintendent during a tense administrative period, I had many concerns. That's why there are subordinate officers; to carry out such chores."

"By the way," interjected Doyle, "who is the person ultimately responsible for any order to turn on the heat into the pipes that lead to Klondike?"

"The heating of the isolation unit starts from a steam pipe connected with the boiler in the engine room . . ."

"This is not a plumbing class, Mr. Davis," barked Coroner Glass. "Answer the question you were asked. He asked you who was the responsible person to turn on the heat in Klondike?"

"The heat was turned on by engineer Rediker," said Davis, "George Rediker."

"Thank you," said Doyle. "Now, have you been informed who ordered Rediker to turn on the heat?"

"Yes, after I learned the heat had been turned on, I asked who ordered the heat."

"And who was that?"

"Sergeant Hartzell," the superintendent replied.

Some in the courtroom grimaced and shook their heads in dismay. Recognizing the importance of the statement, reporters busily recorded every word of the verbal exchange. The evening papers would lead with "Davis Blames Hartzell for Giving Prisoners Steam," and "Superintendent Tells Inquest Jury Sergeant Hartzell Issued Unauthorized Instructions."

Assistant District Attorney Doyle now spoke up and asked, "Did Hartzell have authority, of his own initiative, to order the heat turned on?"

"No."

"Did he have to procure permission from a superior to warrant the heat being turned on?"

The superintendent replied, "The use of heat may be required during cold winter months if someone is placed in the building, but as far as summer is concerned there should not have been any heat. No heat should have been turned on."

"Did you ever make it clear to your subordinates, including captains, sergeants, and guards, that such measures should never be used?"

"The question of heat in the Klondike never came up," said Davis. "The only time heat was used in Klondike was the wintertime. I never heard that heat was used as a form of punishment."

"And how long have you been superintendent?" Doyle asked.

"Five years."

"Amazing," was the assistant district attorney's shocked reply.

In response, Davis went on to state that Warden Stryker never informed him the heat had been turned on, and as far as he knew the ventilation of the facility was left to the condition of the weather. He once again argued that the isolation block had only been used twice since 1934.

"Are you sure of that?" Coroner Glass pointedly replied.

"Well, no," said Davis. "I'm not absolutely positive."

"Warden Stryker was there Friday night, was he not?" asked Glass.

"Yes, he was."

"And you were there Friday night?"

"I was."

"Then you and Stryker were both there Friday night when the heat was turned on?"

"Yes."

"Then how is it," demanded the coroner, "that both of you are in the prison and neither of you knows the heat had been turned on? We're told Sergeant Hartzell gave the order, you and Stryker are both there with overall authority and have no knowledge of what is being done? What is your explanation for that?"

"I have none," said Davis. "I do not know."

Coroner Glass grimaced, his frustration obvious. Others on the bench displayed similar consternation. Glass then asked Davis, "Have you ascertained whether Stryker ordered Hartzell to have the steam turned on?"

"When I was notified by Warden Stryker on Monday morning that men were dead in Klondike, I immediately went there and found that it was true. That was the first time I knew the heat had been turned on. It was very hot when I got in there—"

"Enough with the evasive answers already," demanded Glass. "I asked a simple question. Did you confront Warden Stryker? Did you ask him if he gave the order?"

"I did, and he said that he did not give it."

Coroner Glass sat back in his chair, disgusted. Equally frustrated, Deputy Coroner Ferencz decided to pursue another line of questioning. "Tell me," asked Ferencz, "would you say that there is too much radiation in that building?"

"I do not know," said Davis. "My only knowledge is that the radiators were installed to provide a minimum temperature of seventy-five degrees in Klondike when the temperature outside is zero."

"And how much radiation is in that building, Superintendent?" said Ferencz. "How many radiators are in Klondike?"

"There are five large and two small radiators."

"Seven radiators, five large and two small, in a single-story, fifty-foot long building? A bit much for twelve cells, wouldn't you say?"

"I wouldn't know," the superintendent replied.

"Well, it sure as hell was that weekend," barked Ferencz.

Cheers and applause broke out from many in the courtroom. One female shouted, "He's the guilty one. Put him in jail." Glass brought down his gavel and demanded silence.

"And, as a matter of fact," added Ferencz, "we've come to learn the heat was turned on regardless of the weather outside."

"I do not know why they turned the heat on."

"Well tell me," Ferencz continued, "are there specific orders for guards that, after inspecting the inmates in Klondike, they shut all vents, windows, and doors when they leave?"

"The ventilation is left to the condition of the weather at the time," said Davis. "There are no printed regulations because the place has only been used twice since 1934."

The comment drew visible expressions of doubt from members of the inquest panel. "Aren't you mistaken about that, Mr. Davis?" inquired the deputy coroner.

"Well, maybe, but I don't think so," Davis lamely replied.

"Well, let's see if we can finally resolve this matter," said Ferencz as he was handed a sheet of paper from the coroner and began to read from it. "Isn't it true that subsequent to 1934, Anthony Scarpa and Leonard Williams were locked up in Klondike from January 10, 1935, to January 18, 1935?"

Appearing puzzled, the superintendent replied, "I do not know."

"Isn't it true," Ferencz continued, "that in January 1937; February 1937; May 1937; August 1937; October 1937; and November 1937, prisoners were celled in Klondike?"

Befuddled, Davis seemed unable to speak. The deputy coroner pressed on as all in the courtroom observed the superintendent's hesitance. "Mr. Davis, I didn't hear your answer."

"Well I . . . I asked the warden how often it had been used and his recollection was twice."

Ferencz passed a sheet of paper to a bailiff, who handed it to the witness. It contained the names of twenty-two men imprisoned in Klondike during the years in question. Davis admitted that he recognized many of the names. Some, he claimed, were state prisoners who had rioted at Eastern and were then sent to Holmesburg in an effort to restore order at the state institution.

"Do you know whether heat was applied in the summer of 1937?" Ferencz asked.

"I would not know that."

Perturbed by the reply, Coroner Glass interrupted his deputy and asked, "Were you not the superintendent of the prison in January 1937; February 1937; May 1937, and all the dates we have just mentioned when men were held in Klondike?"

Davis sheepishly replied that he was.

"And yet you have no knowledge as to whether men were in the punishment unit—or the 'isolation unit' as you call it—and subjected to the heat treatment?"

The coroner sneered as Davis mumbled a few inaudible words. Whispering could be heard throughout the courtroom. Glass rapped his gavel and told his deputy to continue.

"Superintendent," asked Ferencz, "did you notify the Board of Prison Inspectors of any of the problems occurring in the prison during the last couple weeks?"

"Yes, since they're my superiors I was obligated to inform them that certain events were occurring in the jail regarding food."

"And what did you tell them?"

"I told the chairman, Dr. Sawyer, what the problem was, what might happen, and if we didn't have too much interference from inspectors, I would be able to handle it better."

"And Dr. Sawyer's response?"

"He was fine with that," said Davis.

"And tell me," asked Ferencz, "how did things turn out?"

Davis appeared angered by the question. He did not reply. The deputy coroner allowed the moment to sink in before asking the witness, "By the way, did you ever inform Dr. Sawyer and the other five members of the Prison Board that they were negligent in their official monthly tours of the three city prisons?"

Once again, Davis was placed on the defensive. He started to reply several times and then abruptly stopped.

"Or did you maintain an attitude that the less one is bothered by the Prison Board the better?"

"No, that's not true," Davis replied. "We meet monthly as a group and discuss relevant issues of policy and personnel."

The deputy agreed they had but informed the superintendent that prison inspectors appointed by the mayor were supposed to visit one prison a month, and not one member of the board had accomplished that modest obligation, including the chairman of the board. "Apparently," said Ferencz, "you were satisfied with a board that only took a passing interest in carrying out their official duties."

"I cannot compel board members to fulfill their official duties."

"But you can encourage them," Ferencz replied.

In another of what was becoming a series of embarrassing moments, all Davis could do was bite his lip and contemplate an appropriate reply. Before he could respond, Coroner Glass asked Assistant District Attorney Doyle if he had additional questions for the witness.

Doyle said he would like to return to the design and use of Klondike in recent years. He asked, "Is it true that the punishment unit known as Klondike was originally built as a twelve-cell, one-man-to-a-cell facility?"

"Yes, I believe that's correct," said Davis.

"Isn't it also true," interjected ADA Doyle, "the Klondike cells are only four feet by eight feet in size, and only one mattress can fit inside?"

"Yes, I believe so."

"Then how do you justify putting three men in a cell?" asked the assistant district attorney.

"Well, I didn't really know there were."

"And when did you discover there were three men in a cell in Klondike over that tragic weekend?"

The superintendent paused for a moment and then replied, "On Sunday, I learned there were sixteen men in Klondike, but I did not give it any serious thought because there were twelve cells in the structure. I did not know until after the bodies were found that there were three men in a cell."

"And if my information is correct," added Doyle, "there were three to a cell because many of the cells in Klondike were being used for storage—odds and ends, from ladders and pipes to paint cans and scaffolds—that made them inoperable as housing areas. How is it that you were not aware of that over that critical three-day period? I guess I'm asking whose duty was it ultimately to determine at the time how many men would go into a Klondike cell?"

"The question was never brought up."

"Well, whose responsibility would it be?" asked Deputy Ferencz.

"Probably mine, in the last analysis," Davis meekly replied.

"And would you agree," asked Doyle, "that any more than one man in a cell over that brutally hot weekend in Klondike would be too many?"

"Probably, if conditions were as described."

Confused, Deputy Ferencz interrupted again and asked, "Do you still have doubts about the conditions inside Klondike that weekend?"

"No, not really."

Doyle went on to ask, "When the prisoners were taken to Klondike, was there any specific official who had oversight concerning who was taken, how many men were placed in a cell, and their condition while in the building?"

"It should have been—"

"I asked you who it was," said Doyle, "not to who it should have been."

Davis hesitated. His inability to answer simple questions rankled many in the courtroom. Particularly troubled by the superintendent's wandering and evasive replies, Coroner Glass angrily spoke up.

"This is all pretty incredible," said Glass. "These are some of the most peculiar statements I've ever heard. Ridiculous, really. Here is a large institution that harbors about 1,400 prisoners, and there are no rules, regulations, or guidelines. When we ask who put the men in Klondike, nobody knows. When we ask who gave the order to turn on the heat, nobody knows. When we ask who gives these orders, nobody knows. Well, what are the heads of the departments there for? They're supposed to know what's going on.

"Who is to know if not the superintendent?" Glass continued. "You were placed there for that reason, and if you don't inquire, nobody will. Hell, they could walk away with the damn place and nobody would know about it from the testimony you've given us. We haven't gotten anywhere here today. There are no restrictions or guidelines on anybody; not for the guards, the captains, the warden, the superintendent. It seems they all do as they please. And as for the man at the top, we have a frustrating series of 'I don't knows' to an array of important questions. Seriously, what good is there in having a superintendent if he doesn't know what's going on?"

Suddenly, cheers and applause erupted throughout the courtroom. Several observers shouted epithets at the superintendent, "He's the guilty one," "Davis should be the one going to prison," and "Put Davis behind bars. He's the cause of this."

Glass banged his gavel in an attempt to restore order. Davis's face flushed; he appeared flustered, beaten down, and looked around the courtroom in total bewilderment. The coroner momentarily pondered the superintendent's fall from grace. He tried to imagine how Davis was understanding his becoming the target of such anger. The coroner struck his gavel and said, "If there's any more disorder we'll have to clear the room. We don't want anything like that to happen again." With many in the restive audience still irritated by the superintendent's exchanges with panel investigators, Glass thought it best to announce a brief five-minute recess.

Though many in the courtroom used the recess in the court proceedings to stretch their legs or take a bathroom break, the majority remained for fear of losing the most valuable seats in town. Looking bewildered, Davis huddled in the corner of the room with his attorney. He sensed his answers to the panel's questions were not going over well. The two discussed how they could right the ship and restore his image as a competent criminal justice administrator.

When the courtroom was gaveled to order, the coroner recognized Cyrus Black, the superintendent's attorney, who had raised his hand.

"Primarily for the jury's benefit as well as everyone else," said Mr. Black, now standing and assuming an authoritative posture, "I would like to remind everyone that we're talking about the dregs of society, criminals all, the robbers, the burglars, the murderers, the rapists—they would shoot your life out for the few dollars they could take from your pockets. These men, these prisoners, demanded through their inmate committee that they be allowed to run the prison, dictating the kind of food, the kind of discipline, and demanding the discharge of guards—"

Suddenly, the coroner's gavel struck the wooden block and Glass informed Black, "This is no time for speeches or closing statements. Such eloquent commentary should be saved for a criminal trial, if the jury so determines one is warranted."

Though Black mildly demurred, the coroner insisted he take a seat. He then asked Superintendent Davis if he would care to respond to his pointed remarks just before the recess.

Emotionally drained but determined to explain himself, the prison superintendent said, "I never ordered the heat turned on as a method of punishment. In addition, I never knew of the heat having been turned on while I've been at the helm of the prison."

When asked by Assistant District Attorney Doyle if he had informed his subordinates never to use heat on the inmates, Davis stated that he had not cautioned his officers about the practice because the question never came up. "No one," he re-emphasized, "had ever been subjected to extreme heat or steam before."

Glass, along with members of the jury, wore expressions of disbelief at such a claim.

"I'm fairly sure of that, and equally sure no additional radiators have been installed in the building since I took over, as some have implied. The building was constructed in 1929, but I wasn't aware there were more radiators than needed for normal heating purposes in the winter. There's no thermostatic control on the radiators, which, to the best of my knowledge, were designed to provide a minimum temperature of seventy-five degrees when the temperature outside was zero.

"And let me be clear, and to answer the charge made by Secretary Enteen earlier this week," Davis boldly stated, "it was physically impossible for steam to be sent through the pipes leading to the toilet. The toilets do not send heat into the cells as reported in some newspapers."

"But as to the isolation unit's purpose," Glass shot back, "wasn't Klondike designed and utilized as a punishment facility?"

"No," David replied. "Prisoners were not sent there for punishment, but to separate them from prisoners who were orderly and wanted to behave themselves. We wanted to quiet and end the hysteria."

"What hysteria?" Glass responded. "On whose part was there hysteria, the prisoners or management?"

Davis gave Glass a withering look. "Among the prisoners, of course.

It was used for prisoners who yelled and screamed and tore out the plumbing in their cells. It was punishment only in a sense. The objective was to put disruptive prisoners, those who destroyed property in their cells, in a separate unit. To get them away from more cooperative inmates."

"But the inmates who died over the weekend in question didn't destroy any property," said Glass. "The inmates thrown in Klondike didn't riot, they didn't attack any guards. They just refused to eat their meals."

Once again, shouts and applause rang out in the courtroom. The coroner banged his gavel to restore order and asked the superintendent if he'd like to reply.

"Well, that would have been established during the course of hearings," David replied, "but, owing to conditions in the prison at the time, hearings were unable to be held in a timely manner. If the deaths had not occurred, the men would have been returned and given regular hearings on Monday."

"Surely you're not saying the deceased died too quickly to be given a hearing?" said Glass "Are you telling us you have some sort of star chamber process where you charge, punish, and then days later have a hearing on the charges?"

Once again unrest and shouts of "He's guilty," "Put him in jail," and "Davis should be charged with murder," emanated from attendees in the courtroom.

The coroner struck his gavel and issued another warning before returning to the superintendent. "'Isolating the men,' as you call it, is bad enough," said Glass, "but what is the idea of shutting the water off on them?"

"I was unaware the water had been turned off, but the practice is occasionally done when disruptive prisoners flood their cells."

"But it would have been impossible for the Klondike prisoners to have flooded their cells," Glass replied, "as the water had been turned off upon their arrival and never turned on again. You can imagine the problems this created as it not only caused the lack of drinking water in cells well over one hundred degrees but also the inability to flush any of the toilets."

Ferencz interjected, "Did you know, Mr. Davis, that one of the men placed in Klondike had tuberculosis?"

"I'm not sure. I may have been told that."

"Since you seem unsure," said Ferencz, "it would appear, regardless of an inmate's physical condition, you still allowed ill men to be placed in Klondike?"

"I did that because there was a revolt in the prison," said Davis. "Established prison authority was being challenged and order had to be restored. We had to take action."

"And men choosing to not eat their meals," interjected the coroner, "is the revolt you're referring to?"

"I object to the question," proclaimed the superintendent's attorney.

"There's nothing wrong with the question, Counselor," Glass shot back. "We have every right to know what precipitated the superintendent's actions."

Superintendent Davis appeared despondent and on the verge of commenting but ultimately just stared at the floor.

Glass asked if there were any additional questions for the superintendent. Hearing none, Davis was excused and informed he may be asked back later if the panel or jury desired him to clarify a matter.

Due to the curiously convenient unavailability of Mr. Samuel Sawyer, chairman of the Board of Prison Inspectors, Mrs. Henrietta Lake, board secretary, was called to the stand. The wife of a prominent businessman and longtime Democratic Party donor who founded Lake Industries, Mrs. Lake smiled at both the jury and newsmen as she took her seat. Attired in a navy-blue dress and small matching hat, she dutifully swore to tell the truth and said she was honored to represent the prison board. Asked about her interest in prisons, she said she had been on the board for just over two years and had found her board duties "very educational."

"Have you been interested in prison work long?" asked Ferencz.

"No, not really," Mrs. Lake replied. "I had never been in a prison before."

"Well, could you tell us how you got on the prison board?"

"The mayor just appointed me. He may have talked to my husband first."

When Deputy Ferencz asked Mrs. Lake how she heard of the Holmesburg Prison food strike, she surprised many by saying she read about it in the newspapers.

"Are you telling this inquiry that you never received a phone call or any communication from Board Chairman Sawyer or Superintendent Davis?"

"That's right," replied Mrs. Lake. "I received no word about the strike. I read about it in the papers."

"And did you receive any notice when the dead Holmesburg inmates were discovered?" Ferencz inquired.

"No, they didn't apprise me of anything," Mrs. Lake replied. "I found out about it from the newspapers."

Appearing increasingly perplexed, the deputy coroner asked, "Do you mean to say that you're an officer of the prison board, a board that oversees the direction and operation of the city's three prisons, and you learned about one of the worst events in the system's history through the papers?"

"Yes, I just read about it," said Mrs. Lake matter-of-factly.

The panel seemed a bit stunned by the news. Ferencz then asked if she called Sawyer or Davis for information as to what had happened. On hearing that she did not make any calls, Ferencz inquired if she had gone to the institution itself to gain information for herself.

"No, I did not. I just read about it."

Members of the inquest panel sat back in their chairs, exasperated. Many in the audience appeared to be equally struck by the witness's lack of curiosity and the prison board's general disinterest.

"This is all very disappointing," said Ferencz. "We seem to have a government oversight body that is neither informed nor desirous of being informed."

Obviously offended by the comment, Mrs. Lake opened her mouth as if to respond but just bit her lip and remained silent. Whispering could be heard throughout the courtroom, and reporters scribbled notes regarding the revealing exchange. "Now, do you, as an official prison inspector," Ferencz asked, "contemplate doing anything about that?"

"Well . . . well I . . . I really don't think that's the right kind of a question to ask anybody in my position."

Troubled by what he was hearing, Coroner Glass interrupted and asked, "Mrs. Lake, if I may, what do you think we should ask? What time is lunch being served across the street today at Wanamaker's Crystal Tea Room?"

Uproarious laughter broke out in the courtroom, and Mrs. Lake's face turned crimson. She started speaking rapidly, but no one could hear what she had to say with all the guffaws and side comments being expressed in the courtroom. Even news reporters found the exchange humorous. The crashing of the gavel several times finally restored order, allowing Mrs. Lake's last few words, "resent the inference" to be heard.

Glass offered a modest apology but also stated, "It's a sad state of affairs where no one of authority seems to know or wants to know what is going on in a large municipal department that holds over 3,000 people captive. A vast prison system can't be run like a Chestnut Hill garden party."

Once again, applause and snickers followed. The embarrassed witness appeared on the verge of bolting from the witness stand. Clearly not used to being the subject of laughter, when order was restored Mrs. Lake said she was insulted by the coroner's insinuations, and as chairman of an official inquest panel Glass should take his role more seriously. The coroner's expression turned from annoyed to bemused as he glanced at his colleagues on the panel, and then back at the witness.

"Your criticism is correct, Mrs. Lake. I need to do a better job," Glass admitted. "But maybe we all do. And on the subject of taking assignments seriously, may I ask if you do?"

"Why, yes, of course I do."

"And you attend every meeting of the Board of Prison Inspectors?"

"Yes, I most certainly do."

"And I'm sure the monthly dinner meetings are swell," said the coroner, "but do you visit one institution a month as scheduled to examine their operations, procedures, and care of the prisoners?"

"Well," replied Mrs. Lake, "I certainly try to."

"Try harder," said Glass, almost in anger. The sharp retort caught everyone's attention, especially the witness's. Offended by the tone of the coroner's comment, Mrs. Lake again voiced her objection, but Glass cut her off. "Do you realize," he said, reading from a logbook, "the last time you entered any of the county's three prisons was last March?"

"Well . . . well I . . . I'm a busy person."

"Apparently so," said Glass. "You've been busy for over one hundred fifty straight days. In fact, everyone on the prison board appears to be busy. According to prison logs, not one member of the board has made an official visit in months. In fact, two of your colleagues have only made a couple of visits the entire year. Could it be prison inspectors mistakenly took their monthly assignments to be quarterly or bi-annually?"

Flustered, and resentful of the snickers audible in the courtroom, the witness gathered her handbag off the floor and clutched it close to her chest, practically begging for dismissal. Observing her demeanor, Coroner Glass asked his deputy if he had any more questions for the witness. Ferencz nodded affirmatively and asked Mrs. Lake if the prison board had met since the discovery of the dead inmates.

"No," she shot back angrily.

"Is any meeting scheduled now?"

"No."

"Superintendent Davis testified it was up to him to run the jail unless given contrary orders from the Board of Prison Inspectors. Was he given any orders?"

"Not that I'm aware of," answered Mrs. Lake.

"I have no more questions for this witness," said Ferencz in obvious frustration.

"Before you are dismissed, Mrs. Lake," said the coroner, "I'd like to know whether the abandonment of the Board of Prison Inspectors and cessation of any prison oversight board would prove detrimental to prison operations."

The witness appeared stymied by the question. Anxious to leave the courtroom, Mrs. Lake replied, "I don't know. I'd need some time to consider the question."

Exasperated, the coroner shook his head and dismissed the witness.

Chapter 24

Interrogation of Holmesburg Warden

Though everyone in the courtroom was already alert and fully engaged when Coroner Glass called Warden Victor Stryker to the stand, there was an air of expectation. A man of medium height and weight, his dark-black hair swept straight back, Stryker wore an expressionless countenance that some found inscrutable, others threatening. Asked to recount his career as a prison guard and his rise through the ranks to the position of warden of the city's largest jail, Stryker said he became a prison guard in 1922 and made sergeant five years later. By the time of the 1929 Holmesburg food strike and riot, he had risen to captain, and deputy warden not long after. "Superintendent Davis appointed me warden when he took over in 1933," said Stryker, "and I've tried to fulfill the job's many demands to the best of my abilities."

"Could you inform us what your days look like?" asked Ferencz. "What are your duties?"

"I usually arrive at the prison between nine and nine-thirty in the morning and remain there until five or six in the evening," Stryker replied. "However, I'm on call all the time regardless of where I'm at."

"And your duties?" inquired Assistant District Attorney Doyle.

"I try to keep the prison in order, see that it is kept clean and that the prisoners keep themselves clean and dressed properly. I also inspect the guards for appearance and uniformity. I try to maintain discipline at all times and make sure the institution runs smoothly."

"What do you mean by discipline?" said Doyle.

"To see that the guards act like gentlemen and are not unruly—and to see that the prisoners do the right thing."

"When you say 'discipline,' does that mean quiet and orderly or does it involve something more?"

"The prison is run like a city," Stryker replied. "There are rules and regulations and procedures that everyone follows. Order and discipline are very important. Every day at one o'clock I hold hearings and try to do the square thing for both guards and prisoners who are cited for violations. If I believe a prisoner should be punished or a guard disciplined, I take action. Sometimes a guard may be prejudiced against a prisoner and bring charges against him, but by these hearings we try to give justice to both when giving out punishment."

"In this walled city," asked the assistant district attorney, "how do you determine if a hearing is necessary?"

"I don't determine that," the warden replied. "A punishment slip is made out by a guard, and from the guard it goes to a sergeant, then to the captain, and then to me."

"Tell me, did any of the prisoners sent to Klondike have hearings?"

"No."

"Why not?" Doyle inquired.

Beginning to display the first signs of irritation, Stryker said, "The privilege of a disciplinary hearing was suspended due to the emergency. The food strike and the disruption that followed impacted standard practice."

The assistant district attorney then told Stryker he'd like to question him about his decisions and whereabouts on the weekend of August 19 through August 22. "Where were you," he asked, "during that period?"

"I was there, in the prison, the entire time."

"When did you sleep?" asked Doyle. "Where did you sleep?"

"I slept very little," said Stryker. "Maybe an hour or so in a chair at Center or in my office."

"So, generally, you were at the scene of the action or in the center control area. Is that right?"

"Yes."

"Good," said Doyle, leaning forward, his focus on the witness growing more intense. "Maybe you can explain to me how you knew nothing of what was occurring inside Klondike during that weekend. All of your comments in the newspapers and to investigators are that you knew nothing about what was occurring in Klondike. Did you enter the punishment unit at any time? Were you in the vicinity when guards entered Klondike and apparently displayed little concern for the men housed there?"

Stryker became visibly annoyed and tried to interrupt the assistant district attorney, but Doyle appeared intent on showing Stryker as a manager who prided himself in running a tight operation but did not know what was occurring inside the prison's punishment unit.

"I was in the vicinity the entire time," said Stryker.

"And being so close to Klondike you still did not feel the need to check on the prisoners there?"

"It wasn't necessary," Stryker replied. "I received no notice of trouble there, and my main concern was the prison proper. Holmesburg contains over 1,400 prisoners; Klondike held just five at the time."

"Of the first group of prisoners sent into Klondike on Friday night," asked Doyle, "was it you or your guards that sent them there?"

"I gave the orders," Stryker replied. "The guards do not have the authority to place men in the isolation unit."

"How did you determine they were the ones to be sent to the punishment unit?"

"They were heard hollering by the guards," said Stryker. "They were causing a disturbance."

When Doyle inquired how anyone could tell who was hollering on cellblocks containing nearly two hundred men, Stryker replied that his guards were experienced and trained to discern who was creating mischief in the jail. They also had ways, unknown by the prisoners, such as standing in the prison yard outside individual cells or going underneath the cellblocks, where they could hear all that was being said.

When Doyle asked about the lack of any due process or formal hearing procedure before sending men to an isolation unit, Stryker replied, "Holmesburg is a prison, not a college or Center City hotel. We have tough, dangerous men in Holmesburg. There are occasions when routine and going by the book just isn't possible. Yes, sometimes paperwork is not fully completed or filed and decisions are made on the spot, but if you were there and saw what we have to deal with on a daily basis, I suspect your attitude would change."

Seeing jury foreman Gilbert Hendricks raise his hand, Glass immediately recognized him. "Why don't you, as the prison's top official, visit a building as important as Klondike?" inquired Hendricks. "Why don't you check to see that the guards assigned to such a building are doing their jobs correctly?"

Warden Stryker replied that his officers and guards such as Trent, Smoot, Crawley, Bridges, and Morris were experienced and knew their roles and duties.

He did not feel the need to observe them. "Besides," he further argued, "the greater threat was that something would break out on one of the cellblocks in the prison proper. That's where I needed to be."

Miss Giovanni raised her hand from the jury box. After being recognized, she directed her question to the witness. "I have to admit," said Miss Giovanni, "I'm a bit shocked that Klondike inmates only receive three cups of water and a slice or two of bread per day. Isn't that a bit harsh?"

"I don't think so," the warden replied. "Klondike inmates receive bread and water plus a regular meal every third day. It's sufficient."

"But don't you think—"

Cutting her off, Stryker responded, "I have no problem with it. These are rough men. Most are well-known troublemakers. We have few other ways to discipline or punish them."

"Good, let's pursue the issue of punishment," said the coroner, anxious to initiate a new line of inquiry. "Warden Stryker, who ordered the heat turned on in Klondike?"

Those in the courtroom who were growing weary of questions and answers regarding missing reports and meager food rations now perked up and paid close attention. The warden did not hesitate and immediately replied, "Sergeant Hartzell."

"And who ordered Hartzell to turn on the heat?"

"No one," said Stryker.

"But, according to your earlier statement, Hartzell had no authority for turning on the heat. You or Davis were the only ones who had such authority. You were at the prison Friday night, as was Davis. At that time, did Hartzell ask for authority to turn on the heat?"

"No."

"Did you ever tell Hartzell that heat was part of the discipline and punishment routine when men were housed in Klondike?"

"No," said Stryker. "I never told Hartzell to turn the heat on as a method of punishment. I never discussed turning on the heat with Hartzell."

"Did you ever caution any of the guards or line officers against turning on the heat?"

"No."

"Did you ever issue any orders about Klondike windows being closed when occupied?"

"No, the only orders I ever gave were to see that there was not too much heat and there was enough air in the cells. I told the guards I didn't want the men uncomfortable."

"Liar, you're a goddamn liar," screamed a man from the rear of the courtroom. Glass immediately stood up, brought down his gavel, and ordered deputies to remove the disruptive individual. While sheriff's deputies subdued the man, Jack Ryan, Stryker's attorney, rose and yelled out, "Objection. We'd like a brief recess." As the officers struggled with the protester and dragged him out of the room, he continued to yell epithets and scream, "Stryker, we know what you did! You murdered eight men!"

Suddenly, an explosion and bright light further startled those at the front of the courtroom. Many ducked for cover, but it wasn't a bomb—just a photographer's flashbulb exploding as he tried to capture the courtroom disruption.

Once the photographer was seated and the protester removed, Ryan raised his objection again, but the coroner curtly ruled, "Objection noted. The inquest will continue."

All that could now be heard was the sound of the coroner's gavel and whispering from many shocked observers in the courtroom. Glass looked to see if jury members were ready to proceed and recognized the assistant district attorney, who said he'd like to return to the first night men were taken to the isolation unit.

"Was the heat turned on in Klondike on Friday evening?" asked Doyle.

"I don't know."

"You don't know?"

"I was busy at the time," Stryker replied. "We had a major problem on our hands. There were other things that needed to be done. But if the heat was on in Klondike, it was only to dry out the building."

Showing his dissatisfaction with the answers he was receiving, Doyle asked, "Did Sergeant Hartzell report to you that the heat was on?"

"No."

"Did you know that heat was being pumped into Klondike on Saturday as well?"

"No."

"Did you know that heat was on in the building on Sunday?"

"Yes. I learned sometime that day."

"And how did you learn of the heat being on in the building?"

Stryker shrugged. "I don't recall."

Coroner Glass cut off the district attorney at this point and forcefully asked the witness, "Isn't it true that it was actually a prisoner on C Block who informed you?" When the warden didn't reply, Glass said, "Mr. Stryker, I didn't hear your answer."

"I don't know . . . it's possible."

"Wasn't it a prisoner who told you?"

"It's possible," said Stryker, glaring at Glass.

"C'mon, Warden Stryker, didn't an inmate tell you there were men in a bake oven over in Klondike and they needed help?"

"No, I don't think so."

"Isn't it true inmate McCabe told you vapor could be seen rising over the isolation building? Didn't he tell you heat could actually be seen pouring out of the vents atop Klondike?"

"I don't recall."

"Let me see if I can help refresh your memory," said Glass. "Weren't you told that the men in Klondike were being cooked to death? Others seem to have known as well. They told us when we interviewed them the heat was so intense inside the building that steam vapor could be seen by anybody in the prison yard, the guard tower, and any structure that had a window facing Klondike."

Many in the courtroom murmured that the warden's silence spoke volumes. When he first took the stand, his responses to questions from the bench and jury were immediate and authoritative. Now he was hesitant, waffling, and non-responsive. Reporters listening to the two city administrators do verbal battle were quick to record the significance of the exchange.

"Tell us," said Glass, "what did you do after your conversation with McCabe?"

"I went out to Center and told Captain Brennan to go out to Klondike and see if the heat was off and if everything was all right."

"Why didn't you go down yourself?"

"The situation in the prison made it necessary for me to remain."

"Do you mean to tell me, after being told a building holding sixteen prisoners in five tiny cells was so hot vapor could be seen shooting twenty-five feet in the air, you couldn't walk the fifty yards to check on it yourself?"

"It was my belief Captain Brennan could handle it," said Stryker. "You can't expect a superintendent or warden to perform every mission, check on every alleged incident. Look, I'm only one man, and it was impossible for me to attend personally to everything. I was compelled to depend upon my guards to help me keep order. That's why there are line officers. Delegation to subordinates is part of the job."

"Thank you for that managerial tip," said Glass sarcastically. "Now tell me, what were your exact words to Captain Brennan?"

"I think I said something like, 'Go out there and see that everything is okay.'"

"And what did Captain Brennan report to you?"

"He told me the heat was off and everything was all right."

"Did you ask whether the place was hot?"

"No."

"Did you ask whether there was any air in the building?"

"No."

"Did you ask whether the men were crying and pleading for water?" asked Glass, who was growing increasingly angry.

"No."

"Did you ask whether any of the men needed a doctor?"

"No."

"Did you ask anything at all?"

"No."

After the rapid-fire exchange resulting in a series of unsatisfactory replies, the coroner grimaced, took a moment, and then asked, "Warden Stryker, don't you think it was your duty to delve more deeply into the situation?"

Visibly trying to contain his annoyance with the coroner's aggressive questioning, Stryker replied, "If I had any idea anything was wrong, I would have."

"But couldn't you conclude something was wrong?" asked Glass. "In fact, as we all know now, that something was very wrong?"

"As I just said, I didn't know the heat was on," the warden replied in as sober a voice as he could muster. "I just didn't know."

"You mean you didn't wanna know," yelled an outraged observer from the middle of the courtroom. Such sudden outbursts from outraged courtroom observers was a recurring event. Glass and sheriff's deputies did their best to prevent their occurrence without much success.

When quiet was restored, he asked Assistant District Attorney Doyle if he'd like to continue questioning the witness. While the coroner scanned the several hundred spectators for any additional troublemakers, Doyle asked the witness, "Was Sunday truly the first time you knew the heat was on in Klondike?"

"Yes. I was completely unaware of any problem there."

"And you want us to believe that not one guard reported to you that conditions were bad in the punishment unit?"

"No one informed me of such."

Still unpersuaded, Doyle asked, "Didn't anyone tell you there were ill men in Klondike?"

"Positively not," said Stryker.

"Isn't it true that Dr. Hankins asked you whether he should go down to Klondike?"

"Yes."

"What did you say to him?"

Stryker sighed. "I said, 'They're all right, Doctor. A little later will do.'"

"Well, tell me, how did you know the men were all right?"

"I had no reason to think otherwise."

"But you knew there were sixteen men in just five cells. Cells originally designed to hold one man. Moreover, the ventilators and windows were closed at all times, except when guards visited. You must have known that."

"No. I didn't know that."

"But the rules of the prison, as many have told us, provided that as part of the punishment they should be closed—you knew that?"

"No, sir."

"For Christ's sake, who knows the rules of this prison?" trumpeted Coroner Glass, shocking everyone in the courtroom. "We had the superintendent here on the stand yesterday, and he didn't know the rules. Guards have testified they didn't know, or what they thought they knew wasn't correct. And here you are, the warden, with all these years of experience, and you don't know. Aren't there any damn rules in this place? And if so, who would know them? Or do folks just walk around the institution and make them up as they go?"

Applause and cheers once again burst throughout the room in reaction to the coroner's eruption. Reporters rose to look behind them and gauge the sentiment of the several hundred onlookers. Many had been on the edges of their seats; they were now standing and applauding. The only section of the courtroom unmoved were those few rows at the front, filled with prison employees.

Glass, red-faced, called for order. Banging his gavel, he demanded everyone take their seats. He then asked the witness if he'd like to respond.

"The rules are very simple," replied the warden. "We are not to harm anyone."

Considering the savagery of what had taken place in Klondike, Stryker's statement brought immediate gasps, chuckling, and muttered comments. Even several jurors winced. Glass and other members of the panel were incredulous at such a self-serving statement. "Not harm anyone?" repeated the coroner in disbelief. "You really want us to believe you didn't know until late Sunday afternoon that the windows and vents were closed, and the water was turned off?"

"That's right," said Stryker, showing little emotion.

"From your long experience and knowledge of the jail, didn't you take it for granted Klondike captives were being given the treatment? That they were being sweated—actually steam fried like shrimp in a Chinese skillet? Isn't that the real reason why you told Dr. Hankins not to go there? You feared what he would discover? You feared you'd have to turn the heat off and send the men back to their original cells?"

"No, that's not it at all."

"Did you investigate any further?"

"No, as I said before, I sent Captain Brennan there and took my captain's word."

"So why didn't you let Dr. Hankins go over and check on the men in Klondike over the weekend? Didn't you tell him not to?"

"I didn't stop him."

"But, Warden," interjected Deputy Coroner Ferencz, "you and others already told us it was standard practice to check the health of men in Klondike every twenty-four hours."

Stryker remained mute.

"Then tell us," interjected Assistant District Attorney Doyle, "why didn't you tell Dr. Hankins it was okay to check on the men? You knew that some men had been in there since Friday evening."

"There was no reason to think anything was wrong."

"But why didn't you let him?" Doyle responded. "He approached you. He asked if he should see the men."

Stryker shrugged and said, "I didn't stop him."

"But you didn't say okay, go over, did you?"

"No."

"Maybe you can then explain to us," asked an increasingly exasperated ADA, "how you as the warden, an official with ninety-six guards and several sergeants and captains under your command, remain uninformed about something of this magnitude? Totally ignorant until a lowly inmate tells you there's a problem?"

Stryker appeared momentarily embarrassed but did not answer. Recognizing the warden's dilemma and not willing to let him off the hook, Doyle pushed the issue. "Don't you think it strange that a convict informed you of something your entire command was either ignorant of, or worse yet, knew of but kept silent about?" When the witness did not answer, Doyle said, "I asked you a question, sir."

"I've given you my story."

Grumbling and nervous laughter could be heard in the courtroom. Doyle quickly shouted them down. He then turned back to the witness and asked, "Warden Stryker, did you tell Superintendent Davis about your exchange with Dr. Hankins?"

"No, I didn't think it was necessary."

"Warden, if I understand correctly," said Doyle, "it was about five-thirty or six P.M. Sunday afternoon when all this was occurring. Do you think that this tragedy could have been averted if something had been done then? If proper measures had been taken?"

After pondering the question, Stryker finally said, "Maybe."

"Thank you for that," said an agitated assistant district attorney.

At 12:20 P.M. and the lunch break nearing, Doyle said he had no more questions. Coroner Glass asked if the attorneys representing the two arrested guards if they'd like to question the witness.

Herman Rosen, the portly, dark-suited attorney for Albert Bridges, raised his hand and the coroner recognized him. The attorney stood up and asked the warden, "Sometime Sunday afternoon, did Mr. Bridges approach you after calling you away from Superintendent Davis and tell you several prisoners were begging to see him, saying they could not stand it much longer?"

"No."

"Did you tell my client at that time, 'I don't give a damn, I'll put four men in a cell if necessary'?"

"No."

As Coroner Glass listened to the surprising exchange, it was clear the once-solid wall of unity amongst Holmesburg custody personnel was showing cracks. Tough, ruthless prison guards like Albert Bridges, who now faced time behind bars, were growing nervous. They were not willing to be the fall guys for what everyone considered an appalling crime. And if they did, they weren't going down alone. Their attorneys had convinced them that there was no honor in maintaining a fiction to save their superiors, especially if the top brass originated the brutal policies in the first place.

Glass then recognized Edwin Lassiter, the attorney for Joseph Smoot. Small in stature, but rather eye-catching in a navy-blue three-piece suit with a gold watch chain running from a button to a vest pocket, Lassiter asked Warden Stryker how many men he had sent to the isolation unit over the years. Stryker replied he didn't recall.

"I guess we can assume it's quite a few?"

"I don't really know," said Stryker. "Not that many."

"And I guess we can safely presume many, if not all of those, sent to Klondike received the treatment?" said Lassiter. "You know, the Klondike steam bath."

"No," replied Stryker forcefully, "that's not correct."

"Well," said Lassiter, pursuing the matter, "would you say twenty percent, fifty percent, eighty percent were punished with extreme heat?"

With a pronounced sneer, Warden Stryker said, "None."

"Sure," Lassiter replied, "just like those shoved in Klondike between Friday, August 19 and Monday, August 21 who didn't receive the heat treatment?"

Stryker glared menacingly at the attorney but did not respond. More than one in the courtroom must have wondered if the prisoners sent to Klondike that sweltering weekend had received that same baleful glare. Glass, who had repeatedly glanced at his watch during the warden's testimony, contemplated whether to continue the current line of questioning or call another witness. He knew Warden Stryker had been put on the spot, but was it enough for prosecution? He eventually decided to announce a one-hour recess.

When the inquest reconvened after lunch, the coroner gaveled the room to order and announced the first witness for the afternoon session: Captain Richard Brennan. A bespectacled man of medium build, Brennan said he was a graduate of Roman Catholic High School and lived in the Fox Chase section of Northeast Philadelphia.

"How long have you worked at Holmesburg Prison?" asked Coroner Glass.

"I've been captain of the guard for nearly three years," said Brennan. "I was a sergeant for three years before being promoted to captain, and a guard for five years before making sergeant."

"Can you tell us where you were when inmate strikers were placed in Klondike on August 19?"

"I was in Wildwood on vacation."

"And you weren't called back when the food strike erupted?"

"I believe they did try to reach me," said Brennan, "but I was off fish-ing with friends, and my wife was visiting some friends of hers in Cape May. Neither of us was available to take a call about the situation at Holmesburg."

"Well, when did you finally learn of the food strike and that you were needed back at the prison?"

"When I reported back to the prison around noon on Sunday, August 21."

"Is that when you learned there were men in Klondike?"

"Yes, I went to Center, and the warden, superintendent, and several guards were there. I learned men were in Klondike, but nothing more."

"Did the warden or superintendent say anything about the heat being on in Klondike?"

"No."

"When was the first time somebody said something to you about the heat in Klondike?"

"I guess it was around six o'clock when the warden called me over," said Brennan. "He told me to check the heat and report back to him."

"After you went to the punishment unit, what did you tell him?"

"I told him it was pretty damn hot out there. I had the guards open the windows and ventilators and told Bridges to shut off all the radiators. The radiators were on full blast. You didn't dare touch 'em."

"Did you tell Stryker anything else?"

"No."

"Tell me," asked the coroner, "did you see Superintendent Davis there?"

"No. He was somewhere else in the prison."

After turning the questioning over to Assistant District Attorney Doyle, the captain was asked if intense heat was a routine part of the Klondike experience.

"Yes."

"Who told you it was part of the punishment routine?"

"Ever since it was built, it has been kept warm when prisoners were in there."

"Do you mean warm or hot, Mr. Brennan?"

The captain did not answer, and Doyle asked if he heard the question.

"It was to be kept hot when prisoners were celled there," said Brennan finally.

"So, according to your experience, the building was designed or at least used to make inmates suffer?"

"Yeah, I guess you could say that."

"When you were made captain," asked Doyle, "did you get any instructions on Klondike?"

"No, not really."

"You must have been given some instructions when men were placed in Klondike."

"Only that when I take men to Klondike I was to strip them and turn on the heat."

"Who told you that?" interjected the coroner.

Brennan sheepishly glanced at the Holmesburg contingent and then the pool of reporters.

"I asked you a question, Captain," said Glass sternly. "Who gave you that directive?"

"Warden Stryker," Brennan replied.

"Did the warden give you instructions regarding the windows, ventilators, and doors?"

"There was a general order that the windows, ventilators, and doors be closed when prisoners were in there."

"And that general order came from whom?" asked Coroner Glass.

"The warden," Brennan replied.

Many in the courtroom sat back and digested what they had heard.

"Captain Brennan, can you give us an example of when Klondike would be used?"

"In 1934, we got a bunch of rioters from Eastern State," the captain replied. "They were tough state cons, and the warden wanted to show them right off we weren't gonna tolerate their foolishness. They were taken right to Klondike."

"And how did that work out?" asked Glass.

"We had no trouble with them," said the captain barely able to contain a slight smile.

"Have there been other times since then when Klondike has been used to punish prisoners?"

"Yes."

"And when would that be?" asked the coroner.

The captain hesitated and glanced over at his Holmesburg colleagues.

"I didn't hear your answer," prodded Glass.

Brennan turned to the bench and said, "Every year since."

"So, if I understand you correctly," interjected Assistant District Attorney Doyle, "1934, 1935, 1936, 1937, and 1938 are all years where inmates were placed in Klondike and given the heat treatment?"

When there was no reply, Glass pointedly said, "Captain, is that statement correct?"

"Yes."

"Captain, let me ask you," said Assistant District Attorney Doyle, "as commanding officer, have you ever ordered the heat to be turned on?"

"No, only Davis and Stryker had the authority for that."

"And how about the closing of windows and ventilators?" asked Doyle. "Who had the authority for that?"

"It was a general order to keep everything closed tight even though the heat is on," Brennan replied, turning from the jury to his questioner. "But I want to make it clear, Mr. Doyle, I did not take men to Klondike on August 19. And I didn't tell the engineer to turn on the heat. I wasn't even in the city; I was down the shore on vacation. I did not come back until I was due to report on Sunday, the twenty-first."

Glass tried not to show his disappointment, but the captain's alibi—which he didn't doubt was true—left a sizable hole in their case. Finding the individual or individuals who ordered the heat treatment for the inmates imprisoned in Klondike on August 19 was critical. Testimony pointed to Sergeant Gary Hartzell as that person, but earlier interviews suggested there were others. The coroner had his sights set on Davis and Stryker. Hartzell was the key link between the Klondike guards and the prison's top officials, but he had managed to go into hiding and avoid a subpoena. Without him, the coroner feared his inquest would be similar to what happened so often in Philadelphia corruption investigations—only the low-hanging fruit prosecuted, if anyone at all. Glass knew guards were involved in torturing the prisoners, but he wanted the bosses. Brennan had certainly implicated Stryker, but the captain wasn't even there when the Klondike episode began on Friday the nineteenth. A jury at a criminal trial could be easily influenced by a slick defense lawyer and led to believe there was insufficient evidence to convict the superintendent and warden. The prospect that they might go free alarmed Glass, but there seemed little he could do about it without the missing piece: Hartzell.

Assistant District Attorney Doyle continued to fire questions at the witness. He sought the names of others who came in contact with the deceased prisoners and asked Brennan, "Who went with you on Sunday evening to check on the men in Klondike?"

"Albert Bridges, Joseph Smoot, Bob Trent, Joe Barnwell, and a few other guards."

"When you entered, you found the interior hot, didn't you?"

"Yes."

"It was actually terribly hot, wasn't it?"

"Yes, it was pretty hot," Brennan replied. "You were perspiring immediately and didn't dare touch the radiators."

"Let me ask you, Captain," said Doyle, "do you think you could have withstood it? Could you have stayed in that brick oven any length of time?"

"No, I don't believe I could," said Brennan. "I was not only sweating from the time I went in there until I left, but it was difficult to breathe. Yeah, it was pretty bad. The whole place smelled from the men's perspiration, their urine, and . . . and you know . . ."

"Finding it unbearable," said Doyle, "what did you do?"

"I ordered all the radiators turned off, and all the windows and ventilators opened."

Captain Brennan continued to be peppered with questions about the condition of the men inside Klondike, and his subsequent conversation with Warden Stryker. Though initially comfortable that his role in the inquest was minimal, observers could sense his growing nervousness. Pressure was being applied, and even those on the periphery of the Klondike deaths were feeling the heat.

Chapter 25

New Allegations of Fault

It was in the midst of the Doyle–Brennan exchange that tipstaff handed the coroner a note. After reading it, Glass excused himself and immediately left the bench. He practically trotted to his office on the other side of City Hall, where Miss Renwick informed him an attorney named Meyer Cohn was waiting for him in his office. He claimed to have contact with someone vital to the Holmesburg puzzle. Grim-faced, she advised her boss, "Watch yourself with this guy."

Glass was familiar with the prominent criminal defense attorney and excited by the prospect that Cohn had something the coroner wanted. Looking prosperous and comfortable as he sat on a well-worn sofa in the coroner's office, Cohn cut right to the issue. "I've been contacted by Gary Hartzell," said Cohn. "He wants to come in. He's prepared to name names."

"Great," Glass replied. "Have him come in."

"Not so fast," said Cohn. "He'll come in just as soon as you agree to give him immunity from prosecution."

"Are you crazy?" Glass replied. "You must be kidding. Eight men are dead, and he wants a pass? He's gotta be nuts."

"No, not nuts," said Cohn. "But he is scared."

"And rightfully so," Glass replied. "He's complicit in the operation of that medieval torture chamber. He's not getting a walk on this."

"Then you won't get Davis and Stryker," Cohn said matter-of-factly. "I've been in the courtroom, Hesh. I've heard the testimony and been reading newspaper accounts. You've got a good case against a bunch of no-name, low-level screws. But the superintendent and warden? That's another story."

"Where's he at?"

THE KLONDIKE BAKE-OVEN DEATHS

"I don't know," said Cohn. "I've only had a couple of phone conversations with him."

The expensively attired attorney with two large cigars sticking out from the breast pocket of his gray suit jacket, looked earnestly at Glass and asked, "Tell me, Mr. Coroner, will you be satisfied with nailing a couple of two-bit shmucks while the guys who ran that dungeon go scot-free and hold on to their jobs? Do you really want to go through this again three or four years from now?"

"I have enough to get both the guards and the big shots," said the coroner, his face taut and nearly crimson.

"Hesh," said Cohn, shaking his head in disagreement, "this is Philadelphia. You've been around as long as I have; you know what the record is when they go after the big boys. First of all, it's not done that often, and secondly, on those rare occasions when it happens, it proves a waste of time, not to mention taxpayer money. And this isn't even a criminal trial—it's some quasi-legal coroner's investigation."

"Yeah, thanks to sharp defense attorneys like yourself."

"Appreciate the compliment," said Cohn, "but my practice isn't solely built on defending crooked cops and politicians. I've seen enough of these cases to know your chances of getting Stryker and Davis without Hartzell's testimony are as likely as you becoming pope."

"But—"

"No buts, Hesh," interrupted Cohn. "Look at the last time they went after one of these demented prison superintendents. A decade ago, that guy, McSorley, was probably worse than Davis. And look what happened to him. Before they could even prosecute the guy, they managed to get him tucked into a mental ward at Byberry. He's never appeared in a courtroom."

The counselor continued to make his argument, but Glass was no longer listening. He knew Cohn's assessment was accurate: Philadelphia was an ethical swamp. Brute political force usually prevailed. The mayor, several city councilmen, and a number of high-ranking police officials were currently subjects of an investigative grand jury for an assortment of public corruption allegations, but few expected anything significant to happen. Bold headlines, salacious stories, and public condemnation were practically weekly events, but indifference and inaction were the bedrock of the Philadelphia political scene. Glass feared his inquest would result in the same.

If he were going to lose his position, he'd like to be remembered for more than a controversial hearing and a few guards losing their jobs. The many hours interviewing guards and inmates strongly indicated Sergeant Hartzell was central to the Klondike unit's operations. The sergeant was that key link between guards who steamed the prisoners and the top brass like Davis and Stryker who sentenced prisoners to Klondike.

Glass admitted to Cohn he wanted Davis and Stryker, but a pass for Hartzell was out of the question. "Besides," Glass argued, "I don't even have the power to strike such a deal. That's a call only the DA can make."

"I know, but you have influence with him," replied Cohn. "If Doyle and his boss want the big shots as much as you, they might go for it. You know the DA is up for reelection, too."

The coroner laughed and then provided his own lecture on contemporary politics in Philadelphia, and the Holmesburg case in particular. "I'm about to lose my job because of this case," said Glass. "If you think the DA wants to follow me out the door, you better stick to the law and forget forecasting political elections."

"I'm not as naïve as you think, Hesh," replied Cohn. "Look, you pressed this case. You could have let it die on the vine like the mayor, the police commissioner, the DA, and quite a few judges wanted you to do. But you took it on and made a damn crusade out of it. Now you've gotten your inquest, and even the DA, the newspapers, and some judges are on your side. You might as well go all the way. Seriously, what can you lose?"

Glass found the prospect of giving Sergeant Hartzell a pass for his testimony against higher-ups nauseating, but he wanted to put the blame where it belonged. He wanted the superintendent and warden to pay; they were the ones who set prison policy, formulated the rules, and gave the orders. There was no question they belonged behind bars. The Klondike guards were repugnant sadists, but they never would have committed such atrocities if the prison bosses had not sanctioned such cruel treatment of prisoners.

Glass finally conceded and told the attorney he would discuss Hartzell's offer with Assistant District Attorney Doyle and get back to him. "I won't promise anything. But if Doyle goes for it, we'll expect Hartzell in court tomorrow morning. He should be prepared to testify at the inquest and any criminal trials that may come out of it."

"Fair enough, Hesh."

After the men parted, Glass hurried back to Courtroom 653 to see if Doyle thought his boss would go for the deal in order to acquire Hartzell's testimony. A brief recess was called, and the two men left the rostrum to discuss the matter.

To his surprise, Doyle was supportive; he had expected the hard-nosed prosecutor to shun such a controversial move. Apparently, Doyle was moved by the testimony, and they were both concerned about the lack of incriminating testimony tying Davis and Stryker to the order turning on the heat inside Klondike on August 19.

The coroner was further amazed minutes later when Doyle reported back that the district attorney, Augustus J. Campbell, had gone for it. Hartzell would receive immunity in exchange for his testimony linking Davis and Stryker to the order to fire-up the ovens. Glass was gratified. Though occurring at a glacial pace, key players and institutions were coming around and seeing the inmate deaths for what they were: a savage mass murder that needed a serious investigation and vigorous prosecution.

In the coroner's office the next morning, Glass came face to face with Gary Hartzell, the sergeant of the guard who had managed to avoid being handed a subpoena. "I want to testify," said Hartzell. "They're trying to pin this on me. It ain't true. I'm not the one who killed those guys. Put me on the stand."

The sergeant was told he was expected to tell the truth, name names, and be available for any criminal trials that may result from the coroner's inquest. Hartzell agreed and extended his hand. Glass refused the handshake and with a steely expression informed him sheriff's deputies would soon arrive and escort him to Courtroom 653.

At ten o'clock Saturday morning, September 3, the courtroom was packed once again for what was expected to be the final day of testimony in the "Klondike Bake-Oven Deaths" inquiry. With the usual complement of newspapermen and thrill-seeking crime voyeurs in the audience, Coroner Glass called Sergeant Gary Hartzell to the stand. Led by two sheriff's deputies from a rear anteroom, the sergeant's appearance stunned those aware that Hartzell had been in hiding for several days. In order to avoid being handed a subpoena, the sergeant had gone into hiding in the basement of his sister's house in West Philadelphia. Prison colleagues were surprised; they knew he desperately wanted to avoid testifying about his role in the Holmesburg deaths. His attitude suddenly changed when newspaper articles identified him as the officer who ordered the heat turned on the Klondike prisoners. Headlines like "Holmesburg Sergeant Named as Ordering Heat on Prisoners," "Davis Blames Prison Sergeant For Turning On Heat That Killed 8," and "Warden Names Hartzell as Giving

Death Order" sparked panic. Being named by fellow officers and top brass as the individual who gave the order resulting in the Klondike calamity abruptly altered his naïve plan to lay low and avoid giving testimony.

About six feet tall, heavyset, and in his mid-forties, Hartzell quickly took his seat on the witness stand and peered across the room, paying particular attention to the large number of newspaper scribes seated in front of him and the six jury members off to his left.

Deputy Coroner Ferencz began the questioning by asking the sergeant when he first came to be employed at Holmesburg Prison.

"I became a prison guard in 1931," Hartzell replied. "I lost my job at Philco Electronics when the Depression hit, and the prison job was the first thing I landed. For the last two years and nine months, I've been a sergeant at Holmesburg."

"Let me get right to the point," said Ferencz. "A number of witnesses have named you as the officer who ordered the heat to be turned on over the weekend in question. You have been cited more than once as the officer who determined when heat was employed on inmates in the punishment unit. For the record, did you order George Rediker, the Holmesburg engineer, to turn the heat on in Klondike on Friday night, August 19?"

"Yes, sir."

"What exactly did you tell him?"

"I told him there were some men going out to Klondike," Hartzell replied. "I told him to turn on the heat."

Faint whispers could be heard in different sections of the courtroom. Someone had finally owned up to their involvement in the inmate deaths. Glass watched Selwyn Rossman and the other reporters feverishly take down every word. He then searched the faces of jury members for reactions.

Ferencz quickly followed up with questions regarding the sergeant's conversations with Rediker and Warden Stryker.

Hartzell admitted the engineer got back to him to confirm heat was being sent through the pipes to Klondike. He said he then reported back to Stryker.

"So you're telling this inquest, Sergeant Hartzell, that you ordered the heat turned on and made Warden Stryker aware of it?"

"Yes, sir."

"Tell the jury, sergeant, what authority did you have for ordering the heat to be turned on in Klondike on Friday, August 19? Can you make that determination yourself?"

"No, sir, I don't really have authority myself. I get it through my commanding officer—in this case, Warden Stryker. When I was promoted to sergeant in December 1935, I was told by Stryker that when there were men in Klondike the heat was to be turned on. He said the heat was purposely used to make unruly prisoners pay a price for their actions. He said very few people could withstand a day or two of the heat treatment."

"Did you interpret that to mean it was to be employed all the time?"

"Yes," said Hartzell, "whenever there were men in Klondike. I remember soon after that first conversation we put a colored prisoner in Klondike, and I asked Stryker if he wanted the heat turned on. He said, 'Yes, what the hell did I tell you before?' He was pretty mad I brought it up. He thought I should've known. When someone is in Klondike the heat goes on. There was a similar incident not long after when a couple of men were placed in Klondike for hiding in one of the exercise yards. Because it wasn't a serious offense I wasn't sure they should be given the heat treatment, so I asked Stryker about it. He looked at me angrily and said, 'If men are in Klondike the heat goes on.' He then told me, 'Hartzell, if you can't remember that, maybe I need a new sergeant.'"

The deputy coroner asked, "Was that standing order ever rescinded?" The sergeant replied that it wasn't; it was still operational.

"Were you acting Friday night on the basis of that instruction?"

"Yes," said Hartzell. "After we put the strikers in there, I immediately informed the warden that the heat had been turned on."

"So, as far as you are concerned," said Ferencz, "you did not order the heat turned on of your own volition?"

"I don't have the power to punish prisoners. I must act on the orders of my superiors. There is a strict line of command, just like the military."

Like many in the courtroom, Glass periodically glanced at Warden Stryker to gauge his reaction to the sergeant's testimony. A model of composure through the two days of testimony, Stryker remained cold, impassive. Glass had expected the warden to show his displeasure or at least quietly curse his former subordinate, but Stryker's demeanor remained unfazed.

Assistant District Attorney Doyle asked the witness, "Had you ever ordered the guards to adjust the radiator pressure or the windows and vents?"

"No," Hartzell replied. "Standard procedure has always been when there are men in Klondike the heat is on and the windows and ceiling vents are closed. I've never seen the windows and vents open while Klondike was occupied."

Coroner Glass asked Mr. Hendricks, the jury foreman, if the jury had any questions for the witness. A couple of members raised their hands, but the foreman said he'd like to first meet with his colleagues, discuss what they had heard from several witnesses, and then proffer questions to certain individuals. The coroner agreed and announced there would be a brief recess.

As the jury moved to an anteroom, there was much discussion revolving around Sergeant Hartzell's testimony. Observers commented on his self-serving explanations, how his testimony squared with the alibis of Superintendent Davis and Warden Stryker, and the questionable veracity of guards who had direct contact with the dying prisoners. Some took sides, defending certain individuals over others, but many expressed dismay with the entire assemblage of prison personnel. As one disgusted courtroom observer was heard telling a friend in the corridor, "No one's clean in this horror. They're all guilty."

As soon as the recess was announced, newsmen scrambled to the press room on the second floor to call in the new account presented by Sergeant Hartzell. The previous evening and that morning, newspaper headlines had trumpeted the day's highlights and forthcoming conclusion of the special blue ribbon inquiry into the "Holmesburg Torture Deaths." For two days, entire pages had been devoted to word-for-word testimony from each witness. Articles entitled "Doctors Claim Ignorance," "Prison Inspectors Knew All About It, But Didn't Take Action," and "Rigid Torture Decree Denied By Stryker in Final Testimony," captivated newspaper subscribers.

From the very first, tabloids and broadsheets seemed to be competing with each other regarding the titillating Holmesburg drama. With a key piece of it—the coroner's investigation—coming to a close, news outlets planned saturation coverage. Sergeant Hartzell's provocative addition to the storyline only contributed further complexity to the mystery and greater difficulty in assigning blame. Evening editions screamed, "Higher-Up Linked to Prison Killings," "Sergeant Names Warden as Killer," and "Prison Warden Fingered as Issuing Roasting Order."

When the inquest was reconvened a short while later, it was Warden Stryker—not Sergeant Hartzell—who was called to the stand. Though not expecting to be confronted for a second time with questions, Stryker maintained his usual stoic, businesslike demeanor.

"Warden Stryker, I've been informed members of the jury have additional questions for you," said the coroner. "Mr. Ferencz, would you please present the jury's questions to the witness?"

"According to Sergeant Hartzell," said Ferencz, "you did not specifically tell him to turn on the heat on Friday, August 19, but you did tell him three years earlier, in 1935, that there was a standing rule that when anyone was in Klondike the heat was to be turned on. And that after he turned the heat on Friday, he immediately reported back to you what he had done. Was this the case, and did Hartzell tell you the heat was on?"

"No, sir," Stryker replied.

"And that is your answer?"

"Yes, sir. If he had reported to me that heat was on in Klondike, I would have told him to turn it off."

"Let's be clear about this," said Ferencz. "Sergeant Hartzell testified that in 1935 you issued a standing rule that heat should be turned on when prisoners were sent to Klondike. Did you tell him that?"

"I positively never told anybody it was a standing rule."

Stryker was then dismissed and Captain Richard Brennan called to the stand.

"Knowing the pitiful condition of the men and the extreme punishment they had endured," said Ferencz, "why did you not remain until the place and radiators had cooled?"

"I'm an officer," Brennan replied. "I was told to go out, turn off the radiators, and report back immediately. I told Mr. Stryker that the heat was off, and he said okay."

"So, in your opinion, further punishment had ended around six P.M. Sunday afternoon?"

"Yes."

"But actually, Captain," said Ferencz, "that was when the worst of it was about to begin."

The Holmesburg captain adopted a vacant stare and never replied.

Chapter 26

Inquest Verdict

After Coroner Glass rapped his gavel and dismissed the witness, he announced there would be a brief recess. While jurors and those in the gallery discussed the case among themselves, Glass, Doyle, and Ferencz stepped into the judge's chambers and debated whether they were ready for the jury to deliberate. They quickly agreed they had heard sufficient testimony for the jury to reach a verdict.

"Carl, do you feel capable of delivering the charge to the jury?" asked Glass.

Ferencz was surprised the coroner would offer him such an important assignment. He was sure previous coroners would not have been so generous with what most saw as the office's biggest stage in years. He presumed his boss had his reasons for passing on the opportunity, but it was also another sign he had earned the coroner's trust and the added responsibility.

When the men returned to their seats, Glass requested silence in the courtroom and announced they would now proceed to the inquest's final stage. He then asked the deputy coroner to give the jury their deliberation instructions.

"Ladies and gentlemen of the jury," said Carl Ferencz, "you have been called from among the citizens of the city to sit in judgment on the death of eight men: James McBride, Bruno Palumbo, John Webster, Paul Oteri, Jake Smyzak, Timothy O'Shea, Calvin Crouse, and William Crawford.

"As jurymen of this special coroner's inquest, your duties are greater in scope than other juries. Your duties are even broader than those of the Grand Jury. We want you to go farther than just determining the cause of these deaths. If you think it advisable, you may make a first presentment as to the causes of these deaths, and then continue your investigation so as to prevent the occurrence of a similar tragedy. You may also decide who is culpable for these deaths.

"It is possible that the Grand Jury of Philadelphia may take some steps in this case. Your decision will be critical to that venture. But at this time your concern is chiefly the cause of the deaths of these eight men, and who was responsible. I will now briefly discuss what has occurred before you.

"The strata of society from which you were selected indicates yours will be a common-sense approach to the situation. I think you can accept as fact that extreme heat was applied on imprisoned men despite any credible statement of witnesses to the contrary, and that this heat was injurious, if not fatal, to humans.

"Homicide is the violent taking of the life of a human being. There are degrees ranging from manslaughter up to various degrees of murder. You will have to determine in this case whether these men met their deaths in a lawful or unlawful manner. You must also consider whether criminal negligence has been committed with regard to the law. Superintendent Davis has the ultimate responsibility. He is in charge of not only all the prisoners but the prison guards as well. He alone is supreme in the prison. He not only has power over the prison but is also in charge of and responsible for the building known as Klondike. You heard his statement that he was in control of 1,400 prisoners over the weekend when eight men died in an extremely brutal fashion.

"Ladies and gentlemen of the jury, you must determine whether there was a complete abandonment of the welfare of the prisoners and whether the situation was not only unreasonable but also fraught with danger. It is for you to determine if Superintendent Davis was responsible and criminally negligent. Eight men were found dead Monday morning. Hence, some of you may feel a compelling prima facie criminal case has been made against him and he should be held for the Grand Jury.

"Warden Stryker admitted that he was in direct charge of Klondike and that he did not see fit to visit Klondike while the prisoners were there. Nor, according to testimony, did he allow physicians to make their normal visits to examine Klondike prisoners. Hence, you may feel he exhibited at the very least criminal negligence, and therefore he should be held for the Grand Jury.

"Now, as to Captain Brennan, it has been testified that he was in charge of the guards and went to look at the prisoners on Sunday night. By Davis's own testimony, Brennan should have taken it upon himself to stop the punishment if he thought it necessary and prudent and to ensure that it not be re-employed. I, therefore, must recommend to you that a prima facie criminal case has been made out against Brennan and he should be held for the Grand Jury.

"Sergeant Hartzell has testified that heat was part of the punishment routine for many years and that he was acting under previous orders when he directed engineer Rediker to turn on the heat in the building. The fact that Sergeant Hartzell was not in the building after Friday night is of note, but the statements of engineer Rediker and others that heat was turned on to take out the dampness in the building is completely absurd. In fact, there has been much testimony from other witnesses that discredits such claims and the equally fallacious claims of authorities. Therefore, if you feel that Hartzell's actions were in accordance with general orders, you must exonerate him.

"Joseph Smoot and Albert Bridges were in charge of the prisoners in Klondike and visited them regularly. I feel that a prima facie criminal case has been made against them and they should be held for the Grand Jury." The deputy coroner continued in the same manner regarding officers Trent, Barnwell, and the others. He summed up by stating, "If they knew the sufferings of the men, and like Smoot and Bridges did nothing, I recommend that they be held for the Grand Jury."

On the matter of the others, Ferencz stated, "As to Oliver Hankins and George Rediker, neither is a member of uniformed custody; one is a physician and one an engineer. However, they both played a role in the deadly events of August 22. By one's sin of omission and the other's sin of commission, eight men died. If you should so agree, both should be held for the Grand Jury.

"I am now leaving this matter in your hands for discussion and debate. Upon your shoulders rests a grave responsibility. You now represent the people of Pennsylvania. I ask you to consider this case reasonably, honorably, and dispassionately."

Gilbert Hendricks and his colleagues—four men and two women—were escorted to a conference room to deliberate and thrash out who, if anyone, should be held for criminal prosecution in the death of eight county prisoners. There was a smattering of applause as they departed the courtroom. The hundreds of spectators in the gallery seemed undecided whether to stay and wait for a verdict or leave. The fact that there were so many potential defendants whose actions required examination only complicated the process. Assistant District

Attorney Doyle and Coroner Glass briefly answered journalists' questions and then departed for their respective offices in wait of a jury decision.

As the minutes passed, Heshel Glass talked with staff and several newspaper reporters who gathered in his office. Almost all congratulated him for a job well done—a job no one else in the city's criminal justice community would embrace. But there were still cynics, and the coroner understood their skepticism. The Quaker City was a wasteland of corruption, nepotism, and inexplicable decision-making. Cases stronger than his Holmesburg gambit had been fixed, jettisoned, or just wiped from the books as if they had never occurred.

Selwyn Rossman of the *New York Times*, knowing of Glass's concern about the coming primary and the slim chances of his reelection, told the coroner he could rest a little easier now. His generally well-received special investigation into the Klondike murders would prove a strong counter-measure to any party opposition that surfaced. The coroner expressed his appreciation for the sentiment but quickly set the out-of-town newsman straight. "In New York, maybe, but not Philadelphia," Glass replied with a forced smile. "Philly and New York are only ninety miles apart as the crow flies, but politically there's a world of difference. Voters here answer to a higher order. Ward leaders control the ballot box, and the mayor controls the ward leaders."

Rossman and a few others tried to reassure the coroner everything would work out, but he wasn't having any of it. "Gentlemen, thank you for the encouragement," said Glass, "but I've been part of the political system here for most of my adult life. I know what can and what can't be done."

Despite his gloomy perspective, privately, the coroner had not conceded his reelection.

In fact, he periodically excused himself to enter his private office to make or receive a phone call with a ward leader, union activist, or civic leader. Glass knew there probably wouldn't be a better time to approach people and ask for their support. He was front-page news, someone people were willing to entertain, if only for a brief phone call. As one politically savvy North Philadelphia ward leader told him in regard to the mayor's efforts to end his career as an elected official, "Hesh, got to admit you've gotten some good press lately. The average rowhouse voter may remember your name if the papers continue to play up your inquest. But if your jury can't make a decision or the Grand

Jury chooses not to follow up and prosecute, you'll be like the last guy in that office—out of a job."

When it was announced that the jury had reached a verdict after deliberating just over three hours, everyone returned to the courtroom. It was a few minutes past five o'clock when the coroner slammed his gavel and asked sheriff's deputies to escort the jurors in.

Everyone tried to read the jurors' mannerisms and facial expressions. Reporters and photographers with pencils, notebooks, and cameras in hand were ready to record the outcome as an air of expectation filled the courtroom. Coroner Glass waited for everyone to be seated. He then requested there be no vocal demonstrations of support or disfavor when the verdicts were read. Turning to the jury, he asked Gilbert Hendricks if a verdict in the Holmesburg matter had been reached.

"Yes, sir," replied Hendricks.

"And your decision is?" asked the coroner.

Hendricks rose and glanced at the contingent of Holmesburg administrators and guards directly across from him. He then put on his eyeglasses and began to read from a sheet of paper. Many in the courtroom leaned forward, some practically standing in order to get a better glimpse of both the jury foreman and those about to learn their fates.

"We, the members of the coroner's jury," said Hendricks in a firm voice, "unanimously find that James McBride, Bruno Palumbo, John Webster, Paul Oteri, Jake Smyzak, Timothy O'Shea, Calvin Crouse, and William Crawford came to their deaths through heatstroke caused by criminal negligence. Moreover, we hold criminally responsible Superintendent Warren Davis, Warden Victor Stryker, Captain Richard Brennan, and prison guards Joseph Smoot, Albert Bridges, Robert Trent, Emil Morris, Alex Crawley, Joseph Barnwell, and Thomas Burnley."

Applause and cries of both triumph and anguish could be heard throughout the courtroom as families of the deceased and friends of prison personnel respectively celebrated and cursed the jury's decision.

Coroner Glass banged his gavel and repeatedly called for order. With those in the courtroom angling for a better view, reporters frantically scribbling notes of the jury's findings, and photographers quickly snapping pictures, Coroner Glass demanded silence and instructed everyone to take their seats. Not till Glass called Superintendent Davis before the bench did the room grow quiet.

After being asked to identify himself for the record, and appearing confused, Davis awaited the next step in the embarrassing legal process, knowing hundreds of eyes were on him and two dozen news reporters were anxiously awaiting his fate.

"You have been found responsible for criminal negligence in the death of eight men," said Glass soberly. "I hold you without bail for action by the Grand Jury."

As the blood drained from Davis's face and his shoulders slumped, a wave of cheers and applause swept through the courtroom. While Glass tried to restore order, Davis's attorney could barely be heard as he came to his client's side and told the court, "As you know, you have no legal right to set bail, but I will ask you for commitment papers as soon as you are able to prepare them. I will also be filing a petition for bail for my client."

The coroner told the superintendent and his attorney to step back and then called to the bench Warden Victor Stryker. Following the same procedure as he did with Davis, Stryker was informed he was being held for action by the Grand Jury, which set off another round of applause and expressions of general satisfaction. Stryker's attorney quickly joined his client at the bench and said he would also be filing petition papers for bail.

For the next several minutes, the process was repeated as each of those found responsible was called before the bench. Though most had lost their swagger, a few were heard to mutter their disgust and curse both Glass and the jury. The coroner proceeded expeditiously, and when the last guard was informed of his fate, Glass looked over the large room with a sense of accomplishment.

With the inquest requirements completed, the coroner turned to the jury and said, "Ladies and gentlemen of the jury, you have sat here for three days and listened with great care to the testimony of numerous individuals, some of it particularly dark, regarding a terrible tragedy. I want to compliment you on the service you have rendered regarding this horrid crime. You have performed a wonderful service to both the City of Philadelphia and the Commonwealth of Pennsylvania. Your role in this disturbing case shall not go unrecognized. And I would like to personally thank you for taking on a difficult assignment that many would have shunned. You deserve our thanks and appreciation. Congratulations on a job well done."

"Lastly," said Glass, looking over the courtroom, "I feel that a case like this might have gone unnoticed had it not been for the assistance of the District Attorney's office, and particularly Mr. Doyle. We, the citizens of Philadelphia, now look to Mr. Doyle and his office for the appropriate judicial resolution of what we have learned over the last few days."

After declaring, "These proceedings are now closed," and banging his gavel one last time, Glass rose from the bench along with other members of the inquest panel. The jury quickly followed. There was a flurry of applause and a mix of friends, family members, and reporters moving to offer congratulations, ask questions, and take reactions from participants. Several reporters encircled Assistant District Attorney Doyle to ask his reaction to the jury's decision and how his office would follow up.

"We shall move quickly," said Doyle. "I'm having the defendants taken in front of Judge Fleetwood, where I will be asking for substantial bail for each of them, especially the superintendent and warden." When asked his reaction to the coroner's inquest, Doyle replied, "We've learned a great deal. We shall present the evidence to the Grand Jury. It will be up to jurors to decide who is to be indicted and the nature of the charges. I'm fully confident a trial regarding those responsible for the Klondike deaths will be held in the very near future."

By far, the largest gathering of newsmen, well-wishers, and spectators surrounded Coroner Glass as he left the bench and attempted to exit the courtroom. Questions for him centered around his take on the result of his blue ribbon inquiry and the likelihood of District Attorney Campbell following through with a Grand Jury investigation. Knowing the mayor's animus toward him and promise to remove him from office, questions also arose concerning his thoughts on the inquest's impact regarding his chances for reelection.

Glass provided very brief answers. "I only did my duty, nothing more," was a recurring response when asked by reporters if he felt good about his effort. As he tried to escape those crowding around him, a space gradually opened and a thin, gray-haired woman pushed her way forward. "Thank you," she said, tears running down her cheeks. "Thank God somebody in this town had the courage to do something . . . to do the right thing."

The coroner immediately recognized Mrs. O'Shea, the mother of Timothy O'Shea, one of the prisoners who lost his life. Reaching for the coroner's hand, her grasp was almost as firm as it was the day she and other distraught relatives sought justice from elected officials in City Hall.

Tearful and occasionally sobbing, Shirley O'Shea tried to communicate her gratitude but was too emotionally wrought, and relatives helped escort her away. Reporters had jotted down her comments and several followed her, but most continued to pepper Glass with questions. "Do you have faith the district attorney's office will pursue the case aggressively?" "How many of the men found responsible today do you think the district attorney will actually prosecute?" "What are the chances the mayor will attempt to block a criminal trial?" and "What yet needs to be done for Philadelphia to take criminal justice and prison reform seriously?"

By late evening on September 3, front-page newspaper headlines were proclaiming "Davis, Stryker, 8 Aides Held in Torture Deaths," "Inquest Finds Negligence In Roasting of 8 Prisoners," and "Top Prison Staff Arrested, Coroner Denies Bond To Those Responsible." Photographs of dejected and glum-faced prison staff appeared alongside the stories. The *Philadelphia Record* had a large front-page photo of the Holmesburg contingent under the headline "Davis and 9 Staff Arrested; Inquest Finds Criminal Negligence in Roasting of Prisoners."

In addition to the banner headlines announcing the outcome, editorials underscored the importance and correctness of the jury's verdict. "The testimony before the Coroner's Inquest," wrote the *Philadelphia Evening Bulletin,* normally no friend of Democratic officeholders, "developed a horrible example of how a modern penal institution ought not to run. It is indisputable that the isolation building served as a place of extreme punishment where unruly convicts were subjected to severe discomfort, meaning intense heat. Such punishment could rise to the level of torture and death as proven by the demise of eight inmates—a thing for which modern penal administration has no place."

The editorial went on to acknowledge the coroner's post-verdict comments concerning the inherent difficulty of such a chore. "A high degree of sensitivity cannot always be expected of prison guards," said Glass. "The intractable nature of the desperate men with whom they are brought into daily contact would soon blunt that. But humanity and common decency are indispensable."

Albeit brief, the *Evening Bulletin's* editorial concluded with an unprecedented tribute to the coroner and his role in investigating the embarrassing prison drama. "We are forever indebted to Coroner Glass for seeking out and illuminating the terrible facts of this case. Punishment of those on whom guilt certainly can be fixed is necessary, but for the sake of the City's reputation there ought to be a drastic change in methods of discipline and of internal administration in the prison."

Radio broadcasts and newspaper accounts informed interested citizens around the country about the latest chapter in the "infamous Klondike killings." Selwyn Rossman's *New York Times* article not only cited the high points of the proceedings but also made the poignant observation that convictions may prove difficult as "everyone involved in forthcoming trials will either be a convicted criminal serving a prison sentence or a penal employee under indictment and facing many years behind bars." He underscored "Philadelphia's recent corruption challenge, and its tolerance for elected and appointed officials making immoral and dishonest decisions." He went on to ponder how juries would "evaluate the testimony of witnesses, all of whom either worked or were confined behind high prison walls."

Some longtime political observers, noted the reporter, were so cynical they wouldn't be surprised if some dramatic event or judicial ruling short-circuited the entire process. "After all," they argued, "this is Philadelphia."

⚯

Just weeks later, on September 21, 1938, a Philadelphia Grand Jury—propelled by resounding public support for the outcome of the coroner's blue ribbon inquest—delivered murder and manslaughter indictments to Judge Theodore Wexler of Quarter Sessions Court in the infamous Klondike Bake-Oven Murder Case. In all, sixty separate bills were brought against ten defendants who were held culpable. The Grand Jury found both murder and manslaughter indictments against Superintendent Warren B. Davis, Warden Victor Stryker, Captain Richard Brennan, and guards Joseph Smoot and Albert Bridges. Manslaughter bills were brought against guards Robert Trent, Alex Crawley, Joseph Barnwell, and Emil Morris. Jurors could not agree on the culpability of Dr. Oliver Hankins and city engineer George Rediker.

The Grand Jury's conclusions came as a shock. Manslaughter indictments were fully expected, but the additional bills charging murder sparked surprise among the public and legal community. It was the general feeling by seasoned observers that grand jurors were moved by the "hardness of heart and disregard for the rights of others" displayed in the harsh treatment accorded to the prisoners. This allowed the jury to "impute malice," and thereby justify murder indictments. The manslaughter bills involved "negligence and callousness in carrying out a lawful act in an unlawful manner."

After Judge Wexler commended grand jurors for a "careful and conscientious job," Assistant District Attorney Vincent Doyle said it was his goal that the defendants be brought to trial as promptly as possible. Davis and Stryker were placed under $10,000 bail. Brennan, Bridges, and Smoot received $5,000 bail assignments, and the others were placed at $2,500.

Chapter 27

Criminal Justice in Philadelphia

It was not long after when the DA's office announced that Victor Stryker would be the first of the Holmesburg defendants to be put on trial. Almost immediately, official shenanigans were detected. Reports were coming into the coroner's office that inmate witnesses were being harassed—and threatened with being sent back to Holmesburg from their less-hostile confines at Moyamensing Prison—if they did not alter their recollections.

Both Glass and Doyle sought judicial intervention, specifically requesting potential inmate witnesses for the prosecution be temporarily removed from Philadelphia County and placed in a nearby penal facility. Though the mayor had made no bold public comments during the inquest and Grand Jury investigation, it was well known that behind the scenes Clarke remained livid, opposed to the criminal trials, and vigorously working to thwart any chance of the coroner's reelection. The fear that the mayor was behind Moko guards pressuring inmate witnesses was shared by both Glass and Doyle, but there was no evidence to support such an explosive accusation. The guards didn't need any encouragement from City Hall, however. They were already united in opposition to inquests, grand juries, criminal trials, and any other court-related tribunal that undermined their authority.

Stryker's attorney repeatedly bemoaned his client being the first of the Holmesburg defendants to be tried, and so soon after the coroner's inquest and Grand Jury determination. "Minds were inflamed and already made up," argued Jack Ryan. "The public is enraged, and passions are white-hot."

When he moved for a trial delay, it allowed Assistant District Attorney Doyle to argue, "Witnesses were in certain terror at the prospect of testifying against guards and prison officials." He claimed, "Pressure was being exerted on inmates to change their stories," and asked the Pennsylvania Supreme Court to intervene.

In response, the court ruled that inmates scheduled to testify in the Philadelphia Bake-Oven Death Trials would be immediately transferred to the Bucks County Jail located in Doylestown, and housed there prior to and during the course of the trial. Moreover, the court granted defense counsel a short delay with the understanding the trial would commence no later than mid-January.

As observers had become accustomed, the former warden would display little emotion during the eight-day trial as numerous witnesses recounted Stryker's role in sending inmate protesters to the punishment unit and then presiding over their harsh treatment.

Despite the Grand Jury filing murder charges against the warden, Judge Frank Kavanaugh threw out the more severe charges of murder and voluntary manslaughter for the lesser charge of involuntary manslaughter before the trial ever began. The momentous legal decision occurred most unexpectedly when a female juror informed the judge she could not serve due to her opposition to capital punishment. "There is no question of capital punishment involved in this case," Judge Kavanaugh replied. "Neither the electric chair nor life in prison would be appropriate in such a case."

The jurist's decision stunned many court observers, but the decision drew little public comment. Coroner Glass was upset with the decision, however, there was little he could do. He wasn't even a member of the bar. When he voiced his concerns to friends and colleagues, they usually replied that he had done more than anyone ever thought possible. "Without you, Hesh," said one sympathetic supporter, "there never would have been an investigation in the first place. If it wasn't for you, they'd still be putting people in Klondike." The praise was appreciated, but it did little to dissuade the coroner from believing things were returning to normal. Glass feared the chance for real reform in Philadelphia was slowly drifting away.

Even newspaper editorial boards that had recently called for justice in the "Holmesburg horror" were silent. Citizens were similarly unmoved; they had grown used to executive decisions and court decrees that sowed confusion, protected the comfortable, and maintained the status quo. Most seemed satisfied there would be a criminal trial and some form of punishment, albeit modest.

Judge Kavanaugh instructed the jury that if it was "determined the decedents died of heat exhaustion, then you must examine the conduct of defendant Stryker to find out whether he failed in any duty, and whether his failure in that duty resulted in the death of prisoners. If his actions were reckless and wanton, then your verdict must be guilty of involuntary manslaughter."

Defense counsel Ryan presented a vigorous case, putting much of the blame on Superintendent Davis, bringing in two industrial hygiene experts to argue the men died of violent external forces and not heat. He also brought in three dozen character witnesses to amplify Stryker's reputation as a "decent, God-fearing man of good character." When on the stand describing that last fateful day when the men died, Stryker would claim he fell asleep in the jail from exhaustion after four days of constant vigilance, and after telling the superintendent "the heat had been turned off in Klondike" and all was calm in the jail.

In summation, Ryan told the jury, "Stryker was not a vicious man. He was efficient, probably too efficient." He'd go on to say, "The warden and his wife are both religious people, and Stryker did not attempt to avoid responsibility by putting the blame on others."

Vincent A. Doyle would be equally aggressive in prosecuting the case. He talked of the defendant's "callous indifference" that led to a "charnel house effect similar to the Black Hole of Calcutta." He called on many of the witnesses who testified at the coroner's inquest and Grand Jury. He repeatedly emphasized that Stryker was the true head of Holmesburg, the real orchestrator of the Klondike horror. Doyle told jurors, "Stryker was there all the time during those three days of horror. He was giving the orders; he was the boss. The guards had to do what he said."

After deliberating a relatively brief two hours and twenty-two minutes, a jury of five women and seven men found Stryker guilty of involuntary manslaughter. Though the warden displayed little emotion on hearing the jury's verdict, his wife fainted and had to be carried from the courtroom. The conviction came with a $1,000 fine and a sentence of eighteen months to three years behind bars. A discussion then ensued as to Stryker's safety—Where would he serve his sentence? Philadelphia County was out of the question. News articles quoted prison inmates boasting, "The chances are 10 to 1 Stryker will be knifed within a few days of his incarceration." There were reports that prisoners in state prisons across the Commonwealth were of a similar mind. The DA made no recommendation regarding a penal facility and left the decision up to the trial judge.

On April 14, 1939, Holmesburg Prison Captain Richard Brennan was exonerated of any responsibility in the deaths of eight prisoners interned in

Klondike. After deliberating two hours and forty minutes, a jury consisting of ten men and two women returned a verdict of not guilty of involuntary manslaughter. As in the preceding trial, murder and voluntary manslaughter charges had been ruled out by the court.

When the jury reached a verdict after a long day of testimony, the court-room was nearly empty. Brennan had been one of the trial's chief witnesses and described when returning to the institution from vacation the orders he had been given by Warden Stryker. The captain repeatedly said he had no role in sending prisoners to Klondike or in their treatment once incarcerated. More-over, he claimed to be the one who actually opened the windows and turned off the heat the only time he ventured into the building.

When the verdict was delivered, Brennan bolted from the defendant's table and proceeded to shake hands with each member of the jury who had given him freedom.

Two weeks later, on April 29, 1939, Warren B. Davis, former superinten-dent of the Philadelphia Prison System, was acquitted of involuntary murder. A jury of eight men and four women deliberated ten hours before arriving at a decision.

In an effort to avoid the emotional impact of jurors hearing about the last hours of the Klondike decedents, Cyrus Black, Davis's attorney, waived testi-mony relative to conditions in Klondike. Judge Lieberthal disagreed and ruled, "The jurors should know all conditions surrounding the prison to determine if Davis failed to perform his duty. That is the real issue."

When Black objected, the judge asked, "Can't you conceive of a case where a man deliberately refused to know what he should have known? Are you imply-ing Mr. Davis didn't know what Warden Stryker and the guards were doing? Do you really think that because a man sits around reading a newspaper or playing checkers, not wanting to know what is going on, he is relieved of culpability?"

With the court previously ruling that murder and voluntary manslaughter charges were inappropriate in such a case, the jury had considerable difficulty coming to agreement on just what Superintendent Davis was guilty of.

The one agreement was that the once-accomplished administrator seemed out of touch and detached from his duties and responsibilities. Eventually, the jury fell back on that one item of agreement and voted for acquittal. Davis, who was unable to hide his nervousness as the jury deliberated, was immediately mobbed by friends and supporters, including many current and former police officials, when the verdict was announced.

On June 16, 1939, Holmesburg Prison guard Joseph Smoot was convicted of involuntary manslaughter by a jury of nine men and three women. After deliberating nearly four hours, the jury decided to reject the more serious charge of murder in the second degree for the lesser charge of involuntary manslaughter calling for a prison sentence of eighteen months to three years.

In his lengthy and detailed charge to the jury, Judge Irving Minkus told the jury a first-degree determination was invalid because "there was no deliberation or premeditation," and voluntary manslaughter was out "because the deaths did not result from the heat of passion." The judge went on to instruct jurors, "The defendant was obliged to take orders from a superior, but if he was asked to do something which would cause death, he would not be obliged to follow that order."

Thirty-nine-year-old Smoot took the verdict stoically. He had displayed little emotion at both the coroner's inquest and his own trial. His frail, blonde-haired wife and daughter, however, wept openly and had to be assisted from the courtroom.

Taking the stand in his own defense, Smoot blamed Warden Stryker for the inmate deaths and said as a guard all he could do was take orders. "I told Stryker to come out and see the men or send a doctor," said Smoot on the witness stand. "He said, 'To hell with them.' I told him all the men were begging for him to come to see them. He told me, 'When I make up my mind I'll go out, and not before.'" Smoot turned to the jury at that point and asked, "What else could I do?"

After the jury returned a guilty verdict, Smoot's attorney said he would appeal the decision and then vigorously argued that his client not be made to fulfill his sentence in a Philadelphia County prison.

To the surprise of many, on June 23, 1939, the last trial growing out of the notorious "bake-oven" deaths resulted in the acquittal of six prison guards. In just fifty minutes, a jury of seven women and five men not only found the defendants innocent of all charges but further determined "all these men be reinstated to their former positions as guards with full back pay."

Of the six, the most surprising defendant to receive his freedom was guard Albert Bridges, who was repeatedly mentioned by surviving prisoners as central to their near-death experience. Even the trial judge was caught off guard by the jury's decision, but apparently Herman Rosen, Bridges' attorney, had sufficiently convinced jurors his client repeatedly turned the Klondike temperature valve down, and on more than one occasion informed the warden of the heat and crowded conditions in the building.

It was while a mystified and frustrated Coroner Glass sat at his desk the next morning reading local newspaper accounts of the last Holmesburg trial that his secretary informed him Selwyn Rossman of the *New York Times* was on the line. Even the *Times* had seemingly grown weary of the story that had once been front-page news. Rossman had not been dispatched to Philadelphia to cover any of the trials, but he was now assigned to do a story summing up what many had argued was the worst example of prison abuse in American history. The two men lamented the trial results; only two convictions and meager prison terms for the murder of eight men. Of equal importance was a discussion of what, if any, long-term impact the case would have for county penal operations and the administration of justice in Philadelphia.

Though there was room for debate on those questions, there was considerably more agreement concerning the coroner's chances for reelection; they had increased substantially. Not only had the coroner's investigation won plaudits from opinion-makers in the city, but something totally unexpected had occurred: Mayor G. Thomas Clarke had been indicted for public corruption along with several top government officials. Further contributing to the mayor's precarious situation was a dramatic downturn in his health.

During the first week of January 1939, citizens were informed Clarke was ill. "Mayor Reported Seriously Ill of Heart Trouble," was the front-page headline in the *Philadelphia Record*. Other papers broadcast similar reports. Though family and government aides initially argued it was just a case of indigestion, word leaked out the mayor had actually "suffered a coronary thrombosis," and his doctors were stating he was in need of "a long rest." In the coming days, more information was revealed, but as usual, much of it was conflicting. Clarke was said to be "unable to rise from his bed" and his "speech slurred as if he had suffered a stroke." The Clarke family, however, proved unwavering in arguing the mayor had "caught a cold while attending a New Year's event," and would "be fine after a week to ten days convalescing at home."

In fact, Clarke had not looked well for some time. And his coughing spells had become more violent and frequent, especially when someone or some incident stirred the mayor's juices. Pressured by his doctors months earlier to take a vacation and relax, Clarke had actually scheduled to take time off during the previous summer, but public talk and newspaper columns hinting that he was under investigation and fleeing investigators caused him to cancel the vacation.

"There is obviously a well-organized campaign of slander and vilification against me," Clarke told the press, "and I feel it is my duty to cancel my plans for a vacation. I want all to know I will continue to wage a fight to the finish against my enemies."

◦•◦

The same week just a few months earlier in late August that Clarke's declaration to stay on the job was uttered to reporters, inmates upset with their monotonous and bland meals at the county's largest prison initiated a hunger strike. In retaliation, authorities began pulling protesters out of population and sequestering them in a separate punishment unit. Three days later, on August 22, eight terribly discolored corpses would be dragged out of a super-heated building the inmates had nicknamed "Klondike."

EPILOGUE

Approximately a year later, on August 12, 1939, Mayor Clarke made headlines once again. This time, however, for a reason no one who knew the ambitious and single-minded politician would have anticipated. As the *Philadelphia Evening Bulletin* announced of the unexpected event, "Mayor Clarke Signs Retirement Papers On His Sickbed."

Citizens were informed the "mayor's health was shattered" and "his life was at risk." Nearly five months before the scheduled end of his term, his condition had grown so serious "physicians were strongly advising him to give up the reins of city government as soon as possible to facilitate his recovery and extend his life."

The rare move left both Democratic and Republican Party activists flummoxed, as Clarke had masterfully played both ends against the middle. As one newspaper columnist opined, "the sudden retirement of Mayor Clarke—a politician who came in as a Republican but increasingly moved toward becoming a Democrat—had precipitated an explosive political situation in City Hall." A week later, on August 19, 1939—one year to the day the Klondike saga began—Mayor G. Thomas Clarke died of a stroke at his home.

Although the mayor's resignation and death presented a conundrum for both parties, his passing allowed Heshel Glass to regain his political footing. In addition to no longer facing the animus of the city's most feared politician and the end of his political career, he would go on to win the endorsement of nearly every major newspaper in the city. Editorial boards that had labeled him "woefully inexperienced" and "an unschooled party hack" four years earlier now sung his praises. He was described as a "breath of fresh air" and "that rare

Philadelphia commodity, an elected official citizens can take pride in." On election day, Glass would handily win a second term as county coroner.

Although Glass would go on to investigate a number of high-profile cases—sometimes beyond Philadelphia's borders as a respected outside expert—and was routinely encouraged to seek higher office, he would never file candidate's papers for anything other than county coroner. As a loyal elder statesmen of the Democratic Party, he would go on to be a role model for progressive forces and help lead a successful political reform movement in the city in the early 1950s.

Glass's deputy, Carl Ferencz, would go on to attend law school at night and eventually win a seat in City Council. Over the years, he would display mastery of subjects ranging from housing and health care to finance and public safety. Many of the bills he introduced to rectify municipal problems became law, and he was viewed as a knowledgeable and sober voice in all public policy debates. Neither his wife nor the coroner would ever learn he had been propositioned late one night by the former mayor to turn on his boss and join Clarke's team.

Though he would escape conviction, Warren Davis's reputation was permanently destroyed, and he became persona non grata in the eyes of most Philadelphians. His once-celebrated career as a military soldier and police official overshadowed by his inept handling of an inmate food strike, he would move to a quiet farming community in South Jersey. Solitary and almost hermit-like, neighbors would occasionally see him on country roads early in the morning and again late at night, walking his dog.

Warden Victor Stryker and guard Joseph Smoot would each serve over two years behind bars. Both men did their time in county facilities outside Philadelphia, Stryker in the Berks County jail in Reading, and Smoot in the Montgomery County jail in Norristown. Encouraged to be ever vigilant, they were always on the lookout for inmates seeking retribution. Upon their release, both men obtained non-criminal justice-related jobs and kept low profiles in their respective Philadelphia river ward neighborhoods.

After graduating magna cum laude from the University of Pittsburgh, David Sandler went to Johns Hopkins Medical School in Baltimore. He would go on to do post-graduate stints at the prestigious Rockefeller and Max Planck Institutes and specialize in bacteriology. As part of the campaign to find a reliable polio preventive, he became a member of an elite research unit that developed a successful live-virus polio vaccine in the 1950s.

Though neither he nor Heshel Glass would ever reach out to the other, Sandler would remember his short time helping to investigate the Klondike murders as one of the most significant experiences of his life. The dedication, teamwork, and commitment to do the right thing, which he learned during the summer of '38 while working in the Philadelphia Coroner's Office, would prove a valuable roadmap for every medical riddle and scientific quest he'd tackle over the course of his career.

Reporter J. Henry Jones not only managed to remain in Philadelphia and cover the coroner's investigation, inquest, and Grand Jury probe, he also used the Klondike tragedy to advance his professional career and foster his literary aspirations. His gripping and well-researched accounts of mass murder in a Pennsylvania prison and its subsequent investigation were so compelling, his newspaper's circulation doubled, and a competitor, the *Richmond Times-Dispatch,* hired him at a much higher salary. Even more significant, the gruesome murder of imprisoned men proved the creative spark he had long been searching for. He would write his first three-act play entitled, *Not Just Devils*, about the incident—under his new pen name, Asheville Jones. The play would be well received, and he would go on to be a highly successful playwright.

Just over two months after the last trial of Klondike defendants and twelve days after the death of Mayor G. Thomas Clarke, the Nazi army would invade Poland. Hitler's desire for European domination would throw the civilized world into unprecedented chaos and destruction. The many crimes and myriad instances of widespread butchery, including the murder and incineration of millions of people, would follow over the next six years and do much to dull the memory of a horrible precursor inside the walls of a Philadelphia prison.

On a sweltering summer day in 1968—a day not unlike one three-decades earlier—William Harper, a career criminal awaiting trial for murder, was taken by several guards from his cell on B Block. He was then escorted with a dozen other prisoners to a small brick building used for storage in an exercise yard between D and E Blocks. Though a couple of the men may have had faint knowledge of the old horror tale, none of them knew the nondescript building they were now standing before was the infamous Klondike of prison lore.

The men were then handed shovels, pickaxes, and heavy sledgehammers and told go to work; they were to tear the building down to the ground. For three days under a broiling sun and the watchful eyes of shotgun-toting guards, the men labored. Brick by brick and cell by cell, the fifty-foot long building was violently demolished. The building's seven large radiators were the first objects to be torn out and broken apart. Approximately forty years after it was constructed and thirty years after it was the scene of one of the worst instances of prison abuse in modern American history, the Klondike was no more.

As with other once-significant but ultimately forgotten pieces of history, lessons once learned were eventually forgotten, impediments to the smooth and felicitous operation of an overcrowded big-city jail. Though there would never be another Klondike-like abomination at Holmesburg, it would continue to have its share of violent riots, clever escapes, and brutal murders, not to mention its quarter-century history of hosting dangerous and unethical medical experiments on prisoners.

The Klondike's destruction passed without public notice. As usual, Holmesburg's high walls kept the media and general public oblivious of such events.

Decommissioned in 1995 and long free of prisoners, the fortress-like Homesburg Prison continues to stand, an ominous relic of a bygone age. The only other structure that harkens back to the deadly incident that once garnered national attention is the Press Bar across the street from the ancient jail. Originally known as McHugh's Tavern, the small basement operation was renamed sometime later in honor of the many newsmen who hung out there during the early days of the tragedy. And like the Klondike incident itself, memories have faded, stories have been forgotten, and not one of the establishment's bartenders or patrons is now able to recollect just how the familiar neighborhood watering hole came by its name.

About the Author

Allen M. Hornblum is the author of seven books ranging in scope from organized crime and Soviet espionage to medical ethics and sports. His work has been featured on news shows such as the *CBS Evening News, Good Morning America,* and on networks such as Court TV, the BBC, and CNN, as well as most newspapers including the front pages of the *New York Times,* and the *Philadelphia Inquirer.* He has also lectured at a cross-section of institutions including the British Medical Association, the National Institutes of Health, the FBI, and a host of colleges and medical schools including Brown, Columbia, and Princeton Universities. Prior to his decision to investigate and write books about controversial and long-neglected subjects, Hornblum had a long career in law enforcement working in the Philadelphia Prison System and Sheriff's Office, as well as the Pennsylvania Crime Commission.

Made in the USA
Middletown, DE
27 March 2021

36361671R00182